MONOHON'S PAPERBACK EXCHANGE
1919-G W. Meridian
WA 98466
(206) 564-7

HEAT FROM
ANOTHER SUN

DAVID L. LINDSEY

BANTAM BOOKS
NEW YORK · TORONTO
LONDON · SYDNEY · AUCKLAND

Although this novel is set in Houston, none of its characters represents or is based on persons living there, or indeed anywhere. All events and personalities are imaginary.

*This edition contains the complete text
of the original hardcover edition.*
NOT ONE WORD HAS BEEN OMITTED.

HEAT FROM ANOTHER SUN

*A Bantam Book / published by arrangement with
HarperCollins Publishers*

PUBLISHING HISTORY
*Harper & Row edition 1984
Pocket Books edition / October 1985
Bantam edition / February 1996*

ISBN 0-553-56790-X

Published simultaneously in the United States and Canada

*Bantam Books are published by Bantam Books, a division of Bantam Doubleday Dell
Publishing Group, Inc. Its trademark, consisting of the words "Bantam Books" and
the portrayal of a rooster, is Registered in U.S. Patent and Trademark Office and in
other countries. Marca Registrada. Bantam Books, 1540 Broadway, New York, New
York 10036.*

PRINTED IN THE UNITED STATES OF AMERICA

RAD   0 9 8 7 6 5 4 3 2 1

To Joyce

For her abiding companionship
these twenty years,
ever hopeful and forgiving

HEAT FROM
ANOTHER SUN

1

The Old Shamrock Hilton loomed broad and heavy into the hazy night sky like an aging mammoth ocean liner, the soft green sheen of her lighted facade fading toward the top to a shadowed silhouette inset with the amber portholes of her rooms; a grand queen of former times, still grand, still queen.

He looked at the hotel through the sparkling clean windshield as he rested his chin on the steering wheel and listened to Paul Desmond's smooth sax floating through "Coracao Sensivel." Below the drift of the music he could hear the girls talking in the back seat in hushed conspiratorial tones. They were speaking what he called Chink-Tex: mostly Chinese peppered with English words and phrases in a distinctly Texas accent. Shit, they were innocents. Two innocents. From his right peripheral vision something pale moved cautiously from behind him. He tensed. A bare leg came over the seats, and an extended toe dangled a pair of panties next to his face. He smiled. A flurry of giggles overrode Desmond's sax. Well, shit, who was *really* innocent anymore?

He took the panties from the toe and shoved the foot back where it came from. He removed his amber-lensed Carreras and began polishing them with the panties. He held the glasses up to his eyes and then threw them onto the seat in frustration. His eyes were killing him, and he had thought the damn glasses might cut the glare of headlights. They didn't. Besides, he looked like a pimp wearing sunglasses at night. He just wanted to close his eyes, maybe catch a few Z's, but he was still so damn wired he wouldn't sleep for a week. And part of the reason he didn't sleep was because he *couldn't* sleep. He was pumped so tight with adrenaline that every time he closed his eyes his mind spit out stop-action stills of the previous two hours, and then he had to open his eyes to stop it. Shit. Just-like-the-movies. It had been one hell of a night. He had never seen anything like it. Never.

The drive-in windows of the bank parking lot were a good place to meet. There were thick hedges and several medians of oleanders to shield them from the traffic on Fannin and Holcombe. The lamps threw their pale light from behind the palms along the street casting needle-shaped shadows on the hood of the car. Natural camo, like the moonlight in Nam. Powell was going to think this was a stupid way to meet, but then, Powell wasn't playing with a full deck, was he. Powell just hadn't been around this kind of thing enough to know when he was into something very heavy indeed. But he would find out.

He reached down and touched the package between his legs in the car seat. Two video cassettes made with state-of-the-art in ENG systems. Hitachi had outdone themselves with this one. Each cassette was sealed in a Ziploc sandwich bag, and the two bags were taped together with fiber tape until nothing showed but the tape. It looked like a bomb, and it was.

Desmond slipped into "Two Part Contention" as Powell's battered cherry Corvette came around the corner off Holcombe and circled the bank toward the drive-in windows. The girls in the back seat quit talking and sat up a little as they watched the car, splattered with primer-gray splotches of Bondo, maneuver between the islands and stop next to their pearl Mercedes. Powell turned off the Corvette's motor and rolled down his window.

He grinned across at them. "Hey, James Bond."

The stupid shit. He just didn't understand. "Can you get into the lab tonight?"

"Sure," Powell said. "Anytime. What's the deal? You been down to tamale land again?"

He ignored the question. "I've got this quarter-inch stuff I want duped and bumped up to one inch."

"How'd the new Hitachi rig work out?"

"Fine. Listen, I need this done tonight."

"So?"

He didn't know how much to tell Powell. He reached up to the dash and turned off the tape deck. Muffled city noises took over, and he motioned for Powell to lean farther out the window.

"I don't want to give them dupes of these," he said.

Powell just looked at him. A collection of gold chains caught the light below his Adam's apple. Sometimes he wondered about Powell. California kid who was no longer a kid but didn't know it. Lived with an absolutely gorgeous chick who was half his age and twice as smart. He couldn't figure it. Powell had been the one who was really going to make it big, but over the years he hadn't even come close. It wasn't going to end up good for Powell. He'd pissed away too many years.

"I want you to dupe these for me, without them knowing about it. If he asks about it tomorrow, tell him I haven't come in, as far as you know. You haven't heard from me."

Powell licked his lips. Even in the washed-out light of the lamps you could tell his skin had been tanned to leather. The blond beachboy hair looked a little out of sync with the face that was stumbling into forty years and not holding up well.

"What's on the tapes?" Powell asked, his head tilted, his mouth hanging open, slack-jawed.

"This is my own deal, Wayne. It's not for them. I'll pay you separately. This one is just between you and me. You've got the equipment I need. It's like moonlighting."

"You didn't go to El Salvador?"

"Yeah, I did, but this is something else. I do other things too, you know."

"But what about the El Salvador stuff? Don't you have any?"

"Not this trip. Nothing happened."

"But you've already been paid for them."

"Kind of."

"What do you mean, 'kind of'? Money ain't 'kind of.' Money's payment. You screw around with these people and you could mess up my situation up there. I don't want to lose that kind of dole, man."

Powell's problem was that he was too damn literal. That's the way it had been in film school. At the heart of it all he was never anything more than a good camera mechanic. Absolutely no creativity. But he was a good mechanic.

"Look, Wayne, I'll explain it to you tomorrow."

Powell looked into the back seat of the Mercedes at the two pairs of unsmiling Oriental eyes staring mutely at him from the half-light. He seemed to think it over, and then he shrugged and stuck his opened hand out the window. "What can I say?"

For a split second he almost changed his mind, and then he told himself it would be a mistake to lose his nerve now. He wanted the tapes in the one-inch format, and he wanted to see what a really good technician could do with the enhancement. There was no reason for anyone to think they were anything different from what the others had been. It was like mailing a million bucks in a shoe box. Sometimes routine procedures were the best disguise, and therefore the safest. So long as Powell didn't let them out of his hands. He took the package from between his legs and handed it through the window.

"There's two of them there. Almost a full sixteen minutes. Those new Hitachis only get eight minutes."

"I know that, man," Powell said with tired sarcasm. "You forget who the hell put you onto 'em?"

"Just run them through and see what we get at one inch. Enhance them, whatever it takes. As soon as you get through, call me from up there and tell me how it looks. I'll tell you what to do from there. Okay?"

"Whatever," Powell said.

"And, Wayne. They're special, okay? Hang onto them. Your eyes only, okay?"

Powell didn't seem particularly impressed by that. He started the Corvette, revving the engine cockily as the car's front left fender vibrated wildly where it had been shattered and temporarily patched with gray swatches of unpainted fiberglass. He looked hard at the girls in the back seat of the Mercedes. They simply stared back at him in blank silence. More revving. More passive staring from the girls. Then Powell popped the clutch and shot away from them in the deafening roar of his exploding engine and the acrid stench of burnt rubber. The 'Vette's tires continued to squeal as he blasted out of the driveway, slamming the rear of the car's chassis against the dip where the cement met the asphalt street. He disappeared into the traffic on Fannin.

The girls burst into screeching laughter and rapid-fire Chink-Tex.

The man was nearly forty years old. It was hard to believe.

2

The first thing he had done was to clean out the library. It had taken an entire month. Haydon did not throw things away easily. His desk, files, and book shelves were filled with esoterica, memorabilia, and items of seemingly small or no importance for which he had formed a sometimes undefined attachment. Everything with which he surrounded himself was evocative of another space and time, and nowhere was this more true than in the library.

For the first few days he mostly thought about it, randomly pulling from the shelves books that he hadn't looked at in years. He opened the covers and read the owners' names, usually in their own handwriting. He read his father's name, his mother's name, and his own. His father's handwriting was elongated, thin, resembling the kind of decorative script one could learn from books sixty years ago. He often made eccentric remarks below his name and date: comments on the weather the day he bought the book, or if he had successfully concluded a particular case, or if something re markable had occurred in the news or affected the family. His books were the marginalia of his life. His mother's handwriting was small, clear, and exact. Name and date. Nothing more.

Haydon's own handwriting was stylistically inconsistent, partly because there were books in the library that ranged from his childhood to the present. One could easily distinguish the awkward scrawl of youth and watch it grow steadier through a succession of books. But even as a man, Haydon's handwriting had always varied in appearance, a fact that privately annoyed him. There had been times, when he was going through the family papers after his parents' deaths, that he hadn't even recognized his own letters.

In this haphazard fashion, he slowly reacquainted himself with what Thomas Carlyle had called "the articulate audible voice of the Past." He came to view the library itself as an aging personality in whom the key to his own threatened memory was fortuitously secured. This discovery was immensely calming to him and was a major factor in his emotional restoration, which was to require several months.

After nearly two weeks of this self-indulgent rambling, in which he spent long days reading whatever he happened upon of interest and letting that, in turn, lead him to some other loosely related book, Haydon began a systematic review of the library's contents. He examined every single volume, journal, and pamphlet that crowded the room's shelves, adding notes to their cards in the catalog that had been religiously maintained from the beginning by his father. In this process he discarded a variety of material that had seemingly found space on the shelves solely by virtue of the family's habit of saving everything that loosely could be classified as a book, journal, or pamphlet that fell into their hands. He eventually threw away three large cardboard boxes of useless material, which he dragged out on the terrace for Pablo to haul away.

Finally, he consumed one full week selecting and ordering more books from the list he kept in a spiral notebook. It was nothing less than a bibliographic binge.

Toward the end of the second month, Haydon turned his attention to the long greenhouse that lay just beyond the citrus grove. For a good while it had been at the back of his mind to expand his collection of bromeliads to take up the entire space. So, with the moping assistance of Pablo, who regretted this new enthusiasm that had turned his lazy mornings into a sweating purgatory, he began the renovations. Huge chunks of limestone were brought in to build small outcroppings, and sphagnum moss was carted in by the hundreds of pounds. Electricians came with rolls of wiring, neatly packaged instruments, ladders, and scaffolding and installed the necessary devices to create a hermetically accurate rain forest, complete with varietal wind currents produced by electrically timed fans mounted in the ceiling beside an automated sprinkler system that simulated mists and periodic rains.

He scoured every nursery in the city for varieties of bromeliads that he did not already have and placed orders for others. At the end of six weeks the renovation was complete. Slate paths wound through the length of the greenhouse amid tiers of hundreds of species of bromeliads that fell from the ceiling to the spongy earth. High up, clinging to palms and the broken stumps of old trees, were the epiphytes, the air breathers, whose roots served only as a means of attachment while they absorbed food and water through a system of scales common to all bromeliads, and which often gave to their leaves a silvery blue hue. Abundant clumps and clusters of them draped down to the boulders upon which the saxicola lived, clinging to the crevices and lichen surfaces of the stones. The terrestrials flourished in the boggy osmundine of the greenhouse floor, among them the shimmering Cryptanthus "earth stars," dazzling against the dark green of moss and peat.

By the beginning of the fourth month, Haydon's days had settled into a comfortable regimen. He rose early and exercised briefly on the bedroom balcony over the terrace before going downstairs and out the front gates to jog three miles through the boulevards in the tenuous morning coolness. When he returned, he showered and ate a light breakfast with Nina as he restlessly scanned both Houston dailies with little interest. Eventually, he fell to daydreaming.

While the cooler temperatures of late morning hung in the citrus grove around the greenhouse, he spent his time there, cataloging his new imports and transplanting the pups that sprang up from the older plants. Often in the morning hours he was simply idle and would lie in a hammock in the lime trees and try to think of nothing. It was an objective he seldom achieved.

From lunch until evening, during the hottest part of the day, Haydon worked in the library. As with the bromeliads, he cataloged the new books he had ordered, which came in a steady stream of boxes every few days. He unpacked them, put the empty cartons outside on the terrace, and stacked the new volumes on the refectory table. Then he sat with his back to the French doors, beyond which the summer heat swelled to an intensity so fierce that even the cicadas seemed to scream in defiance of it, and immersed himself in the new books with an exhilaration he had almost forgotten was possible.

Another month passed in the natural cadence that his life had now assumed. The frantic need to stay busy that had obsessed him in the early months gradually subsided and, like a debilitating fever, left him drained and tranquil. But the routine of his days, carefully orchestrated by Nina, had been regenerative. His anxieties were fewer, less immediate. Those that remained would never go away. They were as much a part of his makeup as the rhythm of his heartbeat. For the first time in longer than he could remember he felt his life coming together with a cohesiveness that long had been absent and, he now realized, had been sorely missed. Nina meant more to him now than ever, for it was she who had patiently and unobtrusively structured his recuperation. After nearly twelve years of balancing her marriage and her career, Nina pushed aside her own work. Commissions from architectural firms were routinely rejected, and for weeks at a time she never walked through the doors of her studio. What work she did, she did at home. She never crowded him; she understood better than he did his need for periods of solitude, but she was never far from reach.

As always, she had seen clearly not only for herself but for both of them. For his present peace of mind, Haydon felt an indebtedness to her of the dearest sort, beyond reason or hope of repayment.

3

He assumed the worst.

His eyes didn't burn anymore. The pain was overridden by the cloying odor of blood, which he tried to wash from his nostrils by rolling down the car window and letting the muggy night air rush in against his face. The girls were subdued in the back seat. He sure as hell hadn't anticipated this. The initiative had almost been taken away from him. Almost.

He considered the options. The streets were empty, and he could think. He could bail out right now, deal with the rest of it from Zurich or Hong Kong or Katmandu or some such damn place by turning over the rest of the tapes and saying he was backing out. Big mistake. Sorry. No offense. Or he could try to salvage the whole thing. To do that he would have to move fast. Go back to the condo right now, pile everything he could into the cars, and drop out of sight until he could engineer a new approach. If he did that, if he could get away in one clean hour, he could make it work.

Shit, when did he ever walk away from a long shot?

It was surprising how much you could get into two cars. In the gray, lifeless hours before dawn, they backed the girls' Audi and his own Mercedes to the back door of the condo behind the wall of English ivy and began loading them. The girls went to their closets and frantically scooped up their clothes and shoes, which took up the entire back seat of the Audi, almost blocking the rear window. They got the stereo, speakers, and records into the Audi's trunk along with paper sacks filled with toilet articles from the bathrooms and other sacks crammed with cooking utensils from the kitchen. They would buy food later.

When they started on his things, he told them to throw all the clothes into the Mercedes' trunk, hangers and all. He had already gotten the suitcases from the closets and was filling them with his tapes, the hundreds of dupes he'd made over the years. Everything. He put the suitcases on the floor in the rear to build it up to seat level for the equipment.

Back in the spare bedroom he began unhooking the cables, not even taking the time to keep it organized, just getting the damn stuff apart. All the cables in one pile; he'd worry about sorting them later. The girls helped him carry the television monitor out to the car and brace it against one door. The Panasonic U-Vision recorder/editor was next, only barely fitting in the space remaining in the back seat. The new Hitachi quarter-inch recorder sat on the front seat beside him along with the two SR-1 VTR cameras. They took sheets from the beds and threw them over everything. No use advertising what they were doing.

By six o'clock they were loaded and ready to go. But not to the Oriental districts. That would be too obvious, the kind of move they would be expecting. It would be better, and easier, to melt into the vast sea of Houston's apartment dwellers, where the flux of residents was so constant that *all* faces were new. While the morning traffic was still light, they pulled onto Bellaire and followed it out to Hillcroft and then turned north, under the Southwest Freeway, left on Harwin, left on Fondren, circling, looking out over the endless rooftops of apartments and town homes that formed the massive and homogeneous society of Sharpstown rent payers.

Having come full circle to Bellaire again, they stopped at a coffee shop and ate breakfast just as the traffic began to stir in sporadic clusters inbound for the city. The girls were quiet. Their greasy American breakfasts were hardly touched in favor of several large glasses of orange juice and grapefruit halves.

He looked at his watch. It was almost eight o'clock. They would find the mess at eight, or shortly thereafter. He would like to be off the streets by ten. Then he needed sleep. And then he would work on the tapes.

While the girls stared passively out the window like Siamese cats, he opened his briefcase and checked the papers he would use. He had two false driver's licenses and two false passports, one set in the name of Richard M. Kaun and the other in the name of Richard K. Malik. He had used them all over the world, and they had served him well. And they should have. They were German productions and had cost him nearly a kilo of the-most-popular-drug-of-choice. The names were a stroke of genius, something that had come to him just at the last minute when he'd turned in his request for the documents. The Boche engraver didn't give a shit. He would have put Quasimodo's signature under Ferdinand Marcos' photograph if the little butcher had paid for it. Curiously, no one had ever questioned the disparity between the names and the photograph that went with them.

They left the coffee shop and the girls followed him as he circled back around the way they had come before he finally committed to a street and went farther into the maze. He wanted just the right place, not too expensive, not too tacky. Something anonymous. He saw a vacancy sign outside a place called Southwest Manor Village that looked like it wanted to have overtones of Old Williamsburg. He pulled into the drive.

The place was probably built when Sharpstown was a ritzy new development nearly fifteen years before. Toy walked through a breezeway in the front section of the quadrangle and into the courtyard. A small pool with most of the paint flaked off the bottom and encircled with a chainlink fence was the main attraction. He followed the red arrows to the manager's office.

The manager was still in her terry-cloth robe and was watching David Hartman over a cup of coffee. She had a two-bedroom available. Three twenty-five a month, no bills paid. Hundred-dollar deposit. She got the key and took him around the quadrangle to see it. Unfurnished except for the kitchen, which had everything. Was he married? Yes, and his sister-in-law was with them. Good thing there were two baths, the woman said. Have any pets? No. Well, they didn't allow them, she said. Any kids? No. Didn't allow them either. Toy looked around. It would do. He followed her back across the quadrangle where residents had worn bare trails in the grass taking shortcuts to the pool.

In a daze from the lack of sleep, they began unloading the cars, everything in reverse of a few hours before, into the empty rooms that smelled of pesticides and pine-scented air freshener. The video equipment went into the living room, along with the stereo. When everything had been unpacked, he went to the bedroom where the girls had put his clothes and collapsed on the carpet, vaguely aware of the depressing surroundings.

When he opened his eyes again, he stared at the dull lighted ceiling, momentarily disoriented. Then he smelled the familiar odors of heated sesame oil and stir-fried vegetables, looked at the empty room, and remembered. His watch said seven thirty. He had slept all day. He got up and walked down the hall to the kitchen, where Yue was standing at the stove in her underwear stirring something in the wok, her long jet hair hanging to the top of her white panties. The cabinets were crowded with freshly purchased produce.

He turned away from the door and walked into the living room. Lai, also in her underwear, was sitting on the floor untangling the wires for the stereo.

"You been awake long?" he asked.

She flashed a smile. "Sleep okay?"

He nodded.

"We are awake two hour. Have nice bathe, hair wash." Another smile.

Jesus.

"Yue cooking."

He nodded again, turned, and walked back to his bedroom. His toilet things had already been put away in the bath. He took a long shower.

They ate standing around the kitchen cabinets, the stereo rolling out Olivia Newton-John. He watched the girls and wondered if anything had been on the six o'clock news. After he finished eating, he went into the living room.

He lined up the three components along one wall. First he hooked up the TV monitor and turned it on, with the sound off. To the left of that he wrestled the old Panasonic U-Vision recorder/editor into position, plugged it into the wall outlet, and attached the cables to the monitor. Then to the left of the editor he placed the new Hitachi player/recorder designed for the quarter-inch Hitachi cassettes recorded on the SR-1s. He plugged this into a wall outlet also and attached the audio and two video cables from the player to the editor.

From the briefcase where he kept his false papers, he took the twelve remaining video cassettes that he had planned for Powell to process. They were part of the latest development in Hitachi's line of electronic news-gathering equipment, the SR-1 video camera. The system was designed to be light and compact so that it could be easily used by a single cameraman in the field. Part of the reason the package was light and maneuverable was that it used quarter-inch video cassettes rather than the larger-formatted and more widely used half-inch or three-quarter-inch cassettes. The only drawback at this point in the package's development was that the cassette was capable of holding only eight minutes of information.

He and Lai had captured almost an hour's worth of film. That meant that during the shooting each of them had had to snap in seven separate cassettes, giving them a total of fifty-six minutes of footage each. Though almost sixteen minutes of the opening action was stolen from

Powell, Toy had made a copy as a precautionary measure. In light of what happened, it had proved to be a prudent decision.

Now he began the process of duplicating the quarter-inch cassettes onto the more popular three-quarter-inch format, which also allowed the multiple eight-minute cassettes to be consolidated on a single sixty-minute cassette. He loaded a blank three-quarter-inch cassette in the U-Vision recorder/editor and the first of Lai's Hitachi quarter-inch cassettes into the Hitachi player/recorder. The final sixty-minute cassette would be rough cut, but that was all he needed now. It would be enough to get the narrative on one continuous tape. It wasn't a damn art film.

By the time he had completed duping onto the last of the sixty-minute cassettes, the girls had finished in the kitchen and were sitting silently on the floor behind him watching the TV monitor. The tangy odors of Yue's Oriental cooking that had gradually filled the den had been replaced by the faint smell of hot electrical wiring. Now that, too, was interrupted by an occasional refreshing waft of the girls' fragrant bath oil.

Now to see the action in one unbroken piece. He went to the stereo first and took off Olivia Newton-John and picked out a Billie Holiday album and put it on. Then he returned to the cassettes and put the three-quarter-inch cassette that held the footage that had been shot from Lai's camera into the U-Vision. He punched the button. There was static on the television monitor, and then it began.

It was the most remarkable footage he had ever seen. The violence, calculated and steamy and desperate, had a dimension of unreality about it that was nauseating in a way that the violence of war and torture never was. And it wasn't the suffocating, clinical violence of the infamous snuff films, of which he had actually seen only one and probably only half a dozen had ever existed. It would have been easier to watch this film had it fit into a convenient framework that would have allowed its brutality to be excused or complacently dismissed with traditional explanations. Society had long ago provided stock responses to most kinds of violence, convenient responses that didn't require anyone to look directly into its face.

But this was different. With an irony that Toy relished, they watched the final gruesome minutes of the tape as the hauntingly melodic voice of Billie Holiday filled the darkened room with the searing words of "Strange Fruit."

4

On a Saturday morning in the first week of July, Haydon rose early, slipped on a pair of old soccer shorts that cinched with a drawstring at the waist, and pulled on some ragged and soil-stained espadrilles. He was careful not to wake Nina, who had read a novel late into the night and probably would sleep until midmorning. He descended the curving stairs, in the flat pale light that seemed to come from nowhere and everywhere at once to fill the white space of the entrance hall, and made his way out to the terrace where Cinco lay, waiting for him. Haydon bent down and stroked the old collie's head, and then stood for a moment on the cusp of the steps, letting the cool dampish air wake his naked torso and legs.

He and Cinco went down the steps and through the wet grass beneath the lime trees to the greenhouse. At a faucet near the entrance, he vigorously splashed water on his face and arms and let them drip dry as he spent the next half hour filling the bird feeders that hung from the surrounding trees. When that was done, he took what he needed from the toolshed and went into the greenhouse.

It was nearly ten-thirty when he heard the jangling of the bell that hung in the ebony tree outside the entrance. He finished packing the osmundine around a pup he had separated from a larger plant, and carried his tools to the corner near the door, where he washed them and left them to dry on a gravel pad. He checked the dials on the watering and cooling stations just inside the door and stepped outside.

Cinco, who had been sleeping under the ebony tree and had been waked by the bell, had no intention of responding unless he was forced to. He raised his old grizzled head, without getting up, and looked at Haydon through squinty eyes. Haydon knelt down and scratched him behind his ears and softly stroked his brindled hair. At first the collie licked the salty backs of Haydon's sweaty hands and then gradually laid his head down again and luxuriated in Haydon's attentions, his eyes closed.

Haydon looked through the rows of the citrus grove to the house, half expecting to see Nina waiting for him on the terrace. A pair of blue jays squabbled and squawked somewhere in the dark green branches of the lime trees. The humidity was high, almost as high as in the greenhouse. The summer was shaping up to be one of the hottest in the city's history. It didn't matter. After a certain point it was just hot. Ten degrees one way or the other didn't make any difference.

"Come on, old friend," Haydon said. "We've got to go to the house."

He stood and waited for the collie to drag himself to his feet. When Cinco's hindquarters failed to respond, Haydon reached down and gently gave the dog a boost. They started off together under the arbor of the trees moving slowly as befitted the dog's old age and the summer heat.

Before reaching the terrace Haydon turned off on a small brick path flanked by a dense growth of cherry laurels and entered a white bathhouse with an open-air shower protected by latticework. He removed his sweaty shorts and went into the shower and turned on the cold water. Quickly lathering with aloe soap, he bathed in the icy spray, rinsed off, and dried with one of the clean towels kept in the bathhouse cabinets. He walked into the next room and picked up a clean pair of ecru summer pants from the daybed and slipped them on, along with a fresh white shirt with a banded collar. As he shoved his bare feet into loosely woven mat shoes, he tucked in the shirttail and rolled the sleeves to the elbow. He strapped on his watch and combed his hair. Stepping outside, he lighted his first Fribourg & Treyer of the day and started up to the house.

Nina was sitting in the breakfast room at the end of the terrace, drinking coffee and talking with someone partially obscured by the fan of a small potted palm. Her light-cinnamon hair was loose, having not yet been put up for the day, and she had pulled it around to one side so that it fell across the front of her left shoulder. She wore a simple cinnabar morning dress of Jacquard silk with no jewelry or makeup, and Haydon thought she was the most exotic woman he had ever seen. He was so preoccupied with the sight of her, the luxuriant sweep of her hair and her large, almost Mediterranean eyes, that it was not until he was about to open the glass door to the breakfast room that he realized her guest was a man, and Nina was not smiling.

Lieutenant Bob Dystal's presence in the sun room reminded Haydon of a circus bear at a children's tea party. He was too big for everything. He sat in his chair with an upright politeness that proved he was well trained and would make no bearish mistakes that would upset the civilized decorum of his situation. But one could sense, too—perhaps it was something in the contrite slope of his shoulders—that he would rather be in more bearlike surroundings. His chocolate-brown suit coat was still buttoned, causing his lapels to gap awkwardly, and his muddy close-cropped hair was coerced into precise and orderly directions by the morning's abundant application of Brylcreem.

"Hello, Stu," he said, smiling. "Sorry to mess up your rat killin' down there." He put both hands on the arms of his chair and made a feint to stand. It was like tipping one's hat in polite company by touching the brim without actually taking it off.

Haydon smiled back. "It's good to see you, Bob," he said. He pulled out a chair and sat down beside Nina, who was already pouring him a cup of coffee. She freshened Dystal's cup and he immediately sipped the scalding coffee, which Haydon thought must seem like weak tea to him.

"How's your flowers?" Dystal asked sociably. It wouldn't have been good manners to come visiting and have things fall into an unpleasant silence right from the start. "Nina tells me there's a whole new setup down there. Got everything like you want it?"

"It's looking good," Haydon said. "Better every day." He stirred cream into his coffee, taking his time. He put the spoon on his saucer and tried it. It was thick, dark Colombian. Nina had made a fresh pot to accommodate Dystal's taste.

"This is a good place for recuperatin'," Dystal said, looking across the terrace to the citrus grove. "All those lime trees." He shook his head. "I remember when I was a boy I'd go to my uncle's down in the Valley for a couple of weeks every summer. They had lots of orange groves and some lemons and limes, too. It was a real paradise for an old West Texas boy, I'll tell you. Me and my cousins would lie in the shade way down in the groves away from the house an' peel oranges an' talk an' listen to the mourning doves. Those were long, long days." He thought about it, remembering; then he raised the china cup, so fragile in his bear paw, and said, "But they weren't long enough."

They all sipped their coffee as if on cue.

"Well, Stu," Dystal said, jutting out his chin. His shirt collar bound his neck like a corset. "Thought I'd drop by and let you know old Mooney's getting along fine. He's teamed up with Lapierre now. You know, opposites like that can work purty good if everything clicks just right. Mooney's a homicide natural anyhow. Shoulda been in there a long time ago. I 'preciate your speaking up for him the way you did. It probably got him in." He looked at Haydon with a sideways glance. "Haven't heard a whole lot about Hirsch. Suppose you keep up with him."

Haydon nodded. "He's happy. I think he's finding it a little tough after having been out of law school for so long.

But he's making it fine. He was able to keep some of his credits, so he's not having to start over from the beginning."

"Good, good. The boy's sharp, no doubt about it. I hated to lose him, but I can understand why he got out. Cases like the Guimaraes thing don't come along much in a man's career, but when they do you gotta be ready for 'em. I guess it came too early in his. He didn't have enough experience under his belt to handle it."

Haydon noticed Dystal still had his American flag lapel pin. He was the only man Haydon knew who actually wore one of those things. He looked at the ashtray on the table. There wasn't a single generic butt. Dystal probably wouldn't smoke in Nina's presence. He was an old-fashioned man's man. His deference to women, especially "ladies," often seemed oddly chivalrous.

Nina put her hand on Haydon's. "You want a hot Danish?"

"Fine."

"How about you, Bob?"

"Oh, no. No, ma'am."

"I'll be right back," she said, and went into the kitchen.

Dystal shifted slightly in his chair. It was his call. He bore the responsibility of getting on with it.

"Well," he grunted. "We covered the other two boys. Now how are you doin'?"

"All right. I haven't missed anything."

"That's good." Dystal wrinkled his eyebrows as he stared past Haydon to the trees outside. They were both listening to Nina in the kitchen. Gabriela was with her, and the two alternated between English and Spanish.

When Nina returned she set the Danish beside Haydon's cup and spoke to Dystal.

"If you'll excuse me, I'd better get dressed. It was good visiting with you again, Bob."

"Oh, my pleasure," Dystal said, leaning forward slowly and feinting with his hands on the arms of his chair again.

"Don't wait so long next time."

Dystal's smile broadened. "No ma'am," he said. "I won't."

Nina gently touched Haydon's neck with the back of her hand and was gone.

"I appreciate that woman," Dystal said. "She's good people."

Haydon poured both of them more coffee and started on the Danish.

Dystal cast another look at the lime trees and then said, "I'm not going to beat around the bush, Stu. We need your help on something."

Haydon chewed the bite and looked at him. It was no surprise.

"I want to tell you about it."

Haydon took the cup and saucer in his hand and leaned back in his chair. "I've got another month left."

"I know you do."

"They agreed to six months' leave of absence."

"It still holds, Stu. I was the one who wanted to come talk to you. Nobody up there's trying to renege on anything. I asked if it'd be all right to come and sound you out on some things, and they said go ahead. This is just man-to-man here, and it hasn't got anything to do with the department. I mean it's a case, but I'm coming to you unofficially."

Haydon looked at Dystal. The big man was cool about it. He had been a policeman too long not to be. He was better at it than anyone Haydon had ever known.

"I meant it when I said I haven't missed anything, Bob."

"I know you did, Stu. You got to know me good enough by now to know I'm not goin' to get slick with you. The thing is, you're in the best position to help me out on this deal, and you know that I go straight for the best way to get at the bottom of something. It's that simple. If I get a little crap on my britches in the process, then I'll just have to live with that."

Dystal pushed his cup and saucer carefully to one side, leaned forward with his forearms on the glass table, and locked his thick fingers together.

"Stu, I know you got problems with this business, and

that you'll either deal with it somehow or you'll get out. That's the way it'll be. I guess you wanted to make that decision when your six months was up, but I'm going to force your hand a little early. Now hear me out on this, okay? Let me explain the rules on this little deal.''

Dystal paused, his head tilted forward slightly as he peered upward from under his eyebrows in anticipation of a nod from Haydon before continuing.

Haydon waited. He felt a disquieting mixture of eagerness and dread, as if he were about to hear a story he knew he had heard before, a drama that was at once seductive and horrible, like the medieval passion plays that dealt with sadness and agony and, ultimately, death. All the ambivalence of the previous five months seemed finally to be balanced on his decision to hear once more the tragic narrative that would never cease, not until man disappeared and time spun itself into oblivion.

''Go ahead,'' he said.

5

Still leaning on his forearms, his voice low and coming from deep within his barrel chest, Dystal began the rundown.

"You see in yesterday's papers about the knifing at Langer Media downtown?"

Haydon nodded.

"The call came in around eight thirty in the morning," Dystal said. "That was Thursday. Mooney and Lapierre were first out; they caught it. By the time they got downtown the two patrol officers at the scene had everything under wraps, and Mr. William Langer himself had got everybody back to their offices prim and proper, so that when Mooney and Lapierre walked in there was no sideshow to deal with. There were no reporters. Langer, bein' the savvy boy he is, had it all zipped up tight. For a few hours at least. A PR business has gotta be one of the worst places in the world for a man to try to keep something secret.

"The advertising agency takes up the whole thirty-second floor. The elevators open up right in their own private lobby, which is in the middle of the building in the same position as the crossbar in an H."

Dystal traced the letter on the glass with a stubby thumb and punctuated the location with a thumbs-down gesture on the spot.

"Each department in the agency—copywriting, graphics, photography, et cetera—have outside entrances that open into the two hallways that run either side of the lobby. They all connect on the inside too. Langer, always on the ball, I guess, had stationed a gofer down in the street to guide the ambulance into the underground garage and to make sure they used the freight elevator there so as not to attract attention. When these boys got to the thirty-second floor they were hustled out of the elevator real quick and rushed into the photography lab, which just happens to be about as far from the main entrance as it can be.

"The lab was a mess. Equipment kicked around, stuff turned over and spilled. Wayne Powell, the photographer, was sitting propped against the wall with all his clothes on in one of those table-high developer sinks. It was full and running over with developer and Powell's blood, damn near all he had in him. He'd been stabbed a couple of times around the chest, a deep one just under the chest bone here, and his throat was cut. Mooney thinks maybe his throat was slit while he was sitting in the sink struggling, because most of the blood was gettin' globby right there in his lap.

"They found his wallet in the jumble of crap on the floor. No money, but there was a little packet of cocaine still there. A California driver's license, credit cards, phone numbers on little pieces of paper, a few business cards. Lab boys went through and did their thing. Mooney and Lapierre spent the rest of the morning taking statements from the two gals who worked with Powell and from the guy who heads the photography department. He's the one who opened the lab that morning and found the body."

Dystal straightened his back and gave his cup a nudge.

"Could I have another little refill?"

Haydon poured the coffee and took another bite of

his Danish. Dystal quickly sipped the scalding brew. Haydon watched him, wondering how he could do that.

"This Powell, it turns out, had been working for Langer Media for over six months," Dystal continued. "Came to Texas from the West Coast about that time. Had wonderful recommendations from people out there. He was the main motion picture fella working for Langer. A couple of kids worked with him, but I think they just kind of toted things around."

Dystal finished off his coffee with a couple of big swallows, wiped his mouth with the blue linen napkin, and shoved them both to one side again. He pulled a thick hand down over his face, which was so closely shaven it glistened.

"Okay, just the high spots now. Lapierre was going over his questions again yesterday with one of those little gals who worked with Powell, and she let on about how Powell just came there out of nowhere. I mean he didn't go through the personnel department and the regular interview process like ever'body else who goes to work there. Their previous motion picture man had been fired, and Mr. Langer just came in one day and told the guy who headed the photography department at that time, guy named Dean Warner, that they'd hired Powell and that he'd start soon. That kind of ticked off Warner 'cause he didn't get a shot at picking his own man. As it turns out, the two men didn't get along.

"The gal said Powell hadn't been there two months when he had a run-in with Warner about Powell coming up to the office at night and working on his own stuff. That's a company no-no. Warner went to Langer about it and came out of the meeting burning up. Powell kept on with his night work, and a couple of weeks later Warner quit.

"Lapierre questioned Langer about this, and he kind of shrugged it off. He said he had hired Powell on the very high recommendation of a friend in the business in California and that Powell's night work was related to some special project Langer Media was sharing with a California company. We called the guy in California, and it all checks out.

"We've put Powell through the works: LEIU, NCIC, TCIC, Warrants and Arrests . . . no show. We thought maybe we had some dirty movies going on here, so we went to Powell's place and went through it. It's a little two-bedroom job. One of the bedrooms was a woman's. His had been rifled. Nothin' dramatic, it hadn't been ransacked or anything, but the drawers had been gone through, cabinet and closet doors left open. It didn't look like burglary because there was a stereo there and a lot of expensive-looking camera equipment. In the woman's room everything was in order, but it looked like she might be gone. There was no suitcase or makeup kit in the closet. No toothpaste in the medicine cabinet, no toothbrush, no razor. They did find an antibiotic prescription in the medicine cabinet for a Jennifer Quinn. They're tryin' to get her pinned down now."

Dystal stretched his chin again and pushed his hair back from the table a little to reposition his booted feet. He looked pensively out the window and down the length of the terrace at Cinco dozing in the shade.

"How old's the dog now?" he asked.

"Fifteen."

"Hundred an' five. He looks a little weary."

Haydon nodded.

"The thing is," Dystal said, still looking at Cinco, "I don't think this smells good at all. There was no sign of forced entry at the agency or at the house. Most likely he let the murderer in, or else it was someone who would have access to the place, someone who works there too. But he was a loner around there . . . except, maybe, for some kind of outside relationship with Langer. Langer brings the boy out of nowhere, and then he dies. I think our story lies in that direction, and I think Powell may be just the ragged edge of something more interesting. I know that's hunch talking now, but it's strong hunch."

On the terrace Cinco began a slow stiff-legged stretch without raising his head. He scratched his muzzle by scraping it on the flagstones. He licked his lips, flopped his tail twice as a comment on his contentment, and went back to sleep without ever having opened his eyes.

Dystal sighed heavily. "Here's the deal: you don't

come into the office at all. Everything regarding this case is kept in duplicate, and a copy comes to you here. This's your office, and this's your only case. You get Mooney and Lapierre when you want them, but you can work alone all you want. You have full access to our technical services. Just go through Lapierre and Mooney. Anytime the case is mentioned they'll be the ones named as the investigating detectives, and it'll be their names that appear in the news accounts. Good or bad. We've been over all this with them, and they've agreed." He grinned. "Lapierre was a little cautious about it, but that's the way the man breathes. Mooney, he just thought it was a hoot."

Haydon smiled slightly, but not about Lapierre. He didn't doubt it was Dystal's idea to come to him, but he wondered about the newspaper bit. He guessed the administration had wanted him to throw that in. There was no such thing as a guarantee like that, but it was a thinly veiled message to let him know they wouldn't parade him around in front of the news media anymore. On the other hand, thinly veiled messages like thinly veiled promises were usually thinly supported.

Dystal crossed his legs and massaged the instep of the boot that rested on his knee, making the leather creak. He looked at Haydon knowingly.

"Well, there's a lot of bullshit in this business, isn't there. The thing is, the captain and the chief and all those boys think the situation here is a little delicate. You know how Langer stands. His company has done public relations work for some real powerful people, and he runs with a purty high-profile crowd. I think the administration's piss-in-their-boots scared that this little investigation could put the department's titty in a wringer. It doesn't look real good for Langer, and it could go beyond him to God knows who or what kind of embarrassment. Some still think it's dirty movies, and those're always a little tender to deal with high-society-wise.

"The fact is, we need a special touch on this one. When necessary we'll leak a little confused shit to the media about how the investigation is cripplin' along, whine about how the leads are so puny, and all that. Meanwhile, they want you in there hangin' on like a bulldog.

Nobody you talk to is goin' to go tattlin' to the news people that they're bein' questioned about a murder, so you should be able to work in relative isolation. Mooney and Lapierre will take whatever heat might come from the press."

He dropped his foot to the floor, took a deep breath, and let it out. "That's about the size of it."

Haydon wanted another cigarette. He took the mignonette-green and gold box out of his pocket and set it on the table, but he didn't take out a cigarette.

"It was your idea to handle it like this?" he asked.

"Yeah, sure was."

"I'm surprised they went along with this kind of arrangement."

"So was I." Dystal almost grinned.

Haydon looked at the cigarette box. He touched it idly with his long fingers and moved it slightly into a bar of morning light that cut through the glass like a laser. The gold letters ignited against the green.

"What if I don't take it, Bob?" Haydon said, concentrating on the cigarette box.

Dystal grunted, thought a moment. "I guess you just wait on out your six months. I'm tellin' you, there's no strings attached to this."

Haydon had known Dystal for a long time, and he wasn't doubting the big detective's word. Dystal was misreading his hesitation, but Haydon wasn't going to clarify the mistake even though it would have been kinder to do so. Instead he hid behind the misunderstanding, letting it veil his own doubt and confusion. He would rather have the lieutenant believe his reluctance to answer was a result of hard-nosed calculation than have him recognize it for the uncertainty that it actually was.

Bob Dystal was not a man given to introspective soul searching, and he had little sympathy with those who were. Questions of ethics and morality, problems of theodicy that teetered on the sharp edges of philosophical deliberations and could not be resolved by the useful exercise of good common sense, were of no value to him. He quietly believed that the consideration of such questions was nothing more than pretentious posturing, of no use to himself and with no practical application to the living of life. The truth, Haydon thought, would be as uncomfortable for Dystal as it was for him, though certainly for different reasons.

There was no reason for Haydon to return to the department at all. When he had asked for the six months' leave of absence it had been in the back of his mind that it was simply a prelude to total severance, a separation without the responsibility of the final divorce. He would think about that later. But now Dystal had caught him off guard, and he was surprised and confused by the contradictory emotions of eagerness and dread, of excitement and sudden fatigue. He couldn't sort them out. Nor could he escape the uncomfortable intuition that there had never, ever, been a question of his resigning in the first place.

Haydon pulled a cigarette from the box and then pushed the opened box across to Dystal. They smoked one cigarette each in total silence before Haydon answered him.

6

Haydon stood at the front door and watched Dystal's car move away on the cinder drive and leave through the iron gates onto the boulevard. He watched long after the car had disappeared beneath the unbroken canopy of oaks that stretched the length of the street, his eyes seeing nothing but the shifting mottle of morning light that made him think of Monet.

As he turned and started back toward the hallway, Nina came down the stairs, her hair now in the familiar chignon, her sandaled feet showing slightly from beneath the cream percale skirt with each descending step. He waited for her.

"It was good seeing him again," she said.

Haydon nodded, and they walked across the hall and through the wide arched doorway into the living room. High ceilings enhanced the light, airy feeling of the white room, as did the tall windows that looked onto the circle drive.

Nina went to a pale titian sofa and sat down as Haydon crossed to the windows and looked out. He turned after a while and wandered over to stare at a red conté drawing. It showed well by the late morning light and was one of several he had bought over the years. They hung throughout the house, mostly nudes. After a moment he returned across the sisal-covered floor and sat near the opposite end of the sofa from Nina. He turned toward her and crossed his long legs as he leaned back with his shoulders in the corner.

"Well, I guess I'm going back," he said.

She looked at him. "What's the matter? Is it something special?"

He told her everything Dystal had said, as well as his own suspicions about the administration wanting to make peace with him, which was why he suspected Dystal was able to get away with such an unorthodox request. The lieutenant's visit seemed legitimate. He simply wanted to get to the bottom of the case, and he felt Haydon was the best man to do it.

"He probably assumed that whatever I might have decided to do at the end of five months would not change substantially at the end of the sixth," Haydon said. "He's probably right."

"You'd already decided to go back?" Nina asked. She took one of the sofa pillows into her lap and started picking at a loose thread. "We never talked about it."

"No. I hadn't given the decision much thought at all. I've thought about everything else, I guess, but not really about whether I would quit, or not quit, when the time was up."

"What about . . . all your other interests? The things you've gotten involved in over the past five months."

"I didn't develop any interests I didn't already have," Haydon said.

"I know," she said. "It's just that I'd hoped you might find something related . . . something that might hold your interest exclusively."

Haydon's eyes wandered around the room. He was uncomfortable with her going at it obliquely like this. It didn't sound like her. Evasiveness was his forte. But he didn't have to listen to it very long. When he didn't respond, Nina confronted the issue head on.

"Stuart," she said evenly, "do you think you're stable enough to go back?"

He let his eyes rest on his mother's baby grand, which glistened black in the bright room, its top laden with family pictures in an assortment of silver and tortoiseshell frames.

"What kind of word is that?" he asked. "Stable."

"How would you phrase it?" Her voice was calm.

"Not like that."

She waited, then said, "Stuart, during the past five months you've grown more relaxed, less distant, less secretive. I hate to see you go back."

"You want me to quit?" It wasn't a challenge. He really wanted to know.

"I don't want you to change. That work changes you. In the past I've never come right out and said I wanted you to quit. I didn't want to put you at odds with your work and with me. That's one conflict I knew you didn't need. But now, yes, I wish you wouldn't go back. I don't think it's worth it. It takes so much out of you, and it takes so much away from us."

Haydon waited a moment and then uncrossed his legs. He leaned forward and tossed a cigarette box on the low table of burled rosewood that sat in front of them. He put his elbows on his knees and clasped his hands together, staring at them.

"Nina, I need to do this. I've had enough time to pull myself together. Now I'm ready to go back." He stopped. He wanted to choose his words carefully. "I need the work, Nina. This work. I wouldn't feel right about turning away from it now. Not after all these years, and not like this. God knows I'm aware of the psychological . . . problems in it for me. If I could explain it for you, I would. I'll have to learn to handle the problems better."

"You can't, Stuart." Her voice was flat. She was stating a fact, a stark fact. "For you, this work is destructive."

"That's a strong view."

"It's not a 'view.' "

"I need to do it," he said. "If it's a strain I'll just have to live with it. I don't know what else I can do about it."

"You could *quit*, Stuart." She put down the pillow and sat forward on the sofa too, leaning toward him as she spoke. "Be available on a consultancy basis for special cases, but not every homicide that comes your way day in and day out, week after week, month after month. You're not made for that kind of nonstop pressure."

"The other men do it. They all live with it."

"You know better than to give me that kind of justification," she said.

"Dystal *is* offering me a special arrangement. I'll have only this one case, and I really want to look into this one. There's something especially interesting about it."

Nina looked at him a long time. "Do you have any idea how many times you've said that about a new case?"

Haydon didn't know how to respond to that. He just sat there.

"Okay, Stuart, let's get to the heart of the problem."

He looked at her, knowing what was coming.

"I don't know how many more times I'm going to cover for you . . . for the times you simply disappear when the pressures get too great. I'm not unshakable, Stuart. Don't expect too much of me; don't assume too much. One day those episodes are going to break one of us. I used to think it would be you, but I don't know anymore. I don't know what you go through when you're away, but I know what I go through. Stuart, don't ask me to give to you until I'm empty. Share this thing with me, whatever it is. Give me a reason for doing what I'm doing."

He studied the expression on her face, acutely aware that he was responsible for it being there.

"It won't happen again," he said.

Nina was at a loss. She simply stared at him.

"It won't happen again," he repeated. "I told you, the leave of absence was what I needed. It gave me time to pull myself together, decide how I was going to live with the stress of the job. It's not impossible. I can do it. I'm not going to ask you to go through another one of those episodes. I'm not."

That was it. He looked away from her, but he could feel her eyes on him as he stared out the window to the green lawn scribed by the gentle arc of the driveway that led to the gates. He felt her pulling at him like a magnet, and he hated himself for what he couldn't give her. Suddenly, all the intensity seemed to drain out of her, and she reached back and did something with her chignon. It took her a long time to adjust whatever it was she was adjusting, her eyes diverted. Haydon turned to her and noticed the slight color in her cheeks. Finally she finished and dropped her arms and looked at him again.

"I shouldn't have gone into it," she said. "We'll leave it here, Stuart. I won't take it any further."

There was a tone in her voice that made him uneasy. And it wasn't only the tone that disturbed him, but the fact that once again it was Nina who conceded in the face of his implacable silence. But this time, there was a subtle difference. In acquiescing now, in this way, she clearly had placed the security of their relationship in his hands. He was responsible for the consequences. It was obvious that she was willing to withdraw into her own silence to avoid an argument that neither of them wanted to engage in, but in doing so she gave him the lead to honorably diffuse the tension. He should have leveled with her. He should have discussed with her his reasons for going back to a job that had driven him to a nervous breakdown, not once but several times: breakdowns from which she alone had nourished him to recovery, and which she alone had kept secret without his having to ask her to do so.

In spite of this, he continued to hold back. His deep reserve was a dividing rift, a crevasse as frightening for what it represented as for what it concealed. During the past five months he had wanted to change that by telling her everything. He had wanted to, but he didn't. Not then and not now.

7

The Powell files were sent over late that afternoon accompanied by a note from Dystal, saying he had talked to Mooney and Lapierre again and they would be expecting to hear from Haydon. Haydon sat in the library and read them through, underlining a point here and there, making a note in the margins about a cross-reference or an item he wanted to go back to later. Lapierre had done the introduction, scene summary, and coroner's report; Mooney had interviewed the witnesses. There was very little to add to what Dystal had already told him.

When he was through reading, Haydon went to the stereo and put on a selection of Bach's "Well-Tempered Clavier." He took the box of scene-of-crime photographs and began spreading them over the refectory table. He first arranged them in a sequence that he imagined was a possible scenario for the narrative of the murder. It was a complicated scene. The blood that had spilled on the floor had been stepped in and tracked around by whoever had done the killing, or by someone there at the time or shortly thereafter. It would be some time, if ever, before the lab technicians would be able to determine which footprints going in which direction had been laid over the top of the others and thereby establish a sequence of movement.

After studying several of these scenarios, Haydon arranged the photographs in groups of perspectives: all the shots taken from the door, all the shots taken from the sink where the body was found, all those taken from the side of the room where the tape-editing machine sat and where most of the blood had splattered, with the exception of the gore in and around the sink. It seemed probable that the initial attack had taken place while Powell had been editing tape. There was, however, no tape in the editor.

There were more than a dozen photographs of the footprints in the blood and of the splatters on various portions of the walls and the equipment. They had also videotaped the scene. Haydon took the cassette into the television room and slipped it into the recorder. There was static, HPD identification signals, and then the scene shots. The camera moved from the outside door of the laboratory into the room and began panning from the left side where the editing machine sat. Haydon was glad they had had at least that much foresight. The camera made a complete circle of the room back to the door, and then the cameraman advanced to the body and made a similar sweep, starting at the door again and going to the editing machine, which was now on the right, and around to the door again. One last complete pan was made from the editing machine itself, starting at the door and going clockwise.

Haydon returned to the library and sat down at one end of the refectory table with the diagram Lapierre had drawn of the scene. The main door to the lab where Powell had worked and died opened off an inner hallway within the Langer complex. It was not a large room, and the sinks where Powell's body was found were not even used by him in his video work. They were actually used as secondary facilities for the larger still-photography lab next door, to which there was access through a second door at one end of the sinks. In Lapierre's drawing the hallway entrance was at six o'clock, the editing machine at eight, the door into the larger photography lab at ten, and Powell's body was in the sink at one. From one to six was a wall of counter space with supply shelves above. The bloody footprints crisscrossed each other roughly around the center of the room and then ended in a pile of paper towels about five feet in front of the hallway door. A single trace was found right on the threshold, but beyond that the killer had walked out with clean feet.

There was a coroner's report with Dr. Harl Vanstraten's signature. According to the report, Powell had died of the throat wound, not of the several penetrations in the thoracic region. Any of those, however, would have proven fatal in time. The postmortem showed no traces of drugs, though there was some alcohol in the blood. Powell had been a heavy smoker. He had prostatis. He would have needed triple bypass heart surgery in another fifteen years, if not sooner, and his liver had been exposed to too much alcohol. He had a very fine tattoo of an oversized *Phthirus pubis* (Vanstraten would not call it a crab louse) just where his pubic hair started in his right groin. Very funny story behind that, no doubt. He had only one testicle. Probably a not-so-funny story. Whatever Wayne Powell had been in life, he made an only mildly interesting cadaver.

Haydon noted that Vanstraten had put the approximate time of death at two o'clock in the morning. He put the coroner's report aside and picked up Mooney's interviews.

Raymond Tease, the director of the photography department of Langer Media, had found the body. He had come in a little after eight o'clock on Thursday morning and opened the still-photography lab. After checking for messages on his desk, he put water in the coffee machine to let it start heating and then went out into the hall and walked down to the snack area to get a quick cup out of the vending machine. He stopped and chatted with the receptionist a minute and started back to the lab. On his way he decided to check and see if Powell was in and found him. He slammed the door shut and ran back to the receptionist's desk just as Mr. Langer was walking in.

The three of them went back to the lab, and the receptionist and Tease stood at the door while Langer carefully entered the room to check Powell's vital signs. When he came out, he stationed Tease at the door to keep anyone from going in and had the receptionist call the police.

The receptionist corroborated Tease's story and had nothing else to add. She had been the one to open the offices that morning and hadn't noticed anything out of the ordinary.

William D. Langer also corroborated the sequence of events and added his efforts to keep the discovery as quiet as possible by keeping it from the others who came in that morning, at least until the police could arrive. Mooney had added notes of his own regarding the extent to which Langer had gone throughout the morning to keep the excitement and publicity to a minimum.

There had been brief follow-up interviews with Tease and Langer, and with a girl named Patricia Beamon who had worked with Tease and Powell in the photo section. Another girl, Alice Parnas, had also worked with Beamon and the others, but she was not helpful and was reluctant to talk at all. The follow-up stories were just as Dystal had recapped them. He had omitted nothing of significance. However, there were additional points Haydon wanted to pursue, and he began making notes. He organized the questions under the names of the persons he wanted to interview and arranged the names alphabetically.

And then there was the question of Jennifer Quinn. Mooney and Lapierre were still trying to find her, and there was a stakeout of Powell's house in case she returned. They were supposed to call him immediately.

Haydon leaned back in his chair and looked at the pile of research on the table. Bach's clavier had fallen silent long ago, and the light coming in through the French doors had lost its white intensity and given way to the muted tones of late afternoon. The color photographs of Wayne Powell's violent denouement were scattered before him, their bright tones of violence fading with the weakening light.

As he looked at the jumble of grisly photographs, it occurred to Haydon that there was something beyond the stealing of life that made homicide repugnant. Perhaps an even crueler aspect of the act was that of the murderer's intrusion into the victim's death. Nothing in life was more intrinsically intimate, more privately sacred, than the process of dying. By imposing his involvement in this process, the murderer forever violated that privacy and forced the victim to participate in the brutal degradation of his own passing. In the frenetic, searing moments of killing, the most intimate act of man's existence was made a garish spectacle and thereby tragically debased by the red ferocity of violence.

Haydon thought about that as he turned out the lights and wondered why Powell was in the sink.

8

The next day was Sunday, and Haydon went with Nina and Gabriela to the early church services. His family had always gone to early services, and Gabriela believed that anything the family had done before his parents' death automatically fell into the category of tradition upon their decease. For an hour he watched the sun on the stained-glass windows, stood when everyone else stood, sat when everyone else sat, bowed when everyone else bowed, and tried not to think about Powell.

Driving home he remained preoccupied as the royal-blue Jaguar Vanden Plas filled with the saccharine fragrance of Juicy Fruit gum, which Gabriela parsimoniously administered in half pieces from the back seat as she had done every Sunday since Haydon was a boy. He and Nina took their pieces from the old Mexican woman and dutifully chewed them as they listened to her review the details of the dresses of the women she had seen at church. Nina was patient with her, attentive to her comments, reciprocating with her own observations. As they pulled into the gates and circled the drive to the porte cochere, Gabriela changed the subject and gave a single pointed opinion about a specific aspect of the morning's sermon. This was always done in conclusion to the drive home, and in a manner meant to bring to their attention that her morning in church had not been totally devoted to the superficial appraisal of women's fashions.

Throughout the afternoon Nina was reserved. She took her pad and pencils into the living room to sketch in its abundant north light, while Haydon roamed around in the library cataloging books, paging through the new arrivals he had not yet shelved, and listening to more of Bach's clavier.

On Monday morning Haydon met with Dystal, Mooney, and Lapierre for one of Dystal's celebrated breakfasts at the JoJo's on Loop 610 near the Galleria. All three men were already there when Haydon walked in. His late arrival had been deliberate. He wanted to see all of them together, to try to get a feel for the group's collective attitude toward him, and toward the unusual arrangement Dystal had put together. Although Haydon had talked with Mooney once or twice during the past five months, it was the first time he had seen Lapierre since he had been on leave. He was especially concerned that Lapierre should feel comfortable with the roles each of them had to play.

They ordered but did not go directly into the business they had to discuss. Instead there was small talk over their first cups of coffee and on through breakfast. The detectives told Haydon about changes in departmental policy and personnel that had come about, or were anticipated, since Haydon had been gone. Lapierre said they had torn the squad room ceiling out again because the new air-conditioning system had not met with building codes. The place was going to have to endure another summer under construction with telephone and computer cables draped from the superstructure of the lowered ceiling and their only cooling coming from the tunnel fans set up in the hallways. Mooney relayed some choice bits of gossip about the personal lives of some of the division's Don Juans and reported a couple of rumored divorces. These he speculated about with a few theories of his own thrown in to back up his hunches. Dystal listened to all this with good-humored distance.

They did not need to say that the speculation about Haydon's leave of absence had been the main subject of similar gossip for weeks on end after his departure. He could, and had, imagined the extent of such theorizing.

When they had finished eating and Dystal had poured fresh cups of coffee, it was time to get down to business. Haydon looked at Mooney and Lapierre.

"I know we've all been briefed about how this is going to work, so we don't have to review the arrangement that Bob's already set into motion. But I wanted both of you to know that I appreciate your willingness to work with me under these circumstances. We've worked together before, so I don't think there'll be any surprises about my approach. I'm sensitive to your vulnerability regarding the press, and you know my own attitudes about that. If somewhere down the line you begin to feel uncomfortable about the way I'm handling things, then feel free to come to me with it at any time. I mean anytime."

Haydon looked at Mooney. "Okay?"

Mooney nodded, seeming to feel a little awkward but taking it seriously. He cleared his throat. "Everything sounds good to me."

He looked at Lapierre. It was for the cautious Lapierre that Haydon had the most concern, and despite Dystal's earlier assurances Haydon wanted all of them to face the issue in one another's presence. It was essential that they feel comfortable with Haydon's position.

Pete Lapierre was of medium height and stocky, with thick black hair that he kept short in an effort to control it. He had smoky eyes that never portrayed anything but calm self-possession. In manner he was as circumspect as Mooney was loose, and though he was a neat dresser his clothes were reflective more of sensible economy than style. He had a reputation for writing the most lucid reports in the division and was a stickler for precision. Some people thought he was humorless, too stern, but Haydon understood his impatience with the locker-room bullshit that was part of the squad-room atmosphere. He was perceptive and thoughtful and never failed to offer his help or express sympathy and concern whenever it was appropriate. Although he kept very much to himself, he was liked by everyone.

"I don't have any problems with any of it," Lapierre said, looking Haydon in the eyes and seeming to understand what he was trying to do. "I'm looking forward to it."

"Well," Dystal said with elephantine expansiveness, relieved that all that had been gotten through. "I guess we ought to kind of get on to this Powell thing then." He picked up the coffeepot, but everyone refused. He poured some for himself. "Awright. Ed, why don't you start it off with the latest on Jennifer Quinn."

Mooney slid back in his chair to get his belly away from the unyielding edge of the table, took a toothpick out of his shirt pocket, and stuck it in his mouth. "Okay. The reason Quinn hasn't showed up is because she's out of the state on a job. She's also a cameraman—woman—and she works for another advertising agency, Cline, Lacey and Lee. A lot smaller than Langer's operation. She's been in New Orleans for one week on a two-week assignment. Had been gone about three days when Powell was killed. We've contacted the police down there, and they're keeping an eye on her for us. She seems to be carrying on with business as usual.

"According to a gal who works with her, she's been living with Powell for about six months, which means she's been with him almost as long as he's been in town. The gal didn't know if Quinn knew Powell before he came down here. Quinn's been with this agency a little over a year. Everybody seems to like her. They say she's a hard worker, sharp, good at what she does, no nasty habits. She's a Houston gal, so we can probably go as deep on background as you want. There's a picture of her in their little bungalow. She's a good-looking redhead.

"That's about it, except that several of the people I talked with at her office had met Powell and thought he was an asshole. I asked if any of them had told her about Powell's death, and they said no. That was late Friday. I suspect they have by now."

Haydon nodded. "I think you're probably right. Let's

go ahead and have the New Orleans police contact her and send her back here. We want to avoid making her feel threatened. Just a message from the police that there's been some trouble at home and she needs to return to Houston.''

"Okay," Mooney said.

"You said you saw a picture of her in their house. Where was it?''

"In the living room.''

"Were there any pictures of her in Powell's room?''

"I don't remember. There were a bunch of pictures tacked up on one wall. I don't remember if hers was there. His place had been gone through, you know, but besides that I got the impression it was probably already messed up from his being kind of a sloppy guy.''

Haydon looked at Lapierre. "What did you come up with, Pete?''

"So far all the blood that was taken from the random samples has been Powell's," Lapierre said, unconsciously realigning the tableware beside his plate, "although they still have a little more to run through. There was a lot of it. The footprints in the blood appear to have been made by two different-sized shoes. Both leather dress shoes. Not a synthetic sole, nothing funky or unusual. Just dress shoes. Actually, there are only five prints of the smaller shoe. They were found going from the door to the editor and then back to the door. Three going to the machine, two going back to the door. None of them really left much of a track. In fact, they just barely identified the two going back to the door.

"The prints leaving the heaviest blood residue were the ones made by the bigger shoe going to the recorder. And they are the only ones of that size that are a single set, not tracked over. Looks like he went from the recorder to the shelves of film and moved around there a lot. There was another trip to the recorder from the shelves and back. A trip to the door that goes into the other lab. Each trip past the sinks he got into the blood again. Tried to get it all off with the paper towels, and left.''

"He had to get the paper towels with his hands," Haydon said. "Any prints from there?''

Lapierre shook his head. "Nothing. And all the fingerprints they've lifted from the place so far have belonged to employees. There's still a few more of those to check out, too."

"The reports said there was no tape in the editor. Was anything missing from the laboratory?"

"We've got the people in the lab there cross-referencing the jobs Powell was working on with the film and tapes he had in the files."

"There was no security breach?"

"Not that anyone can determine. The agency has the usual arrangement with a private security firm, and the security people say there's no record of a breach. It seems to me there are several possibilities, though."

He put his closed fist on the table, palm up, and unfolded one finger with each point.

"Whoever did it had a key. Or they hid somewhere within the complex until after hours and waited for Powell to come in. Or they jumped Powell someplace outside, like in the parking garage, and made a forced entry at gun- or knife-point. Or Powell knew them and brought them there of his own free will. Or they knew how to manipulate the warning system."

"Maybe he was meeting a baby doll up there," Mooney said. "Quinn was out of town."

The waitress came and took away their empty plates, and Dystal poured more coffee from the private reserve that was a permanent fixture at his table. The restaurant was busy, but no one rushed them.

Haydon had often wondered at the wisdom of Dystal's establishing this kind of routine and familiarity. It was a natural thing for the lumbering lieutenant to do, but Haydon thought of how easy it was for anyone to find him there. Over the years a policeman makes a few enemies. Some of them were crazy.

They reviewed other possibilities and potential leads, posed theories, and guessed about which way it would go. Haydon asked a few questions about the interviews at Langer Media. At the end of another half hour, Haydon took his Mont Blanc from his pocket and began writing on his paper place mat. As he wrote, he explained the approach he wanted to follow and outlined the directions in which he wanted Mooney and Lapierre to move. He told them what he was going to do and then asked what they thought of his plans. They exchanged a few more ideas, made some additions, some adjustments, and they were through. Haydon tore off the half of the place mat on which he had been writing and put it in his pocket. By ten o'clock they were gone.

9
....

The executive looked at the profile of the man sitting in front of him. The sharp silhouette was leonine and strikingly distinguished, though the details of his features were cast into darkness by the glare coming from the casement windows. The executive could see that the man's hair, combed back in long thick waves from his handsome forehead, was beginning to take on the contours of a widow's peak. He knew the hair was trimmed immaculately around neck and ears. He looked at the straight bridge of the nose, the ridge of the small mustache, the rounded curve of the dimpled chin. He also knew that the man's firm jaw, which grew a heavy black beard that was shaved twice a day by a barber, bore a perpetual charcoal cast.

Neither of the men had spoken for several minutes, and the capacious room where the man at the desk spent his oddly disciplined days was as silent as a casket. The executive moved around in front of the desk to get away from the brilliant light of the window, one of four on the long wall that provided the only illumination in the room.

The wall spaces between the windows were covered with photographs, both black-and-white and color.

Now the executive was directly in front of the other man and could see clearly one half of the other man's face as he studied something in front of him. The other half remained in the dark.

"Do you want me to warn the others?" the executive asked finally. "They should be told something. What if—"

"*T-t . . . t-t . . . t-t . . .*" The other man looked up, smiling; the soft sound trailing off.

When he didn't go on, the executive continued. "There were five of us that night. Shouldn't I—"

"*T-t . . . t-t . . . t-t . . .*"

The executive stopped, inwardly frustrated, even angry, but outwardly calm.

The other man continued to smile with disarming frankness, not taking advantage of the interruption he had created to speak himself. The attitude of his expression and the anticipatory angle of his head made him seem to beckon the executive to continue, even though he had just intervened. The executive examined the half of the man's face that was in good light and saw the strong white teeth behind the smile. He also saw one eye, the iris of which was so dark it was indistinguishable from the pupil, so that the man looked at him from a black hole that robbed the eye of any personality or feeling of communication. His smiling mouth opened slightly more, his handsome head tilted slightly farther back, his eyebrows jerked higher, inviting the executive to speak.

The executive didn't.

It was a familiar if perplexing exchange. He had experienced it many times, had witnessed it with other executives who had access to this man. The noble head would tilt back and the soft "*t-t, t-t,*" would begin, almost inaudibly at first so that the speaker ignored it. When it persisted, growing in volume, the executive would assume he was being politely interrupted and stop. So would the soft fricative sounds. Silence. Puzzled, the executive would try to sort out what was happening. When the silence continued, he would assume the interruption was not going to be followed up and he would begin again, only to be once more interrupted by the soft fricatives, the tilted head, the smile that made the executive wonder if he was being ridiculed. Another silence, which, this time, the executive would not break.

Eventually, the man himself would begin to speak in a voice so subtle that the executive prayed that some slight noise, a closing door, a cough, would not obscure a word or phrase. The strain of concentrating on every word, of even trying to read his lips, added to the tension of the meetings. The speech pattern was erratic: phrases followed by ellipses, the fricatives, the smiles. The executive would be forced to follow a good deal of the conversation by inference. No one ever attracted attention to the fact that they had difficulty hearing him.

Now, as he waited and looked into the void of the black eye, the executive didn't understand this odd method of communication any better than he had the first time he witnessed it. Still, he had survived dozens of these encounters. But now he was tired. Impatience was playing an increasingly larger part in the range of emotions that affected him when he was summoned to this moody estate hidden deep within a wooden section of the city.

He waited, his hands clasped behind his back. He tensed his arms and pulled his muscles against the vertebrae in his lower back as he met the stare of the man across sloppy stack of papers that slid into one another and formed an unstable mound of debris that rambled from one end of the crescent-shaped desk to the other. Paper clips on the edges of pages snagged other pages in the shuffle and dragged them out of the piles to contribute to the slide. A china cup and saucer were half hidden by the ever-spreading paper floe, and the derrick of a miniature copper oil rig, the kind found at arts and crafts fairs, was almost totally submerged. In among the white documents the executive saw pale green and blue slips that he knew to be undeposited checks. Sometimes they stayed on the desk for months until their writers issued new ones, which also disappeared into the white refuse. The persons who sent these checks were uninitiated and naive.

"The footage is the problem," the man said softly.

The executive moved forward. "I know that. I'll—"

The man smiled and patted the reel cans stacked on one end of his desk.

"I meant these. I wanted to show you these . . . t-t . . . but Bechtel didn't get them out of the vault in time and, uh, I've got to put them back into the air lock to warm up. We'll see them tomorrow." He laughed a little. "They're fascinating. From, uh, Sri Lanka. The first from there. A Sinhalese cameraman tried to sell them to, uh, a network reporter. They wouldn't touch them. T-t . . . t-t . . . Bechtel bought them on his last trip to Paris."

The man was toying with him, of course. He *had* been referring to the other footage, then pretended not to be.

"But we'll see something else this afternoon," the man said.

The executive's heart sank. He was hoping that just this once he wouldn't have to watch a film. He didn't want to see it, whatever horror it was. Today, especially, he wanted to be spared the besotting violence.

The man stood and gathered up the canisters of film. The executive watched him come around the desk and start across the long room. Over the last two years he had grown accustomed to the man's appearance, almost forgetting to notice its unusualness. But today, he saw him again as if for the first time and was stricken by the incongruity: the noble, masculine head so dramatically larger than the slight, preadolescent body upon which it seemed precariously balanced. The man's entire frame appeared to have stopped growing at prepubescence, before the changes of adolescence stirred and injected its cells with the hormones necessary for masculine development. His shoulders lacked squareness, and his torso did not carry the settled weight of adulthood. His hands were devoid of delineating tendons and veins, pudgy in the palms, with little fingers that tapered toward the ends. And yet his body was not ill-proportioned or effeminate; it was simply puerile, lacking any sign of strength or maturity. Conversely, his head was everything his body was not. The physical disharmony of the whole was startling.

The executive followed him, feeling absurd as he lum-

bered behind this little boy/man who habitually wore tiny
black patent-leather evening slippers, tuxedo pants with
satin stripe, wing-collared tuxedo shirt with knife pleating,
no tie, and suspenders. They were the only clothes he ever
wore when he was at home, and they were always soiled.
The shirtfront was dingy with old laundered stains, and
the pants, slightly dusty at the sagging knees, were wrinkled to a permanent pucker at the crotch.

The man opened a wooden door in the middle of the
room on the wall opposite the windows. There was an
adjoining metal door on the other side of the jamb. This
he opened also, and entered a smaller room with wall
shelving holding dozens of canisters of movie reels. The
temperature in this room was 55 degrees Fahrenheit. The
man laid the canisters from his desk on one of the shelves
and took a heavy coat from a hanger on the wall and put it
on. He opened a second door and entered another vault.
The executive followed, not bothering to take one of several similar coats of a larger size, making sure the air lock
was closed behind them.

The vault beyond the air lock was nearly four times
larger, with hundreds of feet of open shelving stacked
with film cans, some aluminum, some plastic, depending
on the age and type of film they contained. The temperature here was 40 degrees Fahrenheit, with 30 percent relative humidity. The archive shelving was arranged by year,
with subcategories of geographical location in alphabeti-
cal order. Each canister was labeled with date, cameraman
(if known), source, location, context, and brief descrip-
tion of the film's subject.

The man quickly disappeared around the corner of
one row of shelving. The executive stayed near the door
with his hands thrust down into his pockets, waiting. He
could hear the man pulling cans from shelves, putting
them back, killing time. In a few minutes, the man appeared around the end of another row of shelves twenty
feet away and stopped in the aisle, looking at the executive. The room held the same close silence of a meat
locker.

"T-t . . . t-t . . . you suppose Toy has the rest of it?"

he asked. His breath hung in front of him like a puff of smoke.

The executive looked down the aisle at him. "Of course he does."

The man thought a moment. His slight frame was bolstered by the bulky coat, and its fur collar, turned up, hid his childish neck.

"Do you suppose he got all of our faces?"

"It wouldn't make sense if he hadn't."

"I suppose he'll make a lot of duplicates," he mused softly.

"I'm sure of it," the executive said. He was tired.

"Do you think he will approach each of us? Or just me?"

"Maybe everyone. I don't know."

"I suppose he'll want a lot of money." The black eyes looked somewhere past the executive's shoulder.

The executive didn't answer. He didn't want to get into that. He just wanted to know what he was supposed to do.

"How much would you say the footage was worth?" The man crossed his tiny slippered feet at the ankles and leaned against the shelving, his small hands in the big square pockets of the coat.

The executive was getting cold now, and couldn't help hunching his shoulders. The damn film was priceless and the man knew it. He was asking a silly question.

"What would you pay for it?" the man said to the executive. He was smiling. *"T-t . . . t-t . . ."*

"Whatever it took."

"But there's a point beyond which you would not be willing to pay."

"I'm sure. I don't know. I'd have to hear what he wanted."

The man shrugged somewhere underneath the coat. "I guess we'll just have to wait until he contacts us."

Again the executive said nothing. He had long found these oblique remarks maddening. The man knew damn well he was already taking care of it, had been working on it since Thursday morning.

The man's lower face was blue with beard and cold,

and a bright red blotch had appeared on each cheek. He seemed so frail the executive supposed it wouldn't take much for him to freeze to death.

"Toy was a superb cameraman," the man said.

The executive agreed. He felt his jaw jump with cold as he looked at the man to see if he could read anything into the black spots he used for eyes. There was nothing there, of course, nothing that helped the executive understand whether the man had used the past tense deliberately or accidentally. Who knew what Byzantine arrangements he had made elsewhere? His life was so compartmentalized the executive marveled that he was not impossibly lost in the maze of his own plottings. But that was the way he maintained the necessary distance. The man's hands were always clean because his executives were his surrogate hands and the surrogate hands obeyed the mind, insofar as they could read the mind. And if they happened to misread it or became overzealous in their wish to accommodate him? What could he do? Certainly he personally could not be blamed for the misjudgments of others.

All that duplicity hid behind the murky wells of his eyes. He couldn't be blamed for anything with eyes like that.

"We should have had him tape those things from the beginning," the man said. "That would have preempted this sort of thing, and we could have controlled the circumstances. And he wouldn't have filmed the people he shouldn't have filmed," he added with a wry smile.

They stood looking at each other. The man pursed his lips and blew out a jet of foggy breath as if he were exhaling the smoke of a cigarette. "Well," he said, and looked aimlessly around the vault at the shelves stacked with film, millions of feet of carnage. It seemed as if he were halfheartedly trying to decide what it was he wanted to do next.

Finally he stirred himself and walked past the executive, who was shivering uncontrollably now, and went into the air lock. The executive followed him and closed the vault door behind them. They stopped at the shelves in the air lock, and the man looked over the stacks of cans that had been in the room for twenty-four hours or longer. They had to warm to the room's temperature slowly to avoid minuscule amounts of moisture forming on the film as a result of condensation.

"We've got some Lahore footage from the sixties," the man said. "There's some Idi Amin interrogations, some Argentine interrogations in La Tablada army installation in 1977 . . . this one has bestiality in it, naked girls and trick rats." He grinned at the joke and then returned to his recitation. "We have a Ku Klux Klan lynching, some Beirut things. . . ." He was trying to decide, standing with his arms folded, still wearing the heavy coat. Finally he reached out and slipped one can out from under several others. "We've been talking about Mr. Toy. Let's watch some of his Guatemalan stories. Huehuetenango. There are interesting things in this one too."

The man handed the executive the reel, hung his coat on the rack, and preceded him into the big room. The executive closed the doors behind them and went to a projector permanently installed in a cabinet in the center of the room. The man crawled onto one of the several sofas arranged in a semicircle in front of the projector and facing the far end of the room. The executive flipped a switch, and the movie screen descended from the ceiling with a soft electrical *whirr*. It took up the entire far end of the room.

The executive threaded the film and then pushed a button on the cabinet that caused the enormous drapes over the windows to close slowly. He flipped on the projector, and the film began to run.

The opening shot is an aerial view of the jungle, the horizon tilting slightly first one way and then another as the aircraft banks. Then the camera pans forward, taking in a string of four blue and white Jet Ranger helicopters trailing down toward the jungle in a wide swinging arc. The camera is apparently in the last ship. The picture vibrates slightly from the pounding rotors. It is a good shot, watching the sinister machines dropping down into a valley, over a river, and between jungle-covered hillsides. Then there are puffs of smoke coming from the open doors of the first Ranger, and then from the others, until the film shudders heavily and the camera swings around to film the door gunner a few feet away raking the trees.

Suddenly the camera records chaos as the ships land with unexpected speed, disgorging soldiers. There is a shot of sky, then grass, then legs, and finally ground-level footage of Guatemalan soldiers running into tall highland grass and emerging into a village firing their recoilless rifles. The camera catches soldiers screaming at one another, pointing, running. A shot shows the Rangers lifting off in a hurricane of dust. A helmet sails across the screen, and the choppers are gone. The film jars to a blur and then, incredibly, there is a close-up of an old Indian man trying to pick up his arm, blood ejaculating from the ganglia at his shoulder. He can't do it, and he turns helplessly to the camera, crying open-mouthed like a child. Then an old woman, wearing a torn dress, runs up and gets it for him and they run off together for a few yards until she is suddenly picked up and propelled forward with her feet off the ground to fall in a heap with the arm. The old man does a hysterical hopping dance over her crumpled body and then bends over and takes his arm by the fingers, but he can't lift it and he trails it along behind him on the ground as he runs again until his legs go rubbery and he plows into the dirt. The camera fast-pans and stops on two Indian men kneeling with their hands tied behind them. They seem young, more like boys. A soldier comes up and begins sawing at the throat of one of them with a knife. He hits the jugular vein and the blood shoots out onto him. He jumps back and kicks at the boy, who is pitching and bucking wildly as if to get away from his own death. The second prisoner inexplicably falls over, and the other soldier runs up and begins stomping his head as if it were a beer can and continues until it is misshappen and red and bears no resemblance to a head at all. In the background people run back and forth in smoke and fire. The camera jogs to one side and follows two soldiers dragging a naked Indian woman along the ground by her feet. Her face wears the passive serenity of shock as she calmly tries to sit up and keep her entrails from getting into the dirt.

The executive turned away from the rest of it. A tiny,

brilliant silver of light came through one of the windows where the curtains did not quite meet near the top. He fixed his eyes on this shard of light and concentrated on it. He clung to it with his heart as well as his eyes, as if it were the only thing in the world that could save him.

10

....

She had agreed to meet him at James Coney Island, downtown at Travis and Dallas streets across from Foley's department store. That would be best, she had said, because it was far enough away from her office that they were not likely to run into anyone she knew, and yet it was close enough for her to walk there and back on her lunch hour and still have time to eat.

Haydon had gotten there first and was sitting at a window table, watching the people come in and wondering if he could pick her out of the crowd before she started looking around and gave herself away. He did. Outside on the sidewalk she had paused at the door, assumed a determined expression, and then leaned against the chrome bar and pushed her way inside.

He half stood; she saw him, stopped, looked at him with a slightly surprised expression, and started toward him. He watched as she made her way through the tables. She wore a lavender shirtwaist dress that went to midcalf and had shoulder pads reminiscent of the styles of the forties. Her taffy-colored hair was pulled back and upward at both temples and fixed with combs in the style of Betty Grable. A white beaded purse was tucked under one arm as she approached.

"Could I see your identification, please," she blurted. She said it with the mechanical determination of a much-rehearsed speech that was not to be denied.

"Of course," Haydon said. "We'd better sit down." He reached into his breast pocket and unobtrusively laid his wallet on the table. She leaned over and looked at it. Her face was oval and her eyelashes were taffy like her hair.

"I'm sorry," she said, relieved, pushing it back to him as she looked up. "I guess that could be forged. I've seen that on TV. Forged I.D.'s." She gave a short laugh, a little foolish grin. "I did call the police station to make sure you were real."

"It's all right," Haydon said. "It's good that you checked it out. We don't have much time. What would you like?"

"Oh, just a coney and a Seven-Up, sugar free. A bag of chips, maybe."

He stood in line and took a plastic tray and slid it along the chrome railing, getting two of the same thing, napkins, and a couple of straws. The black cooks with little white paper caps worked with the economy and swiftness of machines, their eyes never looking up as they sweated in the nearly visible smells of hot franks and mustard and onions. At the end of the line he paid and came back to the table and unloaded the tray. She waited.

"Go ahead," he said. "I'll talk while you eat, and then you talk while I eat. I learned a long time ago that it's the most economical way." He smiled.

"I guess so." She looked at him curiously and then began eating her hot dog. She darted her eyes around the crowded lunchroom. It was a good place for a quick meal, and the small tables had a constant turnover of the men and women who poured out of the office buildings at noon to stretch their legs, catch some sun, and get a bite to eat.

"I've read your interview with detectives Mooney and Lapierre," Haydon said. "I'd like to go over a few additional points with you. I'll be brief, and you can answer in any order you like when you're ready." He paused, and she nodded, chewing and looking at him with wide, expectant eyes. "I'd like to know if Wayne Powell ever brought anyone to the office with him. Like a friend, someone who might hang around for a few minutes at the end of the day waiting for him to finish so they could go home. Anyone after hours. Were you ever there at night when he was working? Have you ever met his girlfriend, a woman named Jennifer Quinn?"

He paused at this point to let the questions settle a little, then continued.

"Did you ever get a look at what it was that Powell worked on at night? What was his attitude toward his night work? Was he protective? Indifferent? Are you aware of any meetings between Mr. Langer and Powell? Did you ever see them talking together? If so, do you know what about? How did Powell get along with Tease? Any tension there? Do you know if he ever discussed Powell's night work with him?"

Patricia Beamon raised her hand to stop him as she chewed quickly and wiped her mouth. She swallowed and took a quick sip of her Seven-Up.

"You'd better stop right there and let me cover what I can. I'm not sure I'm going to remember all your questions."

She took another sip of her drink, looked out the window to the bright hot sidewalk a moment, and frowned slightly in the glare as she gathered her thoughts.

"The negative points first. I never say Wayne talking with Mr. Langer. I was never there at night when he was working. There was no tension between Wayne and Tease, but I would say that's more likely because Ray's a marshmallow. If Mr. Langer said he should keep hands off Wayne, then Ray would never rock the boat no matter how much Wayne might goof off on the job."

"Did Langer tell Tease to keep his hands off Wayne?"

"Well, I assumed it was something like that. That's what he told Dean."

"Dean Warner?"

"Right."

"Did Warner tell you that?"

"We—Alice and I—assumed that's what happened. I mean, after Dean talked with Mr. Langer, Wayne went right on doing what he was doing. It made Dean furious, but he didn't do anything about it. And Wayne kind of rubbed it in too, when Dean was within hearing distance. He'd make little comments about 'other' stuff that he had to work on 'later.' Wayne tended to be a real smartass. He and Dean didn't get along too well from the beginning. Of course, that didn't go on long. Dean quit, you know, a little while after his talk with Mr. Langer."

"Has Tease ever said anything about Powell's night work?" Haydon was eating now. The coney was good, with sweet onions.

"No."

The musical chairs in the lunchroom had picked up speed as the twelve o'clock lunch hour overlapped with the one o'clock crowd starting to come in. Chrome chair legs scrubbed across the floor by the dozens, and people shouted at friends when they saw a table opening up. The line at the counter stretched back to the door, where people had crowded in a knot so they wouldn't have to stand outside on the blistering sidewalk.

"Did you ever inquire or hint about it?" Haydon had to raise his voice.

She shook her head.

"You've never seen Powell bring anyone to the office? No one ever came to see him for any reason?"

"I saw his girlfriend once. A couple of months ago. Alice came into the lab and told me she'd been at the snack bar when this girl came up to the receptionist and asked for Wayne. Alice said she was sitting out there waiting for him. So I went and pretended to get something. Boy, was I surprised."

"Why?"

"She was young, and really pretty. Good build, beautiful white skin that just glowed, and gorgeous red-gold hair that you could tell she really took care of. Green eyes. I mean *green*. Dressed in classy clothes. I remember she was wearing a really nice rust-on-rust striped dress with bateau neck and dolman sleeves." Patricia Beamon shook her head and her eyes sparkled with admiration. "Looked like a million. Sharp." She nodded.

"Why did that surprise you?"

"Well, Wayne . . . it's kind of weird talking about him now." She shrugged. "Wayne was sleazy, in a way. He wanted to be cool, but his idea of cool was about twenty years out of style. He came off kind of third-rate. A loser." She shook her head. "But this girl, she was something else. I just couldn't see them together. But that happens a lot. Really classy girl with some squirrel. You ever notice that?" She leaned toward him earnestly, waiting for him to agree with her.

"Sometimes," Haydon said. "You never saw anyone else up there with him or coming to see him?"

"Our clients would come to see him sometimes, but I know them. No one other than her, and I only saw her that one time."

"What about Alice?"

"What?"

"Has she ever commented about noticing anything?"

The girl winced one side of her face in an equivocal expression that said Alice was another story.

"I'm not sure Alice is all that observant," she said. "She's kind of mousy; in character, I mean. Timid, quiet. She's a sweet girl, but she's not real quick about social nuances. I mean, I'm not sure she'd notice something subtle, like secret interoffice romances. The meaningful-glance sort of thing."

"You said you were never there at night while Powell was working. Did you ever see what he was working on?"

She casually pulled a potato chip from its sack and munched it carelessly with her front teeth as she thought about his question. A wispy tendril of her taffy hair had pulled loose from her combs and floated like a piece of seaweed near her eyes.

"I don't know," she said, with a kind of grimace and scrunching of her shoulders that meant she was walking on eggshells.

"What do you mean?"

"Well . . . ." She paused, trying to decide how she could put the best light on it. "One morning I was the first one to get to the lab. Whoever comes in first is supposed to get things started. You know. I was going around making the coffee, turning on the drying drums, starting the water in the sinks, all that, and I went into Wayne's office. I didn't have anything to do in there, I just—you know—stuck my head in. Well, I was curious. The VTR was sitting there, and I just punched the button. It was Vietnam news footage. Combat footage. Some pretty heavy stuff. You could actually see people getting shot, being killed. It was something. I saw a little of it, and then I shut it off and ran it back a ways hoping he wouldn't notice. I guess he didn't; he never said anything about it. But that was the only time I ever saw anything that wasn't company footage. I guess he was working the night before and inadvertently left the tape. I don't know. It never happened again."

"Were you surprised at the footage?"

"Well, yes, I guess. I don't know."

"What do you think he was doing with it?"

She ate another chip, sipped her Seven-Up. "I don't know." She tilted her head a little. "Maybe he was working on a documentary for someone." That sounded good to her. "Yeah, that would be my guess."

Haydon finished his own hot dog while the girl munched her chips.

"This is really wild," she said. "I've never been involved in anything like this before. Do you have any idea who did it?"

"We're looking into it," Haydon said.

The girl studied him. Then, as if she had decided to change the subject of her thoughts, she said, "We've got the creeps up there. At five after five that place is empty. No one hangs around anymore. Poor Alice isn't even coming to work, claims she has the flu." Suddenly she looked at her watch. "Say, do you have any more questions? I've got to get back."

"No. That's it for now," Haydon said. "I appreciate your taking the time." He reached into his pocket and gave her a card. "Will you call me if you think of anything else you might want to add to what you've already told me?"

She looked at the card and then up at him. "Sure." Her eyes stayed with his a moment. "Oh, I owe you for the coney," she said, and started digging in her purse.

Haydon shook his head. "My pleasure."

Patricia Beamon looked up at him again. Haydon could see her mind working. "I'll bet you need my home telephone number, don't you."

"That's okay. I can get you through the office."

"Oh," she said. "Look, I'll be glad to give it to you." She touched her combs.

"It's not necessary," Haydon said. He stood, and she stood too, tucking her purse under her arm. She swiped at the tendril of seaweed.

"Well, I guess I'll probably see you later." She hesitated.

"Thanks," Haydon said.

He watched her work her way through the crowded diner, through the wad of people at the door, and out to the sidewalk. She gave him one last glance, through the plateglass window, and smiled before she disappeared around the side of the building.

11

·······························

The strident midafternoon sun cut sharply against the angles of the city's buildings as Haydon stood on the east side of Louisiana Street with the Pennzoil towers at his back and looked across at the mammoth arch that was the entrance to the lobby of RepublicBank. The most recent of the city's downtown architectural wonders, and Haydon's favorite, the RepublicBank Center was one of two dissimilar skyscrapers designed by the Johnson/Burgee team that had just been completed in Houston. They had already garnered enough attention in the press to qualify them as national spectacles.

Beyond the fact that it occupied a solid block of prime downtown real estate, the RepublicBank Center was totally unlike anything built in the city before, and it stood out in the Houston skyline like a Gothic cathedral in a city of glass cylinders. Faced with Napoleon red granite, the Center actually consisted of two interconnecting buildings that evoked the architectural designs of the late Renaissance. The taller wing of the two buildings rose fifty-six stories and was comprised on its northern side of three graduated sections stairstepping down to forty-seven stories and then thirty-two stories, creating a three-tiered roofline. Each section was crowned with steep Dutch gables, giving the building an illusion of being three towers in one. The bank lobby itself, at which Haydon was now looking, was actually a smaller, separate building nestled into the eastern flank of the larger structure and connected to it by a dramatically vaulted arcade reaching high above the floor.

Carefully weaving his way through the sluggish traffic, Haydon crossed the street in the middle of the block and walked straight into the bank's main entrance, which loomed above him in an immense arch of fanning stonework as if it were hewn out of a mountain of granite. Once he was inside, however, the weight of the mountain lifted magically as the bright Texas sun flooded the bank's lobby with oblique illumination from a profusion of skylights set in the gabled roof eleven stories up and running the width of the entire building.

Haydon walked toward the elevators just beyond the enormous four-faced street clock that sat in the intersection of the two arcades and gave the immense lobby the feeling of a European village square. Three and four stories above the floor, open walkways with wrought-iron railings crossed the vast spaces of sunlight beneath the arched ceiling. The echoing of hundreds of footsteps on the inlaid design of white and red granite made him smile. He remembered the sound from walking through the vast cathedrals of Europe. The echo had been imported along with the stone and, like the stone, had been adapted to the American way. From the cathedrals of the past to the banks of the future. The only way to go.

Frank Siddons' law firm occupied a floor three quarters of the way to the top of the building. His office faced Rusk Street with a full view of downtown and a clear shot of what appeared to be a second downtown six miles away to the southwest. The Post Oak area, which archly considered itself the nave of the city's elitist spirit and had a skyline rivaling the one where Haydon now stood, was further distinguished by yet another newly completed Johnson/Burgee landmark creation. The elegant art-deco-inspired shaft of the Transco Tower stood above all the others in the hazy summer heat like a taunt to the future that the present was close on its heels. So imaginative was its design that it gave one the uneasy, though alluring, feeling that in this city fantasy was inexplicably evolving into reality.

Siddons stood at the window with Haydon and made a sweeping gesture with an unsteady arm.

"By God, Stuart, a man my age doesn't expect to see this kind of madness."

It was the first time Haydon had been to Siddons' new offices, and the old man was still clearly enjoying the spectacles visible from his windows.

"We old men sometimes contemplate what the world will be like when we're gone," he mused. "It's kind of like whistling in the dark as you walk through a graveyard. We need to prove to ourselves that we're not afraid to entertain such a fabulous concept. After a little practice, we're able to do this with at least the appearance of equilibrious pragmatism." There was a tone of amusement in his voice, followed by a more sober inflection as he said, "But it's pretty damn disconcerting, I'll tell you, to wake up in the morning and discover that the future does not consider your demise a matter worth waiting for."

He pointed a finger crooked with age into the city to their left.

"In there, just down the street there, this hotshot German architect's going to build 'the second tallest building in the world.' Wonderful. I've seen the design. Spectacular. It tapers upward with lighted tiers that'll make it visible all the way to Moscow. Glass and marble, black and white steel." He shook his head, his hooded old eyes fixed on the street below. "I tell you, son, this is Oz, and everybody thinks it's for real. Your daddy would have had something to say about all this. I'd like to have the benefit of his observations right now."

The old man snorted, took one last look at all that lay before him, and turned back to his desk.

"Sit down, Stuart. Let's talk."

Frank Siddons was the last remaining founding partner in Houston's second largest law firm, Siddons,

Wayberry and Wright. All three men had been close friends of Haydon's father, to whom the firm had made a standing offer to include him as a fourth partner. Webster Haydon had never taken the option. Like his son, he had always preferred the flexibility of independence. Nevertheless, the four men had constituted an unorganized firm of sorts, meeting regularly for lunch or dinner at the various private clubs to which each of them belonged. Among them they had commanded a vast resource of knowledge, both legal and otherwise, with more inside information about Houston's past and future than any other four men in the city.

Now only the frail but tough Siddons remained. The old man leaned back in his leather armchair, gnawing on a corona maduro his doctor would not let him light, and listened to Haydon relate the circumstances that led him to seek advice and information. Siddons lent his attention with a poker face and unblinking gray eyes sunken into a face that in the last few years had begun to betray the skull beneath it. His fair skin was speckled, and his thinning gray hair was sharply barbered and combed straight back from his pale forehead.

When Haydon finished speaking, Siddons reached a thin hand to his mouth and removed the cigar. His wrist showed small and blue-veined from beneath the starched French cuff. Before he spoke his eyes glittered.

"William Hemsley Langer the Fourth. He's a very important man, as he will readily tell you. I know you remember he's about your age. He and Sean were at Rice together."

"Yes. In fact, I met him a couple of times at your place, when I would come home for holidays and go to see Sean. If I remember correctly he was a tall, kind of husky blond."

"That's right. Bill was the athletic sort. Stout. Just like numbers One, Two, and Three. That family's old blood. They had already accumulated enormous wealth from land speculations when your daddy moved here in the 1940s. They had tied themselves to the fortunes of real estate when land could still be traded in lots of thousands of acres within a fifty-mile radius of downtown. Shrewd people. Over the years they always managed to hang on to the choicest properties for themselves. The years went by, the city limits went out, and the population went up. They acquired tremendous leverage. They still have it."

He worked his mouth into a pucker, relaxing, puckering, relaxing, savoring the aftertaste of the tobacco in an old man's way.

"Bill's grandaddy and daddy were only children too, you know. The family's loins were as stingy as their pocketbooks. All of them stayed right in there with the family business. Then Bill came along and kicked over the traces. After college he refused the empire. He used his rightful dollars to wedge his way into an advertising and public relations firm, believing—correctly so, as it turned out— that it would be a potential growth industry for Houston during the seventies. After a decent apprenticeship he formed his own company, Langer Media. He showed a lot of pluck. He fought and clawed and played the games and eventually became a howling success. He also became pretty damned obnoxious."

The telephone on Siddons' desk rang, and he leaned forward and picked it up. He listened, holding his corona in his right hand, and then said "No" and hung up. He sat back again and pulled thoughtfully at a long, pendulous earlobe.

"The wheel turned. Langer Media got in trouble. Overextended or whatever it is you do in the advertising and PR business. Bill lost beaucoup money and was on the brink of losing the business. Now, because he had crowed so much during the fat years about how he'd made it on his own and was a self-made man in his own right and all that kind of thing, when the crunch came he just couldn't bring himself to go to the family to bail him out."

Siddons put the cigar back into his mouth and clamped down on it. He sat in his high-backed chair of old leather and stared at something that neither Haydon nor anyone else could see. He was like a little bird in a man's clothes. His collar was stiff and correct, but too big for his scrawny neck. Haydon waited. Frank Siddons had not forgotten where he was, and he was too old to care if he looked as if he had. He was simply thinking, and his thoughts ran in the delicate streams and strata of his own fading world.

"He did the worst possible thing," he said abruptly, speaking around the cigar. Then he took it out of his mouth. "It was the classic move of a vain and desperate man. He sold his soul in exchange for something infinitely less valuable, the hollow admiration of his own times. Josef Roeg secretly bought a controlling interest in Langer Media and put the company back in the chips. I suspect the night before he signed that contract was the last good night's sleep Bill Langer has had."

Haydon didn't need any background from Siddons about Josef Roeg. Roeg International was a multinational corporation that spoke for itself. Its headquarters were in Houston, and its flagship building was visible behind the old lawyer's back.

"When did this happen?"

"Four years ago, I guess. Maybe a little more."

"But the business is flourishing, isn't it?"

"That's right, Stuart," Siddons said, nodding pensively. "The business is flourishing. But there's just one further point. When Josef Roeg acquires a company, its corporate executives are eaten alive on the spot. They achieve tremendous status in the business world, but in reality they're a hell of a lot less than they were before they signed on. They're dead men, actually. Roeg uses their bodies however it suits him. He just throws away their souls. He's got little use for something as amorphous as that. If they ever want to live again, they have to give it all up. Forever. Roeg will see that they never achieve that status again, with his operations or anyone else's. It's amazing how many men are willing to negotiate under those conditions. Greed and vanity are wonderful things."

"Did Langer's advertising agency mean that much to him?"

Frank Siddons sat up in his chair a little and put his forearms on the leather top of the massive old desk he had bought in middle age and carted around with him as the firm grew into ever larger quarters. He too had made a fortune while he was still young, and he had been given

a long life in which to enjoy it. It had made him a thoughtful old man.

He smiled, lending a kindlier expression to his nose,
which had begun to hook with age.

"You know, Stuart, you and your daddy never did
quite see the world like most people; neither did Cordelia,
for that matter. You're a true eccentric, son. You're bred
to it."

The old man took his soggy cigar and threw it in the
trash. He reached for his aged Amboina pine humidor,
which had sat on his desk as long as Haydon could remember, and opened the lid. He took out one of his rich
maduros, offered one to Haydon, who refused, and softly
closed the lid. Since he wasn't going to smoke it, he didn't
bother to bite off the tip. He put it in his mouth, rotated
with his fingers to moisten it, and finally chewed on it
lightly. Haydon watched the motions of habit. The old
man paid no more attention to what he was doing than he
did to breathing.

"I'm going to wax philosophical a moment," he an-
nounced. "Bill Langer is a very fine product of the twenti-
eth century. By that I do not mean that what he is is
necessarily laudable, but simply that he is a distillation of
the elements of his own time and place. He is the issue of
commerce, both of commodities and ideas. He may look
ahead a little way, but only because commerce by nature
has an anticipatory function; and he may look back, but
only as far back as his great-granddaddy. He's got no sense
of history. Bill lives for what he is right now, and what he is
right now is a 'businessman.' Well, I happen to believe
that the 'businessman' and the 'politician' are the giants
of the past and present century. Once again, that's not
necessarily laudable, it's just fact. They are the ones who
affect the direction of world history. That may sound a bit
overblown, but I'm an old man and it doesn't bother me
like it used to to say what I think.

"Anyway, overweening pride and greed are two things
that have not been in short supply in this city for a long
time. I've seen a lot of both sitting right across from this
desk, and I've felt them myself from this chair.

"Well, Bill Langer played by the rules of the game and

the rules of the game are rough. He's no longer his own man, but he's tremendously successful.'' Siddons smiled at that, as though he had seen something obvious that everyone else was overlooking.

"What does all this mean, exactly?'' Haydon asked.

"He's a toady.''

"Is he involved in questionable enterprises with Roeg?''

"Roeg does not have a good reputation.''

"Do you know anything for a fact?''

"No.''

"But you can speculate.''

"Endlessly, but I won't. It would serve no purpose. I don't want to leave the impression that I think Bill's operation is a sink of corruption. I have no reason to believe that. I do know that Josef Roeg is not a good man to do business with. He does not negotiate unless the other party is at a *desperate* disadvantage. In such a situation the opposite party relinquishes more than would be reasonably expected in any other circumstance. A good, successful businessman is shrewd, tough, and opportunistic; he is not necessarily execrable. Roeg is.''

Behind Siddons' back the afternoon sun had fallen to an angle that brought its white fire full against Roeg's building, rendering its enormous sheets of blue glass impenetrable. It became a colossal mirror, revealing nothing of itself while reflecting the images of the surrounding powers. An appropriate metaphor for the man who built it.

"How do I learn more about him?'' Haydon asked.

Siddons leaned forward in his chair again, took an ink pen from the holder on his desk, and wrote something on a clean square of vellum notepaper. Haydon could see the embossed names of the firm from where he sat.

"We represented this man about two years ago. I'll sign my name, and he'll know it's all right with me if he talks. Whether it's all right with him is something else.''

The old man stayed in his chair as Haydon stood and took the piece of paper from his unsteady, puckered hand. They exchanged a few words and Haydon started to leave, then paused a little way from the desk.

"How's Sean?" he asked softly.

Siddons met Haydon's eyes full on. "He talks about the whores in Saigon and tells the punch lines to dirty jokes. Not the whole joke, just the punch lines. He's emaciated. Last year his muscles started contracting for some reason. He's twisted now, and small. Most of his hair has fallen out. He looks like a monkey. Just a monkey."

The old man stopped just before his voice cracked and continued to look at Haydon. Haydon stood there, feeling an empty, hopeless expression come over his face, and then Siddons swiveled his chair around toward the windows. Haydon stared at the back of the chair for a few moments before he walked out and softly closed the door.

12

·····························

Haydon pulled the Vanden Plas to the curb across the street from the bike shop and parked in the shade of the buildings blocking the afternoon sun. He was far out on Bissonnet near Fondren, and the blistered asphalt was giving off shimmering, vaporous waves that seemed thick enough to ignite. The traffic leaving the city was already heavy at four o'clock, its lavalike flow of chrome and glass splintering the sunlight through the smothering heat.

He left the motor running for a moment with the air conditioning going and looked at the customers behind the plate-glass window. There were a couple of young boys milling around the rows of bicycles and a woman in a dark skirt and light blouse standing at the counter, talking with a man on the other side. The shop wasn't fancy. Haydon guessed it was more of a neighborhood operation than a hangout for serious racers in tight black shorts and sporty gear.

Turning off the motor and locking the car, Haydon walked to the end of the block, crossed the street at the traffic light, and doubled back to the bike shop. A sign hung over the sidewalk said FELTNER BICYCLES and had a drawing of a sleek racer with the rider bent forward, grasping the campy downward-bent handlebars.

As Haydon opened the door to go inside the woman was coming out, stuffing something into her already bloated purse. She wore her hair pulled back and tied with a ribbon, and her sunglasses were pushed up over the smooth hair. He held the door for her as she stepped past him, continuing to dig for something in her purse. She never looked up.

Haydon removed his sunglasses and rubbed his eyes as he made his way to the sales counter.

"You guys have to squeeze the brakes on *every* bike?"

The man was leaning with his forearms across the top of the cash register, addressing the two kids. They quit but kept going over the bikes.

Haydon walked up to the man, who shook his head and grinned sideways. "Little farts," he said.

Haydon looked at the boys, who had now migrated to the far corner of the shop, where they no doubt hoped to avoid such close observation. "Future customers?" he asked.

"Nah. Summertime hangouts. The air conditioning's a good place to beat the heat. When they get ready to buy new bikes their parents will take them to one of the discount houses. No guarantees, no service. I'll make up for the lost sale in repair charges." He sighed. "What can I do for you?"

"Are you Jack Feltner?"

"Sure am."

Haydon reached into his pocket and handed Siddons' note to Feltner. When the man finished reading the note Haydon showed him his identification.

"Can you spare a few minutes for me?" he asked.

Feltner looked at Haydon. His eyes reflected nothing. They belonged to a man who wasn't easily caught off guard; he had already heard and seen everything.

"What are we going to talk about?"

"Josef Roeg."

"Regarding what?"

"Bill Langer."

Feltner looked at the note and tapped it contemplatively against the thumb of his other hand. He was a couple of inches shorter than Haydon and was wearing a tattersall shirt that looked as if it would begin to fray at the collar the next time it was washed. His hair, the color of a paper grocery bag, no longer bore the measured shaping of the regulation executive haircut but was tapered at the neck, enabling him to stretch out the time between trips to the barber. Like many men in their late thirties, his face was at that stage in life where, if you looked carefully, you could still see the once-hopeful boy behind the emerging sober face of middle age.

He closed his eyes and rolled his head around his shoulders, loosening the tendons in his neck. He stopped.

"Let's try a Vietnamese doughnut and see where that gets us," he said.

He turned and walked around a corner into the back of the shop. Haydon watched the two boys, who were opening all the flaps on the bike bags and looking inside. They didn't buckle the flaps when they closed them.

Feltner was gone long enough to make a telephone call, and when he came back around the corner he was talking to a boy who followed him with an expression of extreme disconsolation.

". . . and kind of keep an eye on these two little farts up here," Feltner said. The boy, wiping his greasy hands on a red rag, was easily a head taller than his boss. He was skinny, with stooped shoulders, an Adam's apple of truly heroic proportions, and a pimple that had gotten out of control right between his eyes and made him look like Dr. Frankenstein's monster. He wore a T-shirt, and when he turned sideways you could see the inward curve of his stomach and chest.

Haydon and Feltner walked out into the heat and followed the sidewalk half a block to a Dunkin' Donuts shop. It was too hot, and the wrong time of day. The place was empty. From the back they heard the tinny blare of the music as Feltner slapped the bell on the counter. A middle-aged Vietnamese man came to the front, wiping his hands on an apron. His harried face broke into a tired smile when he saw Feltner, who spoke to him by name.

They exchanged a few words about nothing in particular while the man got what they ordered, bobbing his head rhythmically in sweaty accommodation and grinning bravely as if they might go away without paying if he relaxed a muscle.

A plate-glass window looked into the kitchen and Haydon saw two Vietnamese teenagers pushing doughnuts around in a vat of hot grease while they gyrated to the music. The boy, whose straight hair was heavily oiled and roached back in the front, wore lime-green parachute pants and a pink T-shirt. His pink heart-shaped sunglasses had a missing arm and kept tilting to the side of his small oily nose. The girl wore a Day-Glo red miniskirt and a powder blue T-shirt with a picture of Princess Di in a compromising posture. The girl's hair was put up in two clumps that spurted out of the sides of her head like Pekingese ears, and she viewed the world through the thin slits of wrap-around sunglasses. They poked occasionally at the doughnuts and periodically choreographed a smooth movement that put them in tandem, their torsos leaned back, pelvises forward, legs gliding in a pattern that produced a flawless vignette before they broke up again and, still moving to the music, gouged at the doughnuts some more.

Haydon sat at one of the yellow plastic bench-tables near the front door where he could still see the two kids. Feltner came over with two coffees and two apple fritters and saw Haydon looking into the kitchen.

"His niece and nephew," Feltner said. "Good kids, but America has them by the ass. It's hard to believe that eighteen months ago they staggered out of Cambodia. Mama dead. Papa dead. Old Vu got them over here real quick. I helped him get the franchise to this place."

When the record stopped so did the girl, who went over to a little portable turntable and started it again: The Kinks singing "Come Dancin'."

They took a few bites of the fritters, which were a little hard, and Haydon explained what had happened at Langer Media and part of what Siddons had told him. Feltner listened and eventually pushed away his fritter, half eaten.

"Siddons told me you might be able to add something to what he told me about the Roeg/Langer relationship," Haydon said. "He said he'd represented you before, but that was all. I assumed it was something regarding Roeg or Langer."

Feltner nodded. "I used to work for Roeg." It was a tired admission. "I ran around in the same privileged crowd with Bill. That was a long time ago." He pulled his mouth down in an ironic smile. "Only yesterday."

He seemed suddenly to slump, and the soft flesh under his eyes took on additional weight.

"Roeg is rough, but . . . I mean, I know he bent the law sometimes, but mostly he was just morally reprehensible. He didn't go around taking out contracts on people, but he never let the illegality of kickbacks stand in his way for arranging a good deal. I've heard rumors that Roeg's lawyers were involved in money-laundering operations for the drug trade. Cayman Island deals. It doesn't bother him to ruin lives, but I've never heard that he was responsible for taking one. But then, really, what the hell do I know?"

Haydon studied his face. "Frank Siddons indicated Langer may have paid a high price for his association with Roeg."

"I'm sure he did. We all did."

"What kind of price?"

"It's nothing you haven't heard before. Josef Roeg doesn't manage people, he manipulates them. If you want the money, which is extraordinary, you submit to the damnedest things. He pits his executives against one another so that they're all kept off balance, suspicious, fearful, aggressive, jealous, and greedy. You become aware of a hierarchy after a while. There's an inner circle, close to Roeg, that changes from time to time. In favor, out of favor. Once you fall out of favor you never get back in. You can imagine the kind of pressure some men put on themselves to stay at that level once they get there. Money is the only reward. That, and the prestige of having access to Roeg."

"How does Langer stand?"

"At the top. He has access, which means they handle

things no one else knows anything about. Langer actually sees the man.''

"Most executives don't?"

"Oh, hell no. He's a recluse. Yeah, like Howard Hughes," he said wearily.

"Then all the influence Roeg has on most of his people is executed by proxies?"

"Absolutely."

"How many men would you say have access to him?"

"Seven."

"Worldwide?"

Feltner nodded. "Bill Langer's got a lot at stake."

The Kinks' song ended again, and Haydon looked up. The girl grooved past the window, one hand white to the wrist with flour. The old man came out of the kitchen, carrying a tray twice his size filled with particolored doughnuts, and began stacking them in the display racks. The music started again, and the girl cruised back past the window.

Haydon looked at Feltner. "If you had to guess, where would you say Langer was feeling the most pressure in his association with Roeg?"

Feltner started shaking his head slowly. He looked out the window at the traffic. His forearms were on the plastic table and his coffee rested between his hands. He didn't speak for a long time, and the expression on his face was the weary mask of a man who has swallowed gallons of bitterness and survived, but not without life-shortening scars.

"The *most* pressure?" Feltner said. "I wouldn't know. I'm not familiar with the inner workings at that level. But I know Bill pretty well, and I can guess at some of his tensions. Those few men close to Roeg are like clones. It takes a certain personality to suck ass the way they do and still think you're somebody important and not feel debased by continually exchanging your personal honor for . . . money. Those men are extremely intelligent, selfish, aloof, and amazingly petty. They come as close as any I've ever known to fulfilling the popular image of the hard-as-nails corporate executive.

"Bill can be like that, *is* like that, but it doesn't come

natural to him. In addition to his fourth-generation obligations to be successful, he married a woman who probably expects more of him than Roeg. She was a Merriam.
Her family has been around town as long as his. Their
marriage was the sort of union the parents dreamed
about, Louise herself coveted, and Bill—well, he knew it
was the right way to go. If Roeg had never come along to
put the big pressure on Bill, the cumulative effect of years
with Louise would have done the same thing. Now he's
got both of them. The point is, he's not ever going to be
able to back down. He may wig out, have a nervous breakdown, but he won't back down with that kind of stuff
behind him."

Outside, the traffic had come to a standstill. They sat
behind the glass and looked at the frustrated drivers
twenty-five feet away in the street. In front of them a
pickup jacked high on its axles was beginning to throw
steam. Behind the wheel a beaver-faced man with side-
burns glared straight ahead, his gimme cap pushed back
on his sweaty forehead. On the other side of the seat a girl
with stringy brown hair leaned her head against the window frame and cried.

Feltner pushed aside his coffee and looked away from
the pickup. "Langer's situation would make most of those
execs just that much harder, that much more unreach-
able, as they dug in for the long haul, elbowing people out
of their way. Bill has one basic flaw that prevents him from
surviving like that: He wants to be liked. None of the
others give a shit as long as they get what *they* want. Bill
wants to stand on his own two feet, but he sometimes
looks down to see whose juice he's got on the soles of his
shoes. According to the game rules, that's a mistake."

"How long has he been this close to Roeg?" Haydon
asked.

"It's probably been about four years since he sold out
to Roeg, but he didn't really get into the inner circle until
a couple of years ago. I guess Roeg saw something he
liked. Probably all of Bill's weaknesses."

"Is their only connection through Langer Media?"

"It was initially. I'd guess it's gone way beyond that

now. Usually when Roeg makes a new acquisition, he already has in mind how he'll put it to work for him, though it may take him a while to act on it. Each company is rejuvenated—they're always in dire straits when he gets them—and allowed to function awhile and regain their balance. Then Roeg utilizes their leverage."

"What do you mean?"

"Roeg's operations are multinational: petroleum, mining, shipping, agriculture, computer technology. When he acquires, it's in related fields: he buys steel mills that forge the ore from his mines. These are in third world countries where labor is cheaper. His oil holdings are here, but the oil is shipped to third world countries on his tankers. He uses his petroleum to make fertilizer in his chemical plants, which then nourishes his crops, both here and in third world countries. He owns farms and ranches in Latin America. He is a major force in several computer technology research consortiums. These products are used in all his other interests. He's so diversified that whatever happens in the stock market, or on the world money markets, he's going to gain *somewhere*."

"So Langer probably has some healthy contracts with other Roeg companies for advertising and promotion," Haydon said.

"No doubt."

That didn't lead anywhere as far as Haydon was concerned. The incessant repetition of "Come Dancin'" bled into an endless loop of sound. The traffic moved a little. When Haydon turned his face toward the street he could actually feel the combined heat of the sun, the straining automobile engines, hot metal, and asphalt.

"Not much help, is it," Feltner said.

"You never can tell." Haydon looked around at the wobbling shoulders of the Vietnamese girl as she passed the window. The air conditioning in the little shop couldn't offset the sun, magnified through the plate glass, and the heat seeping in from the kitchen. The sweet, heavy smell of yeast and hot sugar became oppressive. Haydon noticed beads of sweat beginning to show on Feltner's upper lip.

"What you need is the other ninety percent," Feltner said. "The rest of the iceberg. Men like Langer live another life, the one that revolves around the presence of Roeg. Like I said, they have deals going nobody else knows about."

"You said once someone in the inner circle falls from grace they never regain it. What happens to them?"

Feltner grinned. Haydon could see he'd been waiting for that.

"It's the most soothing fall from grace anyone could imagine. It's the only time Roeg uses kid gloves. He doesn't want any kiss-and-tell from that group. Suddenly you're denied the presence of Josef Roeg, but by the time you realize what's happened to you, you've been offered the damnedest deal any executive might hope to experience. If you're old enough, it's early retirement with lots of stocks and benefits. If you're middle-aged it's a plush position that will help you save face, lend prestige, plus lots of stocks and benefits. When the time comes, he knows you well enough to know what he needs to do to buy your silence. He lets you down easy and treats you nice. You know you're out of the picture and it's irrevocable. You might as well settle back and enjoy what you get for it. No one has ever talked about 'what it's really like to work close to Josef Roeg.' "

"No one?"

"Not a single soul."

Haydon talked with Feltner a few more minutes, thanked him for his help, and put a couple of dollars on the table as he stood.

"I may want to ask you a few more questions later on," Haydon said.

"You know where to find me. I'm mortgaged to the hilt, so I'm not going anywhere."

Haydon walked into the afternoon furnace and headed for the end of the block. The light changed and the traffic stopped grudgingly. He crossed to the shady side of the street and got into the Vanden Plas. The air conditioner blew hot air for a minute or so, and then it was a long time before anyone let Haydon pull into the traffic. He made a quick right turn, deciding to double back through the neighborhoods rather than having to endure the traffic on the main arteries. It would take him about forty-five minutes to get home. He thought about the doughnut shop.

13

He had not driven straight back from talking with Feltner, but had cut through the residential sections of Bellaire and West University Place, taking his time, his mind wandering as he drove through the shaded streets. When he reached Kirby Drive, he turned impulsively and headed north, intersecting Bissonnet again where it was now deep into the wooded boulevards not far from his home. He continued with the slackening traffic, passing under the elevated Southwest Freeway, crossing Richmond Avenue and Westheimer. On San Felipe he turned right and pulled up to the art gallery of Mears, Simon & Company. They were closed, but he knew they were still there, and he banged on the front door. Spencer came from the back, cautiously, his expression half wary, half belligerent at the after-hours interruption. When he saw Haydon, he broke into a grin and unlocked the door.

Haydon stayed thirty-five minutes, mostly with the canvases of the late-nineteenth-century American impressionists, and then he left, making a mental note to return for the upcoming exhibition of Eugene Atget photographs. He circled over to West Gray and stopped at the Marchand Gallery. They were closed. He knocked again and was let in, as before, with cordial familiarity. He stayed only a short while, restlessly wandering through the gallery's collection of modern Latin-American artists.

The traffic had diminished considerably as he cut back on Shepherd Drive and returned to the section of Bissonnet where a number of quality galleries had established themselves along the approach to the Museum of Fine Arts at the Main Street intersection. He was unable to raise any response to his knocking at the next two galleries. At the Anton Busch Gallery a special exhibition party was in progress. Haydon wanted no part of the crowd and drove past without stopping. Then he changed his mind, pulled to the curb, and walked back. He made his way through the crowd, which milled around the cheese and wine like cattle, and went straight to the canvases. He did not care for the work of the new artist who was the subject of the show and quickly searched out the other rooms. There were still the two small things by Klimt that Haydon had been tempted to buy and probably would, and then there were the canvases of a young photographic realist named Wiman, who had recently moved into a variant, looser style of portraiture, with elongated figures interestingly reminiscent of Modigliani and Giacometti. He liked these, spent a while with them, and then left.

By the time Haydon was nearing home, the sun had died to a gold wash that streamed through the trees along the boulevards and cast long shadows whose edges were melting away into a blue evening. The limestone pillars at the gates were caught in a brief light of rose madder that was quickly deepening to perse. As he pushed the remote control for the wrought-iron gates, they parted slowly, moving like black lace across the swarthy flesh of dusk.

There were two notes on the refectory table in the library. One in Gabriela's handwriting said simply *Mooni* and gave a telephone number. The other was from Nina.

>   *Stuart* . . .
>   R. Mandel called AGAIN. Wants very much for
>   me to work with him on the Nordstrom design.
>   You know I've been putting him off until now. I
>   guess it's time for both of us to go back to work.
>   I'll be at the studio with R. Call if you want, or
>   come by. I should be home around tenish.
>
>   *Love you* . . .
>   *Nina*

The R stood for Race. Haydon didn't like the name or the man to whom it belonged. Mandel knew that, and Haydon sometimes believed that Mandel's silly grin, which reminded him of the graceless humor of a man who read scatological double entendres into every simple remark, was a conscious, taunting goad at the core of which was Mandel's access to Nina. Race Mandel was one of the few persons, perhaps the only person, whose very existence was offensive to Haydon.

He disregarded the telephone number under Mooney's name and called him at home, where Haydon knew he would be by now. It rang four times before Mooney picked it up. He was out of breath.

"Hey!"

"Ed, I'm sorry. Did I get you out of the shower?"

"Naw, naw. No problem." He took a few more heavy breaths. "Listen. I wanted to tell you that Jennifer Quinn is coming in tonight from New Orleans. Continental Flight Two-twenty-four arriving here at eleven-thirty. Their people are going to make sure she gets on the plane, and we'll have somebody out there to stick with her when she lands. How long you want a tail on her?"

"I'll try to see her in the morning. I'll get in touch with you after that."

"Good enough," Mooney said.

Haydon hung up. It was too dark to read the notes now. The lamps would be on at the gates. A splash of yellow fell through the library door from the hallway, and he could hear Gabriela in the kitchen across the hall and through the dining room. The house seemed empty. He wouldn't have noticed it if he hadn't read the note from Nina. If there had been no note, he would have assumed she was there, and it wouldn't have seemed empty. He thought about that, how he would have been happier because of a misconception. A mistake. He wondered how many times he had operated under false assumptions without ever knowing the difference, and he wondered how much of one's life was like that. What was the average percent of time one spent operating within false premises? The percentages no doubt varied dramatically from person to person, but it seemed inevitable that in the end some people will have lived out their lives under the burden of more than their share of misconceptions. Fate, the consummate con, will have cheated them in the ultimate shell game and left them none the wiser. They won't have known the difference. No complaints.

He stood and walked upstairs to wash for dinner.

He ate alone in the dining room, sitting at the end of the table that allowed him a view of the terrace. There was nothing to watch. The terrace lights were on, but not those that lit the lawn and the trees. He could see nothing beyond the balustrades, and in the light there was only Cinco, who lay sleeping at the top of the steps that led down into the dark.

Haydon lifted the wine bottle and poured only enough Chablis for one or two sips into the small ribbed bistro glass. He raised the glass and took a drink and held it in his mouth. How could he have forgotten the messiness of investigations? He had told himself that he would approach Wayne Powell's death strictly as a cerebral proposition. He would take the problem, put it through its paces of equations and theorems, and try to follow it to its proper solution. That was exactly how he had intended to look at it, and how he told himself he must look at it if he was going to be able to handle it at all. And yet now, at the end of only the first day on the case, he had already begun to doubt his ambition to remain meticulously analytical. How could he have forgotten the messiness of these things? Homicides were always messy. They had to be because they were about people, and people were unbelievably messy creatures. Their public lives were messy, their private lives were messy, their businesses were messy, their affairs were messy . . . their minds were messy. Even after five months away, Haydon seemed to taste the coppery staleness of it as he swallowed his wine.

Still, he wondered, who *had* crumpled Wayne Powell into the sink of developing solution and then cut his throat and held him there while his life spilled out into his lap? Despite the messiness, or maybe because of it, he wanted to know who had made garbage out of an aging beachboy.

Haydon looked to the terrace again. Cinco was gone. In his place he imagined Powell's wasted body lying for all to see in the undissembling glare of wrongful death, offensive and pitiable. And just beyond him, the menacing descent of the stairs that led, if not always to the light of truth, then certainly, inevitably, to a darkness that never disappointed in its enormity.

Haydon was sitting in a high-backed chair in front of the French doors that opened to the balcony of the bedroom. He had loosened his tie and unbuttoned his collar, his shoes lay next to his chair, and his feet were stretched out on the cushions of a small sofa. A Tanqueray and lime sat on a marble coffee table just to his left. He had been looking at an exhibition catalog of selections from the *Divertimento per li regazzi,* a series of drawings known as *capricci* by the eighteenth-century Venetian artist Giovanni Domenico Tiepolo. The pen-and-ink drawings overworked with washes in tones from blond browns to red browns featured scenes from the life, death, and resurrection of the harlequin Punchinello.

He had laid down the catalog and was staring vacantly at an etching on the white wall across the room when Nina opened the door. She was carrying her oversized portfolio case under one arm and carefully held a fresh drink in her other hand. She smiled at him and gently pushed the door closed with the back of her foot.

"You saw my note?" she asked. She walked over and

kissed him, still holding the portfolio. Then she laid it down flat on the sisal flooring and kicked off her shoes.

"I saw it," he said. "How did it go?"

"Marvelous." She came around and sat on the sofa, swung her stockinged feet up, and stretched them out to touch his. "Oh, this feels so good." She sipped the drink and unbuttoned the waistband of her skirt as she sighed.

"How marvelous?"

"Well, you already know it's an important account for Mandel's firm. The Nordstroms have made sure everyone's heard about their new project. The house had been discussed for months over afternoon tea at the Remington and the Four Seasons, over dinner at Tony's, over dinner at the Carlyle, over drinks at Boccaccio's, over drinks at the Rivoli, and on and on. Francis Nordstrom asked specifically for me to design the atrium portions. Essentially, I get free rein and a big budget."

"Congratulations," Haydon said. He raised his glass to her.

"And how about you? How was the first day back in harness?"

"Marvelous."

"Come on," she laughed. She set her glass on the table and raised her hips slightly and slipped off the skirt. She tossed it on an empty chair and began unbuttoning her blouse.

"It was all right. Like I'd never been away."

Nina took off the blouse and tossed it on top of the skirt. "Is that good or bad?" she asked.

"Both," he said. Her half-slip and bra were peach.

"Same amount of each?"

He watched her reach back and begin taking the pins out of her chignon, putting them in her lap. He loved watching her do this, the angle of her head, the lift of her arms, the way she crooked her wrist to hold her hair. Always reminiscent of Dégas women. It was a shocking moment for the image of Powell's grisly body to pop into his mind, but it did. It was there as unexpectedly as the murder itself must have surprised Powell. Real, but inspiring disbelief even as it happened. It could have been anyone; no one was exempt from the possibility of a sudden, violent death. Then he imagined, in the moment of the graceful upward movement of her arms, in a single brutal instant, Nina's lap awash in blood, a torrent of purplish grume, splashing, filling the depression in the silk between her thighs, a string of black droplets splattering across the bare rib cage.

"Same amount," he said quickly.

His voice was wrong. She looked at him, her eyes flashing up, pausing, and then down again from under her bent head as she continued to remove pins. Haydon tried to turn his mind away from the gory all-too-vivid image. He was stunned at the strength and clarity of it, an idle mind game threatening to go out of control, needing to be put back in its place the way a defiant demon must be sent back to its source by the conjurer who summoned it.

Nina looked up at him. "What do you mean?"

He couldn't speak. He shrugged instead and took a drink of the Tanqueray, hoping to dissolve the knot in his throat. He was afraid his face was coloring.

She straightened up, her hair falling in wonderful cinnamon folds, unrestrained, uncombed, shiny.

"Stuart?" There was an edge to her voice.

He clenched his teeth and looked at her, clearing his throat to relieve the tension in his vocal cords.

"Swallowed the wrong way," he managed to say.

"Are you all right?" Her puzzled expression passed into something more like simple concern.

"Sure," he said putting down his glass and rubbing his face. He cleared his throat again. "Sure."

Nina ran her fingers through her hair and waited while Haydon reached for his glass again and took another drink.

He continued. "I mean simply that nothing ever changes. The work's always the same, and now is as good a time as any to be going back."

"Actually, I wouldn't have thought you'd be ready," she said.

"Aren't you ready to go back to your work?"

"Well, sure, but—"

"So am I. We don't need to analyze it, do we?"

"No," she said. "We don't need to analyze it."

Having extricated himself, Haydon didn't know what to do. He leaned over in his chair and closed the exhibition catalog, which was now lying on the coffee table. He stared momentarily at the drawing on the cover. It was a detail from a drawing entitled "Punchinellos with Donkey Before a Farmhouse" and was done in golden-brown ink and golden-brown wash over black chalk. Like much of Tiepolo's narrative *Divertimento,* it was not easy to understand the context of the narrative depicted. Haydon studied the shaky strokes of the ink pen, the coloration of the wash that created shadow and mood, and looked into the faces of the strangely clothed harlequins whose beaked dominoes, humped backs, and tall conical caps gave them the appearance of melancholy clowns, whose attitudes seemed eerily reminiscent and familiar.

"Haydon?" Again Nina's voice had an edge to it.

He looked up with a blank expression.

"I asked about the case," she said.

"What about it?"

"Who was killed?"

He leaned back in the chair again. "A fellow who works for Bill Langer."

"You mean in the advertising business?"

"Yes."

"Anybody we've heard of?"

"No. He was one of Langer's photographers. Motion picture cameraman."

"So why did they come get you for that?"

"He was killed in their offices downtown. They think it'll be easier to keep quiet this way. Langer's anxious to keep it quiet."

"I'm sure he is. Are there any leads?"

"Nothing. There are some places to nose around in, but there's no evidence. Nothing at the scene. We're going to have to talk to a lot of people."

She listened attentively as he explained to her what Dystal wanted to do, how he wanted Haydon to handle it. Occasionally she sipped from her drink, which she rested in her lap, the sweat from the glass making a dark circle on the peach silk.

When he finished she said, "If you're going to have to do it, then this is the best way. It's better that you don't have to go to the office."

"It's just for this one case," he said. "After this I'll go back to the regular schedule."

"Still, for this one case it's good. The longer you put off getting back into the grind the better."

He didn't say anything.

Nina finished her drink and set the glass on the floor beside the sofa.

"Hey, mister. You ready for bed?" She rubbed his foot with her toes and nudged him.

They undressed, leaving their clothes scattered over the furniture, and got into bed. Haydon reached up and turned out the light. The sheets were crisp and cool. Nina was finicky about fresh sheets. He lay on his back and stretched out his arm as she automatically rolled in next to him, folding one arm between them and laying the other across his chest. He could feel her skin touching his in a continuous unbroken line from his head to his toes. She massaged her pelvis against his leg as she settled in.

He lay with his eyes open until gradually he could make out the silhouettes of the furniture, emerging hesitantly like earthbound spirits from the dark. The ceiling fan created a soft movement of air. He could tell from the rhythm of Nina's breathing that she was not going to sleep. She waited with him, feeling, he imagined, his apprehension, even his bewilderment. Together they waited in the sapphire light, and he could almost feel her mind searching toward his, wanting to help, silently offering her empathy for whatever it was that threatened him. He held her closer, as if to absorb her serenity, her soundness of mind.

14

Haydon arrived at Jennifer Quinn's address in northern Bellaire shortly after eight o'clock the next morning and pulled the car to the curb in front of the house. Farther down and across the street, a light tan car sat under a camphor tree, the low sun glazing its dirty windows. A hand and forearm came out of the driver's window and made a slow arcing acknowledgment. Haydon didn't respond, but looked through the passenger window of the Vanden Plas at the house.

It was in an older neighborhood with small neat houses that had been homes for the young families that swelled the nation's population following the close of World War II. Haydon immediately decided that the place was Powell's. It was a zinc-white Spanish stucco affair that belonged in Glendale in the 1940s. It had a flat roof, an arched recessed front door with a wrought-iron porch light. Two ragged Mexican fan palms sat on either side of a red cement step-up porch that was only slightly wider than the sidewalk. Carpet grass of a rich thick green was neatly trimmed and spread from house to house in both directions, broken only by sidewalks and the two parallel ribbons of cement that served as driveways. The Jennifer Quinn that Patricia Beamon had described seemed out of place here.

Haydon got out of his car and started down the sidewalk. He had come early deliberately, hoping to wake her. Down the block someone started a lawn mower. Haydon pushed the yellowed doorbell button, but it didn't seem to work. He opened the screen and knocked on the door. Around the corner of the house the compressor on a window air conditioner kicked in. He knocked again and heard a telephone inside the house begin ringing, then stop abruptly. When he knocked again a little slot opened behind a square grill in the wooden door.

"Yes?" The girl's voice was husky, unemotional.

"Jennifer Quinn?"

"Yes."

Haydon held his shield up to the grill and introduced himself. "May I come in?"

"Now?"

"Please."

"Well, I just got up. You woke me."

"I'm sorry, but I'm sure you know why I need to talk with you."

There was a pause. "Yeah, okay," she said. "Just a minute." The slot behind the grill closed.

Haydon looked around toward the unmarked car down the street. A few houses over, a woman in a housecoat was standing in the middle of her yard momentarily preoccupied with the headlines of the newspaper she had just picked up. Without looking up, she turned and slowly started back to her opened front door.

In a few minutes the wooden door opened, and Haydon turned around as the girl pushed open the screen.

"Come on in," she said. He stepped past her through the door, and she leaned to look outside. "Where's your car?"

"In front. It's not a department car."

"That's for sure," she said. "Have a seat. I'm not going to be able to talk to you until I get some tea."

She wore a long-sleeved khaki safari shirt with epaulets, tucked into a pair of pleated khaki pants. The shirt was freshly pressed, with creases in the sleeves. She rolled back the cuffs as she walked into the kitchen. The boxy little house had been remodeled so that the dining room and living room were one large area. The wall between the kitchen and the dining room had been cut in half and served as a bar that allowed the kitchen to look into the larger room. A skylight had been added, giving the expanded spaces an even more open feeling. There were bookshelves, a fireplace, and a huge xylophone next to one wall. Camera equipment, tripods, and a variety of lenses were scattered around over the furniture and in corners.

Haydon watched her moving around in the kitchen. She put water in a copper kettle and put it on the stove to heat. Opening the refrigerator, she took out two eggs and cracked them into a dinner glass. She added two spoons of what Haydon guessed was protein powder, and then filled the glass with milk. She beat the mixture rapidly and then, while the drink was still swirling, lifted it and drank it all without stopping.

"Lousy!" she said, leaning on the countertop. She shuddered, rinsed the glass in the sink, and put it in the dishwasher. She took two cups and two saucers from the cabinet, set cream and sugar on the bar, and then disappeared into the back of the house. He heard water running. In a moment she came back into the kitchen still patting her face with a yellow towel. Her timing was perfect; the kettle had just begun to whistle.

"What kind of tea do you want?" she asked. "We have Darjeeling, Ceylon pekoe, Bengal Bay Black, Earl Grey, English Breakfast."

"Earl Grey."

"Cream? Sugar?"

"Cream."

"How much? Well, look, why don't you come fix it the way you want it."

Haydon did, and then she came around from the kitchen and they went into the living room. She motioned Haydon to the sofa, and then she sat to his left in a modern chrome chair with black leather straps for the seat, back, and arms. She sat a little forward in the chair and balanced her teacup on her knees.

"I feel like I should be asking you questions," she said quickly. "This has been a little crazy. The New Orleans police contacted me yesterday and told me what had happened. I was on a job, and they came out on location to tell me. They suggested I might want to come home immediately, and I went straight back to my hotel. I had to call my office here and arrange for someone to go down there and replace me."

She started to sip her tea, but it was still too hot.

"They didn't tell me anything. Can you fill me in?"

Haydon had watched her closely. Mooney was not quite right about her hair. It was not really red. She was almost a strawberry blonde, but not quite that either. There was more honey in it than that, and it was wonderfully thick with what looked to be natural wave. She wore it shoulder length, and this morning had quickly brushed it straight back from her forehead and let it fall naturally on either side of a center part. Her complexion was not the kind that tanned well, and he guessed she protected it religiously from the sun. It was creamy and immaculate. Her eyes were green enough to inspire vanity, and though she had a strong, almost square jaw, she did not have the angular beauty of a model. Rather, she seemed to be all soft curves.

"Not really," he said. "We were hoping you'd be able to help us gain some perspective on the circumstances."

"I don't even *know* the circumstances," she said, her green eyes widening for emphasis. "How do I help you gain perspective? God, I don't even know what happened to him. Was he shot?"

"No."

"Well?" She looked at him impatiently for the particulars. More often than not people were not satisfied until they had them. It seemed to be a psychological need for corroboration, as though it couldn't be real in their minds until they knew "how."

"His throat was cut. It looked like there'd been a struggle."

She showed no reaction to this except to look away.

"Had you lived with him for a long time?" he asked.

She looked at him and took a deep breath as she straightened her back. Her high full bust strained at the khaki shirt. She seemed resigned to setting the scene for Haydon.

"Wayne moved here from California just after Christmas last year. Between Christmas and New Year's. A friend out there had told me about him, that he was coming to Houston and that I should get to know him because he had this wonderful experience in the motion picture business. I'm interested in what goes on *behind* the camera, not in being in front of it," she added parenthetically, as if to second-guess him. "He was a contemporary of Scorsese, Spielberg, Coppola, and that bunch in the film schools out there during the sixties. He knew Scorsese, worked with Coppola a few times. My friend said I could learn a lot from him because he was good. I said great, and she gave him my number. When he got to town he called me."

She sipped the tea. "One thing led to another." She seemed to think that over. "Actually, I was impressed because he had worked with a lot of big people," she said, more candidly. "He put the rush on me. We ended up here, but the relationship didn't last any time. Wayne wasn't a very mature person." She blew on her tea. "Once he got it through his thick skull the sexual thing was over, we got along fine. Anyway, the arrangement worked well, and we stayed with it, but it was strictly business."

She looked at Haydon. "Does that clear up a lot of guesswork for you?"

"Yes," he said. "Thank you. Did he get you the job where you work now?"

She smiled wearily and shook her head. "No."

"Do you know if he was involved in anything that might have a bearing on his murder? Was he involved in trafficking narcotics, even small amounts for friends? Gambling? Anything that might give us some direction?"

"No."

"He didn't use narcotics?"

"Yes, he did. You asked if he was involved in traffic."

"Who was his source?"

"I don't know. I don't like drugs. I don't use them. He never bothered me about it."

"He'd been in town only six months, you said. How did he get the job with Langer?"

"I don't know."

"Did he have it when he came?"

"Yes."

"He never told you how he got it?"

"Okay, let's see . . . it was a friend. A friend helped him get it. Couldn't you find that out from the Langer people?" she asked impatiently.

"Did you know any of his friends? The people he worked with?"

"I've been up to the Langer offices a couple of times to see Wayne. I met his supervisor once, but he's the only one. I didn't have any reason to go there."

"He dated?"

"No one steadily that I knew about. Wayne was a Happy Hour man. It was his social element. All his girls were Happy Hour girls."

"I understand he did freelance work on the side, using Langer's facilities at night. In fact he was doing some when he was killed. Do you know anything about that?"

She looked at him, but he didn't understand her expression. Was she puzzled, hesitant to speak of something she thought was risky? Was she simply remembering something, making a connection between things that her mind had not associated before? Haydon's mouth was cottony from the tannin in the tea. He set his cup and saucer on an end table by the sofa.

"Do you know anything about his night work?" he repeated.

"No, I don't." She seemed to think of something but held it back. "I just never noticed. . . ."

"You never noticed?"

"No, I never paid much attention." She was curt again, but a pretty hand had moved up to her chest, and she began fiddling with a button on her safari shirt.

"Can you show me where he slept?" Haydon asked suddenly.

The green eyes widened slightly and then relaxed again.

"Sure," she said. She put her cup and saucer down on the same end table with his and stood. He followed her past the kitchen to a hallway that joined another that ran the width of the house. Plate-glass windows formed the outside wall of the hall and looked out onto a courtyard that occupied the entire area between the two wings of the house.

She stopped. "I live on that side." She gestured to the left. "We each have a large bedroom and a full bath."

They turned to the right, and he followed her into Powell's bedroom. The room was dark and smelled musty since the air-conditioner unit in one of the windows had been off for several days. Jennifer Quinn flipped on the light switch and stepped to the windows and opened the Venetian blinds. The bed, across the room, was unmade. Above it a gigantic color photograph covered most of the wall. It was taken from inside the curl of a wave, the water forming a luminous aqua tunnel in the center of which a surfer, arms outspread, was barreling down the sheer wall of water. The photograph had been blown up so many times the grain was outsized, making the picture seem almost pointillistic.

Below the windows that looked onto the courtyard was a row of shelving crammed with records. The stereo sat in the center with the speakers at either end. The opposite side of the room was mostly closets, the folding hollow-core doors askew to reveal the nearly empty shelves. Powell's clothing needs were modest. There were jeans, shirts with a slightly western flair, T-shirts. There was one sports coat, a couple of dress shirts, a few pairs of dress pants. Camera equipment was scattered around the room.

"He wasn't a neat person," the girl said. She had folded her arms and was leaning against the doorframe.

Haydon walked over to the bed. A 35 mm Canon had been tossed onto the sheets. He lifted it by its strap and looked at the frame counter. It was empty. He laid it back on the sheets. Walking over to a bureau that had most of its drawers pulled out at odd angles, he started at the top and worked his way down, noticing the dark smudges of graphite left by the lab men. There were very few clothes. One drawer contained girlie magazines, another incidental camera parts, another a few letters from a girl in California. On top of the chest was an assemblage of junk: beer coasters, sticks of gum, a bottle of drugstore cologne, a matchbook from a club, a package of shoestrings, some change, an ashtray with candy wrappers wadded into little pellets.

"Do you know Cindy Thomas?" he asked, holding up one of the letters without turning around.

"An old flame. Totally burned out."

Haydon went to the closets and nudged back the doors that weren't fully opened. There was an old electric guitar in one corner with a dusty amplifier. In the opposite corner photography magazines were tossed in a pile. Most of the closet space was empty. Haydon turned around and looked at the room. On the wall beside the door a jumble of photographs were attached to the wall with thumbtacks. He walked over.

"You know these people?"

"Almost all of them are California people."

"Do you know anything about them?"

"Not the California people."

"Who isn't from California?"

She walked over, studied the group a minute.

"This one." She pointed to a girl on a beach wearing a pair of tailored green shorts and nothing else. She was clutching a beer bottle, which she pointed at the photographer as she sprayed the foamy brew in his direction.

"Who is she?"

"I don't know her name. He never told me. I just knew he brought the film back from a weekend trip with some girl, and this was from that group. He showed it to me and laughed about it." She leaned over and looked at the picture too. "She's not much, is she?"

"When did he take this picture?"

"Fairly recently. Maybe six weeks ago."

"Anyone else?"

She reached across and put her finger on an eight-by-ten that looked as if it had been blown up from a smaller print. A shirtless Oriental man wearing sandals and white ducks stood on the edge of a swimming pool between two women who had their backs to the camera and had bent over so that nothing showed but the backs of their legs, shapely bottoms, and the tiny triangles of their bikinis. He was grinning, as he stood with one foot casually crossed over the other at the ankle and his forearms resting on the girl's hips. His hands had disappeared inside their bikinis.

"That's Ricky Toy. I've only met him a few times, but I know he's another friend from Wayne's film-school days. He's supposed to be a crackerjack combat photographer with lots of Vietnam experience. Wayne saw him quite a bit."

"He lives in Houston?"

"Yes. He's originally from California, but he moved here several years ago, I think."

"What does he do?"

She shrugged. "He used to be with Reuters. Wayne said he does freelance work."

"You don't know him well?"

"No. Wayne introduced us, but it just didn't happen that we mixed socially. Actually, I think Wayne told everybody like that that we were an item."

"Did that bother you?"

She shook her head. "The people he put that on weren't the kind of people I worried about. If he wanted to be a big man with them that was his business. I couldn't have stopped him from saying it anyway."

"Who are the two girls?"

"Ricky's roommates. Two Oriental girls whose faces are just as luscious as what you see there."

"Anybody else?" Haydon asked, looking at the wall again.

She looked over the remaining photographs. "No. I imagine some of those are Houston girls, though."

Haydon began pulling the tacks out of the two photographs. "Where did Powell keep all his prints? Doesn't he have boxes of pictures somewhere? Negatives?"

"He was mostly involved with motion picture work. He didn't have any more stills around than the average person. Maybe not as many. I assumed his reels stayed at his office. We don't even have a projector here.''

Haydon held the two pictures in one hand and looked around the room.

"I guess that's it," he said.

As they walked down the hall to the living room, Jennifer Quinn said, "The house is his. I guess I'm going to have to move out?"

"You know where it's financed?"

She nodded.

"I'd talk to the people there."

"What do I do with his things?"

"Nothing for a while," Haydon said. "We may want to go through everything again. Just keep the door closed. We'll get in touch with his family on the West Coast, and they can arrange to do something with it."

"Do I have to stay in the city? What if I get another assignment?"

Haydon stopped by the sofa before starting toward the door.

"Why don't you call me before you go anywhere." He took one of his cards from his wallet and turned it over and wrote his home telephone number on the back. "Try this number," he said, and handed it to her.

"Will you want to talk with me again?"

"Probably."

She looked at the card. He noticed again how she filled out the safari shirt. Her fingernails were in perfect condition, unpainted, with clean white cuticles.

"Okay," she said looking up. Her green eyes were richer at close range.

"You didn't care for him much, did you?" he said.

The remark made her a little uneasy, but not contrite. "You think I should be more remorseful?" she asked, looking at him evenly. "I can't help it. He was a slob. He may have been a great technician, but as a person he was no good."

15

By the time Haydon got home Nina had already gone to the studio, leaving word for Gabriela that she would return for lunch. He went straight to the library, sat down at his desk, and called Mooney.

"I need a driver's license check," Haydon said. "Can you do it while we talk?"

"Pete's here," Mooney said. "I'll get him to punch it up."

"Good. The name's Ricky Toy. T-O-Y. Chinese-American. It's probably Richard." He could hear Mooney relay the information to Lapierre. The office was small and close to the squad room coffeepot. Haydon could hear other voices in the background.

"Okay, he's sending that through," Mooney said. "Listen, I spoke with that Ray Tease again like you wanted. The guy's such a fuckin' weeny. So upset about poor Wayne. Can't get over it. Such a shock. Ta-da, ta-da, ta-da. Anyway, I swallowed my urge to puke and had a real talky with him. Says he got along real good with Powell, and that, yes, Powell had privileges the others didn't have. He said he didn't see anything wrong with that since it was what Mr. Langer wanted, and after all, Mr. Langer *owned* the company. Right?

"I asked him if he knew the nature of Powell's after-hours work, and he said absolutely not. Like it was honorable that he shouldn't. Did Powell and Mr. Langer ever confer about the outside work during the day? No. How did he know that? Because it was his job to know what his employees did during work hours, and Powell never talked with Langer. . . .

"Just a minute." Mooney covered the mouthpiece on the telephone with only partial success, and yelled to someone to please shut up because he was on the horn and couldn't hear shit.

"Okay. I asked if anyone else had access to the place at night, and he said all the department heads had keys. I asked him if it was usual that people worked at night, and he said occasionally, when there was an account deadline that couldn't be met any other way. But it didn't happen very often.

"Just a minute." Pause with mumbling. "Okay, Pete's got the stuff on Toy coming up on the screen now. Let's see. Richard Man Toy, thirty-eight years old, five feet eight inches, black hair, brown eyes, one hundred and fifty-five pounds. No restrictions on his license. Had several moving violations in the last three years. One here, one in New Orleans, one in Van Nuys, California. All for speeding. Has a 1984 Mercedes sedan and a 1983 Audi sedan registered in his name. Address: Sixteen-eleven Marquis. That's it."

"Have they finished cataloging the footage in Powell's office?"

"Yeah, they have. Nothing unusual there. All the film's for their accounts. Nothing's missing, and there's nothing there that shouldn't be."

"Tease wasn't very helpful, was he?"

"Naw, the little shit, and he's never going to be. He doesn't want to get crossways with his boss. When Langer farts, Tease smells violets."

"What about Dean Warner? Has Pete been able to talk to him yet?"

"He can't find him. He's not home, day or night. You talk to Quinn?"

"Yes. Her relationship to Powell wasn't what everyone thought. Strictly business, according to her. She doesn't know anything about his work, but she put me on to Toy, a friend of Powell's from California days. Also a cameraman."

"You gonna look him up?"

"Probably. Okay, I guess that's it, Ed. Just keep after the other things and call me when you come up with something. I'll type the reports on my interviews and get copies to you two. How are things going down there?"

"Hot. The place looks like backstage-at-the-opera, shit hanging out of the ceilings, cables all over the floors, damned electricians wandering around looking lost. It's a zoo."

"Cheer up. It'll get better."

"You say."

"Stay in touch."

Ignoring his self-imposed strictures regarding cigarettes before lunch, Haydon reached for the green box of Fribourg & Treyers that he had deliberately left at home when he went out that morning. He lit a cigarette with the gold ribbed lighter Nina had given him and inhaled slowly. His eyes fell on two more boxes of books he hadn't opened, sitting at the end of the refectory table. There would be more than that by the time he got around to cataloging them now.

He ground out the cigarette, irritated with himself for having smoked it. It wouldn't have been that difficult not to. He could have done it. It really hadn't been all that good after all.

He turned to the two photographs he had taken from Powell's bedroom. He laid them side by side and looked at Ricky Toy first. Toy was a handsome man, squeaky clean and well groomed, with an open grin that offered no apologies. He was muscular; his stomach and chest rippled and you could see the swell of his pumped-up thighs through the snug tailoring of the white ducks. His hands were draped over the perky upturned bottoms of the two girls with all the self-confidence of a man who never doubted his own worth and who knew that a piece of ass was a piece of ass. Toy was macho. Toy had fun. And Haydon was willing to bet that Toy looked out for Number One.

Though he tried, Haydon could not make out the faces of the two girls whose legs and heart-shaped bottoms were so remarkably identical in size and form. Both had long jet hair that fell over their heads and faces almost to the water's edge.

He looked at the second picture. Jennifer Quinn had been right. The girl wasn't pretty, but she wasn't really unattractive either. She was simply plain. Looking at her, Haydon realized that she would be difficult to describe. She had no distinctive features, only an easily forgettable face whose features were so feeble they almost refused to show up in the photograph.

The girl's body fared no better. Her legs lacked the necessary sinews that created the liquid lines of the taut-limbed Oriental women in the other picture. Her calves were uniformly thin, her knees were too obviously cartilage and bone, her thighs unskillfully joined an androgynous pelvis beneath the tailored shorts. Even the summer light conspired against her as it fell full on her face and breasts, blanching the latter of any shadow that would have given them fullness and roundness, presenting them to the camera like two raisins on her bony chest.

Over the years Haydon had seen hundreds of naked women, as victims, or suspects, or evidence, or in some other way tangential or suspected of being tangential to a case. In every instance he looked at them without their consent. Regardless of which category they might fit into, their nakedness had not been meant for him. He never lost the uneasy feeling of intrusion. It seemed especially uncomfortable to him now. In appraising her this way, he could almost feel her humiliation at being so callously assessed. And, of course, others would have to see her as well. All strangers, all making the same prying evaluations of her anatomy.

But his appraisal told him something, or rather, it alerted his intuition. The photograph of the laughing girl, he felt, had captured a moment totally out of character. It was something that she herself projected in the way she laughed, not with abandon, or ease, or vivacity, but with an almost fearful reluctance. She was unaccustomed to everything she was doing in the photograph, to her open nakedness and to the sound of her own voice laughing.

Then there was Powell's reaction. It had been a simple statement by Quinn: "He showed it to me and laughed about it." Laughed? In what way? Derisively? Affectionately? Self-consciously? Scornfully? Bawdily? Laughter was not a simple thing, and certainly not here. Why did Powell have her picture on the wall? Not, surely, because he lacked for a pinup girl.

Haydon turned in his chair. Cinco was staring at him, his head slightly lowered as he peeped up through one of the frames in the French door. His tail began to swing. Haydon stood, remembered he was still wearing his suit coat, and took it off. He hung the coat over the back of his chair and took another cigarette from the box, picked up the lighter, and walked out onto the terrace. He paused and performed the rituals with the old collie, talking to him in a low voice as he ran his hands over the dog's smooth coat. He straightened up, lit the cigarette, and headed for the far end of the terrace with Cinco shuffling along behind.

Leaning on the balustrade, Haydon stared off toward the edge of the grounds where the high rock wall was encrusted with old and new passionflower vines, their mallow blossoms burning in the late morning light as if to store a portion of the sun itself to nourish them in the shadows of the afternoon. A heavy-bellied house cat moved through the dappled light atop the wall and stopped momentarily in a patch of fire. Cinco, standing by Haydon's leg, saw it and closed his mouth, flicking his ears forward. But the urge passed, his ears relaxed, his mouth fell open, and he resumed his soft panting. He lay down where he stood, his eyes still on the cat though without the brightness of curiosity. Old games for young dogs. He wasn't interested anymore. The cat moved back into the shadows.

Until now Haydon had successfully avoided thinking about Bill Langer. He dreaded having to talk to him, but it was inevitable. Whatever it was that brought him and Powell together could not have been healthy. Langer, the sharp, aggressive, ambitious, executive gamesman, was somehow tied to the aging beachboy who never quite made it. Could it be something as simple as blackmail? It was an obvious probability.

Even though Haydon was standing on a portion of the terrace shaded by a looming oak, the approaching midday heat had already begun to permeate the still air that lay among the trees. The cigarette smoke didn't move. The cicadas, which sang the loudest in the greatest heat, had already begun the quavering droning that would persist throughout the day and into the early night. In the space of time it took him to smoke a single cigarette, he had begun to perspire even though he had stood perfectly still in the shade. It was going to be an unbelievable summer.

He went back inside, and Cinco stretched out on the terrace to absorb what was left of the night's coolness in the slate and stones.

Haydon could not remember Thomas's number. He looked through the H's in his address book, but it wasn't there. He went to the telephone book and then remembered Thomas always had an unlisted number. He hadn't seen him in such a long time he couldn't remember if he still lived in the city. He knew there had been some changes. He sat down at his desk again and called the Reuters office. A girl answered.

"I'm trying to locate Thomas Hennessey—excuse me, it's not Hennessey . . . uh . . ." He had inexplicably forgotten Thomas's last name.

"Herrick," she said.

"Yes, Herrick."

"He doesn't work for us anymore."

"I know that, but he still lives in the city, doesn't he? I've misplaced his address and thought you'd have it."

"Yes, I think we do. Just a minute."

She was gone longer than Haydon thought she would be, and when she came on again she said, "Who wants to know his address?"

"I'm an old friend. I—"

"You couldn't even remember his last name."

"Look, my name is Stuart Haydon. I'm a police detective with the Houston Police Department. If you want to call him first to verify that, please do."

She hesitated a beat and then gave him Herrick's address and telephone number. He thanked her and started to hang up.

"Listen," she said. "If you talk to him, tell him hello for Nancy, will you? He'll remember me. Tell him to give me a call sometime."

Haydon said he would.

He called the number the girl had given him and was not surprised to hear a recording of Herrick's deliberate British voice.

"Hello, this is Herrick. I am presently occupied and cannot speak with you at the moment. However, should you care to leave a message at the tone, I shall return your call as soon as I am able. Thank you very much."

Haydon smiled. "Thomas, this is Stuart Haydon. I'd like to get together with you and pick your brain about something. Will you—"

"Stuart Haydon? Are you *the Detective* Haydon? Good Lord!"

Herrick's voice overrode the recorder and was followed by a full, rich laugh. "My God, man, where the *hell* did you come from?"

"Do you always eavesdrop on your recorder like that?"

"I'm in my pajamas and robe, Stuart." Herrick seemed to think that was an explanation.

"I've been wanting some interesting conversation," Haydon said. "I think you're the person I need to see."

"Well, I'm sure you're right there. Houston has damn few interesting conversationalists. You and me, Busch and Vanstraten. I won't talk petroleum, though. But you don't want to talk about that, I'll wager."

"You win. The dinner's on me. How about tonight?"

"On one condition."

"Name it."

"That you bring Nina. Sometimes you're too moody for my blood, but Nina has *never* disappointed me."

"Done. When shall we pick you up?"

"Where are we going?"
"The Remington."
"I'll meet you there."
"Eight o'clock?"
"Superb."

16

The Remington Hotel was Houston's wealth and elegance at its best. It lay in a wooded setting just off San Felipe in Tenneco's forty-three-acre Post Oak Park adjacent to River Oaks and just across Loop 610 from the Galleria. New and relatively small, the Remington was built with great attention to detail and craftsmanship and was operated in the manner of the Grand Residence, with emphasis on intimacy of service and atmosphere. Its guest list was largely international and the crème de la crème of corporate world travelers.

They drove inside the gates of the walled driveway and passed under the lighted trees to the entrance, which seemed to emit a warm amber glow from within the travertine facade. They left the Vaden Plas with the valets and went inside to the Main Living Room, where Haydon knew Herrick would be waiting for them.

Herrick stood to meet them as they stepped down into the room. He was sitting in an alcove with a bay window at his back, the lights of the Galleria district sparkling behind him. He was dressed *à quatre épingles*, his British suit severely cut, almost Edwardian.

"Nina, you're gorgeous," he said, smiling richly and holding his hands out to her. He kissed her on both cheeks, offered her a seat beside him, and shook hands with Haydon, who took a chair opposite them, facing the night.

"Something to drink? Of course."

They ordered from the dark-coated waiter, who had kept his eye on them from the moment they appeared on the landing and who dispatched his attendants for the drinks.

"Aren't the flowers here absolutely marvelous," Herrick said, lighting a cigarette and settling back as he swept an arm around the room. "These profuse table displays: here, in the foyers, the dining rooms. There's a fortune in bloody flowers. I've read how much a month they spend on these lovelies. Thousands."

Herrick was a stereotype: British foreign correspondent. His manners were Continental, his ideas worldly, if a little jaded. A lifelong bachelor with no regrets, he was satisfied with his past and eager to get on with the future. He was smiling at Nina now, enjoying her, whose presence he had always relished, with the open pleasure of a connoisseur who knows he's looking at the very best of a kind.

"You're looking well, Thomas," Nina said in self-defense.

"My tailor's a damn lush," he said through his preoccupation.

Nina smiled back. For the most part, she ignored his non sequiturs, having learned to pass over them as though they'd never been uttered. She had once said that since they made sense only in Herrick's mind, that's where she would leave them. Haydon managed to ferret out the connections about half the time. In this case, he knew that Herrick's tailor, whom he had met on a trip to London, was an alcoholic and didn't manage his money well. Herrick often commissioned clothes he really didn't need, paying for them in advance in an unselfish act of noblesse oblige. As a result he had more clothes than he could reasonably expect to wear and, being easily bored with the ordinary, often ordered suits and shirts that were more highly stylized than most people were used to.

"So, how long has it been?" Herrick said, suddenly turning to Haydon. "Six, eight months?"

"Almost a year."

"*Good* Lord! I'd not left Reuters, then?"

"No."

"But you heard about it?"

Haydon nodded.

"Of course you did," Herrick brought his arms up and used the base of his palms to smooth the longish graying hair at his temples. "Well, I'd rather tired of it all, though I must admit I miss the esprit de corps and all that. But being on one's own has its advantages. And the years with Reuters gave me wonderful contacts. I go to London every few months, travel some, but mostly I'm here now."

"I've heard you're doing well. I've seen you a couple of times in *Newsweek,* something in *U.S. News and World Report, Paris-Match, Der Spiegel.*"

Herrick grinned appreciatively. "You do your homework, don't you, Stuart. Yes, I've been fortunate. Actually, for journalists like myself things haven't been this good since Vietnam. All sorts of little wars, plenty of dying and tragic stories, big countries and smaller ones plotting amongst themselves and blowing up one another's people. No one ever learns anything. We are all of us troglodytes, and perversely enjoy reading about our continuing stupidities in newspapers and magazines."

"I spoke to someone at your old base who gave me your telephone number. She said to ask you to call her. Nancy."

"There you are! Advantages of contacts."

Haydon had met Thomas Herrick nearly a dozen years before, when Herrick was covering the murder trial of a British RAF pilot who had been training at NASA and had become romantically involved with the wife of a NASA officer. When the affair soured, the RAF pilot convinced the woman to have one last meeting with him. They argued and he lost his temper and strangled her, then stuffed her body in the trunk of her car, which he abandoned on a secluded drive in Memorial Park. The pilot turned out to be the son of a Member of Parliament, adding a lot of spice to the ensuing trial.

At one end of the room a thin young man sat in a straight-backed wooden chair and played subdued selections for baroque guitar against the backdrop of a massive black-lacquered Chinese folding screen with narrative scenes and columns of characters in inlaid gold that glistened in the soft light. Most of the armchairs and sofas in the room were occupied now, and a low muttering of conversation mixed with the strains of music.

They had a second round of drinks, which they finished over stories of the past year and of mutual friends. Haydon signaled the waiter that they were leaving, and they continued to talk as they walked along the central hall done in beige and pastels through a series of arches with imposts and piers of bleached oak. Their footsteps echoed softly on the floors of pale Italian marble and periodically fell silent as they passed over dhurrie carpets recessed into the stone.

The majordomo recognized Haydon when they came into the foyer outside the dining room and immediately led them through the formal area with its French chinoiserie murals to their table in the conservatory. They ordered dinner and, in Herrick's honor, a special bottle of Château Laville-Haut-Brion.

When the waiters left, Herrick carefully moved aside the single blue iris that sat in the corner of the table and leaned back comfortably in his white wicker armchair. He toyed with an unlit cigarette and looked at Haydon with a bemused smile.

"All right, Stuart, I can't tolerate any more of this polite avoidance. What is it you think you can get from me?"

The waiter came with the white Bordeaux and uncorked it. Haydon thanked him and said he would pour, which he did, and then shoved the bottle back into the ice.

"I'm hoping you know someone I'm interested in," he said, taking the first sip from his glass. "When you were with Reuters did you ever come across a man named Ricky Toy? He was a photographer: motion picture, not stills."

"Yes, I did," Herrick answered crisply, a little surprised. "He was a Chinese-American. From California, I believe. I worked with him quite a few times. I saw him get shot in the head."

"He was killed?" Haydon was perplexed.

"No. It was a freak thing. I heard it, actually." Herrick slapped a fist into an open hand. "Just like that. We were all horrified. It was a Twenty-fifth Infantry Division encampment near this little mountain village called Bouk, I believe it was. We'd been Huey'd in the day before, several of us from different news agencies. Really, I believed, the place was so secure that nothing was going to happen there and that's why we were dropped in.

"In any case, late one afternoon we were looking down into this valley from behind one of those huge sandbag embankments, and this silly lieutenant was giving us some really boring information about how they'd pacified the area. Toy saw half a dozen peasants in those coolie hats winding down a trail toward the bottom of the valley. Always flamboyant, he quite suddenly hopped onto the embankment and began filming. We'd been warned, of course, of snipers. The lieutenant shouted a reprimand and then"—the fist in hand again—"*smack!* Toy's head snapped back, and he tumbled off the sandbags. Medics got all over him, and a chopper came in within minutes and took him away. We were lectured by the lieutenant, who was beside himself with rage. For the next twenty-four hours we solemnly spoke of Toy in the past tense. Then we received a radio message that he was going to be all right. Spent round hit him at a glance or something. He had a fractured skull."

Herrick finally lit the cigarette. "Spent round. Sounded odd to me, which it was, I suppose. They said it was probably some primitive low-caliber thing. I worked with him after that, too. It didn't change him."

"Didn't change him?"

"Right. Toy had a reputation for recklessness. That made him unpopular with the backup men who were assigned him, his battery and cable assistants who had to drag all this hardware along behind him in order for his camera to function. On the other hand, it also made him popular with journalists, who always knew that if there was exciting footage to be found Toy would find it, and if you were working with him your story was more likely to get air time because of it."

"He was good at it then?" Haydon asked.

"The very best."

Haydon thought a moment and then roughly outlined the case for Herrick and explained how Toy's name had come to his attention. Just then their dinner arrived, and Haydon poured more wine.

It was a little while before Herrick said, "I can't imagine, of course, what his connection might be, if any. I don't really know what to tell you that would help. Naturally, because he was such an exhibitionist he was controversial. The younger men among us were likely to be awed by his sheer refusal to believe he could sustain injury while filming. That happened a lot with those cameramen. It seems they found it almost hypnotic to watch violence through that little viewfinder. Their concentration was absolute; they literally forgot themselves. They'd walk right into a firefight with that damn camera stuck to their faces filming this fascinating unfolding drama. It was a mesmerizing delusion; they thought they were invisible." He laughed. "Of course, the poor fellows carrying the battery packs and cables didn't have the talismanic protection of the viewfinder and were terrified out of their minds."

"Was Toy wounded just that once?" Nina asked. "He had no other close calls?"

"Wounded just the once, yes, but there were endless close calls. Journalists would relate hair-raising stories after coming in from the field with him. As the Vietnam thing wore on, Toy's antics became absurd, actually. There were some journalists who wouldn't go out with him. They had no desire to see the man blown to pieces. It was nerveracking to watch him work. We all wagered each time he went out that it would be his last. But we were always wrong. He never got it."

Herrick bent to his Lamb Provençal. The conservatory tables with their tearose cloths were watched carefully by the waiters in black and their white-jacketed attendants, who moved silently and unobtrusively among the diners, serving in response to unobserved gestures and inaudible requests. Muted ceiling light fell in pools through potted ficus trees, casting random traceries of shadows on the tables and the diners.

At the first liquid notes of the flute, Haydon looked through the beveled panes of the tall fan windows that separated the conservatory from the formal dining room. He saw the back of the girl, arms raised to one side of her head in the supple posture of a ballet dancer as she held the flute to her mouth. She bent her head slightly as if hearing the Handel for the first time, entranced. Her dress had an open back, and he saw the tiny dusky shadows that defined her shoulder blades. He wondered how old she was. Young. Certainly young enough to live another kind of life from his, a different tempo of different days and nights.

Then, as suddenly as he had done with Nina, he imagined it happening to the girl too. In the gilded light that suffused the room, the blood he envisioned emerging in a single trickle from the wispy hair at the back of the girl's neck appeared black. Slowly it followed a serpentine path between her shallow shoulder blades to the small ridge of her spine and then continued in a glistening track until it disappeared into the downward curve of her dress at the base of her back. Unaware, she continued playing as another trickle oozed from her hairline, and then another, scoring black paths on her ivory skin as they plunged in quickening streams to join the first along her spine.

He felt Nina's hand on his. He looked at her. She smiled awkwardly, sadly. He looked at Herrick, who was holding his napkin midway between his mouth and the table. His eyes were fixed on Haydon.

"You all right, old boy?"

"Sorry, Thomas," Haydon said self-consciously. There was no convincing way to get out of it. "You made a remark that reminded me of something. I guess I just took off with it. I'm sorry."

Herrick quickly showed an ingenuous smile. "Sherlock's preoccupations." He tried to chuckle, but Haydon saw him cast a quick look at Nina. Haydon did not look at her.

Instead, he took the white Bordeaux from the bucket and poured more for each of them.

"Thomas," he said after a moment. "Could you give me your personal feelings about Ricky Toy? How would you assess him?"

Herrick was more than willing to forget the awkward hiatus. He finished chewing the bite in his mouth and assumed a thoughtful expression.

"That's not easy to answer, really. I worked with him off and on over a period of five years or so. We all changed during those years, adjusted our world views to make sense of the times and to justify the ways of God. But Toy changed dramatically. We first met in 1965 in Saigon. Oddly, it was in Saigon exactly ten years later that I last saw him. At that Dantesque madness of Tan Son Nhut during the fall. At that time, however, I hadn't actually worked with him in several years."

Herrick put his hand on the stem of his wineglass and rotated it, watching the pale topaz liquid catch the light.

"I'd been there a year, in 'sixty-five, and he'd just arrived. Terribly brash, gung-ho, ready to capture the best footage of the war. He didn't like being the new boy and was eager to gain the experience that would make him an old hand. Experience was easy to find in those days. Toy made more sorties into the fire zones than any other cameraman during the next three years. And more of his footage got on the air, too, both in America and abroad, than any other cameraman.

"Of course his reputation became such that it preceded him wherever he went. It was a reputation of steel nerves, of getting footage that told the war 'like it is.' An anecdote:

"By 1969 Ricky had had two cablemen killed behind him and one seriously wounded. It got to the point that no one would work with him. A reprimand came down from the agency big boys that Toy was not to run extraordinary risks, et cetera, and that from this point on cablemen could use *their* discretion on a given assignment as to its inherent dangers. In other words, Toy could be only as adventurous as his cablemen saw fit. Toy was livid but not frustrated. He simply requested additional cables and lengthened his umbilical cord so that his cablemen could take cover while he exposed himself to as much fire as he bloody well wished.''

They finished the wine and declined dessert. Haydon ordered coffee and the two men lit cigarettes. Nina was enjoying listening to Herrick. He was a superb raconteur and knew it, and he talked as much to her as to Haydon. There was more than a little thespian in Herrick's personality, and afterdinner talk was his métier.

"I don't know when it was, precisely," he continued, "but at some point around 'seventy or 'seventy-one, some of us recognized a gradual change in Toy's footage. It was still good stuff. Marvelous action. Much of it remarkable. But there was also something else. And his fellow correspondents in the field weren't the only ones to notice it. The networks began using less and less Toy footage.

"In every cameraman's work there is footage that is considered too violent by the network chiefs to show over national television. There are thousands of yards of combat footage in the network vaults that were never used because the chiefs wouldn't allow it. Too rough to see while having one's roast beef dinner during the six o'clock news hour. Of course, toward the end of the war the networks began to fancy they'd some sort of moral scruples about the war and began allowing actual killings to be shown as a kind of 'brutal truth' journalism that made a statement, I suppose, of the war's 'immorality.' ''

"After a period of time, however, Toy's footage was never used. It became too incredible. Not just *some* of his footage was violent: all of it was. And it became increasingly grisly and ghoulish. Some of it was unspeakable. The agency told him to rein in, produce some usable footage. He didn't. The cablemen again refused to work with him, and eventually the agency brought him home and dismissed him.''

Herrick sugared his coffee and ate several butter mints from the small tray the waiter had placed on the table.

"End of Toy's professional career as hotshot war photog," Herrick said. He spread his hands and sighed.

"But I thought you said you saw him during the fall of Saigon," Nina said.

"I did," Herrick responded. "He'd been dismissed about eighteen months before that, but within a few months he'd returned with his own cablemen, operating independently. I can't imagine what he did with that kind of footage. I don't know who would have bought it. Not the kind he was getting."

"Did you speak to him at that time?" Haydon asked.

"Good Lord, no. You know what it was like in those closing days. Sheer chaotic hell. Toy, of course, was filming it all. The licking flames, the lost and despairing souls. Everything."

Haydon didn't hear the flute. He looked across the gold light of the room, but the girl was gone.

17

MacGregor Way was actually two streets. North MacGregor and South MacGregor were rambling drives divided by Brays Bayou and a greenbelt that wound to a dead end into MacGregor Park. The area also constituted the heartline of Houston's largest black community, a roughly triangular piece of the city with its apex just south of Chinatown where state and interstate highways conjoin in a mass of tangled pavement before spinning off in separate freeways. The two descending sides of the triangle were Interstate 45 on the east, stretching south to Galveston, and State Highway 288 on the west, running south past Hermann Park and the Texas Medical Center toward the Loop. The southern Loop itself formed the bottom of the triangle.

The neighborhood that constituted MacGregor Way was known as Nigger Oaks by white racists and by the poorer and bitterer blacks of Houston who were resentful and suspicious of the wealthy blacks who lived there. MacGregor Way had had a rocky history. It became a neighborhood of ostentatious wealth in the 1930s when the city's growing ancient Jewish community found itself barred from the parvenu enclave of River Oaks, then developing west of downtown. They made the winding boulevards on either side of Brays Bayou their own by displaying there the fruits of their vast and growing mercantile wealth. Grand homes, grand lawns, grand ways.

By the end of World War II, the black ghetto of the Third Ward, which had its center along Wheeler Avenue nearly twenty blocks north of MacGregor, was bulging with impoverished and laboring-class blacks. By the fifties, when blacks all across the South were bidding for their rights to sit at the front of the bus and eat a ham sandwich at the variety-store lunch counter, the blacks of the Third Ward spilled across Blodgett Street and headed for the neighborhoods around MacGregor Way. Within a decade they had claimed the serpentine boulevards for themselves, and the young blacks who broke new ground by going to college in ever-increasing numbers in the sixties entered the seventies as the aggressive new elite and moved into the mansions the whites had fled.

MacGregor Way became the center of one of the wealthiest black neighborhoods in the country, occupied by powerful men and women whose lives were still closely identified with the black community but whose influence went far beyond it.

It was nearly ten o'clock at night when the Lincoln pulled to the curb in front of a two-story brick home on South MacGregor and stopped. The driver turned off the car's lights but did not cut the motor. He simply waited. In a few moments the light went out in an upstairs window, and soon the front door opened and a tall black man in a suit stood in its light talking to his wife. He bent down to kiss his little boy, who had wiggled past his mother's legs, and then turned and came along the sidewalk toward the car. It was a long walk. The front door of the house closed behind him.

He opened the door of the Lincoln and slid in beside the white driver. Both men were big. The front seat was full. The car lights came on, and the Lincoln eased away from the curb and moved slowly along the greenbelt.

"We have a problem, Grover," the driver said. "It's serious."

Grover Ellis automatically reached into his coat pocket for a cigarette. He feared conversations that started like this. He lit the cigarette and turned slightly in his seat to look straight at the driver.

"I think you fucked up," the driver said. He was wired. He was finding it difficult to remain calm, not scream at the damn nigger.

"Well," Ellis said, "what is it?"

"A guy sneaked into the warehouse the other night and videotaped the whole show."

Ellis turned cold. He felt the earth shift its center, felt it wobble in its turning, knew that it would shake itself to pieces. "God Almighty," he said.

"It's going to be blackmail, Grover. Lot of money at stake. Lot of reputations at stake. Your ass at stake, Grover."

"God Almighty."

The driver slammed both big hands down on the steering wheel so hard Ellis thought it was going to snap off the column. "Son of a bitch, *boy*! Is that all you can say?" He slammed his hands down again, and the car rocked. "What *happened*? How did he get in there? *What did you do?*"

"I didn't do anything!" Ellis could hear his own baritone. It sounded baritone. It didn't always sound baritone from the inside. "Who you talking about? Who did it?"

"You jiving me, Grover? You nigger-jiving me? You doin' it to da honky, man? You tryin' ta do a job on da white peeples?"

The driver's voice was mocking, syrupy. He was furious. Ellis could almost see the red in his face through the green glow of the dash lights.

Ellis forced himself to present an outward appearance of reasonable composure, to sound calm. Inside, he wanted to open the door of the car and jump.

"If you don't calm down," he said, "and explain this to me in a rational way, we're not going to get anywhere. Are you through getting that nigger stuff out of your system?'' He leaned against the car door and stroked his mustache with a long graceful finger.

There were several reasons why Grover Ellis wasn't intimidated by the racist baiting. Foremost was that he was simply not the sort of man to be intimidated . . . by anything. Handsome, articulate, educated, shrewd, and ambitious, he had almost the identical attributes as his companion in the car. Only their color and their family histories differed; beyond that they were practically brothers. In addition to these commonalities, they had been friends since college. The friendship had been initiated by the white man, not in an ingratiating sort of way but simply because he liked what he saw in Ellis. When Ellis got out of law school, his friend threw a lot of clients his way and a lot of business opportunities. Even the relationship that had gotten him into this cursed situation.

No, the racist baiting did not bother him because it didn't ring true with Ellis' years of experience with the white man. The guy was emotional. He'd probably send Ellis a Rolex watch after the whole thing was over and make a sentimental speech. That was the way he was. The thing about the white man was that he wasn't consistent. He'd pull your fingernails out with pliers and then send you to the best doctors at the Medical Center and have them give you new ones. Maybe Teflon ones, better than what you had. Give you a lifetime pension. A new car.

The driver seethed in silence as he turned left at Calhoun and then turned left again, going back in the direction from which they had come, except on the other side of the bayou, on North MacGregor. They passed the southern edge of the University of Houston. This side of the bayou was losing the status it had once shared with its counterpart to the south. The residents on this side had not been as conscientious about keeping up their deed restrictions, which, in a city without zoning laws, was the only way neighborhood residents could protect their area's integrity. Apartment houses, drive-in groceries, cheap taverns, fast-food franchises were moving in. In the daylight, you could see the litter of the changing ways strung along the bayou, the carry-out boxes of fried

chicken, the glitter of broken glass, beer cans and discol-
ored paper cluttering the dried grass.

Now, in the evening heat, you could see people sitting
out on the stoops of the declining low-rent apartments. A
couple of kids did a self-involved dance on the sidewalk to
the music coming from a suitcase-sized ghetto blaster sitting in an opened window.

The driver's voice was controlled now. Barely.

"Grover, the feeling is, since you arranged the details
at this end, and since it's on this end that the fuck-up took
place, that the monkey's on your big black back."

"Shit!" Ellis' baritone went up to alto, and now he was
having trouble with *his* temper. "Will you please start at
the beginning and tell me what's going on?"

The driver did. With sarcastically slow deliberation,
spelling it out as if to a retarded man, he told him everything, at least everything he needed to know. When he
finished, Ellis was sweating. His mind was bouncing
around the corners of the whole deal trying to find a
place to crouch down and get organized. He didn't say
anything. He didn't know what to say.

They came to a place along the greenbelt where they
could pull off the street a few yards into a little caliche
turnaround that overlooked the bayou. Highway 288 was
behind them now, and the dark expanse of Hermann
Park lay ahead. On the far edge of the park the many
hospitals of the Texas Medical Center complex rose out of
the darkness like self-contained cities, sparkling starships.

The driver cut the motor.

"Grover," he said. "You better not be trying to in-
dulge yourself here. You don't scam him."

"He thinks I'm behind it?" Ellis was horrified. He
pushed his window button. He had to have some air, even
the hot, muggy bayou air.

"I don't know what he thinks, Grover."

Ellis knew the only way to survive this was to try to
come up with answers. He had to get his mind straight.

"That's what it looks like from where I'm sitting," the
driver said. "You made the arrangements. We put it in
your hands. You seemed to be the right man for it. Then

Toy gets in there. The buck stops with you, Grover. I don't know anything about it. And it's a damn good thing."

"I'm not scamming," Ellis said. "Somebody screwed up."

"I don't know anything about it," the driver said, "but I suppose you got somebody to do something, and they got somebody to do something, and they got somebody. . . . How many people are involved, Grover? What'd you do, give half the brothers in the ward a chance to cash in on this?"

"You want to know how I handled it?" Ellis said. It was almost a dare. "You never wanted to know anything before. It's compartmentalized, remember? That protects everybody. He preaches that. You preach that. You want to open the compartments?"

"Well, I'll tell you, Grover. If this shit doesn't get straightened out *yesterday*, I'm going to be ruined. Do you think I'm going to say 'Fix it, Grover' and walk off and trust you with my future?"

"Here it is," Ellis said. "I went to the Fifth Ward with it. A good place to find people like you wanted. Guy named Boney Walker. I defended him a few years ago on a manslaughter thing. I figured he could handle it. I explained the setup. I finessed it. Didn't come right out and say what it was." He glared at the driver. "We're not doing that, are we? We're not saying what it is we're doing. We're not saying just how far we'll go for what we want."

"Get on with it, Grover."

Ellis was having a hard time. He couldn't remember how he had justified it to himself when he'd set it up.

"I told Walker the dollar amounts. What he'd get for each setup. I told him the winner's fee would have to come out of his cut. The cheaper he could get them, the more money he'd keep. The amount of money staggered him. I told him he'd have to take care of the loser. It was his responsibility."

Ellis lit another cigarette and blew the smoke out of the window. "To tell you the truth, I think he's probably been taking care of the winner too. Getting all the money."

"That'd be better for us. That way he's the only one we'd have to worry about," the driver said. "Is that it?"

"Yeah."

"Then it's this Boney Walker. But how the hell does he get in touch with Toy? There's got to be something more to it than this. It doesn't make sense. What else do you know about Walker? Can he know Toy? Is that possible?"

Ellis was quiet, thinking. The tip of his cigarette flared red, died out to a faint glow. After a minute he said, "I don't have the slightest idea. I don't see how it's possible."

"You didn't tell anybody else?"

"Come on! Who am I going to tell? Every time I think about it I'm afraid somebody's going to read my thoughts. I was sorry I agreed to it the day I did it. You think I'm going to drag a lot of people into something like this? Jesus Christ!"

"Okay, okay. All right. Let's think about this. Maybe Walker told somebody, and they told somebody, and—"

"I don't see, by any stretch of the imagination, how that would get to Toy," Ellis said. "I don't believe this thing could have been set up with fewer people." The end of the cigarette flared again. "I'll tell you something. I have every confidence in the way I set this thing up. If it got out from my end, it was because of something no human being could ever expect to control. There comes a point in setting up a goddamn stunt like this when you just have to trust people. Usually people you shouldn't trust, wouldn't trust, and can't trust. That's what kind of deal we're into." His baritone got low, almost to a hiss. "That's why I was a *fool* to go along on this one. God Almighty!"

They didn't say anything for a while. They just sat there in the dark by the muggy bayou, listening to the traffic on the expressway behind them, trying to get it all straight in their own minds, trying to see past the conversation, trying to envision a solution.

"I don't know where it came apart," Ellis said finally. "I don't know, but I can start with the first man and find out."

"Walker?"

"Yeah. If he was the source of Toy's escapade I'll get it out of him."

"If he was, he'll know he's in trouble, and you won't be able to find him."

"I'll find him."

"When?"

"Right now."

The driver started the car. "Where to?"

18

They got on an access ramp that took them up onto State 288 and headed toward the tall other-worldly towers of downtown. The Lincoln banked through the turns of the interchange southeast of the center of the city and glided over Chinatown as they cruised along State 59 going north. To their left the skyline of downtown changed, turning on its axis as they streamed past it, crossing over Buffalo Bayou and onto the Eastex Freeway before they plummeted down into the darkness of the Fifth Ward, down to Jensen Drive.

The Fifth Ward was a place with a past. It was all past. There was nothing else left. Along Lyons Avenue and Jensen Drive memories are about all that remain, kept alive by a few who still remember those sweet times in the ward, back when the streets were crowded with churches, stores, barbershops, and homes, theaters, hotels, and night clubs. The times when almost everybody had a job, the streetcars ran, and Saturday Night got its name. Summer suppers in the dining rooms of the Pullman or Lyons Hotel, a good table by the opened windows looking out on the evening streets. Nighttime jumping at the Up to Date Dance Hall or the fabulous Club Matinee (with dice in the back) where Cab Calloway and the Duke played when they came to town, attracting the high-rolling whites from the other side of the Southern Pacific. Movies at the Roxy and the Deluxe.

All gone.

This part of the ward was mean now. Sullen poverty and hopelessness were lovers here, coupling among the winos under the freeway, in the boarded-up bars, in the gutted hotels where ghosts crouched in musky garbage, slipping needles in their flaccid veins, in rancid little rooms with pink-shaded lamps where succubi transcended dreams and spread their dark thighs in grim reality. It was the end of the line. You couldn't go any farther down. It couldn't be worse.

"There's a place on the right down here," Ellis said. "Rita's Little Can-Can. Our man has a woman who works there. It's the blue neon."

The Lincoln was crawling, almost there, pulling over against the boarded-up storefronts. Before they got to Rita's, three or four girls moved like a swarming shadow from the sidewalk and stepped in front of the car, banging on the windows.

"Hey! Hey! Ooo-weeee! Looka this ca'! Honey! Honey! Letcho winda down!"

A girl moved into the headlights and pulled up her skirt. She backed away, showing what she had. A girl at Ellis' window was banging on it with a key.

"Hey! Hey! Honey!"

Ellis rolled down his window.

The girl wore chalky lavender lip gloss and for some reason smelled like kerosene. She wore a shiny red dress with spaghetti straps. Her nipples punched against the water-thin material. She stuck her head in the window.

"Hey! Ooo-weeee! White boy! You boys wanna Oreo? Zis you ca', white boy? Nigga got a suit on too! Y'all wanna Oreo job? You not gonna fine nothin' else like it."

"No, no," Ellis said. "We're looking for somebody."

"Who?" The girl popped open her eyes. "Who! Who-who-who!"

"I got to put the window up," Ellis said. He pushed the button.

"Hey!" the girl said. "Who-who?"

"Debbie!" Ellis said in frustration.

"She gone," the girl shouted.

"What?"

"She gone!"

"Where? When?"

The girl in front of the headlights had put her skirt down and pulled open her blouse. She waggled her shoulders.

"I'm going on," the driver said. "Shit."

A couple of the girls had begun bouncing the rear of the car, pushing up and down on the trunk.

Suddenly the back door behind the driver opened and a girl tried to get inside. The driver whirled around and shoved her out so hard she reeled backward and skidded across the pavement as he slammed the door, rocking the car. He punched the automatic lock. The girls fell away from the car, screaming and screeching like harpies, then moved back in, kicking the fenders, yelling "Mutha fucka! Mutha fucka!" in a madness of atonal falsettos. The driver gunned the car.

"Hold it, goddamnit, you'll kill her," Ellis yelled. The girl in the red dress had half her body in the window and let out a single bloodcurdling scream that made the driver flinch and slam on the brakes. The harpies came after them, tight dresses pulled up so they could run, teetering on spike heels.

"Lemme ina ca'!" the girl in the red dress screeched, extracting her head from the window.

Ellis pushed open the door, and she dove in over him as the driver gunned the Lincoln and pulled away from the screaming swarm.

Ellis pushed the girl across onto the seat and jerked her up straight between them like a doll.

"She-it! You crazy fuckas," she said. She tried to pull her skimpy dress down from where it had bunched up around her hips, but she couldn't. She put her plastic purse in her lap. "Whatta you guys wont?"

The driver had gotten as close to his door as he could

and she was looking at him, big-eyed, and smelling of kerosene and something that reminded him of toilet bowls.

"I told you," Ellis said, "Debbie."

"Debbie!" The girl snorted. "What about me? I'm hea!"

"Look," Ellis said. "How much you charge?"

"Fo' what?"

"Anything."

"Both? Oreo type?"

"Shit!" Ellis said. "Look, we don't want sex. We want to talk with Debbie, and we'll pay you to tell us where she is."

"How much?"

"Twenty-five dollars."

"Lemme see it."

Ellis dug into his wallet and handed her the money.

"You know how many Debbies they be aroun' hea?" she said. "She-it!"

"You said you knew her," Ellis said.

"Hey, I jus' wanna ride in this fancy ca'. I neva been in nothin' like *this.*" She looked around grinning, thinking they were going to like the joke.

The driver whipped the car over to the curb, and Ellis opened the door, grabbing the girl by the arm.

"Hey! Hey! Which one? Which one? I knows 'em all. All of 'em."

"This one works at Rita's. Real skinny."

"No tits?"

"Right."

"Got a ruby in her nose?"

"Right."

"Less go on," the girl said.

Ellis closed the door, and the driver moved the Lincoln back into the street. They rode a block, the girl moving some of the knobs on the dashboard, turning on the stereo, fiddling with the stations.

Ellis watched her a minute and then said softly, a cruel edge to his voice, "You'd better hump, honey."

"You ain't gonna talk with her."

"Why?"

"She fuckin' day-id!"

The driver snapped his head around at Ellis.

"What happened to her?" Ellis was incredulous.

"Cansa."

"Cancer?"

"Yeahhhh. Ina wound."

"Her wound?" the driver said. "Her *wound*?"

"Wound! Wound!" the girl shouted, hitting her stomach.

"Womb," Ellis said.

"Jesus." The driver rolled his head and looked out the window.

"Okay, okay." Ellis turned toward the girl. "When did this happen?"

"Lass nigh'. Ova ta Ben Taub. She had it long time. Fuckin' up and down this street 'swat did it. Place kill ya." She shuddered.

"You know her boyfriend? Boney?"

"Maybe."

Ellis went to his wallet again. "Another twenty-five. That's all I've got."

"Lemme see it."

Ellis handed it to her.

"Boney be livin' with Debbie's sista. He was. Maybe a coupla otha places."

Ellis looked at her. Suddenly he grabbed her face in his big hand and jerked it around to him.

"We'll be glad to pay you to help us find him, honey," he said through a cool smile. "You find him, and we'll add a hundred to what you've already got. But you mess us around, and we'll sew your twat closed with steel wire. Understand?"

She looked at him wall-eyed, her lips pooched out between his thumb and forefinger.

She nodded, not breathing. He gave her face a quick squeeze for emphasis and let go, flicking her head around forward again.

Sobered a little, not quite so saucy, the girl took them back down Jensen, farther down into the belly of the beast, down into the place called Pearl Harbor west of Gregg where the devastation of decay was vengeful. On

Green Street, a few blocks from an expressway interchange, they stopped at a lonely little stucco house. The vacant lots on both sides of the house were garbage dumps. One side, seemingly designated as a bottle boneyard, glittered like mounds of diamonds in the blue light of the expressway.

The girl got out of the car and teetered over to the house, her spike heels giving her false footing among the garbage. The door was open and its rusty screen was folded down at an angle like a tent flap. A pale light from a television flickered off the walls and somebody came to the door. They talked for a while, and then the girl came teetering back through the garbage.

"We gotta go ta Worms," she said. Ellis put her in the front seat between them again.

They took a back way, passing under the shadow of the columns that held Interstate 10 above the sad reality, past haunted houses and vacant lots and more mounds of smoldering garbage, old refrigerators, car tires, barking dogs, distant radios.

It was a duplex on Worms. Two black brothers sat on the fenders of an old Plymouth parked in front. Hangin' out. Ellis let the girl out and stood outside the Lincoln while she approached them, teetering, her ass sticking out like she had something wedged in it. She talked to them. One of them laughed. One of them said something about titties. Ellis saw her motion toward them, saw their eye whites flash in his direction. She came back.

"We gotta go ta Mystic," she said. She was smelling sweaty now, the night heat, the tension. She had grown bad-tempered. She had to tell them how to get there. Almost to Denver-Harbor, almost to Lockwood, they turned left off Lyons.

An old man sat on a car seat that had been dragged under a chinaberry near a corner of the house. He was drinking jug wine. A car with the back door open sat a few yards from him and the radio was going. Ellis could barely make out the prone forms of a couple lying down in the seat. He saw something white. They didn't bother to move when the girl got out. She talked to the old man while Ellis listened to the couple grunting. She nodded, listened, nodded again. She came back around and got into the car.

"We gotta go ta New Orleans. Not the one's hea. The end's down ta Gregg."

The driver swore, and she shot him the finger as she crawled in beside him. She wasn't enjoying it either.

They were back close to Pearl Harbor now, and the smoky stench of the garbage fires seeped through the air conditioner. They passed a washeteria, an opened doorway with music coming from the inside, a voodoo-hoodoo shop. The street was devastated. They turned right on Gregg, then left on New Orleans.

"Slow up," she said. She was leaning forward, peering through the windshield as the Lincoln crept along the dark street. "I cain't recall," she said huskily, almost to herself. "Go on down, almos' ta De Chaumes."

The Lincoln hit a chug hole, and the driver swore under his breath again.

"Hea," she said.

"Which one?" Ellis leaned forward.

She pointed to a rotting frame house that sat on blocks. There was a little porch with a railing. An oil drum lay on its side in the front yard beside a tricycle with two wheels.

"He be in thea," she said. "That old fucka back ona ca' seat say he got a gun."

They parked across the street and down one house. Both men got out of the car, got the girl out, and locked it. They waited until their eyes were used to the dark and then crossed over. They stopped in the deeper shadow of a mimosa and decided how they were going to do it. Both of them were sweating. Neither one of them felt like they knew what they were doing.

The driver crouched as low as a big man can get and headed between the houses, disappearing in the clutter of junk in the back yard. Ellis gave him a minute and approached the porch. He could hear the television, could see its pale light flickering across the linoleum floor. He waited to see if he could make out if there was anyone in a position to see him if he approached the door. There wasn't, and he moved up the steps, putting cautious pressure on each board, afraid it would cave in or flip up and make a noise that would give him away. He eased across the wood floor of the porch to the screen door. He stood back from the door a little. Listened. *Knight Rider.* The sound of a car roaring at high speed, a robot voice talking.

"Boney." His voice was not loud. He wasn't sure anyone had heard him. "Boney, my man." He made sure his voice had the black inflections. "Boney," he said, and reached out and jerked open the screen door with his extended arm.

The shot sounded like an explosion, and he saw the flash reflected off the glass of a picture hanging on the wall. A woman shrieked, a long-sustained sound of hysteria, and he heard the man running, heard the back screen door slap open, and then the incredibly loud *whump!* By the time Ellis raced through the house, past the naked woman on the broken-down sofa, and burst out the back door, Boney was on his hands and knees on the ground throwing up. His white jockey shorts glowed in the black night.

"Oh, goddamn!" the driver said. "Grover. Goddamn, I thought he'd shot you."

"I'm all right. What happened?"

"I hit him with a board when he came out." He was emptying out the gun.

Boney couldn't stop throwing up. A dog barked frantically a few houses away. *Yap, yap, yap.* He wouldn't stop.

"We'd better get the hell out of here," the driver said. "Somebody'll call the police. That sounded like a cannon."

They got on either side of the sick man, grabbed his arms, and started dragging him around the side of the house. His legs wouldn't work; they just trailed across the garbage. They could smell the vomit as they towed him through the dust across the street.

When they got to the car the girl was gone.

19

················

The Park in Houston Center was a recently completed shopping mall and the last building in the first phase of a proposed thirty-three-block complex of office towers, trade centers, and inner-city domiciles located on the southern edge of downtown. Houston Center was a joint-venture project that had been initiated years earlier when excitable men of influence thought oil was going to sky-rocket to a thousand dollars a barrel and stay there, and the Houston power brokers dreamed of the city's down-town streets multiplying in an unbridled reaction of me-trofission that would not stop until Lamar Street ended in the briny water of the Gulf of Mexico.

A few blocks to the northwest the skyscrapers that lined Smith, Louisiana, and Milam streets provided a ma-jestic paragon of what the Houston Center developers had envisioned for themselves in the more heady days of the oil wars. But just across the street on the southeastern side, where the remaining 90 percent of the mammoth project was yet to be built, a barren urban desert of vacant lots and derelict buildings stretched across the Highway

59 elevated freeway, which marked the beginning of the western edge of the city's sprawling and ill-defined Chinatown. This wasteland was a reminder of another kind: that oil was a capricious mistress and sometimes she made promises she would not keep.

The Park mall was an integral part of an office building, which was itself connected by skywalks—and the ubiquitous underground tunnel system—to a ten-block complex. The mall's glass roof emerged from the taller side of the building and made a quarter turn downward into the roof of the smaller north side, creating an arching dome of glass that spanned Caroline Street and extended a block in either direction. It housed the usual collection of shops, restaurants, and fast-food eateries designed to accommodate the hectic life of the people who worked in the surrounding towers and passed through the mall as they hurried along the skywalks and tunnels in the course of a day's work.

Haydon stood outside Abercrombie & Fitch and looked down into the open well to the third level. The morning sun streamed through the glass panels overhead and the vast emptiness of the mall was peaceful and pleasant. It would be another half hour before most of the stores opened, and Haydon watched the custodians moving along the deserted central esplanade below, pushing oil mops and cleaning trash cans. One of the men dropped the wooden handle of his mop on the brick floor, and the sound echoed up to Haydon clean and sharp before it died high above him against the glass canopy. Someone laughed far down the way toward the other end of the mall.

Haydon turned around and looked for the third time at the silent empty escalators and was amused to see Lapierre's head rising over the treads, followed by his shoulders, torso, legs, and feet as he stepped off the tracks and walked toward Haydon.

"Good morning, Pete," Haydon said.

"You been waiting long?" Lapierre asked apologetically.

"I was a little early."

"There was a wreck on the Loop. I was going to come

around on 59, but I had to get off and come through downtown."

"No problem." Haydon put his hands in his pockets and started moving away. "I'm supposed to meet him outside the Houston Trunk Factory on the next level. I want to be able to see him when he comes in."

They walked slowly along the silent mall, looking down into the next floor with casual disinterest.

"Dean Warner was helpful," Lapierre said, getting right to the point of the meeting without further preliminaries. "Essentially everything went down about like we heard from Langer and the office staff. Warner was still hot about it. He said that it was clear from his conversation with Langer that Powell was going to be someone special and that Warner wasn't going to have even a little control over him. And Powell's personality made it worse. Warner said about a week after his talk with Langer he started looking for another job, interviewing during the day under the pretext of having to go somewhere on business.

"But he began to be curious about the way Powell was hired and then Langer's hands-off directive. He didn't much believe the business about the joint effort with a California company. He called out there just like we did, got the same information. He still didn't believe it, and just to satisfy his personal curiosity he began snooping in Powell's office when he was out. As a result, Warner was able to view two tapes Powell was duplicating on two separate occasions."

"That's what he was doing? Duplicating video tapes?" Haydon asked.

"According to Warner, video tapes often need to go through some kind of enhancing process before they can be played back with clear signals. It's just part of processing. Powell was taking his stuff through this process. He was also converting it from tape to film."

Haydon nodded. They came to a modern sculpture of a cluster of vertical steel pipes painted in a spectrum of warm yellows, oranges, and reds that rose from the floor below and formed a series of graduated downward loops. The sculpture was called "The Big Tree."

"Anyway," Lapierre said, as both men paused and looked at the pipes, "Warner said he found out that if Powell was working on one of his 'special projects' during the day, he'd slip the tape into an unmarked box and hide it on the shelves among all the other tapes when he went out to get a bite to eat. Within the next two weeks, before Warner left, he located two of these tapes and played them when Powell wasn't there. One was a jungle combat thing like Patricia Beamon said she'd seen, except it wasn't Vietnam. The men in the tapes were Latin Americans. Warner said it was pretty rough. Whoever had taken the footage was practically sitting on the gun barrels. Some gruesome close-up stuff. Mutilation of bodies, some grisly humor, I believe he said." Lapierre paused. "I don't really see a tree in that." He was sincere; the abstraction didn't evoke anything in him.

Haydon shook his head, and they moved away from the steel pipes and continued along the railing that overlooked the floor below.

"Warner said the second tape was an interrogation," Lapierre continued. "Latin American militia stuff again. It was a brutal session, and the man being questioned was eventually killed. Warner went into some detail. It really rattled him. Said it reminded him of the snuff films he'd read about."

"Could he tell anything about the soldiers other than that they were Latin Americans? He couldn't distinguish anything on the uniforms?"

"I asked him that," Lapierre said. "He said he just got the impression that it was current stuff. They were well equipped and had good-quality uniforms. Said it looked up-to-date."

They stopped outside a women's dress shop and looked down to the third floor again. They were above a waterfall created by another series of pipes that rose straight from the mall floor and then bent horizontally at different levels. Water streamed from holes in the bottom of the horizontal arm and fell in hundreds of individual pencil-thin streams down to a bed of black fibrous material that prevented the water from splashing or making any noise. It was a silent, moving, transparent veil of water dividing one side of the mall from the other.

The corner entrance of the Houston Trunk Factory was on the other side of the water veil.

"So what did he do?" Haydon asked.

"Nothing. He said he thought about saying something to the police, but then he got to thinking there wasn't anything wrong with having combat videos, and besides, he had other things to do, like find another job. So he blew it off."

"Had Warner gotten along with Langer up to this point?"

"He said there hadn't been any problems."

"What was Langer's attitude about giving privileges to Powell? Was he adamant, nervous talking about it?"

"Warner said he was cool. Just let Powell do what he had to do and that was it."

Haydon propped one foot on the metal railing and looked at the curtain of water. He didn't like the way the tiny spindles of water fell into the fibrous material without making any noise. Across from them on the same level, a record-store employee was sliding back the glass front of the store. The music that had been contained behind the glass spilled out into the mall, growing louder as the opening grew larger. Finally the lurching beat and hermaphroditic voice of Michael Jackson leveled off at ten decibels higher than it should have been, and Haydon saw a couple of businessmen hurry out of the McDonald's on the third level carrying Styrofoam cups of coffee. Behind them they felt and heard the soft rumbling of another glass wall sliding back. The mall was coming alive.

"There he is," Lapierre said calmly.

Haydon looked through the sheet of water and saw Bill Langer just inside the Houston Trunk Factory showing something to a clerk.

"Didn't he play football for Rice?" Lapierre asked.

Haydon nodded. "Defensive cornerback."

"Was he any good?"

"Not good enough for anyone to remember him for it."

"Oh."

"Do me a favor," Haydon said, straightening up from the railing. "Check out the residence of that Ricky Toy I called you and Mooney about yesterday. I want to talk to him, but I want to catch him by surprise. He lives with two Oriental girls, and I don't want them to tip him off that I'm looking for him. See if you can establish some kind of routine around there."

"Okay," Lapierre said. "I'll get right on it."

"I appreciate it," Haydon said. "And thanks for the update. See you later."

He walked past a jewelry store and another dress shop to the escalators and rode them down to a large open area filled with clusters of tables and chairs where people could sit down and eat their Chick-Fil-A's, American Hero sandwiches, McDonald's hamburgers, Potato Works potatoes, Ari's shishkebobs, Roman Delights, Chocolate Chip Cookie Company cookies, or whatever else they chose from the menagerie of catchy food establishments surrounding this end of the mall. He circled around a bank of plants and walked past the water veil into the Houston Trunk Factory.

Langer looked up when he came in the door, smiled winningly, and extended a massive hand.

"Hey, long time, huh, Stuart."

He looked Haydon right in the eye like you're supposed to do in the people business and then immediately used Haydon's first name again, with familiarity, like you're supposed to do in the people business.

"Listen, Stuart, this'll just take a second, and then we'll find some place to talk."

Another big smile before he turned away and told the clerk that the briefcase would be just the right thing, except in the lighter shade of leather, and when that came in would they please send it over to his office. The clerk yessir-ed and Mr. Langer-ed him a couple of times, and they were through.

"If it's okay with you," Langer said as they walked out of the store, "we'll go across to the lounge on the third floor of the Four Seasons. It's closed. We'll have all the privacy we need."

They turned down a corridor that led past a men's

clothing store and entered the skywalk that crossed over Lamar Street to the hotel. The morning sunlight hit them through the tinted glass.

"This is a hell of a way to get together again after all these years," Langer said, walking briskly and looking down the length of the street as they passed over. "It's really too bad. You looked in on Sean Siddons recently?"

"No. I saw Frank the other day, though. He said it's not too good."

"It's pitiful. Sad."

They came into the hotel and turned left to the lounge that overlooked the street and the skywalk they had just come through. The curtains were open, and a clear morning light brightened the dove-gray upholstery of the furniture. Haydon followed Langer through the empty lounge to a second-level tier and a table next to the windows.

"This all right?"

Haydon nodded and they sat down.

"How's Nina?" Langer asked, pulling his chair into a comfortable position. He threw a look around the empty lounge.

"She's fine," Haydon said.

"That's great," Langer said. "Glad to hear it." He didn't take it any farther, but smiled a big warm smile that said he was happy for Stuart and for Nina. Haydon didn't say anything, so Langer let his smile fade appropriately, knitted his brow sincerely, and said, "What does it look like at this point, Stuart? Have you made any headway on this thing for me?"

The sun was coming from Langer's direction, and Haydon had to move his head to the side to keep it out of his eyes. He shifted his chair a little.

"I'm not working for you 'on this thing,' " Haydon said.

Langer's knitted brow vanished.

"As a matter of fact," Haydon added, "I'm beginning to believe you're the major reason we haven't gotten any farther than we have."

There was a moment when Haydon wasn't sure how Langer was going to arrange his face, and therefore his response. It seemed that he first wanted to register shock, then decided against it in lieu of confusion, which he ultimately (and wisely) forfeited for a hard, even stare. He didn't say anything.

"You're holding out on us," Haydon said. "You're the one who hired the man, ignoring established personnel procedures. You're the one who gave him special privileges that contravened company policies. You're the one who said Powell was working for you on a project no one else knew anything about." Haydon stopped and looked down to the street. He sighed and looked again at Langer.

"It doesn't sound good," Langer said.

"No."

Langer's hard look gave way to something else, almost a flicker of amusement. "It seems odd, doesn't it. The two of us in this situation. Back then, who could have ever imagined that something like this would happen and—"

"We didn't know each other that well," Haydon said curtly.

Langer looked at Haydon soberly. "Okay, Stuart. Straight talk, head on."

For an instant Haydon didn't see a hard-driving executive but simply a big not-too-clever ex-jock, headed into an already disappointing middle age, and in trouble.

"I didn't kill him," Langer said. "I'll admit I wanted to. I thought about it. But, by God, I didn't do it."

20

....

The morning light coming across Langer's chunky right shoulder illuminated the tiny blue-gray stripe that ran through his dark suit of summer wool and heightened the clarity with which Haydon saw him, as if the minuscule particles of dust that normally floated in the air had been removed, presenting the man in the sharp, clean focus of an expensive lens. If it hadn't been for the pellucidity of the light, Haydon probably would not have seen the odd quivering of the carotid artery just below Langer's jawline. It was the only thing about him that moved.

"He was blackmailing me." He said it stiffly, as though he expected it to have some terrible impact on Haydon.

Haydon said nothing, showed nothing.

Langer eased off a little, cut back on the drama.

"Last year I was in Los Angeles on business. I, uh, got involved in some stuff out there—"

"Stuff?" Haydon was impatient.

"Group sex." Langer spat it out like a kid gulping a spoonful of medicine to get it over with.

"When?"

"Last summer."

"I need the dates."

"I don't remember the dates, exactly. In August."

"I'll have to have the dates."

Langer didn't ask why. "Okay. I'll check my calendars. I was out there for a week. I was involved twice. I came home and two months later, out of nowhere, I got a package at the office marked *Personal*. I opened it, and it was two video cassettes. No letter, note, or anything. About three days later I got a telephone call from Powell. He introduced himself and asked if I'd received any tapes. I asked him how much he wanted, and he said something stupid, like sixty thousand. But that wasn't all. He wanted to move to Houston, and he wanted a job.

"He said we'd better meet personally, so he flew out here. I paid for the ticket. We met at Hobby, didn't even leave the airport, and settled everything. At first I wouldn't listen to the business about a job. I offered him a hell of a lot of money for a clean one-time payment. He said a lump sum would be good, but what he really wanted was a job and the security and benefits. I couldn't believe it."

Langer looked uneasy, then went ahead. A faint syrupy smell of liquor permeated the empty lounge.

"I tried threatening him," Langer said. "I told him I could be pressed only so far, and I might think it was a better deal just to get rid of him. He said he'd thought of that and that's why he wasn't going to pump me dry. He said he had reasons for wanting the job in Houston. I had the equipment he needed for some other business."

"What kind of equipment?"

"The latest in video technology. First class all the way. A big investment. Anyway, he made it sound innocuous enough. Just the job and the freedom to use the equipment."

"So you did it," Haydon said.

Langer nodded. "Yeah. I really didn't see any way to get around it. I moved him down here."

"Did you get the tapes back?"

"I got some tapes. He claimed they were the originals.

And they may have been, but I'm sure he kept copies. They would have been his job security. Neither of us ever mentioned it again. He went to work for me, and that was it."

"Do you know what his outside work entailed?"

"No, but it was obviously something sleazy. Could have been anything. I snooped around, tried to find out, but mostly I was afraid to rock the boat. He seemed content, and I wanted to keep him that way."

"So when Warner comes to you about Powell's use of company equipment, you told him to let it go."

"That's right."

"You felt like you could trust Powell indefinitely? Didn't you think he would eventually raise the stakes?"

"Yeah, I thought about it a lot. But everything was going okay, and then I didn't have a lot of time to devote to worrying about it. I had to get on with the business."

"Weren't you afraid Powell would get your company involved in some kind of scandal?"

"I thought of that too." He shook his head at his predicament. "You have a lot of fires to put out in this business. He wasn't an immediate threat. He was stabilized, so to speak. I let it go."

A black maid in an apricot uniform and carrying a vacuum cleaner came around the corner from the hallway where the hotel's business offices were located. She saw the men talking, hesitated, and then turned around and disappeared down the hall again. In a moment the vacuum started up, muffled, far away.

Langer was looking at Haydon, waiting.

"From my point of view you're in a worse position now than when you started talking," Haydon said.

Langer nodded. He knew it. "On the other hand," Langer said, "you know full well that I'm probably not the only one who would have liked to see him dead. I don't know what he was doing with that video equipment, but it wasn't anything legitimate."

"That doesn't help you any. If he was blackmailing someone else, we'll never know it now."

Langer only shrugged and looked sorry for himself. "You told the detectives who questioned you that

Powell was doing some work with a California company and that was the reason he was working at night. They called out there and got it verified."

"I'm sorry I did that. I gave them the name of a business associate out there. He backed me up on it. Look, I tried to cover up the blackmailing thing. I'm sorry. I didn't know what to do. I didn't want it to get out, and I thought there was a chance I could bury it."

"Where are the tapes?" Haydon asked.

"I burned them."

"Someone went through Powell's bedroom after the murder."

Langer nodded. "Yeah, it was me. I went over there just before lunch on Thursday. I thought if he had kept a copy I might be able to find it."

"You didn't?"

"No. Either he was telling the truth about me having the original, or he stashed it somewhere else." Langer watched a couple walk by the lounge and go down the staircase that descended under a skylight to the main lobby through a series of white stone terraces planted with ficus trees, bromeliads, and palmettos. "If you come up with them . . . I guess they'll have some bearing on the case until it's cleared up. But after that, can I get them back? I mean, you don't have to keep them, do you?"

"Can you substantiate where you were all of Wednesday night?" Haydon asked.

Langer's face was unreadable. He nodded.

"Where?"

"I had a business meeting the first part of the evening. Then I went home and was there the rest of the night."

The maid was working her way up the hallway, getting closer to the lobby outside the lounge.

"Who was the meeting with?"

"Josef Roeg." There was a combination of self-importance and tension in Langer's response. The name always carried a degree of prestige with it, but at the same time he seemed as if he'd rather it hadn't come up.

"How long have you been working with him?" Haydon asked.

"A little over four years."

"Where do you fit into Roeg's operations?"

For a moment it looked as though Langer was going to protest Haydon's course of questioning; then he let it go and answered without being evasive.

"He owns a controlling interest in Langer Media. I run it for him."

"Do you work closely with him?"

"Not particularly. He gives his CEOs a lot of room."

"Do you like the arrangement you have with him?"

"Arrangement?"

"Your corporate relationship. I believe you're one of a few executives who have regular access to him on a one-to-one basis."

"I'm not complaining."

Again Langer showed mixed emotions. He looked out of the windows and over at the skywalk as if the conversation wasn't all that fascinating, but he began squinting and relaxing his eyes. Squinting and relaxing, a curious tic that Haydon suddenly recognized from nearly twenty years before. He was glad to see it. Up to this point he really hadn't been able to get a true feel for Langer's emotional position. He seemed to have calculated every response up to this point, but now he was unconsciously giving Haydon an undisguised signal of tension.

"I understand Roeg is eccentric, that he makes unusual demands."

"Why are we talking about Josef Roeg?" Langer held his mouth differently, not wanting the anger to show.

"Why shouldn't we?"

"I think we ought to stick with the subject."

"We're getting off the subject?"

"I think so."

"Do you know who killed Powell?"

"Of course not."

"Then how do you know when we're off the subject?"

"Come on, Stuart. A possible relationship there?" Langer snorted.

Haydon reached into his coat pocket and took out a photograph. He put the picture of Ricky Toy and the two girls in bikinis on the table facing Langer.

"Do you know him?"

Langer looked down at the photograph. Haydon watched his eyes, which didn't waste any time on the almost naked bottoms of the girls but locked on Toy and stayed there. It took him too long to answer. Langer was having to think on his feet.

"No."

"You sure?"

"He's Oriental, for God's sake," Langer said testily. "Don't you think I'd remember an Oriental?"

"It took you a while to decide."

"Listen, dammit, what is this?" Langer's face was coloring. It went against his grain to be on the defensive. "What do you think I'm hiding? Can you be a little more specific about what you want from me? I'd like to hear something specific. What is it you think you're getting at here?"

Haydon didn't say anything but reached into his coat pocket again and pulled out a second picture and laid it on the table. Langer shook his head in disgust and then looked down at the photograph. He quickly looked closer, squinting.

"Shit!"

"Who is it?"

Langer seemed to be trying to figure out why the girl was in the photograph, not that she was practically nude but that she was there at all.

"She works at the agency," he said. "Yeah. Where'd you get this?"

"I got both photographs from Powell's bedroom. They were tacked up on his wall. I'm surprised you didn't see them when you were there."

"Me too," Langer said. The tone of regret was unmistakable.

"Who is she?"

"I think her name's Alice. Yeah," he said, looking at her closer. "That's Alice Parnas."

21

········

Langer said he had a meeting elsewhere in the Four Seasons, so Haydon left him going down the terraced staircase as he walked back across the skywalk to the Park. By this time he was needing a cup of coffee. He passed up the quickie places in the mall and took the tunnels to First City Tower. He had several choices of coffee shops in the corridors that ran in four different directions from there.

He stopped at a sidewalk shop called Kip's in the underground junction. The coffee was in a self-serve urn at the cash register and you had a choice of sizes of Styrofoam cups. He got a small, filled it, added cream and, for the hell of it, sugar, while the girl at the register got his change. He took the cup over to a table for two that was next to the brass railing separating the shop from the subterranean plaza. There was a sandwich bar across the way, a tobacconist, a newstand/gift shop. A couple of young executive types were having coffee at another table, identical suits, identical ties, white button-down collars, blow-dried hair cut short above the ears, college rings on their right hands. One also wore a wedding band.

Haydon lit a cigarette and thought about the conversation with Langer. The whole thing rang false. Bill Langer told of his blackmailing by Powell with all the contrition one would expect, but Haydon missed a crucial emotion. Embarrassment. Langer tried to portray unease at being held hostage by his own indiscretions, but he was a B-movie actor. He never tried to soften what he had done, never said it was a stupid stunt, never chastised himself for getting into such a mess. Men in his situation, sincere or not, usually found it necessary to go through the routine of cursing their hard luck or their stupidity. Langer never even considered it.

In fact, his timing was too good. He was too quick to make himself a prime suspect in Powell's killing. And yet he said he had alibis for that night. Maybe it wasn't that he wanted to implicate himself in the homicide as much as he wanted to portray Powell as a blackmailer. If Powell was blackmailing him, maybe he was blackmailing others. Langer even suggested it. There were other suspects, then, unknown persons. Haydon had the feeling Powell was being set up, posthumously.

A young woman in a dark pearl business suit and tortoise-shell glasses was reading a newspaper at the table next to Haydon. She was reading an article illustrated by a photograph of a woman in black tights, white leotard, and a Farrah Fawcett hairstyle grinning inanely at the camera as she demonstrated "tummy tighteners." The headline read: REGULAR EXERCISE A MUST FOR TODAY'S SUPERWOMAN. An advertisement above her pictured another woman in tights and leotard standing sideways to the camera, showing a flat stomach and breasts that looked impossibly perky, while the copy promised that "you" could lose six to thirty inches in one hour if you gave the cute girls at Slim World twelve dollars and fifty cents and let them wrap you in hot plastic sheeting.

Haydon put out his cigarette. Langer's stratagems had the smell of a diversion. From what? There were two points in their conversation when Haydon felt Langer had reacted honestly: when they talked about Roeg and when he identified the photograph of Alice Parnas. Haydon could see any number of reasons why he would want to avoid involving Roeg, but the question of Alice Parnas was different.

Haydon did not want to talk to Parnas at Langer's offices, so he called from a pay phone in the tunnels to make an appointment with her elsewhere. The receptionist told him that Alice wasn't there. She had been ill at home since Thursday. He had forgotten.

From the parking garage next to the Four Seasons, Haydon drove through downtown to Washington, just north of the police station. When he reached Studemont, he took a right and followed the old street under the Katy Freeway and into the Heights. The houses in the Heights area had been built during the war, a comfortable middle-class neighborhood that had fought to stay that way as Houston passed through three decades in which it grew from a big town into a city. The old ways of the Heights hadn't survived. The Anglo population that had predominated had gradually given way, mostly in the East Heights, to exploding Latin families who had expanded their territories from the west Loop neighborhoods of Pecan Park, Harrisburg, and Magnolia Park through Denver-Harbor, through the black neighborhoods of the Fifth Ward, and into the Heights. Times had changed.

Alice Parnas lived on Bayland in a white wood frame house with green trim. It was in good shape, better than the others, with two scaly cottonwoods in the front yard that loomed over the house. The trees were presently serving as the sole neighborhood haven for dozens of great glistening black grackles that shrieked and clamored among the branches, their droppings splattering the spiky leaves and the sidewalk.

Haydon got out of the car and walked up to the front door. The door and all the windows of the house were open. A black aluminum grill in the form of a giant spiderweb braced the wood frame of the screen door. He knocked on the doorjamb and looked at the fist-sized aluminum spider in the center of the web. He looked back at his car, then up at the screeching, defecating grackles.

When he turned around again, the small wan face of Alice Parnas stared at him from behind the screen.

"Miss Parnas?"

She nodded. Her eyes seemed larger than he remembered from the photograph. Maybe it was the dark circles. She was wearing a pale yellow cotton robe that she had cinched tightly around her waist. The sleeves were rolled up and wadded at the elbows.

He introduced himself and told her he would like to talk with her for a few minutes.

"I've already told the other men all I know," she said.

"I understand, but I've come across some new information I need to ask you about."

"New information?"

"Do you mind if I come in, Miss Parnas?"

With one hand she gathered the collar of the robe close around her throat.

"I won't stay long," he said.

She unhooked the screen and backed away. Haydon opened it and went into the small living room furnished with things that had been new when the house was built. It was clean but smelled of age, another era. He had the impression she had never moved away from home and that her parents had died and left it all to her, the old house, the old furniture, the scaly cottonwood, the cursing grackles.

He sat on a sofa in front of opened windows that looked out onto a crushed-shell driveway and a hedge of junipers that separated the Parnas house from the one next door. There were no lights on in the house, but he could see well enough when his eyes adjusted. Alice Parnas sat near the opened front door in an armchair in the same style and material as the sofa. The midmorning sun was just beginning to heat up the house.

"I'm sorry to bother you when you're not feeling well," Haydon said, "but I'm hoping you can help me learn a little more about Wayne Powell."

"I hardly knew him," she said. "I just worked with him. Not even with him, just in the next room. I can't help you."

"I think you knew him a lot better than that," Haydon said. "I wish you'd help me. I want to find out who killed him."

"I'm sorry," she said, shaking her head. She was sitting forward on the big cushion of the armchair, her feet flat on the floor, her knees together, the faded yellow robe hanging to the floor covering her feet. Her brown hair was short and fine, without body, and looked as if it hadn't been combed for several days. She might have quickly run a brush over it when she heard him at the door.

Haydon reached into his pocket and brought out the photograph of her on the beach.

"I found this in his bedroom," he said, and handed it to her.

Outside the grackles suddenly stopped their infernal cacophony in the strange way that flocks of birds seem to act with a singleness of mind. In the unexpected silence you could hear the traffic just a few blocks away on the North Freeway coming out of downtown.

She held the picture in both hands as they rested on her knees, her back bent slightly. For a moment she just looked at it, studying it, remembering perhaps, seemingly unmoved. Then her face contorted ever so slowly, and she began to cry, her eyes fixed on the picture. She wept great sobs without attempting to cover her face, her shoulders heaving as she looked at herself in another time and place. She cried openly, for herself, not feeling whatever it was that people felt that made them want to cover their faces when they cried. Tears glistened on her flat cheeks and dripped off her chin like rain. The sound of her crying was painful and unrestrained, coming from deep within that center of feeling we call the heart.

Haydon made no attempt to stop her or comfort her, nor did he turn his eyes away.

The grackles erupted again without warning, their whistling bedlam threatening to destroy the trees by its sheer reckless volume. After what seemed a long while, during which Alice Parnas made no attempt to control her crying, it began to exhaust itself, slowing to a whimper of its own accord. She did not wipe away the tears, made no movement to dry her face, but simply looked at the picture in her hands, resting on her knees.

"He made me feel pretty," she said finally. "Inside, at least." She looked up at him, her eyes beginning to puff.

"I know you've heard all the bad things about him. I know you have. Did you hear anything good? From anyone?" She looked at her picture again. "It doesn't matter. If there's goodness in someone, you can't take it away from them just because no one's told you about it. It's still there."

"Are you going to help me?" Haydon asked.

"We were lovers," she said. "Nobody would've guessed it in a thousand years. Nobody really ever understood him. All they saw was what he showed them. They never took the trouble to look under the surface. They never do, you know. If you don't look just right, people won't have anything to do with you. Not in this city. Jesus. Not in this city."

"How long were you lovers?" Haydon asked. No breeze stirred through the opened door or windows, and he wondered if she weren't suffocating in the old cotton robe.

"Five months. We got to know each other on lunch hours at first. It just kind of developed. He didn't have to strut around me, probably because I'm plain. He didn't feel like he had to prove anything. We got to be close. One night we spilled all this stuff out to each other. I don't know. It surprised us how much we were alike. This whole new attitude came out in him, and he was . . . he was tender with me." Her voice wavered a little. "We became lovers. It seemed even more wonderful because it was secret. I don't know why we kept it secret. It just seemed the natural thing to do. It made us feel special for some reason, when we were around the others at work."

"Do you know what kind of work Wayne was doing at the labs at nights?"

She sighed, a tired sigh that made her shoulders sag. "He was doing work for a Chinese guy named Ricky Toy."

"What kind of work?"

"Duping video tapes. The tapes were shot on quarter-inch cassettes, and Wayne would dupe them in three-quarter-inch and enhance them to broadcast quality. Sometimes he'd convert them to film so they could be shown on a larger screen."

"Toy's tapes?"

"No. Toy shot them for someone else. He sold them—well, really he was hired to shoot them."

"Who hired him?"

"I don't know."

"Did Wayne know who Toy was working for?"

She shook her head.

"What kind of tapes were they?"

She hesitated, looked at him, looked out the screen door to the sidewalk, big junky leaves from the cottonwoods here and there on the ground. She ran her tongue around her lips, straightened her shoulders a little.

"The guy Ricky Toy was shooting for liked war stuff. Ricky had been a war photographer in Vietnam. This guy hired him to shoot war stuff for him. Toy would go down to El Salvador, down in there. The bloodier it was, the better he liked it. I saw some interrogations too, military interrogations. Death-squad stuff. People were killed and tortured in every film I saw. Right there, close up. I may have seen a dozen of them."

"When did you see them?"

"When Wayne worked at night he'd come by and get me and I'd visit with him while he was doing it. It would only take a couple of hours. Nobody ever knew I was there."

"Were you up there the night he was killed?"

She shook her head.

"How often did he process videotapes?"

"Twice a month. Toy would go down every two weeks and bring them back here to Wayne."

"That sounds like an expensive operation."

"Wayne said Toy was making a mint from it."

"Were those the only kinds of tapes you saw Wayne process?"

"Yes."

"Did he ever express the fear that he might be in danger because of his work with these tapes?"

"He never said anything about it."

"Did you know that Wayne was blackmailing William Langer?"

She looked up sharply. "Where'd you hear that?"

"Langer told me."

"He's lying."

"How do you know?"

She flushed, her flat cheeks going pink. "I just don't believe it."

"Why do you think Wayne had access to the equipment on Langer's instructions?"

She thought about it.

"Didn't you ever ask him about that?"

She shook her head.

"Do Langer and Toy know each other?"

"I don't know."

"Did Wayne ever tell you how he got into the arrangement with Toy, or how Toy was tied in with the man he was working for?"

She didn't answer, just looked down at her picture again. She looked at it a long time.

"Who do you think killed him?" Haydon asked gently.

She didn't take her eyes off her picture, and he could see them beginning to fill with tears again.

"Everyone talked about him behind his back, like he was a joke," she said. "Just because he wasn't part of the A crowd. To them he was a loser. Laughed about his hair, about his clothes, the way he acted." She shook her head. "He was just covering up. He didn't feel good about himself. He knew they thought he was a loser, and the harder he tried not to act like a loser the more they thought he was."

The grackles sounded as if they were tearing the tops out of the cottonwoods. The heat was noticeable in the house now and seemed to enhance the odor of age all around them. Old wood, old fabric, old wallpaper.

Alice Parnas looked at her picture in her hands resting on her knees. She looked up at him, out at his car, back at him. Her eyes filled with tears.

"You're a handsome man. You know that, don't you?"

He didn't say anything.

"You know it, don't you?" She waited for him to answer.

He didn't know what to do. It was a strangely discomforting question.

"And rich. That car out there."

He waited.

"Sure you know it. Plain people know they're plain too. Ugly people know they're ugly. Losers know they're losers. I mean, plain people and losers can look around and see that they're plain, and losers—just like handsome winners—can look around and see what they are. They don't kid themselves about it, you know. They know other people think they're plain and losers, and it hurts. It hurts because people don't try to hide how they feel about it."

The tears were all over her flat cheeks again, and she was sitting there looking at him, crying again, not covering her face.

"He wasn't a loser inside, and I wasn't plain inside. We treated each other like we were beautiful winners, and that's what we had going for us. More'n anybody else in the world." She sobbed. "And, Jesus, they killed him."

She looked at her picture in her hands. The tears dripped off her chin like rain.

22

Haydon walked out the screen door of Alice Parnas' little house with the sounds of her sobbing still pulling at him and blending with the screeching of the grackles until it was all mixed up in his mind. A mess. And he was convinced it was more of a mess than she had told. He got into the car and drove away from Bayland Street, not paying any attention to where he was going. Just driving and thinking of the mess of it all.

He wasn't surprised when he found himself getting deeper into the Latin neighborhoods, going under the North Freeway and into the streets between Little White Oak Bayou and Hollywood Cemetery, Holy Cross Cemetery. He drove like the people drove, slow, almost idling. It was nearly noon, the heat had burned away the morning shadows, and the small houses stood defenseless, letting the sun scorch them one more day, make tiny bubbles in the worn asphalt shingles on the roofs, dry out another piece of paint to flake away and expose the wood, heat the dark insides of the cramped rooms to suffocating temperatures so that the ammoniac odor of urine burned your

eyes and the roaches thrived and bred like the time-
surviving creatures they were.

He wasn't surprised, either, when he found himself in
front of the house, motor off, looking at it. It hadn't
changed. He had been to it many times since then and it
never changed, just as the events never changed no matter
how many times he relived them. The people were gone,
those people, and there were children again. There had
been a lot of children since then. Always children. There
or next door or in the next house or down the street or
across the street.

He watched a pot-bellied little boy, a toddler, come
around the side of the house wearing only dirty underwear drooping below the sway of his belly. He absently
grabbed at the low leafy limb of a honey locust as he came
around, dragging a stick in the dirt as a mongrel pup tried
to bite it. The boy stripped the branch of leaves as he
chugged along, letting it pop back, bare, a few of the
tree's feathery amber flowers falling from the vibration.

Spotting something interesting in the dirt of the bare
yard, the boy abruptly squatted, dropping the stick, which
the pup promptly grabbed and shook fiercely like a terrier
shakes a rat. The boy's distended stomach hung down
between his fat little knees as he doodled with whatever it
was he saw. His straight black Mexican hair fell down over
his forehead, a sprig of it going wild at the crown at the
back of his head.

Haydon could see the sticky dirt on the tight bow of
the boy's stomach. It was like the stomach of the small boy
that night who huddled on the lumpy sofa looking at his
sister on the floor. His little sister. So little. Haydon remembered the dirt on her, too, and the other stuff. The
flies. The one big crusty roach sitting where it shouldn't
have been. Ever.

The boy kicked at whatever it was he had found in the
dirt, kicked with one chubby foot from the squatting position, which would have been an acrobatic accomplish-
ment for an adult, but not a little boy. He heard
something behind him and quickly turned around. A
young Mexican woman in a dark shirtwaist dress stretched
shapeless and missing several buttons came around the

edge of the house, her face angry, her hand stretched out at him. She quickly reached up and grabbed the same branch he had just stripped of its leaves and broke it off. The boy didn't wait. He jumped up and headed for the opposite corner of the house that would take him around to the back again, already beginning to cry in anticipation, one fat hand behind him covering his filthy buttocks. The woman marched after him.

Haydon felt panicky. He wanted to throw open the door of the car and go after them. Slowly he closed his eyes and lowered his head to the top of the steering wheel. Images, stark and dark, made a ratcheting procession across his mind, a painful jittering of scenes from a night in that house so long ago and only yesterday. It seemed both. One would think it couldn't seem both, but it did. The movies had it all wrong about things like that. They didn't happen in slow motion. They happened fast. Like an explosion. And then afterward when you thought about it, or your mind wouldn't let it alone, it still wasn't in slow motion but fast again, an endless looping of the same scenes so that you did them over and over and over again.

He looked up. With the air conditioner off, the car was getting hot. He looked through the windshield at the desperate little street. Nobody along here could afford the noisy window units that kept some of the other houses almost cool. Here they used the houses to create a shade, a place to crawl into out of the sun, not out of the heat. You couldn't get away from the heat.

Reflexively Haydon looked around again just in time to see the boy come around the corner of the house, crying, rubbing his eyes as he walked with the rolling gait of a fat man. He wiped his nose with a long sweep of his forearm as he walked straight to the pup chewing on the stick. He bent down and jerked the stick out of the pup's mouth and began hitting him with it, getting down close as the mongrel rolled over on its back in defenseless supplication, exposing its spotted pink belly.

Finally the little boy quit and threw down the stick. He picked up the pup and hugged it and then dropped him. Looking around, he walked over to the spot in the dirt he had been looking at before the woman came and squatted once again, punching something in the powdery dust. Haydon looked at him and imagined that from his navel he could see a thick globule of dark blood emerge and form a fat bubble. The bubble burst and made a thick scribe on the downward curve of the boy's stomach until it reached a point that it stopped and began dripping quickly into the sand.

Haydon started the Vanden Plas and drove away.

Nina's car was not there, so he parked in the drive and went into the front entryway. Gabriela heard him come in and met him in the kitchen, where he had taken a bottle of white Bordeaux out of the racks and was pulling the cork.

"You had lunch?" she asked, resting one hand on the tile cabinet and the other on a well-padded hip.

He popped the cork. "No. Could I get a sandwich?"

"Of course. Ham and Swiss cheese? It's smoked ham. A good one. And good fresh bread from Regina's. Dark bread."

"That would be great. Could you bring it into the library? And olives?"

"Of course. And the little green onions."

She watched him get out one of the ribbed bistro glasses and walk across the dining room to the hallway and the French doors. She came after him.

"You gonna give that stuff to ol' Cinco?"

Haydon went out the door.

She stood in the door as he got Cinco's bowl and moved it out of the sun into the shade. The old dog was pulling himself up from where he had been sleeping next to the balustrades at the other end of the terrace.

"You gonna cut his yeers in half givin' him that stuff," she said from the door, her hands perched on her hips. "Tha's for pipple, not dogs."

Haydon knelt down and poured a third of the bottle into Cinco's bowl as the old collie walked up, swinging his tail, and looked over Haydon's shoulder, touching a cold nose to his neck. Haydon turned, scratched him behind his ears, and stood. Cinco moved around next to the

shady wall and leaned against it as he eased himself down
on the flagstones. He blinked at the bowl and began lap-
ping the wine.

Gabriela shook her head and went back into the
house to start the sandwich.

Haydon walked into the library from the terrace
through the French doors and set the wine bottle and the
glass on the refectory table. He sat down at his desk and
pulled the typewriter table over to him and threaded a
sheet of paper under the platen. He watched Cinco a few
minutes and then began working up the reports from the
morning's interviews.

After a while Gabriela brought his sandwich and left it
beside the glass and bottle on the refectory table along
with a linen napkin. Haydon finished his notes and turned
to the food. The combination of smoked ham and bakery
bread was delicious, with just the right touch of Dijon
mustard to make it taste musky with the salty olives. The
green onions were fresh and light. Haydon ate in silence,
sipping the Bordeaux and looking out at Cinco, who had
gone to sleep beside the empty bowl with his long nose
resting on his paws.

In between bites Haydon pulled a piece of paper and
a pencil over to him and wrote down Powell's name in the
center of the clean sheet. To one side of the name he
wrote *Parnas* and drew a line between them with arrows at
each end. There was an interaction between the two, a
mutually beneficial relationship. He moved up and wrote
Langer. This time the arrow went from Powell to Langer: a
relationship initiated by Powell. Farther around Powell he
wrote *Quinn,* the arrow pointing from Powell to Quinn:
another one-way relationship. She reciprocated nothing.
Farther around he wrote *Toy.* The arrow pointed both
ways, another mutually beneficial relationship. From Toy
another went out to a question mark.

As far as Haydon knew at this point, Langer was the
only one who had an apparent reason to kill Powell. But
according to Langer there should be at least one or more
arrows going out from Powell's name with question marks
at the end of them too. The subjects of Powell's blackmailing. According to Langer. But if that were the case, where

were the tapes Powell was using for leverage? Or, for that matter, where were the tapes he was supposed to be using against Langer?

Haydon didn't believe there were any video tapes. In fact, he didn't believe Powell was blackmailing anyone. For some reason, that idea simply didn't fit in with the profile Alice Parnas had drawn of Powell. And regarding Wayne Powell, Haydon tended to believe Parnas rather than Langer. He looked at the diagram, at the arrow going from Powell to Langer. He erased the tip of the arrow next to Langer and put it at the other end, pointing to Powell. That, he felt, reflected something closer to the truth.

If Powell wasn't blackmailing Langer, then why had Langer contrived that elaborate story about his illicit activities in Los Angeles? As a diversion. From what? From whatever it was Powell was actually doing in the lab at night. But if Parnas was to be believed, what Powell was doing, though certainly odd, wasn't the kind of thing to get him killed. Unless something unexpected had come across on the tapes, something that shouldn't have been filmed and that Powell shouldn't have seen. But would Langer have known about it, and would he have killed because of it?

Perhaps not, but if Langer fell into a secondary position as a suspect, then Toy took his place. Whatever the machinations of the individuals involved, it seemed a very strong probability that Wayne Powell had been killed because of something he had seen and processed on video tapes. And where were the tapes? Two possibilities: Whoever killed Powell had them, or Powell had hidden them.

He needed to talk with Mooney and Lapierre and see what they had come up with. It was time to compare notes.

23

....

"I just walked in," Mooney said. He was shouting. An electric drill whined in the background. "How are things going at your end?"

"Confusing. We need to talk," Haydon said. "Is Pete there?"

"No, he went right on out to Toy's place after he left you this morning. We're supposed to meet for lunch, though. Have you eaten?"

"I'm just finishing, but I'll meet you."

"Good deal. How about Grif's, one o'clock? No, wait, it's almost one now. Make it one-thirty. Pete was going to call me when he got on the Southeast Freeway, and there's no note that he's called in. It'll be one-thirty at least."

"I'll be there," Haydon said.

Grif's Shillelagh Inn ranked among the top three of Mooney's favorite lunch spots. It was a block off Montrose on a small narrow back street called Roseland and was so close to the consulate of the People's Republic of China that you could hit it with a rock. Grif's was a comfortable place, tap beer, two televisions, and a clientele of weekend jocks who talked a good game, whatever game was in season.

Haydon got there first and walked inside the tall wood fence that protected the large raised deck outside the entrance where they set up tables at night, when there was less danger of heatstroke. He went inside and claimed one of the wooden tables with benches by the front windows. He sat with his back to the windows so the light would be on Mooney and Lapierre's faces and ordered a Miller beer he didn't want.

When the two detectives came in about fifteen minutes later, Lapierre came over and joined Haydon while Mooney stopped off at the bar to say something to one of the waitresses, something confidential and humorous, judging from the look on her face, while one of his fat Irish hands rested casually on a portion of her anatomy that made the gesture dangerously close to a misdemeanor. He came over, still laughing, pulled a long piece of folded paper from inside his coat, and tossed it on the table as he climbed over the bench.

Mooney and Lapierre ordered from the same smiling waitress Mooney had spoken to, and she turned in their orders and brought their drinks as Haydon began telling them of his conversation with Thomas Herrick and his interviews with Langer and Alice Parnas. He gave them his impressions of the truth, or lack of it, in the latter two conversations.

By the time he had finished, the waitress brought the hamburgers. Mooney took a bite, chewed a few times, and washed it down with his milk.

"Sounds to me like this Toy is a real serious case," he said. "He could be involved in all kinds of shit here. Guy with a background like that. Hand me that ketchup, Pete."

"He doesn't sound as weird to me as the guy who hires him to get the gory film," Lapierre said, sliding the bottle across in front of him. "Nothing illegal in that, I guess, but it doesn't sound nice."

Mooney shook a thick paste of ketchup over his fries and said, "I'll tell you. I think we ought to get ahold of that little slope and threaten to send him back to fuckin'

Mongolia if he doesn't open up on what the shit's going down here."

"That'll be hard to do," Lapierre said, laying the uneaten part of his burger down in the plastic basket and wiping his hands on a paper napkin.

"Don't tell me," Mooney said, looking at him, a long red fry dangling from his fingers.

Lapierre nodded. "I got over there about ten-thirty. His condo is on Greenbriar, not far off Holcombe. There's almost a solid block of them in there, and Toy's is inside a little drive, kind of a compound. I parked across the street and strolled over, looking for either the Audi or the Mercedes parked around the circle. I didn't see them, so I walked around to the back drive and found Toy's slot numbers in the garages. Nothing. It's pretty private back there, so I went up to the door. It was closed, but it had been jimmied open and the latch had been mangled. It didn't even catch. I pushed it open and went in."

He took a sip of his Coors Light.

"Cabinet doors were standing open, some of the shelves were bare. Looked like pots and pans were gone. Most of the pantry goods were there, but it looked like it'd been gone through. I took a quick walk around to make sure I wasn't going to get jumped. The closets in the up-stairs bedrooms had been cleaned out, as well as most of the clothes chests. Personal effects were gone from the bathrooms. There were marks on the carpet downstairs where it looked like there'd been a television, and there was a square of dust on a bookshelf where there'd proba-bly been a stereo turntable. And I could see where the records had sat too. Mail was piled up under the slot in the front door. I stepped outside and got the newspapers: Thursday's through today's.

"It looked like they'd made a fast move. Almost every-thing else was there. I started knocking on doors around the compound, but nobody knew anything until I came to one woman who said she was pretty friendly with the two Chinese girls. She said she hadn't seen them in several days. They were usually around the pool. I tried to pin her down on how long it'd been since she'd seen them, and she decided the last time was Wednesday. A week ago. I didn't have any luck with anybody else."

"Did anybody around there besides that one woman know Toy or the girls?" Mooney asked. He had finished his hamburger and was using his toothpick while he lazily finished off the fries. In the light from the window, Haydon noticed that the little crimson spider veins in Mooney's nose and cheeks had gotten worse. His face was taking on the raw, tender look of a perpetual sunburn. His Irish ancestors should have stayed away from Texas.

"No. But there are eight residences around the circle there, and I only talked to five of them. I didn't get any response from the other three. Those people might know something."

"Thursday's paper," Haydon said. "And the door had been jimmied."

"I'd guess maybe Toy's got the tapes in question," Mooney said. "And he knows somebody else wants them. What do you suppose the little turd's up to?"

"Pete," Haydon said. "We need to get the licenses of those two cars out to the patrol units as soon as possible. Seal off Toy's condo and go back and try to talk to those last three residences. Ed, why don't you go through the place again and see if you can't find something that will give us a lead. Anything. Get Dystal to let you have someone who can start checking the airports and bus stations for Oriental names departing within the first three days after last Wednesday night. And let's check the car rental agencies too. If Toy stays in the city he might not want to drive around in the Mercedes or the Audi."

Lapierre nodded and made a few notes.

"You got the list of clients from the agency?" Haydon asked Mooney.

"Right here." Mooney unfolded the piece of paper he had tossed on the table and handed it to Haydon.

"It's pretty interesting," Mooney said. "Guess who's on there. Mrs. Harold Wilshire and Mrs. George Ginsberg. Can you believe it? Society ladies hiring a PR agency."

"Happens all the time," Haydon said, looking down the list. "Next few months it'll be someone else."

Mooney looked at Lapierre and opened his eyes wide. "Well, there's politicians on there too. That was easier to take. Those turds need all the help they can get. Lots of big companies. A hell of a lot more out-of-state accounts than I expected. Langer's got a big-deal company there."

"You have a copy of this for your files?" Haydon asked.

"Sure do."

"I'm going to try to get an interpretation of this," Haydon said. "I don't know what Multicorp is. I don't know what Synco is, or Intermark, or TechGroup, or United Merchantile, or half a dozen others. I don't want to go to anyone at Langer's for information because it'll get back to him." He looked at Mooney. "You did take precautions in getting this."

"Yeah. The little gal who sneaked it out for me thinks her religious silence on this matter is the only and absolute hope of catching the mad killer that's stalking Langer Media. She's going to be saying 'What list?' for the rest of her life. She's *recruited*."

Frank Siddons looked at the computer printout on his desk and smiled. He was enjoying having a privileged inside look. One of his earliest pleasures as a young lawyer had been the realization that the confidentiality assured by the attorney-client relationship would open up to him a world of secrets, both pure and profane, and that because of it people requiring his services would be inclined, even compelled, to tell him things they would be hesitant to whisper even in the holy isolation of the confessional. Secrets were wonderful things. He enjoyed them immensely; he even enjoyed keeping them.

This was not the same thing, of course, but still he liked being privy to information that wasn't rightfully his. It reinvigorated him. He had identified most of the corporations, explaining their business, speculating on the contacts Langer had made and massaged in order to get the contract to represent them. A large independent oil company, a young and burgeoning computer firm, a major bank, an electronics firm, a trucking corporation, an airline, a real estate firm, an industrial construction company, a home builder, a textile mill, a lumber company, dozens of retail firms. Langer was strong, stronger than Siddons has suspected.

But the smile had been reserved for the discovery of two specific accounts. He didn't know there would be two of them, but he knew there would be one at least. He took the unlit cigar from his mouth and held it in his left hand while the knobby jointed index finger of his right hand tapped once at each name.

"There you are, Stuart. The telltale signs of the gentleman across the way." He jerked a thumb back over his shoulder at the mirrored building of Roeg International. "Multicorp and Synco."

"He owns them?"

"Multicorp, yes. It's an electronics firm in Denver." Siddons sat back in his old chair. "A few years ago the U.S. military provided our Israeli friends with a new kind of weapon that we wanted them to try out first time they got the chance. Since the Israelis were then in the process of that astonishing drive into Lebanon to rout the PLO, it just happened that they had the opportunity to use this weapon right away.

"It's called the vacuum bomb. The Israelis took it up and dropped it over a building where they claimed Yasir Arafat was hiding. He wasn't. The way the thing works is, you drop it from an aircraft and detonate it directly over the target. The thing explodes and the air rush *implodes* the building, killing everything inside but causing practically no damage at all to surrounding structures. That was what it was designed to do, and that was what it did. They killed nearly three hundred people proving the vacuum bomb was a successful weapon. They're going to make more of those, and Multicorp Electronics makes the detonator. Roeg's got a lucrative contract with the government."

"And Langer has an equally lucrative contract with Multicorp," Haydon added.

"Certainly," Siddons said. "And that mostly consists of defensive PR. Left-wingers love to hassle government-financed 'munitions dealers,' and Langer's firm just tries to help Multicorp keep a low profile. They'd make them invisible if they could."

"Okay. What about Synco?"

Siddons grinned. "Synco's a little more interesting and requires a lot more work from Langer Media. Synco, Stuart, is a dummy company. It's a front for a CIA disinformation operation in Central America. Specifically El Salvador. For the U.S. government, which wants so much to get itself thoroughly involved down there, El Salvador poses an enormous PR problem. The corrupt military factions we support down there, the right-wing death squads that seem to be aligned with the government, the increasing buildup of our military presence, the mysterious civilian deaths, all this and more has to be made palatable to the American public so the public doesn't get on its high horse and force Congress to back out of there. There's a hell of a lot that can be done to adulterate the reportage that gets back to the States regarding these distasteful subjects. Langer has a whole gaggle of CIA-trained people working down there trying to control that sort of thing."

"Why doesn't the CIA do it themselves?"

"Well, the CIA's getting fat again, you know. I mean, they're making a comeback. But Congress still puts a lid on them. They can only go so far. Yet they want to be just a little fatter. So they farm out the stuff they can't do directly for themselves. Disinformation and media control are two areas where this has worked successfully. The CIA says, Here's a fake company, here's the names of some boys we've trained but no longer employ, here's a job we want done, here's a contract."

"It works?"

"Very well. Better than the American public ever suspects. And it works two ways. These Synco people down there also try to defuse the anti-American sentiment by Salvadorans. They've got their hands full."

Haydon reached over and turned the printout around to face him. He studied the list while Siddons chewed on his cigar.

"Then Langer has contacts in El Salvador. People who know the ropes down there and could take you wherever you wanted to go to see whatever you wanted to see."

"Oh, yeah. Most of them are Salvadorans, Central Americans. The CIA uses them just like they've used the Cubans. Always use the natives for covert activities. They'd know their way around all right."

"Thanks, Frank," Haydon said, folding up the paper. "You've been a great help."

"My pleasure. I enjoyed looking over your list." He grinned. "You getting this thing worked out, Stuart?"

"I'm closer than I was."

The old man nodded, rotating the maduro in his mouth with wrinkled, waxy fingers, his calm eyes resting on Haydon.

Haydon paused before he stood. "Feltner told me that none of those executives close to Roeg, or those who had been close to him, would open up about what it's really like to work with him. Talk about his personal quirks, his eccentricities."

"That's what I understand."

"I need to find someone who will."

"Maybe you ought to just drive out there and talk to him," Siddons suggested.

"Not yet."

"You got something specific in mind?"

Haydon thought it over before he spoke. "Wayne Powell was processing video tape in Langer's laboratory at night. Not as a part of his regular work. Moonlighting. His girlfriend said the film was taken by a former combat photographer who had been hired by 'a man' who paid him to go to all the hotspots of the world to get combat footage, the bloodier the better. A lot of it was coming from Central America. Langer pretends not to know about this, says he was letting Powell use agency facilities as a condition involving blackmail. He doesn't know what Powell did in the laboratory at night and doesn't care.

"I think he was processing video tape the night he was killed and that it was the subject of that film that got him killed. The combat photographer has disappeared, and someone has broken into his place and gone through it."

Haydon could almost feel the old man's nerve endings reaching out, cautiously probing the electricity in the air like the antennae of an otherwise motionless insect.

"Langer could be telling the truth," Haydon added, "and whatever was going on with Powell and the photographer is a completely separate operation. But I don't believe Langer's story about Powell blackmailing him. That opens up, in my mind, at least, very complicated possibilities that could easily include Josef Roeg."

After a moment Siddons said, "You feel pretty sure about this?"

"I don't know enough to be pretty sure."

Siddons looked at him. He had taken the cigar out of his mouth, his pale and age-puckered hands resting on the dark lustrous wood of his desk. "Jack Feltner may not have been entirely correct," he said.

24

....

He lived in Hunter's Creek, one of a cluster of incorporated townships within the city of Houston known as the Memorial Villages. Together they encompassed eleven square miles of the city's most tranquil and expensive real estate west of the Loop and along Memorial Drive. His house lay in the middle of two acres of lushly wooded land on Pifer Road off Beinhorn. The pines here were close and crowded with a thick, impenetrable undergrowth. When the sun broke through it came in shattered pieces, fighting shadows all the way down from the overstory to the mulchy earth, dancing briefly before disappearing as though absorbed by the gloom.

Haydon turned into a paved drive behind a split-rail fence and followed it well off the road until it ended in front of a low-built house situated so tightly within the surrounding woods that Haydon found himself wondering how the builders had managed to do it. It was a ranch-style home, maybe twenty years old, with walnut-colored brick and a cedarshake roof whose shingles had weathered gray like the surrounding underbrush. The house blended subtly with its environment, making it seem even more secluded and remote.

There were no other cars in the drive, no apparent garage, and it was a moment after Haydon turned off the motor of the Vanden Plas that he made out a small strip of pavement leading off into the trees and disappearing around the house. At the edge of the paved drive there was a wooden bridge with simple log railings that spanned a kind of ditch, or dry creek, and led to a limestone walk that went to the front door. The pine needles were so thick on the ground that Haydon felt as if he were walking on a cushioned path as he crossed the bridge and approached the front door. He heard a mockingbird singing crazily somewhere in the dense undergrowth as he inhaled deeply the scent of the woods.

He pressed the buzzer on the front door and waited.

"Who is it?" A woman's voice came from the grilled speaker. A middle-aged voice, he thought.

"Stuart Haydon for Mr. Greiner." He wondered if his voice sounded middle-aged to her.

"Just a moment, please."

He waited, looking into the woods to his right, then on the other side. When the door was opened a stout, muscular young man dressed in white stood in the doorway. Haydon quickly determined it was a uniform, a tight-fitting athletic T-shirt, white cotton pants, white belt, white crepe-soled shoes. A male nurse. The young man said hello and glanced beyond Haydon out to the driveway.

"You came alone." It was a statement, but Haydon said yes. "Fine, come in." He stepped back and Haydon walked into a rush of cool air and the faint tangy smell of woodsmoke left over from the winter.

The house was big. The ceilings were not high, but the rooms sprawled and rambled from one to another in all directions. He could see through wide doorways into other areas of the house. Directly in front of them was a glass wall that looked outside, and as Haydon followed the silent steps of the nurse, he realized it was one of three glass walls that seemed to wrap around a vast portion of the woods. The house was totally carpeted, which cushioned the inside from noise as the woods cushioned the outside. The silence was oppressive. Haydon felt vaguely uneasy.

They followed a broad hallway, with the woods beyond the glass on one side and an occasional door on the other. The nurse stopped before double casement doors and pulled them apart. As they disappeared into the walls, the young man stepped into the room and Haydon followed him. It was the last room on this wing of the house, long with a convex outer wall at the far end, also made of glass. In the center of the large bulbous portion of the room sat a man in a wheelchair looking out at the woods.

"Here's Mr. Haydon, sir," the young nurse said.

The wheelchair whirred and slowly pivoted about.

"Philip Greiner," the man said as the wheelchair hummed toward Haydon. "Frank called ahead of you."

He stopped in front of Haydon. It was obvious he was a very sick man. He seemed to be in his mid-fifties, but it was difficult to tell, since his flesh sagged exaggeratedly, giving him loose jowls and revealing too much of the mushy red tissue below his eyeballs.

"Amyotrophic lateral sclerosis," he said. "I got it after I 'retired.' When I was supposed to enjoy the fruits of my many years of labor."

He laughed. It wasn't a bitter laugh. He really seemed to find some humor in the irony. His head bobbed a little and then fell down on his chest the way a baby's does when it is just learning to hold it up but hasn't yet acquired the strength. The young man came over and helped him raise it again until he was looking once more at Haydon.

"That happens," Greiner said. "Hope it's not disconcerting to you."

"I appreciate your taking the time," Haydon said.

"You'll buzz if you need me, Mr. Greiner?" the young man asked. He stood halfway to the door.

"Oh, yeah. Thanks, Mike. Thanks."

The young man walked out and pulled the doors closed behind him. Greiner plucked at a toggle switch on the wheelchair arm, and the chair began turning robotically, moving back to the other end of the room.

"Let's go over here. If I get right out near the glass if makes me feel like I'm outside. It helps."

There were armchairs in a casual semicircle facing out to the woods, a coffee table, a liquor cart with a small icebox, lots of magazines, and a few popular novels tossed on the floor. The man pulled up among the group of chairs.

"Sit anywhere you like, Mr. Haydon. Want a drink?"

"No, thank you."

Greiner smiled shakily. "Frank and I are good friends," he said. "Have been for . . . eighteen years. I worked ten years for Josef Roeg. Five years coming up, five years on the inside." He leaned his head back on a cushioned brace that had been built onto the chair for him. Since his head wasn't erect, he looked at Haydon through slightly lowered eyelids. "Frank said you needed to know something about the inner workings of Roeg the man, and that you were told nobody talked who knew anything. Sure you don't want a drink?"

Haydon shook his head. It was difficult to tell how large a man Greiner was. The wheelchair had a lot of batteries and gadgets on it, and he looked relatively small sitting in it. It may have been because his navy blue robe, which swallowed him, had been bought for the man he had been before his illness. His pale blue pajamas with dark piping showed from beneath the robe at the collar, cuffs, and legs.

"Frank didn't tell you anything about me, did he. Didn't even tell you I was in a wheelchair."

"No, he didn't."

Greiner said, "Are you an introspective man, Mr. Haydon?"

"I suppose," Haydon said. "Reasonably."

Greiner smiled again. "Reasonably. Well, I'll tell you, I never was. But in the last fourteen months I have become the *most* introspective of men. Churchill said that being shot at concentrates the mind wonderfully. He was right, but having pieces of you ripped away does the same thing. I mean *real* pieces of you, not your body.

"I'll tell you what can happen to a man in fourteen months that will concentrate his mind wonderfully. A little over a year ago I had everything. Lucrative career, status, lovely wife, wonderful daughter. In May, fourteen months ago, my wife, Janet, and I were sitting right here where you and I are sitting now. It was a Saturday morning, and we'd just received a call from Denise, our daughter. She was leaving Chapel Hill that very minute. Coming home for the summer. Janet and I had been talking about how eager we were to see her. Janet picked up a new *National Geographic* that had just come in the mail and was looking at it when she suddenly sighed and slumped over on the sofa. Right there. Dead. Massive coronary."

He stopped, as if remembering exactly how it happened.

"You know, it was supposed to have been me. I smoked, drank a little, had a high-pressure executive position. It was supposed to have been me from an actuarial perspective. A few days later I was sitting here again. Alone. A widower. But Denise was here, and we had the summer together.

"Three months later, after her summer vacation was over, Denise was driving back to school in an autumn rain. Her car left the road on a curve, and she was killed. When I got the telephone call I almost died too. I really did."

Greiner rolled his head the other way, looking out to the woods. "Three months later, just before the Christmas holidays, Roeg retired me. Within six weeks of that, doctors discovered this: amyotrophic . . . lateral . . . sclerosis. Lou Gehrig's disease. No cure."

He rolled his head back toward Haydon. "In the past five months I've become . . . . a little more than 'reasonably' introspective. I'll bet you've read about things like that happening to people before. In the newspaper. Somebody suffers a string of tragedies and you shake your head and turn to the sports section. I've done it myself. There's really nothing else you can do."

There was a brief silence and then Greiner touched the toggle switch on the arm of his wheelchair, which moved him to a slightly better angle to see Haydon.

"What is it you wanted to know about Roeg?" he asked. He seemed to have said all he wanted to say about the sad matters of the last fourteen months of his life.

It seemed to Haydon that he should somehow respond to Greiner's story, but he could think of nothing that wouldn't sound trivial in comparison. Instead he followed Greiner's lead, crossed his long legs and slowly began a careful overview of the case, giving it enough continuity for Greiner to see how Roeg might fit into it and why Haydon needed more information about him. He did not mention Langer's name, but it proved to be a naive omission. As he talked the sick man closed his eyes. He smiled once at something but was otherwise motionless.

When Haydon finished, Greiner opened his eyes and touched the toggle switch again just enough to make the motor whirr. It didn't really move the wheelchair. He seemed to do it like a nervous tic, to affirm his presence in the world of the living.

"You're talking about Bill Langer too," Greiner said. "Listen, before I start enlightening you, would you come over here and adjust this headrest?"

Haydon got up and went over to the wheelchair.

"There's a wing nut at the back on the chrome shaft holding this thing up. Just loosen it and tilt the pad forward a little. Good, great. Right there. Thanks."

Haydon returned to his chair and sat down again.

Greiner bumped the toggle switch again and waited a moment before he spoke, seeming to settle his mind on the subject.

"Josef Roeg is an odd man in every respect. He looks odd, acts odd, and has one of the most unusual obsessions in the world. He loves violence. That is, he loves to watch it. A wisely passive observer.

"He has a film archive in that big place of his over by the River Oaks Country Club. A big vault with controlled humidity and temperature to preserve old film as well as the new developments in video technology. He has spent hundreds of thousands to stock that archive with the most violent things ever captured on film. Mostly war footage, naturally, since that's about the only kind of real violence you can get on film legally. He's got pirated copies of most of what the networks couldn't show. He's got Nazi SS interrogation film, gassings, brutality in the camps. Those bastards pioneered that kind of thing. Documentary film. Preserving the history of the Third Reich. They put a lot of horror on film you wouldn't believe. The documentaries you see on television don't even scratch the surface of the kind of stuff that's available.

"As you know, Roeg's corporate headquarters are downtown. But he, personally, works solely from that big estate of his. From there his directives go out into the real world, where he uses the fulcrum of human frailty to move his corporations. He works in a huge long hall. At one end of his desk, his computer screens, all the electronic paraphernalia he needs to communicate with the rest of the world. I'll bet there're as many cables going into that place as a lot of corporate offices. At the other end of the big room is a retractable movie screen mounted in the ceiling. The film archive is located through a couple of doors off one side of the hall. There's a permanent movie projector installed in the center of the room. Most of the video tapes have been converted to film so he can see them on the big screen."

Greiner paused and coughed, trying to maintain his balance against the headrest and the back of the chair. If he slid to one side, someone would have to set him right again.

"What happens is your muscles grow progressively weaker," Greiner explained. "They atrophy. You become totally helpless. You can't even speak, because eventually your vocal cords grow flaccid, your jaw muscles will no longer pull up your jaw. You're in a state of absolute immobility. But of course your mind remains in wonderful shape. It's just imprisoned. You think, but that's all you can do. As time passes your body can't properly keep up its defenses. You get pneumonia, a kidney infection, or something like that and you can't fight it off. Something else gets you, but ALS brings it on."

"I can come back another time," Haydon said. "We don't have to talk now."

"You better get it while you can," Greiner said, grinning. "This is a progressive disease. In my case, later definitely is not better."

He bumped the toggle switch.

"All of us had to watch the films," he continued. "Did you ever read any of those books about Hitler's entourage at the Chancellery or Obersalzberg: the interminable hours spent sitting around in overstuffed armchairs after meals in which everyone ate too much; long afternoons in which nothing happened and people nodded off to sleep, bored, but staying on because that's what suited Hitler? That's what it was like for the privileged executives in Roeg's big hall. Except, instead of dozing boredom, we watched hours and hours of horror.

"What is the effect of this kind of entertainment? At first, when I was introduced into the sanctum of these afternoons and evenings, I was fascinated. No one had enlightened me or warned me about this side of Roeg's nature. God, I'd never seen anything like it. I watched every frame that came across the screen. It didn't seem ghoulish at first, but after a while I began to be uneasy. There was just too much of it. It began to seem sick. I watched the other men. One fellow, if he could get a seat out of Roeg's line of vision, simply went to sleep. Another man really suffered through those things. He didn't like any of it. On more than one occasion a couple of us would go into the lavatory between reels, and this guy would be in there throwing up. He never said anything about it, and we didn't either. He would always be late for the next reel."

"Did no one take pleasure in these things besides Roeg?"

"Oh, yeah. Two or three guys consistently got a kick out of it. And I'm not going to claim a constant position of pious moral indignation. None of us were always revolted. You'd find yourself being fascinated almost against your will. It *was* incredible stuff. The intensity of the violence was frequently mesmerizing. After a while you realize there's simply nothing people won't do to other people, and there's nothing new that can be done in the way of violence. It's all been done before, in endless variation. We just keep on repeating the same atrocities from generation to generation, from one people to another. We never lack for someone to sacrifice to our prejudices.

"Oddly, that constant barrage of violence gave me

some distance from the subject, gave me a new perspective on it. There's no denying it's stimulating. Violence appeals to something primitive in us. In our society we take it in fairly regular doses, in films, books, television, newspapers. We kind of like the little shocks we get from it. But when you sit for hours, day after day, and watch *actual* violence, not just Hollywood's glamorous view of it, you come to see it as a real entity, a specific identifiable force. It's like you've been able to distill it, put it in a test tube, and hold it up and look at it in its pure form. You realize that it is as lethal to society as a deadly bacillus. You don't come to that kind of realization from periodic exposure. It makes you wonder what will happen if the duration between exposures becomes less and less frequent and society one day wakes up and finds itself terminally infected.''

"How did Roeg justify all this time spent away from your executive responsibilities?''

"When you work for Roeg, you have to get used to the fact that he's going to waste a certain amount of your time. The man has no family and no social skills. He doesn't know how to entertain or just sit around and chat, but he wants company. Since he hasn't a single real friend in the world, that anyone knows about, he uses his executives as substitutes. In effect, they are total prostitutes. They're highly paid, but he has the right to call them anytime he wants. Anytime.

"The time you might waste with him is not work time. You do your job or you wouldn't be there. It's the time you normally would have spent with your own family that you sacrifice. Roeg's share comes first. He doesn't hesitate to call you away from home or a family party with friends. Anytime. And when you get over there he might not be able to make it clear what he wants to talk about or do, so you end up watching more film.''

"What do you mean, he can't make it clear what he wants?'' Haydon asked.

"He's socially inept,'' Greiner said, rolling his head more directly at Haydon. "It's that simple. He can talk business, once you learn his quirky way of communicating, but when the business is done and he still wants someone around, he doesn't really know how to keep you there. Except the films." Greiner let his head ease back to a more comfortable position. "It's pathetic."

"How many men were involved in these afternoon sessions?" Haydon asked.

"It varied. Several of the men who are a part of the inner circle live outside the country, so they would not be there regularly. I'd say it fluctuated between four and five. Not counting Langer and Roeg. I've been there when there were as many as seven."

"Did he hire photographers when you were still going there?"

"I don't know. You see, Roeg kept his life compartmentalized. Each executive was in charge of looking after not only his own area of corporate responsibilites but also some area of Roeg's personal life. One guy was responsible for everything administrative regarding the estate: hired the groundskeepers, the gardeners, the servants, authorized the improvements and repairs. Everything. Another was responsible for all the transportation, kept the limos serviced and fitted with the gadgets Roeg would get a notion to have, took care of hangaring and servicing the Lears at Hobby, hired the pilots. Each of us had something. We had our own families, and then we had a piece of Roeg's life also."

"And Langer?"

"You see, remarkably, none of us ever discussed our responsibilities, or the troubles we had with them, with each other. That's hard to believe, I know, but there's a very good reason: If you didn't know anything about it, then you couldn't be held responsible. Nobody wanted to know anything beyond their own realm of responsibility. And that's the way Roeg wanted it, too. He had reasons for that. Legal reasons, practical ones."

"But at the same time, we knew." Greiner smiled wearily. "Roeg would say in front of the others, 'Phil, did you get the new carpet in at the Rue LaMarque?' and everyone would know that I was responsible for Roeg's homes away from home. He had to travel all over the world, and he owned places in about six major cities. I had to look after those, staff them, make sure they were ready when he needed to be there. Or he'd say, 'Wes, did you take care of that thing for Chuck?' We all knew Chuck was the Lear pilot, so we knew Wes was in charge of transportation.''

He paused and let his eyes wander to the forest outside. There was no sound in the house. It seemed completely removed in time from the woods beyond the glass. Haydon had the sensation of being in a large museum in which the trees and underbrush were a diorama depicting a wildlife scene. If you looked closely, you would see a stuffed squirrel with slightly dusty fur, birds with faded feathers sitting at stiff angles on dead branches, and a raccoon frozen beside a pool of off-blue polymer plastic.

Greiner rolled his head toward Haydon again.

"Yeah, Bill was in charge of the archives. He'd be responsible for the photographer." He said it as though the words soured on his lips as he spoke them, his eyes locked on Haydon. "I'm gravely ill, Mr. Haydon. I'm dying. But I'm not nearly as sick as I was while I was working for Josef Roeg.''

There was a long pause. Haydon could almost feel the great expanses of carpet reaching up to absorb any wayward sound, even muffling his own heartbeat.

"It's amazing," Greiner said, "how grown, intelligent men can let themselves be manipulated by . . . someone like Josef Roeg. Their strong desires become their frailties, and a small man can gain enormous strength through their weaknesses.''

25

Ricky Toy walked into the quadrangle through the breeze-way that led from the parking lot. He was precoccupied and heard the girls before he saw them. Actually, he heard the dull *whump* of the diving board before he heard the girls. He looked across the parched grass to the pool and saw Lai coming up out of the water. Yue was lying on a rusty deck lounger with faded green plastic strips. There were three men sitting around in pool chairs talking to her. Lai crawled out of the water, and a guy with a frog-white belly and a can of Pearl struggled out of his chair to give her a beach towel. Lai smiled radiantly and began patting her long bronze limbs with the towel. The guy with the Pearl forgot what he was doing and just stood there watching her.

Toy smiled and followed the sidewalk around the quadrangle under the balcony and under the stair land-ings that led up to the apartments on the second level, past the metal Burger Boy grill, the ragtag lawn furniture, yellowy potted plants put out to sun, a motorcycle being overhauled but temporarily abandoned, a ten-speed Vista chained to one of the landing's support posts. He came to their apartment door and went inside, went straight to the refrigerator, and got a Tecate and a lemon slice. He sat down at the dinette table to watch the girls pump up the local boys at the pool.

They had been there a week now. It hadn't taken the girls long to make the place livable. Their sudden, if temporary, decline in living conditions hadn't depressed them. They were that incomparable combination so often seen in Oriental women: deliciously feminine but surprisingly tough and resilient. They would always make the best of whatever life offered them. If it was abundance, they enjoyed it like true voluptuaries experienced in the creative pleasures of the Sybarites; if it was hard times, they endured with a silent stoicism that never despaired and that most people could not understand. Hong Kong ladies.

The day after they moved in, Toy changed the license plates on the cars and the girls went shopping in the Audi. He told them they weren't going to live in the apartment very long, so they had rented the furniture and had it delivered the same day. They scrubbed the place from top to bottom, washed the windows, shampooed the carpets so they could go barefooted on clean floors, made the air smell fresh. They bought plants. They stocked the kitchen. They settled in. Always upbeat, no matter what. Hong Kong ladies.

They hit the pool on the third day, and the good ol' boys came out of the woodwork like tree roaches. They gathered around to watch, couldn't believe their eyes, couldn't believe these two long-legged, damn-near-naked gals had come to live in *their* little ol' 'partment complex. They couldn't believe it either when a guy named Roy who had steel wool on his chest, a Tom Selleck haircut, and his brains between his legs got himself all revved up and excited and used his Happy Hour moves on Yue. He put a blunt-fingered paw where he didn't have permission to put it, and the two girls ended his adventure by breaking his thumbs. You didn't make one of the girls unhappy without the other one getting unhappy too. They looked out for each other. Number one rule. Of course, it also worked the other way: what one of them liked, they both liked. And what they liked best, with uninhibited affection, was Ricky Toy. He smiled. Hong Kong ladies.

It had been two days since Toy had mailed out the single three-quarter-inch cassette. Roeg had gotten it by now, had contacted his archive factotum, who probably hadn't been able to digest a meal since poor old Wayne was discovered. Toy hadn't sent anything but the cassette. No note. And he had sent the package registered so Roeg would have to sign for it, and it wouldn't lie around unnoticed for a week. Toy decided to give them the rest of the day and tonight. The way the mail was, Roeg wouldn't get the thing until this afternoon. Tomorrow Toy would call Langer and arrange a meeting with Roeg personally.

He ran through a mental checklist. He had been to a lawyer. Not just any lawyer, but a lawyer at one of the firms in town whose name would mean something to Roeg when the time came. He had had his will drawn up, making sure he could do what he wanted to do, that the terms would be honored to the minutest detail, that something couldn't intervene and change the circumstances making the terms he was going to offer Roeg unattractive by virtue of their impossibility. It had to be tight, airtight. His life would depend on it.

He had secured a safety deposit box at TexCorp Bank and deposited his neat little package. Sealed, he hoped, forever. Never to be touched again except to be destroyed, without being opened, after Toy had enjoyed a long and happy life. He had flown down to Panama, with a ticket purchased in the name of Richard K. Malik, and had arranged things with the greedy and greasy Alvaro Nunez Chamaco. Of course, no pro'lem. He had flown back the same night.

The only thing that really bothered him about this deal was that they might somehow find him before he could see it through. But even if they did, now that the will was in effect, now that everything was in place, wouldn't he be safe? No, not until he explained. Not until he had the meeting. And then there were the girls. If Roeg's people got to the girls he would have to back off. Maybe Richard M. Kaun should rent a car and send the girls out of town until it was all in place. He considered that. He looked out to the pool and considered it.

Grover Ellis sat on a wooden kitchen chair with the back missing and looked at the sun streaming in through the dirty bare windows. He had lit a cigarette so he wouldn't have to smell the human urine that permeated the abandoned apartment building that for years had been a den for winos and heroin addicts. His white dress shirt had huge rings of perspiration under the arms, his tie was undone, and he was looking at Boney Walker across from him on the floor.

"You gonna let me have a smoke?" Boney asked. He lay on his side, his hands tied behind him with electrical cord, his feet tied together and stretched backward and joined to his hands. He had spent the night in that position, lying on a bed of rat pills that stuck to his sweaty skin as he moved about on the floor trying to ease his aching muscles. His jockey shorts were soggy and stained yellow where he had gone to the bathroom during the night.

Ellis went over and squatted down and put the cigarette between Boney's lips. He lit another one for himself and stood up, went back to the chair.

"I didn't think you was gonna come back," Boney said, squeezing the cigarette with his lips in one corner of his mouth, talking around it. "I didn't get no sleep. I had ta keep jerkin' around on the flo' ta keep the rats off, man. One of the little fuckas bit me anyways. Down thea, ona toe. You see any blood down thea?"

Ellis looked that way. "I don't see anything."

"Oh, shit," Boney whimpered. He sucked on the cigarette. He was shaking a little. "Wha' you gonna do?"

Boney Walker had been a hustler all of his thirty-eight years. He had been to prison twice. TDC. Brazoria County. Ramsey II Unit and Darrington Unit. He was tall and rangy. There were a few knife scars on his bare body. The man hadn't had an easy life, not by a long shot.

"I guess I'm going to kill you," Ellis said.

"Oh, shit, man." Boney's voice quavered. He was squinting through the cigarette smoke. "I swea ta God I

don't know nothin' about no China man. We *brothas*! You
can't kill me, man."

"Boney, I'm just doing what you'd do in my place,"
Ellis said.

"No, you *ain't*," Boney protested.

"What would you do?" Ellis' voice was quiet, conver-
sational.

"I'd *believe* me, man! I mean, you think I'd let you kill
me ta save a China man's ass? I wanna save my *own*self
ass."

"I don't know what you'd do, Boney. All I know is
you're the only one I involved in this. *I* didn't let the man
in the warehouse."

"Me neitha!"

Ellis didn't like any of this. They had gotten Walker
out of the Fifth Ward and driven to this derelict building,
where they unloaded him in a second-floor room. He had
thrown up one more time while they were standing there
looking at him on the floor and trying to decide if he was
going to be able to get loose. Ellis was afraid he would
choke to death on his own vomit if he continued to throw
up after they left. He didn't want to leave him there. He
was afraid a vagrant would find him and call the police. He
was afraid some kids might find him and call the police. He was afraid Boney might somehow get loose and
get away.

They finally left without laying a finger on him. They
had questioned him for about half an hour about Toy, but
he swore he never heard of the guy. They threatened him,
but it wasn't any good. He said he didn't know what they
were talking about. Finally they tied Ellis' handkerchief
around his mouth and left him there, just walked out
without saying anything to him. But Ellis had to come
back the next day and get to the bottom of it.

He couldn't believe he was sitting in this hole looking
at this stupid shit and telling him he was going to kill him.
He had worked all his life to rise above derelict people,
derelict buildings, and derelict views of life. Now here he
was putting down a hustle on a professional scam man,
and it was coming so easy for him. He couldn't see that
he'd made a hell of a lot of progress beyond the Boney

Walkers. He had nicer threads than Boney's army surplus jockey shorts, but here he was doing dirty business with dirty people in dirty places.

His thoughts were interrupted by blubbering noises coming from Boney.

He was crying and talking to himself. The cold filter of the cigarette was on the floor in front of his long, morose face.

"I jus' a pore unlucky nigga. My God. Come ta this. Layin' in rat shit. Wearin' pissed-in shawts. Neva had no chance."

"Shut up," Ellis said to him. Trucks whined like live things on the expressway a few blocks away. If he didn't get something out of Walker, what was it going to look like? It was going to look like Toy had worked the setup through him. Would it really? Did they really believe he would do that? Did he really believe Walker didn't know what was going on?

He stood up. Walker jerked tight and looked at him as he walked toward the door.

"Wha' you doin'? Hey, brotha! Whea you goin'?" His eyes were rolling like a vaudeville black's.

"Don't start screaming," Ellis said. "I'm going down to the car. I'll be right back."

He walked from the room out into the hallway, around a banister, and down the stairs. He went down a hallway and out into the alley in back of the building. Unlocking the car door, he took a sack with a drawstring out of the glove compartment. He closed it, locked the car, and went back upstairs.

Walker was reared back as far as he could go, waiting for him. Ellis walked over to the backless chair and opened the sack. He took out a Smith & Wesson Chief's Special, .38 caliber, and checked the action. He reached into the sack and took out a long cylinder and began screwing it on the end of the revolver.

"Oh, shit!" Walker said. He whimpered.

"What can I do, Boney?" Ellis said. "You're not helping me any. I gave you a good deal. Fixed it so you could make a bundle, did right by you, and then you screwed me and when I came to talk to you about it you tried to blow me away. That's not good, Boney. You shouldn't have done it.''

"But you ain't beat me yet,'' Walker whined.

"No, I ain't beat you,'' Ellis said. "Why would I want to do that? Get myself all hot trying to work it out of you. Not my way.''

Ellis shook his head and gave a final twist to the silencer. He stepped over to Walker and squatted down close to him.

"The thing is, Boney, I might be inclined to believe you if it hadn't been for that shot you fired through the door. You were expecting me, brother. And the reason you were expecting me was because you'd done something you shouldn't have done, and you knew it. So I bring you here and ask you a question. You don't want to answer me, fine. I'm not going to do it the hard way. I'll simply blow your eyes out and get to work on something a little more fruitful.''

Walker's face was drenched in sweat. His wooly hair had spiderwebs, little bits of sticks, and rat pills in it. The expression on his face was a study in slow enlightenment.

"Why'd you shoot at me, Boney?''

"Man, I didn't know it was *you*. I do business with other peeples needs shootin' at.''

"You didn't recognize my voice?''

"No *way!*'' Boney's own voice was just a few decibels off a squeak.

Ellis thought he would put the silencer up to Boney's face right there, but then he changed his mind. It would work better if he backed off. He stood and stepped back, keeping his eyes on Walker. He raised the gun, the long silencer looking lethal and wicked.

He had it almost horizontal when Walker screamed, *"Okay!* Aaahhhh! *Okay!''* Urine soaked his shorts again and ran down his side. "Ooohhhh.'' Walker's stomach was sucked up tight, his head reared back, and you could see his heart slamming against his rib cage beneath the thin membrane of black flesh below his sternum. He was strung tight as a bowstring, and if you had plucked him he would have vibrated. Ellis lowered the gun and Walker's muscles collapsed. He rolled forward on his stomach, into the puddle he had just created.

"God damn you, mutha!" he said, crying. "I tell you 'bout Ricky Toy."

Ellis stood where he was. Walker sniffled, took a minute to get hold of himself. He talked from where he was, his face looking into the trash and rat pills.

"The fuckin' warehouse in *China*town!" He said this as though it should have been obvious to Ellis, which it was, so Ellis waited for Walker to elaborate. "Afta noon afta the secont time, guy comes ta my do', wakes me up and puts this big-ass gun in my face, and say let him in. He sit me down and give me some pitchas ta look at. They show me with a winna, show me handlin' a losa. All of it. Say he knows what's goin' down an' was gonna tell the police if I didn't give him a key. Say he jus' wont in thea one night. Say he pay me. Say he didn't know what choice I got an' I didn't eitha, so tha's what I did."

"You gave him the key?"

"Yeah. I had 'notha one."

"How did he know we were there? How did he know about you?"

"Tha's what I ast. He say it don't matta. He say if I tell 'bout him comin' he come back an' blow me away. He a mean fucka. Put that nozzle of that gun right up my nose, inside, twis' it 'round, jam it up in thea. Wha' I'm gonna *do*? I wish I neva hea of you guys. I been in nothin' but hot watta since I got ina this shit. Jus' an unlucky nigga. God *dammit*!"

Suddenly Ellis was aware of the stifling heat in the room and the overwhelming odor of Walker's urine. He seemed to break into a heavier sweat. The rings under his arms had already worked themselves into wide dark bands going into the waist of his pants. He heard flies, saw them darting all around Walker.

"Did you ever meet him again?"

"Damn right! Coupla nights back I woke up in the middle of the night and that yella sucka was on top of the *bed*, had his big ol' cannon stuffed up ina my nuts. Ask me if I be keepin' my mouth shut. Yeah, yeah, I say. He jab me with the gun. Good, he say."

"That's it?"

"Nothin' else, man. I don't know nothin' else an' I don't wanna know nothin' else."

"You don't know where he is?" Ellis asked.

"Shit, no! He always knows whea *I* be."

There was a long silence, no sounds except for the noises on the expressway and the tiny sound of the flies.

Walker cautiously turned his head toward Ellis, cutting his eyes as far around as they would go, wondering what was going to happen to him now.

Ellis came over and squatted down. "Now I'm going to show you the kind of people you're dealing with here," he said.

26

The conversation with Philip Greiner left Haydon feeling low, for several reasons. Greiner had had more than his share of personal tragedies, and it was difficult not to be influenced by the disheartening details of his story, despite the fact that he related them with a surprising amount of philosophical acceptance. Somehow Haydon didn't feel that his own introspective bent would have taken him that far under similar circumstances. Greiner was a certain kind of survivor. Whatever it was that made the man endure, Haydon felt no kinship with it. He envied the dying man's ability to reach even deeper within himself and drag up handfuls of strength.

Haydon found himself once again in the late-afternoon traffic. He knew better than to take the Loop. He turned off Memorial Drive onto Chimney Rock and followed it across Buffalo Bayou. Just past Woodway at the Tanglewood intersection, he turned left and followed the broad residential drive to San Felipe, where he turned left again and headed across the northern edge of the Galleria/Post Oak area toward the Remington on the other side of the Loop. He was too preoccupied even to become frustrated by the stubborn traffic, which inched along in the sweltering afternoon heat.

The other depressing thing about the conversation with Greiner, of course, was what he had learned about Roeg and Langer. He was afraid that Langer, whether he knew it or not, was in too deep to get out. The power Roeg offered his executives was an enormous seduction. Every day in this city men succumbed to far less enticement than he had held out to Langer. One way or the other, Langer was in trouble. He knew something about Powell's death, if he hadn't actually killed him himself, and he was covering it up to protect his own interests or Roeg's, if there was any difference at this point.

Haydon passed under the Loop and turned onto Briar Oaks Lane, following the sweep of the drive into the entrance of the Remington. He left the Vanden Plas with the valet and went inside. As he passed the Living Room, he quickly scanned the guests to see if Siddons was there. Sometimes the old man took a few drinks while he waited for his wife to join him for dinner. He wasn't there, and Haydon continued along the corridor to the lounge. He stopped at the steward's booth and left his beeper. He didn't like to have the thing go off when he was around people. The steward would come get him if it was necessary.

Before going into the lounge, he crossed the foyer to the telephone rooms. Gabriela answered, and Haydon asked if she had heard fron Nina. Yes, Nina was having dinner with Mr. Mandel and the Nordstroms at Tony's. She wanted him to join them at eight o'clock. There was not much mail; she read him the envelopes. There had been a call from Mr. Clay, the accountant, and a woman had dropped a package by for him a couple of hours earlier. Haydon tensed.

"Who was it?"

"She didn't leave no name."

"Did you ask?"

"No."

"What's in the package?"

"How do I know?"

"She didn't say?"

"No."

"What did she look like?"

"A woman. What do you mean, 'what'? A woman."

"Can you describe her?"

There was a long pause.

"I guess not. She was nothing particular."

Haydon gave up. He thanked her and told her that if Nina called again to tell her he couldn't make it. He was sorry. He returned across the foyer and went into the lounge and bar. The dark wood-paneled rooms with low-beamed ceilings weren't crowded; he was glad. He couldn't really decide whether he wanted a table or not and walked through the lounge area to try to make up his mind. A couple of his favorite alcoves were already taken, so he circled around to the bar again and took a small table near the back. He had a good view of the bar and the entrance. His eyes rested in that general direction now, past two huge bronze bulls that sat on the backs of the leather-covered wall seats that faced the two main dining areas.

He ordered a Tanqueray and lime from the waiter and lit a cigarette. He was almost embarrassed that the urge for a cigarette had come to him automatically when he ordered a drink. But it was good; it was very good.

Nina knew he wouldn't accept the invitation to dinner, and he was amused at the thought of the panic Race must have felt when Nina insisted on inviting him. He wondered if Race had tried to dissuade Nina from making the offer. If he had, it only irritated her.

His thoughts wandered back to Langer. Alice Parnas had provided Haydon with a sound connection between Powell and Toy and Latin-American war footage. He had the connection between Roeg and Langer and war footage from Philip Greiner. And he had a connection between Roeg and Langer and Latin America from Siddons' knowledge of their activities down there through CIA contracts. It was a combination of a lot of probables. There was no direct proof that Toy was working for Roeg, but it was obvious he had been. And from what Greiner said about Langer's responsibilities, he was probably the one who dealt with Toy and was juggling the Toy/Powell operation. That put him in a bad position.

The questions were: Was Powell killed because of what he'd seen on footage he was processing? Probably. Was it footage Toy had given him? Possibly. If it was the usual war footage, what could the subject have been that would have warranted Powell's death? Something involving the CIA? Possibly. Who would have thought it necessary that Powell die for what he had seen? If it was CIA related, it could have been absolutely anything. Roeg could have wanted him killed if the tapes had revealed something of his companies' involvement with covert activities. Langer could have wanted the tape kept secret too. It wouldn't be great publicity for his company to have it spread about that it worked for the CIA. If this was the direction in which the answers lay, why did they even let it get into Powell's hands in the first place?

Haydon lit another cigarette and nodded to the waiter for a second Tanqueray.

Maybe Toy was running a little game on the side, setting up an extortion scam based on something he had filmed down there that was incriminating to Roeg International or Langer Media. If so, he might have given the video to Powell to process (would Powell have been in on it or would he have been processing the tape innocently?) and then someone (Langer?) surprised him while he was processing it, discovered the extortion possibility, and killed Powell to shut him up and then put out tracers for Toy. That would explain why Toy had dropped out of sight. But if Toy had disappeared, it was because he was aware that his extortion plans had been discovered. And when would he have first become aware of that? He hadn't picked up Thursday's paper, which means he probably had moved out Wednesday night. The night Powell was murdered.

What a damn mess. Why would Toy want to murder the man to whom he'd given the tapes to process? Did he need Powell's expertise, then find it necessary to dispose of him once he had served his purpose? That didn't seem right. He would have done it differently. Why involve Powell like that if you knew you were going to have to kill him afterward? Surely there would have been a better way to handle it.

He needed to talk to Dystal. Go over it with him, let the old bear mull it over in his mind. Whatever was going on, it didn't bode well for William Langer.

Haydon lit his third cigarette and motioned to the waiter. He ordered a third Tanqueray. He finished them both as he watched the lounge and bar fill with the pre-dinner crowd. Some were waiting out the traffic, like himself; some were regulars at the bar who had no use for the white-clothed tables but sat looking at themselves and the others in the reflection of the long mirror.

Haydon watched one couple who, like himself, sat at an out-of-the-way corner table. They were both in their early forties, he guessed, the woman a little nervous as she sipped her drink, the man tensely pensive, dabbing the bottom of his sweating glass on the white tablecloth. The woman said something and the man shook his head slowly, rejecting the remark with hopeless resignation. She turned to him, her eyes no longer evasive, and put her hand on his as she spoke again, her expression pleading. Haydon could almost see the tears. The man listened without looking at her, his face growing emotionless, afraid of showing something. He let go of his glass and rubbed his face with both hands. When he removed them his face seemed more tired, depleted. The woman leaned closer, looked as though she might embrace him, kiss him. She had forgotten everyone else in the room. The man hadn't. He glanced quickly around, caught Haydon's eyes. They stared at each other a moment and then Haydon looked away, took the last pull on his cigarette, and put it out.

When he dared look back their way, the man was dabbing his glass on the cloth again, and the woman had moved away from him, looking nervous once more. Haydon had seen hundreds of affairs. They were all traps. A few rare ones would survive the heat of their sexual excitement, become something more than what they were in spite of what they were. All of them were messy.

Haydon didn't want to leave. He ordered dinner, a sautéed veal steak with morels and chanterelles, which he ate with a glass of red Bourgueil. He was almost through with the last of the steak when he saw the steward come through the door of the bar and say something to the captain, who looked through the amber light to Haydon. Haydon's stomach tightened as the captain walked toward him. He drank the last bit of Bourgueil.

"Your beeper's signaling, Mr. Haydon. Do you want to call from in here?"

"No," Haydon said, getting up. "I'll step outside."

Ed Mooney was standing under the big cottonwoods, the cherry and blue flashers from the coroner's van and the patrol cars alternating across his face as he talked with a couple of patrolmen. The neighbors stood around in little clusters on the edges of the light, watching the men talk. A couple of boys without shirts rested their arms on the handlebars of their bicycles, chewing gum and waiting to see the body. Everyone was waiting, forgoing their favorite television programs, standing in their undershirts, in their robes, slapping mosquitoes, and waiting for a chance to see the body.

Haydon parked behind one of the patrol cars and took his time going up to the sidewalk where the van was standing with its back doors swung open. The early night was close and muggy. White Oak Bayou wasn't that far away. The two patrolmen turned around as Haydon came up.

"She's just like the neighbor lady found her," Mooney said as he turned and went with Haydon to the front door. He pulled open the screen with the spiderweb grillwork and they went into the living room, turned left through a doorway, and across a tiny hallway into the bedroom.

Alice Parnas was on the bed in her little bedroom amid the relics of another generation and the smell of oldness. She lay on her back in a clumsy sprawl, her faded yellow robe pulled open to her waist where it was cinched, then thrown open, again from her waist down. Sweat had matted the hair around her face, and even in death her eyes were swollen from crying. There was a hole worn near the elastic waistband of her faded blue panties. In one of her pale hands she gripped a brown plastic medicine bottle without its lid.

One of the coroner's investigators from Vanstraten's office stood near the opened window that looked out into the front yard. The voices over the radios crackled in the still heat outside.

"Suicide, huh," the coroner's investigator said, winking. His name was Ernest Leighton, and he combed his hair in the oily pompadour waves of the fifties. He smoked Kools and sometimes left the crumpled-up empty packs at the scenes he caught.

"This is all there is to it?" Haydon asked. He was looking at Alice Parnas' swollen eyes, her cheekbones even flatter in death.

"Exactly," Mooney said.

"I haven't touched her," Leighton said. "Not even her temp."

They all looked at her.

"They don't always have ahold of the bottle like that," Leighton said.

"Everybody's a detective," Mooney said, looking at Leighton. "Next-door neighbor came over and found her," he told Haydon. "Said Parnas' old Chevy was in the driveway so she knew she must be here. House was open. She called several times, no answer, so she went in and found her. Officer Weingarten out there got the call, came by, and radioed in. While he was waiting he looked around the bedroom and saw your card on her clothes chest over there. Called it in. Lieutenant called me, I called you."

Haydon heard somebody laugh outside. The sound stayed in his head and mixed with the sound of Alice's sobbing, the extremes of human emotion confused in the crowded little bedroom where Alice's nakedness was once more the focus of strangers' unloving eyes, eyes that didn't really want to see her naked but looked anyway because by dying without an explanation she had forfeited all her rights to stop them.

"Where's the lid to the bottle?" Haydon asked.

Mooney looked around. "I don't know," he said. "You seen it, Ernie?"

"Probably up in that robe somewhere," Leighton said. He didn't move to look for it.

"Go ahead with her," Haydon said. He turned and walked out of the room. He stood in the middle of the living room and looked at the dowdy chair where Alice had sat and cried that morning. The cherry and blue flashers were washing past the spiderweb grill on the screen door. He lit a cigarette. He was smoking too much. He had gotten it down to six a day while he was on leave, and he had already had twice that many today.

"So what do you think," Mooney said.

Haydon shrugged. If he said what he really thought, Mooney would think he was losing touch with reality.

"I was going to come back and talk to her again," Haydon said. "She was holding back a great deal. She knew more about those tapes Powell was working on than she wanted me to believe. I don't know, Ed. I just couldn't press her on it this morning. I should have, I didn't. It was a big mistake."

As they stood in the living room, he told Mooney about his conversation with Philip Greiner.

27

Haydon was halfway home before he remembered that he had not asked Mooney if he had found anything in Toy's condo. It could wait until morning. He was going to call Dystal when he got home and suggest a breakfast meeting. They needed to go over what they had, get the benefit of each other's perspectives on the evidence.

It was just a little after nine o'clock when he pulled through the gates and drove along the crunching cinder drive to the porte cochere. Again Nina's car was not there. He went in the front door and got the mail off the small table in the hall and scanned the envelopes as he went into the kitchen. Laying the mail on the cabinet, he started to open a bottle of wine, decided he had already had enough, and reached for the Melitta coffeepot. He put enough water in the kettle for two cups and heated it while he put two spoons of Arabian mocha in the clay filter holder. When the water was ready he poured it into the filter, watching the rich mocha drip its dark syrupy brew into the small white pot.

When it was through dripping, he put the pot, a cup

and saucer, and the cream pitcher on a tray with the mail, carried them into the library, and set them on the refectory table. There were only two lamps lit, one on his desk and one on the old table. He poured a cup of coffee and stirred in a spoon of cream. While he was tasting the first sip of coffee he saw the package on his desk.

He had totally forgotten about it. Gabriela had said a woman had left a package and a letter. Without taking his eyes of the package, he took his coffee over to his desk, pulled out the walnut captain's chair, and sat down. He took one more sip of coffee, eyes still on the package, hoping.

The package was the right size, wrapped in brown paper that had been a shopping bag. Part of the red letters of the word *Safeway* showed on the front of the package. A plain white envelope was attached to the package with a green rubber band of the kind newspapers are wrapped with.

Haydon set down the coffee cup and pulled the envelope from under the rubber band. He tore it open and unfolded the single sheet of paper. It was a typewritten page with the type going out to wide margins and close to the top and bottom of the page. It was signed by Alice Parnas.

Dear Mr. Haydon,

After your visit this morning, I began thinking about what I was doing. I have no right to keep anything away from you for I know that you are doing your best to find poor Wayne's killer. I can not cry forever and I know deep down that crying doesn't help find Wayne's killer but it is just a selfish indulgence for me.

I can not go back to work at that place for the things they say in their gossiping hurt so much and the wonderful secret Wayne and me had is now a nightmare that just gets worse and worse for they do not know, of course, and I can not listen to the things they say anymore since he is not here to make it not matter. I have an aunt who lives in New Mexico and I will go out there and live with her a while until I decide what to do. But this is of no interest to you. I will tell you what I know about what happened the night poor Wayne was killed.

The night Wayne was killed was the night Ricky Toy was supposed to come back from a trip to El Salvador. Wayne got a call from Ricky Toy a little after 12 that night and Ricky Toy wanted Wayne to meet him at a bank drive-in over by the Shamrock Hilton Hotel. I have told you that I usually go up to the office with Wayne when he processes these video tapes but Ricky Toy does not know that so Wayne dropped me off at a drugstore while he went over to get the tapes from Ricky Toy. When he came back to get me he told me that something was going on because he did not think Ricky Toy went to El Salvador but had some tapes of something else that he wanted Wayne to process but he did not want Wayne to pass them on to Mr. Langer like he always does because this was something Ricky Toy did not want Mr. Langer to see. Wayne thought Ricky Toy was doing something to blackmail Mr. Langer. Ricky Toy told Wayne to process the tapes and then to call him and he would tell him what to do then.

We went back to the lab at the office and Wayne started processing the tapes. He said that he didn't want any part of whatever it was Ricky Toy was doing and that just to prove he didn't have anything to do with it if Mr. Langer should ever think he was part of whatever was going on he was going to make a copy of the tapes for himself and give it to Mr. Langer to show where he stood. Wayne did not want to lose his job there because it was a good one and he was wanting to settle down and someday we would get married.

While he was working on Ricky Toy's tape we heard somebody come into the offices. Wayne was afraid it was Ricky Toy coming for the tapes

(Wayne had given Ricky Toy a key to the offices a long time ago) so he gave me the copy he had made for himself and told me to go on and he would call me later. I couldn't drive his sports cars so I took a city bus. That was about 2:30.

That was the last time I saw poor Wayne and I do not know who it was we heard coming into the offices but whoever it was they must have killed Wayne.

I hope this tape will tell you something. We looked at it and it didn't make any sense to us but you are more experienced at such things and I am sure you will be able to see something here that we did not see.

I hope this helps you get Wayne's killer. I do not want to talk about it anymore but I know that you may want to ask me some more questions so I will send you my aunt's address when I get out there. I won't give it to you now because I may go somewhere else I don't know.

Alice Parnas

Haydon laid down the typewritten page and sat quietly in the soft glow of his desk lamp. He remembered the way Alice Parnas had looked lying on her dingy bed, the faded yellow robe thrown open to them all, her eyes still swollen with crying, the ragged hole at the elastic waistband of her panties. He looked at the typewritten page again, at the last part of the last line: "I may go somewhere else I don't know."

He reached for the package and slipped off the rubber band. He unwrapped the brown paper until a video cassette lay exposed on his desk. It was three-quarter-inch. He picked it up and looked at it. There were no identification markings. He thought suddenly of fingerprints and opened one of the bottom drawers on his desk. He removed a pair of white thin cotton gloves and slipped them on, decided there was no use, and took them off again and put them back into the drawer. He picked up the cassette and walked into the television room.

Turning on the television, he slipped the cassette into the VTR and pressed PLAY. There was static on the screen. Then the tape began. The opening shot was of a door in a large room. The lighting was bad and the only illumination seemed to come from a bare light bulb that hung just inside the door. The door opened a little way, then closed and opened again. Three black men came in and stopped just inside the door, closing it behind them. They stood together a few minutes while one of them talked to the other two, looking as if he was giving instructions. His voice was faint and garbled. Haydon thought the cameraman was too far away from his subjects. Occasionally the other two nodded as if they understood. They seemed ill at ease, looking around into the darker edges of the picture. All three men had sweat rings under the arms of their shirts. The man doing the talking was tall and thin, not old. One of the others was younger, husky, wearing a net shirt bulging with muscles. The third man wore gaudy pimp clothes and seemed the most relaxed of the three, almost sullen.

As the three men moved away from the door the camera followed them, but not far before they disappeared into the muddy darkness. It was far enough, however, for Haydon to see that they were in some kind of warehouse.

In the next shot the door of the warehouse opened again and two men came through. The first was a large black man in a suit. He was handsome, with a mustache and an athletic build. He seemed vaguely familiar to Haydon. He held the door open for another man, also dressed in a business suit, who seemed a little nervous. The camera also followed them along the aisles made by stacks of wooden packing crates until the darkness swallowed them.

Again a shot of the door. This time when it opened William Langer was the first through, followed by a second man. They visited casually as they strolled out of the camera's view. The black man in the business suit passed them and went out the door and returned shortly with yet another man, dressed casually in a knit shirt. Langer's back came into view, and he went out the door also. When he returned he was accompanied by a slightly built individual who hurried into the darkness more quickly than the others.

It was difficult to determine how long this had taken, because in actual time several minutes had probably passed between each entry and exit from the warehouse door. Haydon checked the counter on his VTR. It registered nearly eight minutes.

There was a jump in the tape here, and the quality of the taped image changed dramatically. The first shot was in darkness, and it was a moment before Haydon realized that he was seeing movement in the darkness. Gradually he was able to make out the gray, smoky images of the men he had seen come in through the door. They seemed to be standing or sitting together, all facing one direction. They were talking among themselves. The camera zoomed in on their faces and though the lighting was hazy you could clearly make out each individual. The camera lingered a long moment on each of them, including Langer and the black man.

Then, slowly, the camera panned from the area where the men were sitting across the aisle to an open area. Here the tape almost went white, flaring, washing out everything. Haydon assumed a fast lens had been used to get a shot of the men in the darkened portion of the warehouse and then it let in too much light when panned toward the lighted area. He saw someone moving in the lighted area but could not make out what they were doing. He thought it might be the black man who had been giving instructions at the beginning. The lighted area seemed to be ringed with more wooden packing crates, and just as Haydon was relatively sure of this the camera came slowly around again to dwell on the men in the shadows, once again zooming in on each individual face. Then it went blank.

Haydon looked at the VTR counter. The tape had lasted sixteen minutes.

He did not run the tape again but pushed the rewind button and sat back to wait. What had he just seen? There was nothing there on which to build a blackmail scam. Even if the men Langer had been seen with were known criminals, he could explain his way out of that a dozen different ways. Why were they there? They had come to see something. They were seated facing the lighted area, waiting. The question was, what was it they were going to see and why hadn't Toy filmed it?

The VTR rewind clicked off and Haydon punched the ejector and retrieved the cassette. He turned off the television and walked back into the library. He got his coffee cup, poured the cold coffee into one of the potted plants by the French doors that looked out onto the terrace, and poured the second cup from the Melitta pot. After he mixed cream with it, it was only lukewarm. He sat down at his desk.

Maybe what he had here was only *part* of everything Toy had recorded in the warehouse. That would make sense. He would give only a portion of it to Powell in case something happened to it while it was in Powell's possession. Whoever had killed Powell had gotten the original and might or might not know if additional tapes existed. But surely there was more, and Toy probably had them. Haydon had only the prelude sitting in front of him. Ricky Toy had the rest of the narrative.

Langer had been shrewd. He was indeed being blackmailed, but he had laid the blame at the wrong doorstep. Half-truths. It happened so often. People who tried to lie their way out of trouble often took little bits of truth and mixed them with little bits of lie and tried to pass it all off as a whole reality. It worked against them in the long run because they were likely to forget the exact proportion of the ingredients. Seldom could they re-create the recipe with total accuracy. They would be much better off to fabricate the entire thing, but they rarely did. It was odd how they clung to the little fragments of truth, as if they were good-luck pieces.

Haydon's eyes fell on the cardboard boxes of books across the room and then went back to Alice Parnas' letter.

"I may go somewhere else I don't know."

He suddenly put down the cup and saucer. Alice Parnas was not a woman who toyed with innuendos, and she was not likely to begin doing so at death. It was not suicide she had had in mind when she wrote that last line.

He grabbed a piece of paper from his desk and quickly scribbled a note to Nina that he would be late coming in. He taped the note to the shade of the lamp on his desk and left.

28

Haydon followed Montrose out until it crossed Buffalo Bayou and became Studemont, went under the Katy Freeway to Studewood, and then turned right on Bayland. Alice Parnas' house was closed and dark. There were no police, no gawking neighbors, no sound from the grackles. Only silence.

He parked in front of the house and turned off the motor. Mrs. Spiegler lived in the house across the crushed-shell drive, on the other side of the juniper hedge. Haydon got out of the car and walked along the pavement, across the spill of crushed shell that had worked its way out into the street, and onto the sidewalk that led to Mrs. Spiegler's. Her house was open, trying to circulate the hot night air. She had seen his headlights and was at the front door, craning her head against the screen to see what was happening now.

"Mrs. Spiegler?" Haydon said as he approached the door. He heard her snap the latch on the screen.

"Yes," she said. She was holding a sweaty can of Pabst

beer. A radio was playing somewhere in the living room behind her.

He introduced himself, said he had been there earlier but hadn't gotten a chance to talk to her, and would she mind if he took a few minutes of her time. She looked at him, looked at the shield he held in front of her.

"Can't you come back in the daytime? This's not exactly a prime business hour. Can't it wait?"

"If you could give me just a few minutes. It would be best if I could talk to you tonight."

She had on a pair of green-and-white striped pants that ended just below her knees in little cuffs, and a short-sleeved boat-neck cotton blouse that hung over the pants. The hand that held the Pabst wore a plastic digital wristwatch with a piece of tissue tucked under the strap. Her face was incredibly wrinkled, and she had bags under her eyes. Her lower lip tended to sag away from her gums.

"About Alice," she said, almost reverently and with unexpected tenderness.

"Yes, ma'am."

"God, that poor little girl." Her eyes drifted toward the Parnas house. Suddenly she looked at Haydon, her eyes round and startled. "Was she Catholic? I never knew. Her folks wasn't, but you know kids veer off. If she was Catholic, where d'you suppose they'll bury her? Pope won't let her in, you know. They're funny about"—she tilted her head toward the Parnas house—"that."

"I don't really know," Haydon said. "Do you mind if I come in?"

She looked at him. "Do I have to sign anything?"

"No, ma'am."

"Good," she said as she snapped open the latch, " 'cause I won't do it."

She pushed open the screen and Haydon followed her into the room. The house had the same layout as the Parnases' though Mrs. Spiegler had put her sofa on the opposite wall and her armchair on the opposite side of the room. The radio was loud, and she walked over to a little bookshelf and switched it off. Haydon noticed that she was bowlegged and walked in the self-assured manner of a woman who was used to looking after herself.

"I wasn't looking at the TV," she said. "Wasn't in the mood for a damn situation comedy."

Haydon sat on the sofa and Mrs. Spiegler in an armchair to his side. Both of them faced the blank television. Haydon had to turn a little to talk to her. An old black rotating fan sat on the floor in front of one of the open windows, humming back and forth. Every time it turned to the left it shimmied, rattling the wire grill around the blade.

"Want a Blue Ribbon?" She hoisted the beer.

"No, thanks."

"What is it you want to ask me?"

"There's a certain amount of routine paperwork that has to be done following an unattended death. It won't take long."

"Shoot," she said, and took a swig of Pabst.

"Do you know if Miss Parnas had any relatives in New Mexico?"

"No. I mean, no, I don't know. I don't think they had any relatives in town, though. I've been living next to them for about ten years, and I never heard them talk about relatives in town. Alice's mom died about five, six years ago. Her dad dwindled away after that and died about two years later. They're Greek. Looked Greek. Alice doesn't—didn't—look Greek. I wondered about that, was going to ask her once if she was adopted, but I didn't because she was such a sensitive thing I thought that might offend her or something. I wouldn't have done that for the world. The girl was just an angel."

Mrs. Spiegler's voice cracked a little, and she took another swig of beer. She sat with her feet flat on the floor, her legs spread out comfortably, her pedal pushers pulled up to her knees for coolness.

"Had Alice been depressed a lot lately?"

"Well, she was sick. She'd been sick about a week, home from the office. Holed up over there."

"Did she tell you she was sick?"

"Yeah."

"That's all she told you?"

"Yeah. Why, should she have said something else?"

"I just wondered if she had explained."

"She didn't go into no detail, if that's what you mean. She wasn't a bitcher. Wasn't going to tell me about any female trouble or stuff like that that most women have so much fun telling each other. Not Alice."

"Did you visit with her much during this week she's been ill?"

"Nope. When I saw she'd been home a couple of days I went over to check on her. We've been neighborly that way for years. Said she was sick. I didn't pry into it, but I brought her some broth that night. I don't care what's wrong with you, hangnail or polio, broth's good for you. Funny I should say polio. Nobody gets that anymore, do they. Anyway, I've looked in on her every day, not in a busybody sort of way, but to let her know I was here if she needed me."

"Did you go over there today?"

She seemed to droop, her face sad. "No, I didn't. Wish to God I had. I mean, I found her, you know, but I hadn't gone over before that."

"Are you home all day, Mrs. Spiegler?"

"Most of the time."

"Today?"

"All but about an hour and a half this morning. I went grocery shopping."

"When was that?"

She squinted. "Nine-thirty to ten-thirty, or eleven."

Haydon had been there from roughly ten to eleven.

"Could you tell me, thinking carefully, who you might have seen go to Alice's house from the time you got home to the time you found her?"

Mrs. Spiegler looked at him. She thought a moment as her eyes stayed on him and she took another swig from the Pabst can.

"Why?"

"State law dictates that anytime a person commits suicide, or the circumstances of death are such that they lead to the suspicion of suicide, the body of that person must undergo a routine autopsy to try to verify that suspicion. By the same token the Houston Police Department likes to accompany the medical investigation with one of our own to make sure the deceased was not involved in anything of a suspicious nature prior to death. It's quite routine."

She seemed to think that sounded reasonable.

"Anybody?"

"Right. Mailman, delivery boys, other neighbors. Anyone."

She thought a minute. The old fan vibrated rhythmically, bringing in muggy Heights air heavy with July heat that didn't begin to lighten at night until well into the early morning hours.

"Mailman about one-thirty. That was a little early for him. 'Member when you used to get your mail in the morning? Salvation Army truck came by and got an old armchair she'd had on her back porch for a month. I guess that was, I don't know, two, two-thirty. Nigra boy came around about that time, too, selling magazine subscriptions to go to college on. I never know whether to believe those boys or not, but I subscribed to *Field & Stream* and *Cosmopolitan*. Census lady came about three. That's it, as far as I can remember."

"The mailman just left the mail and went on?"

"Yeah."

"How about the Salvation Army men? Did they go inside?"

"No. Went down the driveway, got the chair, and took it around."

"You saw that?"

Mrs. Spiegler decided not to be embarrassed for snooping. "Yeah, I saw it," she said a little defiantly. She finished the Pabst.

"What about the black student?"

"Stood at the door, same as he did here. She bought something too. I saw him writing out one of those tiny receipts they give you. Hardly read the boy's writing. Takes six months to get the magazines, too."

"He didn't go inside?"

"Nope."

"And the census lady?"

"Sure, she went in. Same as she did here." Mrs. Spiegler stood and walked into the kitchen. "Sure you don't want a Blue Ribbon?" she called back.

"No, thanks."

She returned, folding a paper napkin around the bottom of the can. "Things sweat in this weather. Cans. People. Everything."

"Did the census woman go to the house on the other side of the Parnas house when she left there?"

"No. She came here."

"She spoke to Alice Parnas first?"

"Yeah. In fact, she parked in front of her house. I saw her drive up there, get clipboard and things out of the front seat, and go up to the door. Talked to Alice and then went inside."

"How long did she stay?"

"Nearly an hour."

"Did she stay that long here?"

"No. She said Alice had a lot of complicated family things to straighten out. I guess she meant her parents' deaths since the last census. I don't know. I didn't ask."

"Then how did she happen to mention it?"

"She just volunteered it, why she was there so long."

"How long did she stay here?"

"Maybe fifteen minutes."

"What kind of car was she driving?"

"Kind of a sporty-looking thing. I don't know."

"What color was it?"

"White. It was little."

"What did the woman look like?"

"Cute as a bug. She was a girl, not really a woman. I think of a woman as older. Reddish-blond hair. Fair-skinned. Not thin, particularly. Dressed real good."

"What kind of questions did she ask you?"

"Oh, census-type questions. Age, people living in house, family stuff."

"Did she fill out a form as she questioned you?"

"Yeah."

"You saw it?"

"Well, I saw her writing it all down. I guess it was a form they use. I couldn't see it exactly."

"Did she leave a card or anything?"

"No."

"How did you know she was from the census bureau?"

Mrs. Spiegler studied Haydon for a while, her bottom lip sagging a little more than before.

"That's a good question," she said. "I just took her word for it. She seemed . . . okay. She was dressed real good. I just took her word for it. Nothing suspicious about her."

"You'd recognize her if you saw a picture of her?"

"Sure. She sat right there, and I talked to her fifteen minutes."

"She continued down the street when she left here?"

"No. She went back to her car and left. I guess she'd filled her quota of households for the day," Mrs. Spiegler said helpfully. "You know, she was real nice, though. She was . . ."

Haydon tuned her out, his eyes focusing on the dummy-like hinging of her mouth. He imagined, almost against his will, the blood, dark and arterial, snaking out of her nose. It came from her right nostril first and trickled over her long upper lip. He thought he would stop it at that, and just as he was making up his mind to listen to her again, the other nostril began to bleed too. It sought out the wrinkles and crevices around her mouth, and when she took a drink from the can of beer it got on the can too, pinkish where it mixed with the beer that stayed around the rim of the can. It got inside her sagging bottom lip.

"I appreciate your taking the time to talk to me," he said, standing quickly. "Here's my card. If you think of anything else, would you give me a call? Anything at all could be of help."

"Sure," she said, looking a little surprised at his abruptness, but standing too. "How long do you people keep your end of the investigation open?"

"Usually takes only a few days." Haydon was aware of feeling a little light-headed.

She nodded and looked at the card. "Says 'Homicide.' " He imagined that some of the blood flipped off her bottom lip onto her blouse. She wouldn't have noticed.

"We all do this in our spare time," he said.

She nodded again. "It's going to be odd having her gone, you know. I guess I'll get new neighbors. Probably Mexicans or Nigras, they're pretty well taking over out here now. Minorities. Of course, the Parnases were Greek. Nothing wrong with minorities. It's just that there's not as many regular people out here as there used to be." She raised her can of beer to Haydon as if toasting the idea. "*Tempus fugit,*" she said, and smiled ruefully.

She followed him to the door, chatted with him as he went outside on the little cement porch. He told her good night and turned to walk down the sidewalk as he heard her snap the screen latch behind him. When he drove by in front of her house, she was standing backlighted in the doorway, a wedge of light coming from between her bowed legs, her arm bent, holding the can of Pabst Blue Ribbon. He couldn't see anything on her face. It was in the dark.

29

Haydon rolled down the windows of the Vanden Plas and drove along Heights Boulevard, with the long narrow park stretching for several blocks down its center. There were a few people in the park, lounging in night shadows of the gazebo, smoking on the broad spaces of the grass. He caught a brief aroma of marijuana and then it was gone. He turned right into the smaller streets of the Heights. Dirty yellow light came from the opened doorways and windows, often mixed with the technic blue of a television. He heard children shout, a boozy tune from a radio in a parked car.

If he continued imagining the blood he wouldn't be able to stand it. He could live with the nightmares, with the tension that seized him every time he felt a little funky and feared it was the slow, menacing precursor to a racking season of depression. All this he could adapt to, the way you endured a chronic pain. But not the blood. It was remarkable and unnerving. It was as though the idea of flowing blood had lodged itself in his imagination in the same way horrible and shocking scenes have traumatized and burned themselves into the minds of those who have witnessed them, only to intrude unbidden and unwanted into their consciousness at unsuspecting moments for the rest of their lives. Forceful memories. Scenes to be repressed, but never forgotten.

He turned south, backtracking down Studewood to White Oak Drive, which he followed west past Stude Park and then White Oak Park, that hugged the bayou. He remembered the execution killings down in there. Three chubby Mexicans side by side, shot in a kneeling position in the back of the head, all clutching cheap metal crucifixes. It was summer then too, it was always summer, and that was why the three men were chubby. Mooney had been with him. They were new homicide detectives together then, just as they had been rookie cops together. Dystal had been a part of the group too. So many streets, so many scenes, memories of them scattered all over the city like ghosts that wouldn't close their eyes and you saw them everywhere you went, every time you got in the car, three, five, ten ghosts depending on the route you took, looking at you from a vacant lot, a drive-in grocery, a derelict house, a fashionable home, a gas station, an alley, a bayou, a street corner, a park, a bar. Lonely places. Each with a ghost rooted to the spot. This is where we died.

When he bothered to notice where he was, he found himself idling once again past the small frame house near the Holy Cross Cemetery where he had seen the little boy earlier in the day. It was wide open. Through front bedroom windows he could see deeper into the house where a dim glow backlighted smoky silhouettes in the bedroom. Jungle movements gliding slowly past the torn screen of the window. Silent movements. Naked movements. He knew there was a back bedroom and a back door that came into the kitchen. *Flash-flash-flash-flash-flash!* Not the glamor of cinematic slow motion. Not like that at all. *Flash-flash-flash!* No time to think . . . and then an unexpected second of clarity, time to think . . . and doing it. FLASH! It was over. And then it wasn't, and never would be again.

He wasn't doing a very good job of living with it, although at first he thought he was. On the other hand it had been eleven years now, almost long enough for him

to make himself believe it hadn't happened, except that
he couldn't get away from it. God knows he had tried. He
had shut his mind against it and closed his ears, prayed
that the drumming memory of it would not deafen him,
that once he had turned his back it would not emerge in
the periphery of his consciousness, like some wild horrible thing that had crept off a Bosch canvas. He ran from
it, and sometimes he outstripped it, but it was relentless
and never-tiring. There were only times of reprieve, never
the solace of absolution.

Sitting in the car across the street, he watched the
house. He had removed his suit coat and thrown it across
the seat. He wiped the sweat from his forehead with his
handkerchief, wiped his face. The street was quiet except
for the distant and incessant rumble of the North Freeway. He could smell the dankness of Little White Oak
Bayou, which coiled itself around the neighborhood and
the cemeteries like a marshy tapeworm.

The smell had not changed, probably never had,
never would. It had been a July night then too. An unusu-
ally wet spring had hidden the bayou in lush vegetation;
weeds and saplings gummy with new growth hung over
the sluggish black water swarming with mosquitoes. He
ran, chasing the devil that was chasing him, into the sultry
dark through the flower streets of Jessamine, Marigold,
Lilac, and Goldenrod, the fateful Hyacinth, across Cosmos, and beyond into the silent world of crypts and saints,
ghosts upon ghosts as far as you could see, almost to the
bayou again and Moody Park far away into the night. *I do
not understand my own actions. For I do not do what I want, but
I do the very thing I hate.* And then he went no farther but
turned and faced him, out of breath, full of fear, standing
five graves away, leaning on a leaning stone, hunched and
sucking air, the low dank air from the bayou. He could see
his eyes, white as the canting gravestones scattered all
around them, eyes so recently glazed with the horrors of
Hyacinth and now seeing the horror from the other side
because he knew, could sense, that now he was going to
cross a different Cosmos, and so he watched and waited
with incredulity bulging his eyes. And as he waited he
started toward him, getting closer so there would be no

mistake, stalking over the graves, narrowing the distance between now and the black minute. *For I do not do the good I want, but the evil I do not want is what I do.*

He was glad to see Nina's car. He pulled in behind it, locked the Vanden Plas, and let himself into the front hallway. At three in the morning the house was as still as it would ever be. His footsteps echoed down both halls as he crossed the entryway and started up the stone stairs. Halfway up the crescent he could see the light on the marble passageway that came from their bedroom. Nina would be waiting. She might have dozed, but she would have heard the car coming in the gates and was now looking at the door, waiting for him to open it, anxious to look at his face to see what it would tell her about him. He unconsciously massaged the two vertical creases between his eyebrows, which she said made him look intense even when he wasn't and made him look older than he was.

She was in bed, a book propped on her knees, looking at him.

"When you say 'late' you mean it." She smiled, but her eyes locked onto him, exploring all his features as though they were the sensitive fingers of a blind woman, touching with knowledge the contours of his face that seldom hid everything from her.

"Sorry," he said. He came around to her side of the bed and kissed her, anticipating and finding the fragrance of her bath. "Things are speeding up a little now. I hate to stop when it gets like this."

"I know."

He went over to his closet and began taking off his clothes. "How was your evening?"

"Fun. Going to Tony's is always fun. I was so surprised when you didn't come."

He looked at her. She was grinning. "I'll bet Race was disappointed too," he said, pulling off his shoes.

"No, Race wasn't. But I did enjoy talking with the Nordstroms."

"What's she like?" Haydon was taking the stays out of his collar. The shirt had been steamed in the bayou heat and pressed into a thousand wrinkles.

Nina put a book marker in the book and laid it aside. "She's in her early thirties. Sharp features, but small. Not a large woman, though she gives the feeling of being larger than she is. She would not photograph petite. Natural blonde. I liked her. I only had dinner with her, but she didn't seem to be the greedy little opportunist everyone's been gossiping about. In fact, they seem to be one of the sanest couples I've met in a long time. She's a good deal younger than he is, but neither of them seem to fall into the negative stereotypes people often think of in that situation. They were very nice. They gave me the impression of being very kind."

"Just great people all around," Haydon said, taking his baggy white *calzones* from their hook inside his closet as he walked into the bathroom.

"Great people all around," she confirmed.

He showered quickly, washing his hair, and then toweled dry. He brushed his teeth, slipped on his *calzones*, and walked back into the bedroom, tying the drawstring at his waist.

"And your day?" she asked.

"Met a lot of nice people," he said.

She laughed. "The note on the lampshade seemed to have been written in a hurry. Terrible handwriting."

"It was."

He stopped and put his shoe trees into his shoes and put them into the closet. He hung his belt on a hook inside the closet and took his cuff links off the top of the dresser and put them in their box; the brass collar stays went into their leather case. He stopped at the windows a moment and looked down to the terrace. The early morning hours were blue.

He must have stood there longer than he realized.

"Why was it written in a hurry?" she asked.

"Ed called early in the evening. A woman who worked for Bill Langer, and whom I'd interviewed earlier this morning, was found dead at home. I had to go over there."

"Was she killed?"

"It looks like suicide."

"Looks like?"

"Pills. She was very depressed when I talked with her this morning." He turned away from the windows and walked to the light switch. "You ready?"

She nodded.

He turned off the lights and went over to the bed and lay down. Nina threw off her covers and lay with him on top of the sheets.

"Are you making any progress?" she asked.

"I think so."

"Is Langer going to be okay?"

"No, he isn't."

Haydon lay there, feeling his body slow down. His heart rate returned to a slower, easier rhythm. He shouldn't have stopped jogging. It wouldn't be long before the rate at rest would be quicker. Right now it seemed steady and strong, and even though he was exhausted, it made him feel good to know he was in shape.

Nina rolled onto her side and put an arm across his chest.

"And how about you? Are you going to be okay?"

The question made him instantly angry, but he didn't say anything. He simply lay there, letting her words hang in the air, unstable, waiting. What was the matter with him? Didn't he want her to care? If she didn't care, would he be happier? If he thought she might stop caring, would he be happier? What was it he wanted from her? Did he want her to be perfect, caring when he wanted her to care, not caring when he didn't want her to care? Wasn't he ever going to allow her to be human about him? He had had to catch himself before he said something he would have regretted two minutes later. Why was that? He didn't understand why he continued to return her concern with bitterness. Why in God's name did it cost him so much to be totally honest with her?

"It's gotten old quickly," he heard himself say.

She made a small movement with her hand on his chest and then was still.

"I like it," he added, "but it gets serious too soon. You get caught up in their lives. The messes they've made of them. You look closely at the messes, you've got to, and then you realize you're not all that different. I find myself

feeling hypocritical looking at them under the micro-
scope of the investigation."

He looked toward the blue windows, at the black tops
of the trees on the other side of the panes.

"What do you mean?" she asked. Her voice was so soft
she almost whispered. It was as if she did not want to
intrude into his thoughts beyond planting the question in
his mind.

"In a sense," he said, "an unexplained death gives an
investigating detective extraordinary rights. Private lives
become public, at least potentially and in fact, insofar as
the detective is concerned. As a stranger you are free to go
to the heart of personal things, things you ordinarily
would have no right to ask about and would not ask about
now except for the fact that you think you ought to know.
Suddenly you've got the freedom to look into the corners
of people's lives, study what you find there, make judg-
ments about what you discover. You see things you were
never meant to see, not anything that pertains to the case
particularly, just private little things, things on the edges
that you weren't meant to discover, and you wish you
hadn't."

He waited, but she didn't speak. He wondered what
she was thinking, if she was wondering where he was going
with all this and what it meant. He wanted to say "Penny,"
but he didn't. She fit next to him like an actual part of
himself. She belonged there, breathing along with him,
exchanging breath for breath, keeping him alive. He
imagined that if she were suddenly taken away he would
be sucked into a vacuum of such crushing force he could
not long survive it.

Nothing else seemed important now. He held her,
and sleep surprised him.

30
....

The next morning they overslept. When the alarm rang Haydon blindly slapped it off before either of them had fully awakened. An hour later Gabriela came up with a pot of hot coffee and woke them, then had breakfast ready by the time they got downstairs. Nina hurried off to the studio where she was to meet Francis Nordstrom again, and Haydon called Dystal and made arrangements for the lieutenant, Lapierre, and Mooney to be at Haydon's around eleven o'clock. Haydon then walked out on the terrace to pet Cinco, who was already taking the first of the day's naps against the balustrades. After a while Haydon went in through the French doors to the library, took a photograph from the Langer files, and drove back to Bayland Street.

Mrs. Spiegler came to her screen door and looked at Haydon standing on her small cement porch. She was in her housecoat and held a white glass mug of coffee in one hand and the newspaper folded to the crossword puzzle in the other. Her voice was raspy from sleep and had to compete with the grackles, which were screeching and whistling again in the cottonwoods next door.

"Good God, I can't even 'member your name," she said.

"Detective Haydon."

"That's right," she said. "You're a real bulldog about your job, aren't you."

"I'd like you to look at a photograph and tell me if you've seen this person," he said, reaching into a manila envelope he had in his hand.

"You don't want any coffee? It's got chicory in it."

"No, thanks."

He held up the five-by-seven photograph and Mrs. Spiegler peered at it through the screen. It took her just a moment and then she said, "Yeah, the census lady. Pretty little dipper, isn't she."

"Yes. You're sure it's her?"

Mrs. Spiegler looked again, tilting her head back as if she were wearing bifocals, which she wasn't. She wasn't even wearing glasses.

"Sure it's her. I don't know who else it'd be. I don't know anybody else looks like that."

"Thank you," Haydon said. "You've been a great help."

"Grackles sure raise hell, don't they," she said. "You going to try to get the census lady to talk to you too?"

"Probably," Haydon said. He left her standing behind the screen door just like the night before. She was looking over at the grackles in the cottonwoods.

"The car license check hasn't had a nibble," Lapierre said. "But it's only been about twenty-four hours. They're just now starting the second go-round on the shifts. They could turn up something."

The four men were sitting in Haydon's library. Gabriela had brought them a pot of coffee and pastries from Regina's bakery and left them on the Pembroke table near the center of the room.

"Instead of asking them to keep their eyes open for those two cars," Haydon said, "let's have them *look* for them. We've got registration information?"

Lapierre nodded. "And color."

"Good. Anything else?"

"Car rentals, no; airports, no; chartered flights, no; bus stations, no. But we did locate his checking and savings accounts at Intel Bancshares. He's got a little over sixty thousand in money market savings accounts and a money market checking account that fluctuates around five thousand. On Friday he withdrew four thousand."

"He didn't touch the savings account?"

"No."

"Okay. Get back to them and tell them that if he comes in to make a withdrawal from that account we want them to stall him as long as they can."

"Okay."

"And the neighbors you'd missed before?"

"They didn't know anything about anything. Well, one of them did give me the colors of the cars. That's been added to the GB."

"Ed, you didn't turn up anything else at the condo?"

Mooney shook his head. "Zip. Toy really cleaned out. No loose ends."

Haydon related in detail his conversation with Frank Siddons after he had met them at Grif's the day before. He told them of his visit with Philip Greiner, of coming home last night and finding the letter and the cassette, of going to talk with Mrs. Spiegler, and of returning to see her again that morning.

"Now, before I tell you what I learned this morning, let's go into the next room and look at the video cassette."

They viewed the tape twice before Haydon flipped on the lights and rewound it for the last time.

"Jesus," Mooney said.

"Anyone recognize the black man in the suit?" Haydon asked. "I've seen him somewhere."

"Yeah, me too," Lapierre said. "I think he's a lawyer. Maybe on the edges of city politics or something."

"What about the rest of the men?"

"I'd bet one of them was Roeg," Mooney said. "You ought to show it to Greiner. See what he says. If these guys are Roeg's associates, he'll be able to give us a lot of names of guys we can go to work on."

"Good idea."

"It looked like a warehouse," Lapierre said.

"Yeah, a warehouse," Mooney said. "Terrific. In this city that's like narrowing it down to an apartment, which is nothing."

"I think those boys were gettin' ready to watch something they didn't have any business watchin'," Dystal said. "Some kind of damn nudie thing, maybe. Since Roeg's a violence freak, maybe it was S and M stuff."

"I didn't see any women," Mooney said. "Just those three black bucks. One of them seemed to be giving instructions or something."

"Damn funny film," Dystal said. "The rest of it must be dynamite. Toy took a lot of pains to make sure we saw who was there."

"What do you think is going on, Stuart?" Lapierre asked.

"If Roeg is in fact one of the men we saw, whatever he went there to see is not going to be lighthearted, considering the caliber of entertainment he's used to."

The tape finished rewinding and Haydon snapped the cassette out of the player. They returned to the library and helped themselves to more coffee while Haydon went to his desk and got the manila envelope. He removed the picture and came back over to them and held it up.

"This is the 'census lady,' " he said.

Dystal snorted.

"Son of a bitch," Mooney said.

Lapierre put down his cup. "Is Mrs. Spiegler sure, or does she just think she looks like her?"

"She's sure," Haydon said. "Jennifer Quinn was probably the last person to see Alice Parnas alive."

Everyone thought about that a minute.

"I don't know if this ought to confuse us all that much," Dystal said after a moment. "Seems to me this puts everything this gal said to you out in left field, Stu. If she's involved, she gave you bum steers. Seems the important possibilities are, one: Roeg and/or Langer are being blackmailed; two: probably by Toy; three: the tape or tapes in question are still in Toy's possession; four: the tapes probably record a felony in progress. Which one of these possibilities is going to be easiest for us to crack and drive a wedge into?''

"You don't think Jennifer Quinn is important?" Mooney asked.

"I think she *may* be," Dystal emphasized. "We know these other things *definitely* are. I don't know, maybe if we concentrated on her we'd get right to the center of the thing, but we could spend a lot of time for nothing too. Maybe Powell spouted off something to her one time about what he was doing and she put this and that together and thought she could get some mileage out of something she thought Powell's girlfriend had. Maybe she wanted to ask Parnas some questions for some other reason, thought Powell had left some photographs in Parnas' possession that could possibly be embarrassing to *her*. I don't know. That's my point. Nothing hard to go on with her. We *know* these other points are going to get us somewhere if we can crack 'em open."

"I guess I agree with Bob," Haydon said. "Except I don't know how Quinn knew about Alice Parnas. She told me she didn't know the girl in the photograph. As far as I know, only one person was aware of the Powell/Parnas relationship besides us."

"Langer," Lapierre said.

"That's right. He discovered it when he identified Parnas' photograph for me. When I went to talk to Mrs. Spiegler, I expected her to confirm my suspicions that Langer had visited Parnas, looking for the tapes, for information regarding them, suspecting she knew a lot more than she actually did. But instead I found out that Quinn had been there."

"Maybe Quinn lied to you about not knowing who Parnas was," Lapierre said. "That's simple enough."

"Why would she have done that?"

"Maybe to give herself time to get to Parnas before you did. For whatever reason," Mooney suggested.

"But I talked to her on Tuesday morning. If she was in a hurry to see Parnas, why did she wait until Wednesday afternoon to go see her? Parnas was home, had been home for several days."

"So what do you think?" Dystal asked. He was grinning. He knew.

"Based on the timing of things here, I think we may hae something between Quinn and Langer."

Mooney screwed up his face. Lapierre waited for the explication, and Dystal continued to grin.

"Jack Feltner told me that probably one of the greatest pressures on Langer was his wife. He seemed to think they didn't have a very happy marriage. Langer doesn't need that kind of incentive for an affair, I know, but it's an additional consideration. While I don't believe Quinn lied to me about not knowing Parnas—at the time I took the photograph off Powell's wall, I don't think she did know who she was—I do believe her story of her relationship with Powell was a lie. It doesn't make sense to me that a girl as sophisticated and ambitious as she appears to be would continue to live with a guy like Powell if there were no advantages in doing so. There was no personal relationship. There were no professional advantages. It turns out Powell didn't swing any weight with anyone. They didn't have common friends, their personalities weren't even similar. She doesn't seem to need to share rent to save money. She dresses well and drives a Porsche. He had nothing to offer her, yet she stayed on."

"So she was living with Powell to keep an eye on him for Langer," Mooney said.

"I think so. Langer perceived Powell as unsound, maybe a weak link in the whole operation. Toy was living proof of his professionalism. Powell didn't have the personal stability."

"Langer wouldn't have to be having an affair with Quinn for her to be working for him that way," Lapierre said.

"No, you're right, Pete. And she most likely lied about how she met Powell. I doubt if it was a mutual friend from California. I imagine Langer arranged it somehow."

"Well, I think that's a pretty good reconstruction," Dystal said. He was sitting in one of the green leather winged-back chairs, and the leather groaned as he stretched his chunky boots out in front of him. "But what are we gonna do from here to move this thing along?"

Haydon looked at each of them. They waited.

"All right," Haydon said. "How about this? Pete, you do whatever you have to do to track down the black guy. Get some background on him so we can talk to him. Take the video tape to Murray and ask him to make several duplicates, say, four. Have him make stills of each man in the tape. See if he can go over the tape inch by inch and identify any markings on the crates that are stacked in the warehouse, or anything else that might give us something to go on. When you've got Murray started on that, try to find out what warehouses in the city are owned by Roeg International. I know there will be a lot. Just locate them and spot them on a map."

"Ed, take a copy of the tape to Greiner and see what he has to say about it. Milk him for whatever you can get on those guys."

He turned to Dystal. "Can we extend the GB for twenty-four hours? Give them background on this at Roll Call?"

Dystal nodded.

"I was hoping we could use the tape to panic them. The black guy, the other men if Greiner can identify them, Langer, Quinn. Any of them. All of them. Someone could lose control and spill the whole thing. Someone could be convinced to turn State's evidence. However, the drawbacks are obvious. If we show too much of our hand, they'll know we're grasping at straws and dig in. Nobody talks, and we'll be forced to come up with hard evidence. We may never do it.

"Let's all give it some more thought until we've identified these men. As soon as you've got something, get back to me. In the meantime I think I'll make another call on Jennifer Quinn."

31

....

Ricky Toy stood in the clear plastic cubicle of a pay telephone on Bissonnet and listened to the telephone ring.

"Langer Medi-a. Will you hold, please?"

He wondered why they asked. If you ever bothered to
say no you'd be talking to a glitzy rendition of "Raindrops
Keep Fallin' on My Head." The telephone cubicle was to
one side of a convenience store. He was about twenty feet
from a trash dumpster with its heavy metal lid thrown
open. A derelict was sitting in the garbage just inside the
hatch, looking out. He reminded Toy of a monkey with a
wide-eyed blinking expression, watching the traffic go by.

"Thank you for hold-ing. May I help you?"

"This is Mr. Toy for Mr. Langer."

"Is he expecting your call?"

Toy grinned. "I'll bet he is."

"Thank you-u-u."

She put him on hold again, but it wasn't long.

"This is Langer." The voice was almost brusk, not
acknowledging an awareness of the caller's identity.

"And this is Toy."

There was a split second's hesitation while Langer verified the voice in his own mind.

"Where are you?"

"Did Roeg get my tape?"

"What are you talking about?"

"Look, for all I know you may have some way to trace this call so I don't want to waste time talking cute, all right? Did he get the tape?"

"Yes."

"I want to talk to him."

"You'll have to deal with me. Just like always."

"No. I talk to Roeg in person."

"He won't do it."

"That's cool. Why don't you let the man decide for himself? I'm going to hang up. I'll call you back in exactly fifteen minutes, and then you tell me what he says. When and where."

Toy hung up. He looked at his watch.

The derelict was crawling out of the dumpster hatch. He was slow about it; he was having a hard time keeping from sliding off the earth. With spraddle-legged caution, he made his way around the side of the bin, away from the convenience store but in full view of the street next to it, and opened his pants to urinate. It took him a while, so everyone who had stopped at the traffic light got to watch the whole thing. Finally he finished, shook his business with more persistence than seemed really necessary, then made a series of little squatting and bobbing motions as he stuffed it back into his pants and zipped them. Still keeping his steady grip on the earth, he made his way around to the front of the dumpster and crawled back into the hatch.

Toy felt good. He could tell from Langer's voice that he was scared. Christ, the guy had been scared as long as Toy had known him. A big fucker like that. Scared something was going to throw a kink in his precious business, scared somebody was going to find out about the CIA deal, scared somebody was going to find out about Toy's filming forays, scared that Powell was going to foul up somehow, scared Roeg was going to say *boo*. He didn't have any balls at all. If he ever did anything gutsy it would be an accident.

Roeg was something else. Toy was going to have fun tightening the screws on him. People like that, they thought they were invulnerable. Toy had studied this a long time, and it was working out just like he had planned. The thing with Powell almost screwed it up, but it was all right now. He was back on schedule. He was going to be able to pull it off. He could feel it in his juice. It was going to work.

Toy checked his watch. He put another quarter in the telephone and called Langer again.

"Langer Medi-a."

"Mr. Toy for Mr. Langer."

"Oh, yes *sir*!" Langer has built a fire under her.

"This is Langer."

"When and where?"

"There's a little restaurant and bar in the River Oaks Shopping Center, the Wine Press. It's on the north side of the street, down on the east end where the portico of the walkway comes out over the sidewalk. I'll be parked under the row of palms right across from the restaurant. You know my car. Just come on over and get in. Two o'clock."

"I'll be there," Toy said. "Oh, Langer. You should know that I've got myself covered a hundred different ways. Anything should happen to me, the shit would hit the fan. Okay?"

"Two o'clock," Langer said, and broke the connection.

The River Oaks Shopping Center straddled West Gray at South Shepherd, the intersection where Gray becomes Inwood and limestone pillars mark the eastern entrance to the most posh residential section in the city. The shopping center had been built in the late nineteen thirties, the first one of its kind in Houston and only the second or third in the nation. It was a pure example of the Moderne architectural style, with its entrance off Shepherd consisting of two elliptical sections curving toward Gray and then breaking into parallel wings on either side of the street, flanked by esplanades and files of tall palms stretching toward the skyscrapers downtown. The shopping center had fallen into decline during the fifties, and fake storefronts replaced the clean geometrical lines of its original design. It continued to deteriorate during the sixties when the excitement of the new air-conditioned malls outside the Loop came into vogue and the better stores fled the neighborhood shopping centers for the promise of the perpetual crowd.

Then in the middle seventies restoration architecture came into its own and the River Oaks Shopping Center began a five-year renovation program to bring back the glory of the thirties. The drab fake storefronts came down to reveal the rounded corners, porthole windows, aluminum detailing, and classic deco designs. The entire center was painted white and accented with black glass and tile. The trendier shops, boutiques, accessory stores, and restaurants returned, making the center one of the smartest places in the city to shop and be seen, next door to River Oaks and with a palm-lined view of the dazzling downtown skyline.

Toy came an hour early. He set up shop at a window table in Birraporetti's, nursing a Mexican beer and looking past the two rows of palms at the parking spaces along the esplanade on the other side of West Gray. He was distracted a few times by the well-dressed women who passed the window, long and lean beneath their summer dresses, haughty and horny behind their summer shades. Whatever it was he expected to see by coming so far ahead of time he didn't see, and at a quarter to two Langer's slinky Lincoln oozed its way along Gray to Duffie Street and turned left across traffic into the shopping center. Creeping along, he found a place across from the portico and pulled into the slot.

Leaving a larger tip than necessary on the table, Toy walked outside and stood a minute around the corner from Birraporetti's and watched the Lincoln. He had to laugh. Langer thought he'd come early too, scope things out. Fifteen minutes early. What a duck. Toy looked at his watch. At five before two he eased around the corner and walked down the sidewalk to the River Oaks Book Store. He stood looking into the window, catching the reflection in the glass of the Lincoln behind him. At two sharp, he turned and quickly walked across the first esplanade and row of palms, jaywalked across West Gray, across the second esplanade with palms, and opened the door of the Lincoln.

"Let's go," he said, sliding in and slamming the door.

Langer had turned to stare at him. He was wearing sun shades, not the fashionable gradient kind but the solid dark ones that made him look like one of the three blind mice. He looked at Toy but didn't move to start the car.

"You think you know what you're doing," he said.

Toy didn't respond. It wasn't a question.

"Do you have any idea how dumb you are to think you can do this?"

That was a question, but it wasn't a nice one. "I have some idea of how much money I'll get out of it." Toy grinned.

Langer's dark glasses didn't move.

"Let's go," Toy said.

"He's authorized me to make one proposal. It'll be your only opportunity." He looked solemn as hell, really pissed, and it sounded like he was having a hard time controlling his voice. "You turn over the tapes, he'll give you five hundred thousand, and we'll all walk away from it. We don't see any more of you, we don't hear any more of you. You made a mistake, he lets you out of it. Fine. We're even all around. It's a good offer; it's the last offer. It won't be available five minutes from now. When I start the car, you're in for good."

Toy looked at the Houston skyline behind Langer's head. Billions and billions. Roeg was right in there, a big piece of it. Billions. Toy's tapes could cost him most of it, hell, all of it. Everything. Was it really a contest?

"Let's go," he said.

They left the shopping center and drove between the limestone pillars on either side of the entrance to Inwood. They made a series of quick turns that took them deep into the wooded estates that stood in aloof silence well back from the winding streets. Toy knew where they were going. Curiosity had drawn him here long ago, and many times he had driven by, peering into the dense woods to get a glimpse of the great estate of the man he would eventually encounter. He felt the same giddy eagerness as on a shooting foray, never knowing exactly what you're going to see but knowing it would be death, wondering how it would happen, how it would come flying out of the blind side of nowhere like a devil to claim its meat.

At the gatehouse a couple of men wearing business suits and aviator sunglasses, and who looked like they belonged to the secret service, stepped out of the air-conditioned cottage. One of them stood casually in front of the car while the other one spoke to Langer by name, looked in the car, checked a list on a clipboard, and then stepped back, waving them on. Both men wore sidearms. A wrought-iron fence extended in both directions from the gate, disappearing in a gradual curve along the avenue. Toy had seen a bank of electronic equipment and television monitors through the gatehouse windows and knew the fence was electronically secure. They drove a short distance along a paved drive that passed through thick woods and underbrush, from which the house gradually came into view.

It was three stories of what had once been a dun-colored brick but which time had stained dark apricot. Its style tended toward Georgian, though not strictly, with limestone corners and lintels and a burnt-umber slate roof. The central section of the house was flanked by two wings, also three-storied, that extended at forward angles to embrace a courtyard in front of the house. The tiny matting leaves of climbing fig ivy covered much of the brick on the bottom floors and was carefully trimmed around the tall windows and doorways. The lawn around the house was fine-textured Zoysia grass, which is often planted on the greens of golf courses and has a deep emerald shade.

Langer pulled into the courtyard and parked the Lincoln with the several other cars already there. He got out, checked around briefly as he shut his door, and headed for the main entrance. Toy noticed another plainclothes guard with a radio lingering in the recessed doorway of one of the wings. As they crossed the paving stones, the muffled, chattering sound of electric hedge clippers was the only audible evidence of life besides their own footsteps.

Langer did not ring the bell, but opened the heavy front door himself and went into a rather dark and large entry hall that was a good twenty-five to thirty degrees cooler than it was outside. He closed the door behind Toy and strode down the south wing hall, ignoring Toy's presence. He was pissed, really pissed. Toy figured that would have made him one mean mother back in the old Rice U football days, but now that he was a lot older it had to be putting a real strain on his overstressed pump. They came to a white-paneled wooden door on the left side of the hall, and Langer stopped. He rapped twice, hesitated, and then turned the knob as he pushed the door open and stood back for Toy to precede him into the room.

32

·······························

The room must have taken up a good portion of the first floor of the south wing. It was long, with a comfortable width and tall windows that looked out onto an expanse of grass with woods beyond. To their left was a large curved desk flanked on each side by several computer screens and keyboards. One of the screens was a continually rolling display of stock market quotations. The desk was a rat's nest of confusion. Photographs of war action covered every available space on the walls between the windows, some of them big, grainy blowups, some of them classics.

Looking at them, Toy recognized Capa's Spanish soldier photographed at the instant a bullet exploded his head as he ran across a field; his U.S. soldier sniper victim dying alone in a pool of his own blood on a villa balcony in France; Adams' astonishing photograph of Brigadier General Loan's point-blank revolver execution of a suspected Vietcong commando leader in the Cholon district of Saigon; "Nick" Ut's photo of the South Vietnamese girl running naked and screaming down the center of Route 1, her arms held out from her body burned with napalm;

Ulevich's chilling photograph of a right-wing Thai student using a metal folding chair to batter the bloodied head of a lynched left-wing student hanging by his grotesquely stretched neck while a jeering crowd of young students and children urges him on; Baughman's pictures of South African blacks "subdued" by Rhodesia's Grey Scouts fighting cavalry; the instant captured by an anonymous UPI photographer when nine Kurdish rebels are doubled up and blown off their feet by a volley from the rifles of the Ayatollah Khomeini's Revolutionary Guards, who are squatting in the dust and firing at nearly point-blank range; Price's photographs of the execution of Liberian President William Tolbert's cabinet ministers by Sergeant Samuel Doe's liberating soldiers of the 1981 coup d'etat.

They went on and on, hundreds of them. Toy recognized them all.

In the middle of the room a movie projector was humming, rewinding a film that had just been shown on the huge screen that hung from the ceiling at the opposite end of the room.

"Come on over, Mr. Toy."

The voice was soft, barely audible over the clacking of the rewinding projector. Toy looked around but didn't see anyone. As if sensing his predicament, a white-sleeved arm came up over the back of one of the sofas facing the screen and beckoned him over. Toy walked past the projector and rounded the end of the sofa.

Josef Roeg was lounging on a silk sofa big enough to be his bed. He was wearing a tuxedo, without the jacket or tie, and his small slippered feet were dug into the plush padding of the cushions. His clothes looked as if he had slept in them. It took Toy a moment to take in the peculiarities of his physique.

Roeg sat still, looking at Toy, seeming to wait until Toy had gotten used to him.

"I've admired your work, Mr. Toy. We've worked together for quite a while now . . . without meeting. Perhaps we shouldn't have waited so long."

Toy wasn't going to be humored. "I don't have any regrets," he said.

"No, of course not," Roeg said. The take-up reel finally retrieved all the film and the leader tape slapped loudly until Langer could hurry over to cut off the machine. Roeg waited until all that had been done before he spoke again.

"You might want to sit down, uh, Mr. Toy. Anywhere."

Toy sat on another sofa that ran perpendicular to Roeg's, facing the tall windows and the walls of photographs.

"I really hate to see this end to our relationship, Mr. Toy. You have an uncanny way of . . . capturing the most startling footage."

"It helps to have contacts," Toy said. He didn't smile.

"Our people were helpful?"

"Sure they were. They were mixed up in some of the worst things down there. Or they knew where they were happening."

There was some movement from Langer, who had positioned himself at the end of Roeg's sofa.

Roeg smiled at the remark's unintentional, or perhaps intentional, indictment.

Toy looked at Roeg's smile. He thought he would like to photograph Roeg. He'd never seen such a combination of virile masculinity and childishness. What was the little shit trying to do with that silly grin, psych him out? Toy made a decision. He wasn't going to bring up the proposition himself. If Roeg was trying to put him on the defensive, he'd have to try a lot harder than sitting on his nuts and grinning. No need to be obvious with a guy like this. When he was ready to deal he'd let Toy know. Toy sat still, looking without expression at the smiling Roeg.

"What do you feel when you are . . . filming death?" Roeg asked.

"Nothing," Toy said quickly. He hadn't expected a question like *that*. In his eagerness to appear unflappable he had answered too fast.

Roeg nodded slowly. His smile had faded to something like amusement.

"Then why do you do it?" he asked. "I know what you cameramen are paid. It's not enough to risk your life for."

"You were paying a hell of a lot better, though," Toy said.

"But apparently it wasn't enough," Roeg said.

"What?" Toy leaned a little toward Roeg. Why the hell was he whispering?

"Apparently it wasn't enough," Roeg repeated, not that much louder.

"Nobody ever gets enough money," Toy said. "Do you have enough money?"

Roeg grinned and shook his head slowly.

Toy shrugged, his point proven.

"You don't feel anything when you're filming death?" Roeg got back to his original question. "I hear . . . there's . . . a rush of adrenaline."

Toy looked at Roeg. What was this? Next thing he'd want to know what it was like to screw an Oriental. Roeg trying to rattle him again. It wasn't going to work.

"Yeah, you get juiced up about it."

"Reuters let you go because you were turning in footage that was too violent. What were you doing?"

Toy really hadn't expected this. Wasn't the guy worried about the money he was going to lose? What did he want to know this stuff for?

"I got tired of the hypocrisy. They wanted to show GI Joe comic-book footage. That's not what it was like."

"So you filmed . . . the real war."

"That's right. You know that. You bought all that old footage I had stored."

"You liked the excitement."

Toy looked at Roeg. Chewed at the inside of his jaw. "You get to look forward to it."

"Have you ever seen something so terrible you wouldn't film it?"

"No."

"What's the worst . . . thing you've . . . ever filmed?"

Toy changed his mind. He wasn't going to do this, but he didn't want to seem to be weakening. If it went on like this he was going to be in a defensive position. He would stop it right here.

"Probably the worst thing I've ever filmed was what you had going in that warehouse." He looked right into Roeg's black irises. "The worst."

Everything drained from Roeg's face, curiosity, humor, amusement. The dark shadow of his closely shaven beard turned from jet to ash. But he was an experienced gamesman. He didn't lose his composure.

"What are your . . . terms, Mr. Toy?"

"I want two million dollars."

Something happened inside the black irises. Toy didn't understand exactly what.

"Your terms, Mr. Toy?"

"In exchange for the money, I'll turn over to you all the original tapes. It took two of us to get it all. It was shot with the new Hitachi SR-1, so we had to use eight-minute cassettes. We shot seven cassettes each, nearly an hour each. From different vantage points."

He let that drop, no need to pursue it. He didn't care. Langer's tension was almost tangible. Toy liked having the pompous bastard backed against the wall.

"So," he continued, "I give you all the originals. But I have to have some insurance." At this remark Roeg's black irises assumed a veil. "I want to live to spend the two million. I've gone to Scurlock, Meins and Collins and drawn up a will. In that will I've left instructions that if I die under circumstances that appear in *any* way unusual, if I disappear without a trace and no satisfactory explanation is put forward within one hundred and twenty days, then my executors, who are only named in the will and are otherwise kept secret until my death, will request from Scurlock, Meins and Collins a sealed envelope. In that envelope is the number of a safety deposit box."

Toy turned and looked at Langer, who was still standing beside Roeg. Langer looked like a manikin.

"The safety deposit box is in one of the city's major banks. It contains a single copy of the original tape I will have given you, spliced together into one long narrative just like the one I sent you in the mail. With this copy is a document that tells what the tape is, how it came to be filmed, how I went about shooting the film. It relates the circumstances of my arrangement with you, that you've paid me two million to keep it quiet. Everything. It says that if my executors have gotten this far it should be evident that both of you are suspect in my death. I've had an extensive and major physical. All of my medical records, dental records, everything will be in this box. The name of my physician, dentist."

"I assume you're in excellent, uh, health," Roeg said.

"Excellent," Toy said.

"But what if you die of altogether innocent causes?" Roeg asked softly. "That safety deposit box leaves me forever in jeopardy."

"No," Toy said. "If my death doesn't arouse any suspicion, and my executors are charged with determining this, then they are instructed to remove the package in the second bank box and destroy it without opening it."

Everyone was silent for a moment. Roeg shifted his small frame on the sofa, glanced at Langer, smiled a little, and looked at Toy.

"What happens if the executors you've named . . . predecease you?"

"I've named six executors. It would be a hell of a coincidence. Incidentally, I've handpicked these people. They're not the sort who are likely to be bought off. I'd love to tell you who they are, just for the satisfaction of showing you how well this has been put together, but discretion seems the wisest course right now."

"It always is, Mr. Toy. Always," Roeg said. He thought a minute more. "How do you want the money?"

"I have a Panamanian bank account. I'll give you the number. When my banker verifies that that account has received a two-million-dollar deposit by you, then I'll turn over to you the only copy of the tape in existence, except for the one in the bank safety deposit box that'll serve as my life insurance."

"How do I know there are no other copies?" Roeg asked. "You could have dozens of them scattered around. You could make this appeal to me again later, for additional, uh, contributions to your . . . financial well-being."

"I've thought about that," Toy said. "How to make you one hundred percent sure of what I say. The only answer I can give is that you're going to have to trust me. I mean, that's just one of the things you're going to have to live with. Everything in this world's a trade-off. You want your odd jollies, you run the risks."

Roeg nodded, thought some more.

"You said it took 'two of us' to shoot the footage," Roeg said. "How can I be sure you can always vouch for the . . . other person? What if that person decides to work independently of you? That puts me in jeopardy again."

"You're not going to have any trouble from the person who worked with me," Toy responded. "But it's like I told you, I can't make it a hundred percent safe. It's not *my* fault you're in this situation anyway. I'm just telling you the kind of arrangement I'm willing to make. The way I see it, you've got this kind of problem anyway, with the other guys who were there, even with Langer here, if he ever decides to turn on you."

Roeg smiled. "This is very thorough."

"There's nothing personal in it," Toy said. "You paid me well, but a man can't do that kind of thing forever, so I worked this out. It's just a business deal. I imagine you've lost this kind of money before, by coming out on the short end of a merger or a bad commodities investment. It's not that big a deal to you, two million. But for me, with two million, I'm through working. It's my retirement plan. You're not even going to miss it."

Roeg tilted his head back and laughed silently. "I always miss money I 'lose,' Mr. Toy." He shook his head slowly. "When do you want to start the exchange?"

"Right now, if you want. You can wire my banker in Panama."

"Give me the number," Roeg said.

Toy reached into his coat pocket, took out a piece of paper, and handed it to Roeg. Roeg looked at it and nodded.

"And when do I get the tapes? I can do the wiring from here." He nodded his handsome head toward the computers.

"As soon as I receive an acknowledgment from Chamaco."

"Let's handle the logistics this way," Roeg said. "Why don't you go wherever you have to go to get my copy of the tape, and tomorrow at ten A.M. you meet Mr. Langer in the lobby of the Inland Trust downtown. The two of you will go to the private quarters of one of the officers of the bank who is a friend of ours, where you will have access to a VTR. Mr. Langer will verify the cassette tape, call me here, and I will initiate the transfer. I will tell Mr. Chamaco where he may contact you to inform you of the successful transfer when it is complete. You will wait there for that confirmation. When you receive it, you may both leave, Mr. Langer with the cassette and you with two million in your Panamanian account. Any objections?"

"Sounds okay," Toy said.

"Then we're through with each other, Mr. Toy," Roeg said softly. He picked up a light blue binder that had been lying on the floor beside the sofa and started thumbing through the pale green pages of the computer printouts.

Toy stood and followed Langer, who was already headed toward the door. They went out into the hall, back through the entrance hall, and out the heavy front door. The afternoon heat was like an oven. They walked across the courtyard. Just as Langer started to unlock the Lincoln he said, "Just a minute," and he walked across to the man who had been standing in the doorway of the south wing when they came in. They talked a few minutes while Toy squinted in the sun. Suddenly he heard a high-pitched whining that grew to a powerful whooshing and then a pounding, throbbing *whump-whump-whump*. Toy grinned and shook his head. The little asshole had a helipad back there somewhere.

Langer finally came over, and they got into the Lincoln and drove back along the drive. The two secret service types didn't come out of the air-conditioned cottage, didn't wave at them, just watched from behind the insect lenses of their aviator glasses.

They returned along the avenues the way they had come, onto Inwood, following it to the limestone pillars, then across Shepherd and into the shopping center. Langer pulled up to the exact spot where Toy had gotten in the car. He stopped and pushed a button that unlocked the doors. Toy got out, slammed the door, and heard the doors lock again, and Langer pulled away, out onto West Gray, and headed downtown. He had not spoken a word to Toy since Toy had rejected the initial "proposal" when he had first gotten in the car. And nobody had even mentioned Powell.

Toy walked back across Gray and went into Birraporetti's again. He made a telephone call and then went out the back door and crossed the street behind the shopping center. He walked several blocks toward downtown, cut across to Gray again, and went into the men's room of a service station. He wasn't there more than five minutes when he heard two quick raps on the door. He stepped outside and crawled into the back seat of a Yellow Cab which had pulled up between the restrooms and the street. He stayed on the floor of the cab looking at Lai's ankles, as Yue, her long hair tucked up under her cap, headed into Montrose.

Just past Westheimer, Yue pulled into the four-story parking garage of an office building. On the third floor she stopped and let Lai and Toy get out of the cab before she circled around and drove back down the ramp and headed toward Sharpstown. Twenty minutes later Lai had also put her hair under a cap and applied makeup to disguise her feminine and Oriental features. Toy crawled onto the back floor of a rental car and Lai threw a blanket over him. Within minutes they were following two other cars out into the swelling traffic.

33

Once again Haydon stood on the small front porch of the white stucco bungalow and listened to the air-conditioner unit in one of the bedroom windows around the side of the house kick on and clatter laboriously. The houses on either side of Powell's also had humming window units, and their blinds and curtains were tightly pulled against the afternoon heat. Next door a yellow metal water sprinkler wobbled on a bad bushing and threw water in an erratic, crazy pattern that was originally intended to be a circle.

He remembered the article he'd seen in the *Wall Street Journal*. The previous year Houstonians had paid out nearly three and a half billion dollars for cold air, more than the gross national product of forty-two African nations. The newspaper went on to quote other outrageous but nonetheless accurate statistics, a favorite technique of any journalist writing about Texas, and especially Houston.

More than seven hundred firms replace and install an estimated 90,000 air conditioners annually. . . .

They take up forty-four pages in Houston's Yellow
Pages. . . . Ninety-five percent of the city's four million residents air-condition their homes, compared
with fifty-five percent nationwide. . . . A Houstonian
millionaire enclosed and cooled his entire backyard—
including the swimming pool. . . . Monthly average
usage of kilowatt hours in Houston last year was 1,125
compared to 526 in Chicago, 490 in Philadelphia, 391
in Los Angeles, and 267 in New York. . . . Houston
Lighting & Power Company will spend eleven billion
dollars for the construction of power plants during
the next eight years. . . . The city's skyscrapers are
reflective boxes designed to keep out heat and retain
precious cool air . . . and are built over five miles of
cooled tunnels by forty thousand office workers each
day.

Heat and humidity. Humidity and heat.

He punched the doorbell again. He knew she was
there, having already looked down the driveway and seen
the low white Porsche in the garage.

When she opened the door she stood behind the
screen in bright yellow shorts the exact color of sunflowers
and a green cotton blouse with short cuffed sleeves. The
shirt was tucked neatly into the tailored shorts. She
propped the foot of one bare leg against the inside ankle
of the other foot and looked at him. Her strawberry-blond
hair was casually piled on top of her head, making her
look cool and relaxed. He could see her green eyes even
in the shadow of the room.

"Back again," she said. She didn't seem too surprised
to see him, or too happy about it.

He said, "Mind if I come in?"

She didn't say anything, but pushed open the screen.
He followed her into the living room, which was bathed in
a pale light from the skylight. Boxes were scattered
around the room, some half packed, some already taped
closed.

"Just find a place for yourself," she said, gesturing
hopelessly with her hands. "Can I get you something?"

"No, thank you. You decided to move out?"

"Right. Place gives me the willies now." She perched on a stool at the bar that looked into the kitchen.

"Where are you moving?"

She looked at him. "I guess you can get by with that, being a detective." She smiled.

"That's right."

"Not far, really. In the Tanglewood area."

"Nice," Haydon said. "A little more expensive, isn't it?"

She had crossed her legs indifferently, very relaxed. They were nice legs and she knew it, which made it easy for her to be comfortable on the tall stool.

"Yeah. A little more expensive. A step up. I've had some good luck. This place hasn't been bad news for both of us."

"When will you be completely moved?"

"Tonight. I've moved a little bit at a time over several days, and this is the last of it. Tonight's the first night in the new place. It'll be great to get out of here."

"That's good," Haydon said. "You work hard and you get rewarded for it. That's good. But I'll bet you're exhausted." He looked around at the piles of boxes.

"Not really. Moving little by little has helped."

"Oh, I meant the two jobs," Haydon said. "Holding down two jobs. But it looks like it's been worth it. It got you out of here."

She smiled, but it was shaky.

"You *are* working at two jobs now, aren't you?"

"No."

"You're not working for the Census Bureau?"

For one striking instant her face revealed a startling vulnerability, and Haydon thought she was going to blurt out the entire convoluted story that must lie behind the deaths of Wayne Powell and Alice Parnas. But he may only have imagined it, for no sooner did he see it than it was gone, leaving him to wonder if it had really ever been there at all.

"No," she said again.

"Yesterday morning I had a long conversation with William Langer," Haydon said. "He identified the girl in the picture I took from Powell's room as Alice Parnas, an employee in the photography lab where Powell worked. I went to talk to her and she told me, among other things, that she and Powell had been lovers. She was very upset by his death. Last night she apparently committed suicide. I talked with her next-door neighbor, Mrs. Spiegler. I wanted to know if she had seen anyone visiting Alice Parnas that day. She identified a photograph of you as being a woman who had come to her house and to Alice's house taking census information.''

Jennifer Quinn shook her head. "It wasn't me. The old lady's mistaken. That kind of thing happens all the time to blondes. We all look alike to some people.''

"Then you wouldn't mind meeting her in person.''

"No, certainly not, if it's necessary.'' She hesitated, frowned. "If you thought that was me, what did you think I was doing? You didn't think I was working for the Census Bureau, did you?''

Haydon shook his head. "No.''

She uncrossed her legs and put both feet on the bottom rung of the stool. She clasped her hands together and put them between her knees and looked at him.

"If I'm suspected of something, don't I have a right to know about it? Do I need a lawyer to tell me what my rights are in this?'' She was getting a little agitated; her voice rose. "Are you going to tell me what's going on here?'' Her light complexion was flushed. He couldn't tell if she was angry or frightened.

"Miss Quinn, at this point everyone related in any way in this case is suspect. We've checked on a number of people in a number of situations and this is simply one of them. Whoever the blonde was who spoke to Mrs. Spiegler and Alice Parnas was also the last person to see Alice Parnas alive. We're going to have to verify it wasn't you.''

"Jesus Christ!'' she said incredulously. Her eyes grew red around the rims as though she might cry. "That was a cute little chitchat act you put on about the two jobs. You think that was clever? You think . . .'' She was definitely angry now. She threw her hands up in a gesture of exasperation. "Can't you just question someone right out, be straightforward about it? That's insulting.''

Haydon looked at her. She was glaring at him and

made an irritated swipe at a stray strand of hair that had come loose and wandered in front of her face.

"The last time we talked, you said you had met William Langer. What were the circumstances?"

"The circumstances?" She looked at Haydon blankly, maybe a little flustered. "I don't remember . . . ever meeting Langer. I've never met him."

"But you said before that you had. You don't recall that?"

"I never said that. What the hell are you trying to do anyway?"

"You can verify where you were yesterday, between two and about five in the afternoon?"

"Yes, by God, I can."

"Where?"

"In the darkroom at the office. Working with a guy named Grant Sutton."

Haydon looked around and saw the telephone on a cardboard box on a chair. He got up and picked up the receiver.

"What's the number of your office?"

She blinked and gave it to him.

He dialed it, waited for an answer, and asked for Grant Sutton. As the receptionist told him Sutton was out of town for the weekend, he looked at Quinn, who instantly registered an expression of remembrance and impatience. She hopped off the stool, stepped over, and snatched the telephone out of Haydon's hands. She covered the mouthpiece.

"Dammit, I forgot." Her face was pink. She spoke into the telephone. "Sara? This is Jennifer. I forgot he was going backpacking. Do you know where he was going? Can I reach him?" She listened, nodded. "Okay. Thanks, thank you."

She hung up.

"Colorado. Shadow Mountain national park. He'll be spending one night in a lodge in Granby. There can't be that many lodges in Granby." She looked at him, containing her temper. "Look, I can't help that," she snapped.

"Surely he's not the only one who saw you," Haydon said.

"Yes, as a matter of fact, he was. I had been packing things here, and I was a sweaty mess. I just had a couple of hours of developing to do. I didn't go through the reception area because of the way I looked. I went in through the side door, worked until I had it all done, and left."

"We'll talk to him when he gets back," Haydon said.

"I know how it looks," she snapped again.

"Don't worry about it," Haydon said. "We'll cover it later."

"Well, what else do you want to know?" She had one hand in the pocket of a cocked hip, the other hand coming across her waist and grasping the wrist.

"Nothing," Haydon said. "I'll let you finish your packing."

"When do you want me to meet the old lady? She'll clear it up when she sees me in person."

"I'll get back to you," Haydon said, making his way through the boxes to the front door. "Oh, could I have your new address?"

She told him. "I'll remember it," he said.

When he got to the front door she said, "Look, I honestly forgot about Grant taking a long weekend. I'll try to track him down at that lodge and have him call you. I've got your card."

"You don't have to do that. We can wait until he gets back."

"No," she said. "I want to. I feel like a fool. I want him to tell you. I'll track him down."

Haydon nodded, opened the door and stepped outside. She stood in the doorway squinting into the outside glare.

He said goodbye and went to the car. The steering wheel was so hot it was oily. He left the door open while the air conditioner cooled down and then drove away. He didn't look back. He didn't have to.

Jennifer Quinn was pretty good, but she wasn't good enough. Haydon believed her about Grant Sutton. He had no doubt that Sutton would verify her claim. It really was an oversight on her part that he was going out of town. She didn't have an alibi and then she did, but she didn't. Haydon appreciated the irony in that. But it wasn't working anyway. A slip of the tongue was far more damaging than any number of small miscalculations in a well-made plan. Twice Quinn had referred to Mrs. Spiegler as "the old lady." Haydon had never mentioned her age.

Boney Walker leaned over the old pedestal sink, with crazed porcelain and nicotine stains where cigarettes had burned to stubs, and carefully eased the wooden match-stick into his nose. He probed cautiously, flinching as he touched the blood clots and blinking the tears out of his eyes. He looked at himself in the jagged space of the old mirror where the silver backing hadn't peeled off. Nose all over his face. Eyes like Billy Whistle's, all bugged. Lip sticking out like it was maybe something else growing there, not a lip; didn't look like a lip.

He had been blind tired, but the night hadn't brought him much sleep. His muscles, as tender as boils, had made his whole body throb, and he had had to breathe through his mouth because of the clotted blood in his nose. He had to dig it out. It would help the swelling go down, and besides, it bugged the shit out of him. Just like picking your nose. When there's something there you gotta get it out. He touched a raw spot, and the pain was so sharp his knees almost buckled as if somebody had hit him, and he leaned his head on his arm on the edge of the sink. He turned on the water, using a pair of vise-grip pliers because the handle had stripped out, and let the blood from his fleshy bleeding nose drip into the rusty water and then down the drain.

He stood and looked through the black specks in the mirror. He reached for the brown paper towels he'd stolen out of a service station restroom and wet one and kneaded it to make it soft, as soft as you can get a brown paper towel, and put a little piece of it on the match and poked it in his nose. It was like putting a knife in his nose. He wanted to sit down but couldn't sit on the commode because it didn't have a lid, so he backed away from the sink and sat on the floor in the doorway. He leaned his head back against the jamb, sweat streaming from his hair, from under his arms, slick with it against his sides. He had a wet paper towel wadded in his hand and he began rubbing it over his body, squeezing the water out of it onto him. He closed his eyes, which didn't take much closing, and sighed.

In an instant he realized there were flies crawling on the piece of paper towel in his nose. He shooed them away and slowly slid off the doorjamb and onto his side on the floor. He was so tired. He rolled over on his back on the cracked linoleum. It was a little cooler on the bare floor. He put a ragged undershirt over his face to keep the flies off his nose.

Mother fucker. He would not forget that white nigger. He closed his eyes. He was going to lie there and think about what he could do to that mother-fucker white nigger. If he went to sleep maybe he would dream up something that would be better than anything he could think up awake. Something real good.

34

He looked at the two Gustav Klimt drawings. They were not large. The first was actually a detail study for his mural allegory, "Philosophy," that had been painted for the University Hall in Vienna in 1900. It portrayed a nude woman, her back to the viewer, twisting around to her right as she looked upward, her head thrown back, her right hand on her right breast. It was a conté drawing. The second, "Profile of a Lady Smiling," was signed and drawn in blue crayon.

It was late afternoon, and Haydon was in the gallery waiting out the traffic. He did this occasionally, usually staying past closing time. The rotund and placid Anton Busch simply locked the doors and quietly went up the stairs to his offices, where he finished the day's bookwork while Haydon slowly roamed from room to room. He had bought more than a few pieces of art during these odd hours at the end of the day. Busch had nothing against the curious habits of his clients, especially when they were buying clients.

After starting out with the Klimt drawings, Haydon

had migrated through the other rooms, pausing at other drawings, ignoring the abstracts, pausing at portraits, ignoring most of the landscapes, until he was back at Klimt. He had been studying the two drawings a good while when he sensed Busch behind him.

"Looking at the Klimts again," Busch said.

Haydon nodded.

"You won't buy the nude one, will you?" Busch asked. His hands were clasped behind his back, and he was looking at the blue-crayon "Profile of a Lady Smiling."

Busch's beard, trimmed neatly and identically in the style of Edward VII, was graying on either side of his mouth and into his chin. The rest was reddish brown. He had been born in Vienna a few years before the war and had lived there until after the war when his mother, a professor of art history at the University of Vienna and newly widowed in the last months of the war, left for New York to join her sisters, who had preceded her two years earlier.

"If I recall, you've got three conté nudes from me in the past eighteen months." An eyebrow flickered innocently. "And I don't know what you may have bought elsewhere." One hand came around and wiped his beard downward, contemplatively, then returned behind his back. "I don't know. But unless you want your home, which is a marvelous place with many good areas for hanging fine artwork, unless you want it to become . . . unusual, you should take the blue crayon."

"You saw me looking at the blue crayon," Haydon said without turning around.

"Yes, I saw you looking at it."

"It's more expensive."

"Yes, it's more expensive. But it's signed. And the hair, the way he's done the hair. It's very nice."

Haydon nodded.

"But, if you are really fond of the red nude I must tell you that someone else is interested in it. They're coming back tomorrow."

"No. I prefer the blue crayon. I'd like to take it with me."

Busch made a little bow from the waist and stepped

up and took the drawing off the wall. As they started up the stairs he said, "Being a dealer, I'm supposed to be inured to things coming and going. Somewhat like the administrator of an orphanage, I have to keep my distance from my charges and not grow too fond of them. The children must inevitably leave. And it's good that they do, both for the children and for me." He chuckled. "But these two Klimts. Ah. Do you know I've only had four in all the years I've been down here? These two and two others: "Frontal View of Sitting Nude," also blue crayon, and "Study for Water Serpents," a pencil. Klimt's art is a little mad, of course, like Munch and Moreau and Fuchs—"

"And Fuseli," Haydon said behind him.

"Yes, and Fuseli the intellectual, but he, I mean Klimt, was a fellow Viennese, and despite my studied detachment . . . well, I hate to see his drawings leave."

Haydon sat down in Busch's office and wrote out the check while the dealer took the drawing into another room for his assistant to wrap. When he returned he handed the package, now bearing the large gold-wafer seal of his gallery, to Haydon and smiled broadly.

"A new era for you, Stuart. From red nudes to blue portraits. *Bonne vue.*"

By the time Haydon arrived home it was dusk, and he was surprised to see not only Nina's car in the drive but Mooney's also. He parked, and with the picture under his arm he went into the house. From the entrance hall he headed straight for the library, where he could hear Mooney's voice.

As he stepped in the door he saw Mooney standing at his desk talking on the telephone. Nina was sitting in one of the armchairs.

"What's this?" she said, smiling and looking at the package under his arm. "Uh-oh, you've been with Busch."

Haydon tilted his head questioningly toward Mooney as he went over and handed her the picture.

"Said he's got something for you," she whispered. "He's only been here about ten minutes. He got a message on his beeper, and he called in." She started unwrapping the package and then gasped. "Stuart, my God.

You're crazy. It cost too much . . ." She stopped, glancing toward Mooney, and then looked at Haydon and whispered again, "It's gorgeous."

He smiled at her and then turned to Mooney.

". . . I'm calling from there now," Mooney said into the telephone. "Just have the guys sit tight. We don't want them to do anything. We're on our way."

"What have you got?" Haydon asked as Mooney hung up.

"A patrol unit thinks they've spotted Toy's cars at an apartment complex over in Sharpstown. They've checked out the plates. They belong to a guy in Bellaire. They got his wife on the phone, and she went outside to check, and sure enough, they're gone."

"They haven't made any inquiries around the complex?"

"Nothing. They're waiting for us."

"Great." Haydon turned around again and kissed Nina. "I'll call you."

"You get a new picture?" Mooney asked. He looked over and Nina held it toward him. "Blue?"

"Let's go," Haydon said. Nina was smiling.

As they followed the beads of lights along the Southwest Freeway, Mooney told Haydon what he had found out from Philip Greiner.

"Greiner doesn't know the black guy. But he knows the others. They're all part of Roeg's little inner circle. The guy who came in with Langer at the last was Roeg." He leaned his hand against the window of the Vanden Plas, to catch the surges of light from the freeway lamps, and read from his pocket notebook.

"First guy came in along with the black was Gerald Kemper, handles Roeg's merger deals in the States. Does all the footwork, heads up the legal teams. He's a lawyer. The second guy, who came in with Langer, was Harvey Gage, Roeg's personal factotum. He travels with Roeg, makes sure he's happy with accommodations, screens the people who want to see him, schedules his time. You generally have to go through him to gain access to Roeg, even if you're one of the privileged inner circle. And the last guy, who came in with the black the second time, was

Victor Landa, the CEO of Roeg International directly under Roeg.''

Mooney straightened up and closed the notebook.

"That's it?"

"Yeah. After I saw the tape several times with Greiner I realized there really weren't that many people. The three black bucks at the beginning who huddled under the light at the doorway. The black dude with the mustache who came in with a white guy. Langer with someone. Black dude again with someone. And finally Langer again with Roeg."

"Was Greiner very helpful about background on these men?''

"Not really. The guy was in pretty bad shape when I talked to him, Stuart. Kid with all the muscles seemed a little concerned that I was overdoing it, going over and over the tape so Greiner could look at the faces. Greiner did say that these three guys had probably been with Roeg longer than anyone else in the inner circle. They really played his game. Yes-men."

They rode in silence a few minutes, the car lighting up like daylight as they passed through the interchange where the freeway intersected Loop 610.

"What did Greiner think of the tape, Ed? Did he comment?''

"He was fascinated with it. He really concentrated on it. Wanted me to replay it for him all the way through twice, not counting all the backing up and going forward to look at the faces. I asked him what he thought was going on and he just shook his head. Said it didn't necessarily have to be something sinister. Said Roeg didn't do normal things in a normal way. Could of been doing anything.''

"But if it was simply a clandestine business meeting with his own executives to discuss a major move he wanted kept secret, why would Toy have felt it was a subject ripe for blackmail?'' Haydon said.

"Yeah, that's exactly the point I made to Greiner. He didn't say anything to that. I got the impression he sure as hell didn't think it was some kind of harmless little get-together, but he wasn't going to say so."

"Have you heard from Pete?"

"No."

"The black fellow in the business suit is the only person who isn't identified so far," Haydon said. "Except for the three men at the beginning. If he's in politics of any kind, I think he's our best bet for a squeeze. He could be ambitious to the point of having been sucked into something he'd like to get out of. He might be persuaded to cooperate."

"Maybe," Mooney said.

Haydon took the Hillcroft exit off the freeway and dropped down into a wasteland of architectural homogeneity. During the day, as seen from the freeway that cuts diagonally through the district, the more than three thousand acres of apartment buildings spread out in an endless crust of brown roofs whose cheap composition shingles threw off a vaporous sea of constantly shimmering reflective heat. At night the lights disguised the monotony, at least from a distance.

They saw the patrol car sitting by the Reddy Ice freezers outside the convenience store and pulled up in a slot a few feet away. The patrolmen didn't immediately realize who they were until Haydon and Mooney got out of the Vanden Plas and Haydon flashed his shield as they went into the store. One of the patrolmen followed them while the other stayed back to keep an eye on the apartment building.

They introduced themselves and stood by the cold beer locker at the back of the store while the young patrolman briefly repeated how they had found the cars. As they talked they looked across the food shelves and out the plate-glass windows of the store.

"The cars are around to the left side," the patrolman concluded. His name was Sublette, and he was wearing a short-sleeved uniform that exposed the thick neck and forearms of a weightlifter. "You can't see them from here, but you can see the only drive in and the only drive out. The place is built in a square with a quadrangle in the center. There's a breezeway to get into the quad from the front and another one at the back. Since the cars are on the left side of the building I assumed they lived on that side. The cars are parked side by side."

"Okay," Haydon said. "I want you to get two more units out here and park them out of sight at either end of the block. When you get them stationed, you and your partner meet us on the breezeway at the front."

The patrolman went outside to call the other two units and to pull his car around in the dark out of sight.

Haydon and Mooney walked across the street and up the drive on the left of the building to Toy's cars. They let the air out of a single front tire on each car and then went around the edge of the building to the breezeway where the two patrolmen were waiting.

Mooney and the two patrolmen waited in the breezeway while Haydon followed the red arrows to the manager's apartment. He knocked on the door and waited. When the woman came to the door Haydon showed his shield, introduced himself, and asked if he could come in. The woman's startled face betrayed her anticipation of imminent bad news, and she backed into her apartment as if at gun point, letting Haydon close the door behind him.

"There's nothing to be afraid of," he told her. He hated those expressions of dumb, unwarranted fear. They were usually warning signs of people who panicked easily. "There are two cars out in your parking area that we believe belong to people we've been looking for. Do you have a tenant named Ricky or Richard Toy?"

The woman shook her head. She was thin, with hair dyed so black it looked as if it had been dipped in tar. She wore badly frayed blue-jean shorts cut so skimpily that the white pockets underneath hung out nearly two inches onto her thighs. Her cotton halter top said *Tits for Texas.*

"He's Oriental, probably would have checked in here about a week ago. There are two Oriental women with him."

The woman started chewing a fingernail with a creased brow as if Haydon had just asked her the sixty-four-thousand-dollar question. She started nodding her head.

"Yeah, yeah, the two girls has been hanging around the pool. Showin' off. But their names isn't Toy."

"What name are they using?"

"Starts with a K. I don't know. Let me look."

She went over to a plastic filing box that was sitting on the kitchenette table and opened it. She flipped through the folders until she found it.

"Richard M. Kaun. Apartment One-thirty-two. That's on this side, nearly to the end. I don't know the girls' names." She swallowed, wondering what he would say next.

"You keep master keys, don't you?"

She nodded, eyes widening.

"If you could let me borrow the key to their place I would appreciate it."

Like a robot she reached into the bottom of the filing cabinet, rummaged around, and came up with a paper tag with a key dangling from it. She handed it to him without speaking.

"Do you know if they're home?"

She shook her head.

"I'll bring the key back in a few minutes," Haydon said.

She nodded, and he opened the door and stepped outside, leaving her standing behind the opened lid of the plastic filing cabinet.

35

Haydon walked back around to the breezeway where Mooney and the two patrolmen were waiting.

"Okay," he said. "They're in one-thirty-two, on the left side a little over halfway down. The manager doesn't know if they're in there or not." He looked across the quadrangle at the pool where a man and a woman were swimming, hanging on to the edge of the pool near the diving board. "Ed, I guess you'd better have them go inside. I'd feel better about it."

"One-thirty-two." Mooney turned and looked at the sequence of numbers on the apartment doors. "That's almost straight across from the pool. You think they'll get suspicious if they see me out there?"

"I don't know, but we can't let those people stay where they are." He looked at Sublette. "Why don't you two go around and cover the front. We'll give you enough time to get in place before Ed goes out to the pool, just in case they spot him and try to ease out. Be careful. Give the door plenty of berth. Once we get inside and everything's okay, I'll open up. Call us when you're in place."

The two patrolmen left and Mooney muffled the radio with his hand as they waited for the call. The couple in the pool were laughing. The girl's throaty voice came to them clearly across the surface of the water. In a few minutes the radio crackled. The two patrolmen were ready.

Haydon held the radio as Mooney started across the spotty grass of the quadrangle toward the pool. Haydon watched as he approached them, squatted down at the water's edge, and surreptitiously showed his shield as he began talking. They became still in the water, two dark heads in the liquid turquoise. Haydon tried to imagine the sequence and range of their emotions as they realized what was happening. In a few moments they got out of the pool, and the girl stood in her dripping bikini talking to Mooney while the man walked around to the broken lawn chairs and got their towels. All three of them left the pool together, Mooney putting his arm on the guy's shoulder in a chitchatty manner, as they disappeared behind a clump of honeysuckle on the other side of the quad.

Haydon started down the side under the stairways toward 132, stepping around a Burger Boy grill and a stack of fishing poles. He saw Mooney coming to meet him from the other direction. They approached the door from opposite sides, holding their guns. Mooney nodded that he was ready, and Haydon stretched out his left arm to knock, then stopped.

Mooney looked at him and Haydon pointed to the doorknob. A brass key protruded from the lock. Both men leaned back while Haydon slowly reached up and knocked on the door. He knocked twice. When there was no answer, he turned the door handle and pushed open the door. Mooney reached inside the doorjamb and flipped on the light. When nothing happened, Haydon slowly leaned into the opening. The light carried from the breakfast nook adjacent to the kitchen, into the dining area, and across one end of the living room. It was enough.

"Damn," he said, and charged inside as he flipped on another light in the dining room, bathing the lower half of the woman's naked body in a harsh light, her upper torso still in the darkness on the living room floor. "Damn! Watch the hallway, Ed."

Haydon stepped across into darkness.

"Jesus, Stuart," Mooney snapped.

The ceiling light flashed on in the living room and Haydon was unlocking the front door as the two patrolmen burst in.

"Help him check out the bedrooms," Haydon said, jerking his head toward Mooney, who was still crouched at the entrance of the hallway.

The two patrolmen stopped in midstride and stared at Haydon kneeling over the woman lying face down, her long black hair matted in the pool of dark syrup that had spilled out of her head, one arm tucked under her, the other flung out on the carpet. In the bright light of the almost bare room, the trail of blood that tracked up the wall and ended in a fuchsia starburst caught their attention like the brilliant flash of an explosion.

"Help him, dammit," Haydon yelled, and they ran past him as he put his hand down into the girl's hair around her neck. Her carotid artery was flat. With half his mind he was alert to Mooney and the patrolmen making their way down the hall, opening and closing doors, and with the other half he worked up the courage to turn her over. He could tell there was an exit wound in the scramble of hair at the back of her head.

"It's clear," Mooney yelled, and Haydon heard them returning along the hall. Gently, as if she were asleep, he put his hand on her left shoulder and began turning her over. She was almost all the way over before her face pulled away from the soaked carpet and fell back. He laid her out flat, and with the tips of his fingers picked the hair away from her face. There was a single small bullet hole above her left eyebrow, belying the massive intracranial blast that had bulged and blackened her eye and caused her face to balloon in a grotesquely lopsided fashion. She had deep purple bruises around her breasts and rib cage, and a large one covered most of the right side of her lower abdomen. He looked at her hands. The backs of them and the undersides of her wrists were covered with narrow abrasions.

Haydon stood up. Mooney and the two patrolmen were looking down at the girl.

"Sublette, get on the radio and call it in," Haydon said. "Have them bring the wagon to the front door. I don't want them carrying the body through the quad. We're going to attract a crowd, so get the other two units in here." He looked at the name tag on the other patrolman's shirt. "Moreno, get a sheet out of the bedroom."

"Looks like they questioned her before they shot her," Mooney said.

Haydon nodded. "I wonder if she told them anything. Any signs of struggle back there?"

"It's hard to tell. The place has been ransacked."

They looked around the living room.

"She put up a fight," Mooney said, pointing to the video equipment scattered around the otherwise empty room, and to the blood splattered along the base of the walls. "Blood's scattered around too much for it all to have come from the gunshot wound. They must've shot her against the wall."

He looked at the red starburst and walked over to it.

"Yeah, here's the hole. We'll have the lab guys get it out."

"She had handcuff marks on her wrists," Haydon said.

Mooney came back and looked toward the kitchen.

"She'd been getting supper," he said. "Vegetables on the countertop in there. A wok with oil in it, too."

"You see her clothes?" Haydon asked.

"No, but then you can't really tell. The place is a mess back in there."

"They should be somewhere around here," Haydon said.

Moreno came in with the sheet and put it over the girl.

"Thanks," Haydon said. "Why don't you wait outside the back door. Keep people away. And leave the door open, will you? We need some circulation in here."

They were standing by the girl's body. Haydon felt his heart pounding. The muscles in his neck and shoulders were drawing up, pulling at their roots deep in his back.

He had been inhaling the musky odor of blood since he had seen the girl from the back door. Now he could taste it as well.

Mooney looked around the room, waiting, as Haydon stared at the sheet, which now had several crimson patches forming in it where the blood was soaking through. She was so still. He almost expected to see a gentle rising and falling of the sheet, a sign that she was not dead. He wondered what quirk of fate had dictated that she be the one. Why her instead of the other one? If she had walked across to the convenience store to get a bunch of celery . . . if she had been ten minutes earlier or ten minutes later from wherever she had been . . . if the patrolmen had spotted the cars half an hour earlier . . . if . . . if . . . What would it have taken to have saved her from the motionless silence of the sheet?

"So what do you think," Mooney finally said.

Haydon flinched. Listened a moment, relaxed.

"It's Roeg," he said. "The rest of the tape must be extraordinary." He looked down. "This. I don't know. I'd like to think Langer couldn't do it. He might have had it done."

He heard the first steady whine of the sirens on the Loop, several of them, beginning to waver.

"We might have had a chance to find Toy before." He shook his head. "But not now."

"I guess the other gal's with him," Mooney said.

"Probably. I wonder how he's going to react to this? He may not be satisfied with blackmail now."

The sirens were in the neighborhood. He looked out the front door, which had been left open, and saw the blue and cherry flashes growing brighter against the front of the apartments across the street.

"You think he knows about it yet?"

Haydon shrugged. He looked at the figure under the sheet again, heard the car doors slamming outside, men's voices, equipment being unloaded. Stan Gibbs, one of the coroner's investigators, came in the door with the two men from the crime lab. They looked at the sheet, at the wall, then at the two detectives.

"Haydon? Didn't know you were back," Gibbs said.

He walked over, squatted down, and peeked under the sheet. When he saw it was a naked woman, he lifted it a little higher, looked some more, then pulled it off. He stood, looking at her. "Little Oriental," he said. "Dang, she's really put together."

Haydon turned and walked out of the room, through the kitchen, and out the back door into the quadrangle. Several people had already come out on their balconies and around the lighted pool, staring at the open doorway of 132.

Pulling his cigarettes out of his coat pocket, Haydon offered one to Moreno. The young man hesitated, then went ahead and took it. He mumbled "thanks" and Haydon lit them both. Without speaking, he moved out into the grass and stood alone.

When Haydon was halfway through his second cigarette Mooney came out of the apartment, looked for him, and came across the grass.

"Gibbs thinks maybe a couple of hours. Sublette and Moreno couldn't have missed them by much."

Haydon smoked. A girl in a swimsuit broke away from a group at the pool and made her way over to Moreno, sent to see what it was all about. Moreno bent slightly, listened to her, and then shrugged, nodded his head toward the opened door. She continued talking to him.

"I went ahead and sketched the scene, got the measurements and everything," Mooney said. "The lab boys are checking the key for prints." He was looking at Haydon.

"How the hell did they know where to find them?" Haydon asked. "Either someone told them or they followed them here. If someone informed them, who would it have been? Who other than the two girls knew where Toy was? Who would he have shared that information with? If they followed them, how did they miss Toy, and how did they pick them up in the first place?"

"Maybe they just followed the girl," Mooney said.

"From where? How would they have picked up her trail?"

A couple of other people from the pool area came up and joined Moreno and the girl in the swimsuit, a few more drifted across the quadrangle, two women came along the sidewalks under the stairs. Finally a small crowd had gathered. A woman came around behind Moreno and tried to look in the opened door. When he turned around and saw her he made all of them move back off the sidewalk onto the grass.

Haydon began absently to field-strip his cigarette, his eyes looking at what he was doing but not really seeing anything. He looked up suddenly, fiddling with the filter.

"I'll bet Toy made his bid, tried to collect, probably using the girls, and they followed her here. Maybe she was supposed to make the pickup, and they grabbed her."

"I don't think so. Remember, she was cooking supper in there."

"How do you know it was her? Maybe it was the other girl, or Toy. When Roeg's people come in with her, Toy and the other girl get away. When Toy gets away they try to get more out of her and end up killing her."

"What makes you think Toy got away?" Mooney asked. "Maybe they hauled him off somewhere. Somebody'll find what's left of him in a trash dumpster tomorrow."

"Okay." Haydon sighed. "Why don't you start with the crowd over there. Let's see if anyone saw or heard anything."

He turned and walked across the quadrangle to the manager's office. She was one of the very few people who were not outside their apartments or peeking through their curtains. He knocked and she came to the door, opening it cautiously.

"I need to ask you a few questions," Haydon said.

She nodded.

"May I come in?"

She unlatched the screen door and pushed it open. When he got inside he didn't sit down, but stood in the tiny breakfast nook. He laid the key with the paper tag on the dinette table. She looked at it, her thin arms folded across the bare space between her halter top and the blue-jean shorts.

"You want to tell me who you gave the other key to?" he said.

She looked at him, her eyes slightly too big for the bone structure of her face. She had added a little mascara since he talked to her earlier.

"My husband works night shift," she said. "With the telephone company."

Haydon waited.

She sat down on the green plastic seat of one of the dinette chairs, slumping as if she wouldn't have been able to stand another minute. She massaged a thin hand against her right temple.

"Coupla hours ago guys came to the door looking for that Chinese and his two girls. Said they needed to talk to 'em about repossessing one of the cars. Asked what apartment they was in and then asked for the key. I asked what they needed the key for and they said that was their business. I said well just a damn minute and one of the guys came over and put a hand on my shoulder and squeezed real hard and said they'd like to have the key."

She looked up at Haydon, her eyes wet now, messing up the mascara.

"I mean, they were threatenin' me, you know. Goddamn." She shuddered. "Told me I didn't have to say anything about them to anybody, you know. I gave 'em the key and they left and that's all I know."

"You didn't see them leave?"

"I sure didn't. People like those Chinese have problems, it's none of my business, just like the man said. You can't go around sticking your nose in ever'body's business, and I don't want any trouble. This is just a job, bein' manager, not a damn babysittin' service. It's like running a damn convenience store. Robber comes in, I'm not going to get myself shot over the boss's till. My life's worth more'n a damn minimum-wage job, I'll tell you that. No, I didn't see 'em leave, and I don't know when they left."

"There were two, three of them?"

"Two came in here."

"What did they look like?"

"Just businessmen. Wearing suits like yours."

"You'd know them if you saw them again?"

"I imagine."

"Was one of them a big fellow, sandy hair? In his forties? Could have been a college football player?"

"I don't think so. They were just ordinary guys. Just common guys. Nothing noticeable about 'em."

Haydon thought a minute. "Okay, I appreciate your help. Our people will be through down there in a couple of hours. We don't want anyone in the apartment until we give you official permission to clean it up. We'll put our own locks on the doors."

"Clean it up?"

"One of the Oriental women was shot in the head. I'm going to leave you one of my cards."

"Dead?" The woman's mouth quivered.

Haydon nodded.

"Well, what'll I do?" She looked at him, her eyebrows contorted in knots of anxiety.

"Ask your husband when he gets home," Haydon said. "He'll know."

Outside, Mooney was standing by the edge of the pool talking to a man in a cowboy hat. Mooney waved to Haydon, and they started toward him.

"Haydon, this is Sandy Buckner. He saw one of the girls earlier this afternoon."

Haydon shook his hand. Buckner was in his early thirties, wore a cowboy shirt, Levi's, and boots. The round imprint of a Skol can showed from his shirt pocket, and his bottom lip was pooched out with an oversized lump of the grainy tobacco. He flipped his head toward Mooney.

"He wonted to know if anybody saw sumthin' unusual aroun' this place"—he flipped his head toward apartment 132—"or with the people that lives there. I seen those little ol' Jap gals all the time"—he flipped his head toward the pool—"out here swimmin'. I never saw 'em do anythang but lay aroun' the water or go out with their boyfriend."

He leaned a little to one side and spat.

"This evenin' I was comin' home from work. I drive a truck, and I'd been out in Odessa a coupla days. When I pulled aroun' to the side over here I saw one of those little gals gettin' out of a yella taxi car. I mean she was gettin' out from under the wheel. I didn't know she drove one.

She was wearin' a man's britches and shirt and had her hair all tucked up under a taxi cap. Maybe she just started the job, I don't know, but I never seen her drive it before."

He looked at Haydon. No one said anything.

Buckner looked at Mooney and lifted his shoulders. "Well, that's the unusual thang I seen."

"Is the cab still around there?" Haydon asked.

"Hell, yeah," Buckner drawled. "I seen it while ago."

"Thanks," Haydon said. He started back toward the apartment.

"We'll probably get back to you," Mooney said, moving toward Haydon.

"Lissen, I seen those little gals quite a bit," Buckner said. "I talked to 'em. One of 'em's named Lai and one of 'em's Yue. Wont me to look at her, see if I can tell which one it is? It won't bother me none. I was in Nam. I've seen lots of that kind of shit."

"Maybe later," Mooney said. He wanted to catch up with Haydon. "We didn't know their names though," Mooney said, pulling out his notebook. "Thanks. We'll call you."

Haydon was already inside the apartment door.

36

The Lincoln sat alone in the parking lot of the Houston Arboretum and Nature Center, its lights off, its engine running to support the air conditioner that provided a minimum insulation from Memorial Park's swampy humidity. Bill Langer waited, staring out of the windshield to the wall of woods that rose up in front of the car, his mind dulled by the day's shattering events. He was too tired to think, too disheartened.

In the rearview mirror he saw the headlights pan across the tree trunks and then shine directly on him as they approached across the asphalt parking lot. When the car pulled up beside him it illuminated a sign at the edge of the woods that read WILLOW OAK TRAIL. The Porsche's headlights went out, and the interior light came on as Jennifer Quinn opened the door and got out. A moment of black night, and then she opened the door of the Lincoln and they caught a brief, harsh glimpse of each other as she slid into the seat and slammed the door.

A warm, clammy mass of bayou air came into the car

with her, bringing the odors of decaying pine needles and dark mud. The air conditioner labored to expel it.

He turned on the dash lights, which suffused them in a pale jade glow. She wore a silk shirtwaist dress, emerald like her eyes and unbuttoned low enough for him to see the swell of a pale breast. Her hair, parted naturally near the center of her head, was combed simply and fell over her shoulders. He wanted to take her and hold her, bury his face in the fragrance of her dress, hold her so tight he could feel her heart moving against him. He didn't want to feel anything but the timeless pleasure of making love to her.

"What's happened?" she asked. She leaned back against the door and looked at him.

He felt a sinking disappointment. He should have known he wasn't going to be allowed the luxury of indulging his feelings of vulnerability, even if it was only within the confines of his own mind.

"Toy made his pitch today," he said.

"You're kidding."

"I took him to Roeg myself."

"How much does he want?"

"Two million."

"Christ!" She continued looking at him. "Well, what happened?"

"Nothing. Roeg pretended to be going along with Toy's elaborate system of checks and balances for the payoff, then I took Toy out of there. I'm supposed to meet him at Inland Trust tomorrow for the exchange."

"The tapes for the money."

"More or less." He turned down the dash lights a little. "It'll never happen. As we left Roeg's place one of the choppers lifted off behind the house. They were going to track Toy by air. Two cars on the ground."

"And?"

"I went back to the office. They were supposed to call me when they found out where he was staying." He shook his head. "I never heard from them."

"What does that mean?"

"I don't know."

"Do you think they found him or didn't find him?"

"I don't know."

She crossed one leg over the other and stretched them out toward him, keeping the hem of the dress over her knees.

"Is he cutting you out?"

"I imagine so. I didn't handle this to his satisfaction. It never should have gone this far."

"You didn't learn anything from that black guy, Walker?"

Langer snorted. "No. Toy contacted *him*. I don't know how he knew what was going on. Anyway, Walker was no help. Ellis threatened him, beat him up, and let him go."

"So that's it? You're out?"

"I don't know for sure, but I imagine I'm out, yes." He put one arm on the back of the seat and one arm over the steering wheel, and looked out the windshield to the dark woods. He was half turned toward her. "But that's the least of my worries. Haydon's going to take this all the way. I've got more to think about than being put out to pasture by Roeg."

It was quiet a moment.

"He came to see me today," she said.

"Haydon?" Langer continued to stare out the windshield. Nothing surprised him at this point.

"The old woman next door to Parnas remembered me. He showed her a photograph. He knows I was there before she died."

"Goddamn. What did he say?"

"Nothing. I insisted she was mistaken, but he wants me to meet her in person. I'll have to come up with something, an explanation."

"I wish I knew how much that damn girl told him," Langer said. "I still can't believe they were having an affair. There's no telling how much she knew or how much of it she told Haydon. I've got to think of something to explain my involvement with that warehouse business. I've got to be ready for him to spring it on me."

"Maybe you got your hands on the only tape," Quinn said. "Maybe Haydon still doesn't know what's going on with Roeg and Toy. I didn't find anything in the house, I didn't find anything in Parnas' place. Toy's gone. What can he know? He doesn't know anything."

"Alice could have told him everything."

"You're assuming she knew something. What makes you think Wayne told her? What makes you think he told her what he was involved with?"

"It's just the kind of crazy thing that would happen," Langer said. "Something you can't anticipate. It comes from your blind side and busts you so hard you can't even catch your breath."

"Then what's he waiting for? Why hasn't he moved to do something?"

Langer shook his head. He didn't know, and he could only think about it distractedly in between wondering how Roeg was going to dispose of him. Roeg couldn't very well retire him at his age. Roeg had never before had to get rid of anyone in the inner circle who was too young to retire. It was going to be nasty. Everything was falling apart, steadily, inexorably, like the towers of wooden blocks he had made as a child. He had constructed them carefully, matched the blocks perfectly, one on top of the other. Eventually, at some point, he would add one too many, and the tower made a slight but fateful list. From that instant he knew they were going to fall. It was irrevocable. He couldn't stop them from falling with any power on earth, and he was fascinated by the sight of them holding together in the long arc of their falling, their destruction confirmed far in advance of the actual devastation. That's the way he felt now. He was, at this moment in the long arc of his falling, intrigued by the fact that he was still holding together, though his ruin was already determined.

"What are you going to do?" she asked.

"I'll think of something."

There was nothing he could do. It was over. Roeg was going to dump him unceremoniously. Somehow. It didn't really matter how. His service with Roeg was through, and with it went all the prestige, the money, the power, of the past five years. He didn't own enough of Langer Media to give him any influence on the board. A seat, maybe. A vice-presidency, a silly toy executive, the object of whispered derision. A vice-presidency, maybe. Yes, Roeg would do that to him, because not only had Langer failed but in doing so he had also threatened the entire empire. Roeg would strip him of everything. He would humiliate him.

If he survived that, or even if he didn't, there would be the criminal charges to battle. He would have the best lawyers. His family would buy them if he couldn't. They might get him off, or at the very least they could buy him several years. Years of the worst kind of publicity.

Louise would not tolerate it. That didn't matter. They had long since quit caring for each other. But there was the family: his family, his children. How much did he want to take them through?

He never for a moment believed that Roeg was in any kind of danger at all. He was beyond reach. There *were* men who were beyond reach. Few people realized that. There *were* men beyond reach.

"Like what?" she persisted.

For a moment he didn't know what she had said, and then he didn't know what she meant. By the time he figured it out he caught another pair of headlights in the rearview mirror as they panned across the trunks of the pines and came into the asphalt lot, creeping slowly around the edges of the parking lot until they came up behind them and stopped.

He turned around and saw the insignia of the park police on the side of the door. No one got out of the car, but it idled behind them for a minute and then moved away, around the other side of the parking lot and out the drive the way it had entered.

He heard her breathe a little heavier.

"Is he going to strip you of everything?" she asked.

He felt a sudden sensation of nausea, a weakening of his muscles. She did not ask, "Are you still going to marry me?"; not "Let's run away together, leave it all behind"; not "Hold me, Bill, I love you no matter what happens." She didn't say any of those things, or things like them, or a million variations of them. She said, "Is he going to strip you of everything?"

"Yes, I think so." He was deliberately bleak about it. He didn't want to watch her trying to decide how she should play her options. It was best if she knew that disaster was inevitable. She had to decide how she wanted to meet it.

She was quiet.

He looked at her leaning against the door, looking at him. She had pressed him for nearly a year to divorce his wife, but he had put her off, avoiding the discomfort of an expensive divorce, retaining the respectability of marriage and the eroticism of an illicit affair. She had wanted him so ardently and he took her, everywhere in every way, feeling the aphrodisiac of his own importance and power, of her youth and beauty. He imagined it going on forever in just this way, everything the way he wanted it, she wanted him, he wanting her, the incredible energy of their sex together. He was crazy for it, like a satyr, indulging himself as if he were half his age, thinking he *was* half his age and that she found him as wonderful as he found her. No end, no end in sight.

And then, gradually, he acquired a different perspective, the clouded perspective of a man whose lust and selfishness and sense of power have evolved into emotions quite the opposite. Characteristically, he didn't see the evolution in progress, that his lust had become something deeper and more enduring, that his selfishness was giving way to the pleasures he found in pleasing her, that his sense of his own importance diminished in light of the value he placed in her. He didn't see it happening because for the first time in his life his preoccupations were turned away from himself toward someone else. He began to live for her.

She looked at him steadily.

"From what you know, can they charge me with anything?"

The air conditioner wasn't cooling as it should. It didn't work as well when the car was idling. He could feel the car getting gummy.

"Probably," he said. "You know of criminal activities and you've concealed it. That's a crime somehow. Withholding evidence. Something."

She ran the fingers of one hand through her blond hair to get it out of her face. It fell back where it was.

"You could save your neck by going to the police," he said. "You ought to do it."

She flashed him an angry look, but she didn't say anything.

"They can't get you for anything with Alice Parnas. As far as they're concerned, she committed suicide. It doesn't matter that they can place you there nearly an hour before she died." He took off his suit coat and threw it in the back seat. He loosened his tie. "But you know about Powell, you know about the warehouse business. I shouldn't have told you. You'd be all right if I hadn't told you."

She looked over the back seat, out the rear window. She looked at him. She looked down at her lap where she was nervously turning the rings on one hand.

"So what are you going to *do*?" she blurted, looking up. "You make it sound like it's hopeless. You said you'd think of something. I want to hear it. You owe me that."

There were tears in her voice. If it went too far she would say something he didn't want to hear. She would hurt him. He could sense it near the surface now, in her throat, crouching behind the first sob she would utter.

"You're all right," he said. He would have liked her to go through it with him, to support him, to wait for him. Be there. But deep within he knew the reality of it, and he wanted to spare himself the sight of what he most feared: that she would be unwilling, that she wouldn't do it . . . that she would leave him.

"They don't know that you know about the rest of it," he said. "I'm not going to tell them, so how would they find out? There's nothing they can do to you. They can't charge you with anything. You're all right. If all the other business comes out in the open, just tell the truth. There's no crime in having tried to discover if there were more tapes."

"What about the pills?"

"There were just two of you there. I'm not going to tell anyone that you forced her to swallow them. When all this finally winds down, that'll probably be the only secret to remain intact."

She continued to look at him, and he could see the

mechanism of her thoughts behind her eyes. It wouldn't be an immediate break, but she would stay well in the background. Would she even let their affair come out in the open? Would she try to conceal it? Would she have anything to do with him at all? What would his family think of his affair? What would his children think? None of it was reconcilable. He would lose it all, and he would lose her first.

She was subdued, but he could tell she was relieved. He had cut her loose from any further obligations. It wasn't necessary for her to go through it with him. With no real risk she could once again play the part he wanted her to play. Just go through the motions. He wouldn't think too hard about what she felt inside. He just wanted her to go through the motions with him.

She shifted a little in her seat, not caring too much about the hem of her dress now.

"What are you going to do, Bill?" Her voice was calm, but there was a little edge to it. She really wanted to know. She was concerned. "Bill?"

He looked at her eyes. He thought that in the faded jade fog of the dash lights he could see the deeper green.

"I have an idea," he said. "I think I have something worked out."

37

Mooney had gotten the registration number from the cabby's identification card and had gone back into the apartment to call the company to see if the number was still good. The picture on the card was of a Vietnamese, Hoang Lam.

Haydon had gone through the trunk of the car, looked under the back seat, felt down in the cracks of the front seats, under the front seats, under the floor mats, through the ashtrays, the glove compartment, through the junk in the plastic tray on the dash, and through the papers attached to the sun visors with rubber bands. He was sitting behind the steering wheel with the front door open looking through the windshield at the flashing lights on the patrol units and the morgue van. Policemen were milling around the opened front door of the apartment waiting for the coroner's investigator and the lab men to finish with the girl. A clutch of people were gathered around the outside of the apartment staring toward the policemen and the lighted doorway and hoping to get a glimpse of the sheet-covered corpse on the stretcher or to see some of the blood they had heard was splattered all over the walls.

There was a shuffling movement on the far side of the crowd, and it opened up to let Dystal and Lapierre through. They started toward the cab, Dystal rolling with a heavy-footed gait, Lapierre glancing back at the people.

Dystal approached the cab, bent down with his forearms resting on the windowsill of the opened door, and looked at Haydon.

"Anything of interest in here?" he asked.

Haydon shook his head. "Mooney's checking out the owner. A Vietnamese."

Lapierre came around and opened the opposite door and sat down like Haydon, with the door open.

"The black is Grover Ellis," he said. "He worked for a couple of city politicians and won a lot of recognition in the black community as an up-and-coming young man. He's considered running for the city council next time around. Owns some rental property in East Houston, married, with a family, well liked, well educated. He played football with Bill Langer at Rice. There's a file if you want to read it."

Haydon looked at Dystal, who raised his eyebrows and remained silent, peering through the opened window.

"What about the video tape?" Haydon asked. "Is Murray going to be able to make anything out of it?"

"He said it was going to be tough. When the camera was close enough to the crates to pick up the stenciling, there was a low light situation. When they were standing near the door, there was just that single bulb hanging down. When the lighting was better, where all the men were sitting down, the camera was farther away from the stacks of crates, and the stenciling might be too small. He's working on it. He's going to get good stills of all the men, though. They came in right under that bulb at the door."

"When will he have something for us?"

"Maybe midmorning tomorrow."

"And the list of warehouses?"

"Tomorrow morning too. They're on computers.

There'll be a printout of addresses with property descriptions. That might help. Then I can spot them on a map."

Haydon nodded. He could see a little of the living room through the opened door of the apartment. There were strobe flashes. The crime lab photographer would record her death from every necessary angle. The girl would be uncovered now. Everybody looking. Some people never got tired of looking at something grisly.

"If you're not going to want anything else from me," Lapierre said, "I'm going inside to help Mooney go through the rooms."

"Go ahead, Pete. Thanks."

Lapierre got out of the cab and walked back to the apartment, moving through the crowd and disappearing inside.

"Did you look in there?" Haydon asked Dystal.

"Yeah, we looked. We talked to Ed." Several streaks of perspiration emerged from a clipped sideburn and sparkled in the flashing lights as they trailed down his rounded jaw.

"I think we should come down on Ellis," Haydon said. "We're going to have to find out what Toy recorded. The other men in the film are going to be old hands at stonewalling. They're going to be used to playing games, not so easily frightened. I may be underestimating Ellis, but at least he's not going to have that kind of background, that kind of experience."

"I think you're right. I'd rake him over the coals." Dystal unconsciously fiddled with the outside rearview mirror on the car door. "You don't think they got Toy and the other girl?"

"No. We would have found them all like the girl inside. Or at least both girls."

"You want to have Langer picked up?"

"Not until we talk to Ellis."

"What about Toy? What do you think his situation is right now?"

"He's probably in a real bind. Rental car, maybe. No clothes because everything's in there. He may not have any money with him except what was in his wallet. Of course, he cashed the four-thousand-dollar check, but that was nearly a week ago. We don't know how fast they've been spending it. Ed and Pete may find a chunk of it hidden in there somewhere, or Toy might carry all of it with him just in case something unexpected like this should happen. Or maybe they won't find anything in there, not because Toy didn't leave it behind but because whoever killed the girl found it and took it with them. If we don't find the money it doesn't mean Toy has it. I doubt if he's going to go to the trouble to get another apartment. He'll be traveling light now. A hotel or motel. Or a friend. Mr. Hoang Lam might be able to help us out there."

"There's a lot of fancy video equipment in there," Dystal said. "I guess Toy's got duplicates of that damn tape scattered in hidey-holes all over the city. I'll bet he's got his ass covered on that point."

Haydon nodded.

"How was he registered here?"

"Richard M. Kaun. K-A-U-N."

"Then he's probably got some kind of ID in that name. I'll bet he used it to rent a car. I'll have them start checking the agencies. And the banks too. No tellin' how many bank accounts he's got squirreled away in different names."

"If he rented a car in that name, he will have abandoned it by now."

"Maybe so."

Haydon saw Sublette's stocky frame coming through the crowd toward them. Perspiration was coming through the light blue uniform shirt in dark splotches under his arms and across the top of his stomach. All the beef he had put on lifting weights in the department gym was suffering in the still night heat. He approached the car.

"Excuse me," he said to both men. "Detective Mooney wants y'all to look at something."

Dystal straightened up from the car window and looked at the young officer. There was a salty drop of sweat on the tip of Sublette's nose.

"Hot in there, son?"

"Yessir. There's no circulation back in those bedrooms."

"You look purty damn soggy," Dystal said.

"I always sweat a lot," Sublette said. He grinned a little and wiped his nose on his shirtsleeve with a shrug of his shoulder.

The three men returned to the apartment. The girl's body was covered again and Gibbs's men were bringing in the gurney to pick her up. The crime lab technicians were still occupied in various parts of the apartment. Everyone was soaked with sweat.

"You guys can have it," Gibbs said to Haydon, as he stood back and watched his two assistants fold the sheet under the girl and then lift the whole bundle onto the aluminum gurney. "You're not going to be able to stand it in here in another couple of hours if somebody don't clean this up. Next people rent this place gets a new carpet, new paint job. They'll think, 'All *right*. Lucky us!' And then the first person they meet that lives here is gonna say, 'You know *why* you got a new carpet and a new paint job?' " He laughed. "Think they'll want to lay on the floor there and watch *Love Boat*?"

He laughed again, including them in the humor he imagined at the expense of the next tenants, and followed his men as they wheeled the gurney out the door to give the crowd the brief glimpse of the sheet-covered body they had waited so long to see.

Haydon and Dystal followed Sublette down the hallway to the last bedroom on the left. The room was a mess. Everything that could be taken apart and scattered had been. Mooney and Lapierre were standing in the middle of the rubble looking at something Mooney was holding.

"They really went through here," Mooney said, looking up as they walked in. "Pete and I got to looking around, and everywhere we thought to look they'd beat us to it. Everywhere." He grinned. "Almost." He handed an object to Haydon.

Haydon recognized it instantly, a small plastic ivory-colored box with a false front that looked like an electrical wall outlet. Inside were three keys.

"I see those things advertised all the time," Mooney said. "In those sections stuffed in *Parade* magazine that always fall out when you open it up. Peddle all sorts of nifty gadgets like teeth whitener and fifty-piece tool sets for five bucks." He pointed to the plastic box in Haydon's hands. "Keep your valuables in there and the burglars don't find them. Simple enough to install. Just unwire the real outlet, tape up the wires, push 'em aside, and slip that thing in. I don't even know what made me check it out."

Haydon looked at the keys. "Three different numbers. Three different boxes? They're all Mosler keys. Every safety deposit box I've ever seen has been a Mosler box. They all could be in the same bank, or three separate banks." He handed everything to Lapierre. "Pete, you'd better get down to Intel Bancshares in the morning."

"They didn't have him listed with a safety deposit box," Lapierre said. "Just the checking and savings accounts."

"Then you'd better start calling all the banks and savings and loans in the morning."

"There're some commercial security vaults too. I think a couple of 'em are open twenty-four hours," Dystal said. "That'd be his speed. He could get to it in a hurry."

"The telephone book's in the dining room," Lapierre said, stepping over the junk in the room and disappearing down the hall.

"Anything else?" Haydon asked.

"Nothing yet. Either Toy was a paranoid housekeeper regarding his personal records, or whoever beat us here swept it clean. We couldn't even find grocery receipts in the kitchen trash. The man left no trace."

Haydon stood in the middle of the room and looked around at the stripped mattresses, the tangle of coat hangers and clothes and shoes, the broken and gutted clothes chest. Whoever had been here had left nothing behind but refuse. The girl too. Nothing but refuse.

Lapierre stepped in the door. "There's only one commercial safety deposit facility that's open twenty-four hours. It's way out in Town and Country Village. They wouldn't give me any information over the telephone. I'm going to have to go out there. I don't think it'll take too long if I cut across Gessner."

"Good," Haydon said. "Take one of the patrol units outside with you. If Toy actually has an account there, and he hasn't already beat you to it, take whatever's in the box and stake the place out. Have the patrol unit stay out of sight as backup. Wait all night if you have to. Let me know the account's status as soon as you can." He turned to Dystal. "Bob, can we have someone to start trying to locate those other boxes first thing in the morning? We might get lucky. In the meantime, Ed and I will go talk with Hoang Lam and Grover Ellis."

When he saw the two police cars turn off Fondren ahead of him, he tensed. But he didn't say anything. Lai was fooling with her Walkman, trying to get another station. He slowed and cut in on Clarewood, meaning to come in the back way on Bonhomme. After a couple more turns he eased into the intersection that would give him the first view of the apartments. He saw the flashers bouncing cherry and sapphire off the apartment building across from their front door. His ears began to ring. He rounded the corner and approached the drive into the apartment building. There was a police car at the mouth of the drive and a police officer with his cap pushed back on his sweaty forehead waving on the slowing traffic. As he passed the drive entrance he looked down the row of cars, saw the police cars, the crowd, and the morgue van backed in among the cars. At that moment Lai glanced up, stared blankly a second, and screamed.

He swung at her with an opened hand, missed, then grabbed her wrist with his right hand and jerked her away from the half-opened car door as she tried to get out. With his left hand he whipped the steering wheel around and plunged the car into a drive-through behind another complex. He made two more quick turns, accelerating in the straights down the alleys as Lai screamed and fought him, before he brought the car to a screeching stop near the entrance of another street. He pulled her over to him and held her, squeezing her to him, burying her wailing mouth in his chest, holding tight to keep himself from flying apart as much as to comfort her.

Jesus Christ, how had they done it? They had found her and they had tried to make her talk. That was all it could be. He no more doubted what *had* happened than he doubted what *would* happen. It hadn't had to be this way. There were other ways Roeg could have dealt with it. If he wasn't going to go for it, there were other ways. He hadn't had to do it like this.

Lai fell into a rhythmic, incessant sobbing. She was clinging to the front of his shirt with a gripping rigidity, and he could feel the dampness of her tears through the thin cotton. He let her cry for what seemed too long before he eased her down in the seat. She lay on her side curled in a fetal position, her head next to his thigh. He leaned across and locked her door. Her crying was wrenching, the sound of faraway times and faraway places. He had heard women cry like this in dozens of countries around the world. It was always the same. There was only one language for this kind of emotion.

He slowly pulled out of the alley and made his way over to Bellaire and turned west. Every moment counted now. Everything was shattered, and he had to regroup. But he needed his tools. In a few blocks he reached Gessner, turned north, and headed toward Town and Country Village.

38

Both men were quiet as they drove back to Haydon's house, where Mooney was to pick up the department car so he could go directly home from wherever they finished that night. It was a little after ten o'clock when they turned into the gates and circled the drive.

Haydon pulled up behind the department car and stopped.

"Where do you want to go first?" Mooney asked, opening the door. "Yellow or black?"

"I've changed my mind," Haydon said.

Mooney looked at him.

"I want to talk to Josef Roeg."

"Now?" Mooney frowned and looked at his watch. "We just going to walk in cold? How do you want to handle it? You going to spring something on him?"

"I'll go by myself," Haydon said. "Let's let Grover Ellis wait for now, but you'd better go ahead and talk to Hoang Lam. He might provide a lead to Toy. If it doesn't look right to you, call for a backup."

"What about Pete?"

"I'll keep my radio with me. Let's keep in touch."

"Okay." Mooney sighed. His tone of voice indicated that he would do what Haydon said, but it seemed like strange timing to him. "Keep your head down."

Mooney got out of the Vanden Plas and walked around in front of the headlights, fumbling in his pockets for the car keys. He found them, got in the car, and started the motor. Haydon could see him fiddling with the air conditioner. As Mooney eased the beige Ford around the drive, Haydon followed him and pushed the remote control for the gates. When they pulled out into the street, they turned in opposite directions.

The gates at Roeg's estate were closed too, and when Haydon's headlights raked across the windows of the security house he could see two men in suits look up from their television. Both men got up and stepped outside. One approached the car while the other stood back.

"Yessir, can I help you?"

Haydon already had his wallet out and showed his shield.

"Detective Stuart Haydon to see Mr. Roeg," he said.

The guard frowned and took the wallet and tilted it toward the lights mounted at the gates. Haydon looked at his regulation tie, the pale gray suit with an almost invisible plaid pattern, the close-cropped haircut sprayed in place.

"You have an appointment?" the man asked. "We didn't have anyone listed for tonight."

"I don't have an appointment, but I think Mr. Roeg will want to see me. You'd better check."

"Just a minute." The guard took the wallet, walked back to his partner and said something, both looking at the shield, and then went inside to use the telephone while the other man looked at Haydon from where he stood.

Haydon watched the man inside through the windows. He was looking at the shield, reading something from it. He nodded. He shook his head. He looked up at the bank of television monitors and shook his head again. Finally he nodded again, hung up the telephone, and came back out to the car.

"All right, sir," he said, returning Haydon's shield. "Are you wearing a firearm?"

"Yes, I am."

"I'll have to ask you to leave it here while you're inside, sir."

Haydon looked at him. The silence was long enough to make the man uneasy.

"I'm a police officer," Haydon said, his voice getting soft. "I don't give my handgun to anyone. Now you open that gate, or I'm going to call enough units down on this place to give the newspapers something to talk about for a month, and then I'm going to arrest you for interfering with my business."

He pushed the window button and the glass went up between the two men as they looked at each other. Haydon put the Vanden Plas in gear.

The man stared at him a second longer, then turned on his heel and fast-walked back to the guardhouse. The gates opened, and as Haydon drove through he saw the man on the telephone again. Presumably to tattle on Haydon's ill manners and heavy artillery.

He followed the winding drive illuminated by hooded footlights through the thick woods and soon caught glimpses through the underbrush of the lamps around the house. When the car emerged into the parking area, two men standing in the drive waiting for him motioned to him where to park.

Haydon turned off the motor and got out.

"This way, sir."

Haydon followed one of the men across the paving stones to the large door in the central section of the house. The door opened as they approached, and a middle-aged man in casual clothes smiled at Haydon.

"Detective Haydon?" The man backed inside the entrance hall, allowing Haydon to come in. "Harvey Gage." He extended his hand and Haydon shook it. He recognized him from Toy's tape.

"I hope you'll excuse our precautions outside," Gage said, smiling gratuitously. "Mr. Roeg has a rather elaborate security system. Sometimes the men involved err on the side of overprecaution. We never reprimand on that account. In fact, I sometimes wonder if there *is* such a thing as overprecaution these days. Terrorism is becoming so much more sophisticated.''

He said all this standing with his hands casually rammed down into the pockets of his sporty linen pants. He smiled. Haydon looked at him, but didn't smile and didn't say anything.

Gage's expression never faltered. He simply removed his hands from his pockets and started walking down the hall that led to their right from the entrance.

"Mr. Roeg usually gets ready for bed rather early, though he doesn't actually go to sleep until much later. He's in his robe and pajamas."

They walked the rest of the way in silence.

Gage led him into Roeg's sanctum and Haydon quickly took in the furnishings, the junky curved desk backed by computer screens and keyboards, the wall of windows and photographs, the projectors, the screen, the sofas, the two doors opening off the room in addition to the one they had just come through.

He followed Gage to the arrangement of sofas.

"Please, have a seat. Can I get you anything?"

"No, thank you."

"I'll get Mr. Roeg." Gage walked to the last door at the end of the room near the movie screen and went out. Haydon started to look around, but the door opened again immediately and Gage returned, with Roeg walking behind him dressed in a burgundy robe with silk lapels and collar.

Haydon stood.

"Mr. Haydon," Roeg said. He didn't offer his hand but sat down on the sofa across from Haydon. Gage kept walking and went out the door that led to the hallway, closing it after him.

"I'm sorry to bother you at this late hour," Haydon said, sitting down again. "But I'm investigating a case that involves persons in your employ, and I think it's time to talk to you about it."

"The homicide at Langer Media."

"Yes."

Roeg nodded, kicked off his slippers, turned sideways on the sofa, and buried his feet into one of the cushions.

"Go ahead," he said. Haydon almost didn't hear him.

Haydon quickly outlined the progression of events: the murder of Wayne Powell at the Langer Media offices, the discovery that Powell was doing extra work after hours for Langer, Langer's elevated position in Roeg operations, Powell's relationship with one Ricky Toy, who in turn worked for Roeg, the suicide of Powell's girlfriend, Toy's mysterious disappearance, and the subsequent homicide of one of Toy's girlfriends earlier that night. He listed these incidents with the barest narrative connection, never explaining how he had discovered any of the relationships to which he referred. When he was through, he paused. Roeg did not comment.

"We have three deaths, one a probable suicide. Persons with whom you work closely are likewise closely connected with the other two victims. Graphically it appears as a triangle: you at the apex, Bill Langer and Ricky Toy at the two lower angles. Other persons involved are involved through those two men. You remain at the apex."

He paused again, then said, "I talked with Bill Langer yesterday morning. I asked him if he knew Toy, and he said he didn't. I showed him a photograph of Toy, and he still claimed ignorance. Why do you think he did that?"

While Roeg had been listening to Haydon's discourse, his eyes had roved over the gallery of photographs on the wall to Haydon's left. When Haydon asked the question, Roeg's eyes came down and rested on Haydon. He seemed mildly pensive.

"Sometimes it's redundant for Mr. Langer to claim ignorance," Roeg said. "It's usually evident by his actions long before he confirms it orally." He allowed himself a small smile. "I don't know the answer to your question. I . . . can't answer for Mr. Langer." He adjusted his feet, turned a little more toward Haydon. "But you didn't come here to ask me that. You suggested that I—being at the apex, as you put it—am an integral part of this . . . situation. Would you like to be more specific?"

Haydon simply looked at him and then stood up. It was an unexpected movement and Roeg's eyes grew cautious. Haydon walked over to the wall of photographs, folded his arms, and looked at them unhurriedly. Some of the images were familiar, the way a television personality or a film star is familiar simply because their constant exposure to the viewer has made them famous. These images, however, were famous because of their shocking brutality.

He turned to Roeg. "Can you explain your fascination with this?"

Roeg's reaction was unexpected too. Haydon had anticipated another fatuous smile; then, perhaps, some flippant response. Instead, Roeg turned squarely on the sofa to face Haydon and the wall of pictures. He put his feet into his slippers and sat back. There was no smile. There was nothing at all on his face, but he looked at the pictures.

"Fascination." Roeg thought a moment, his eyes on the pictures. "I'm not sure that's the proper word in this instance. Fascination." He strung out the four syllables, seeming not to have his mind on them. Then he stood, put his hands into the pockets of his robe, and walked closer. He looked at the photographs in silence, his features assuming an almost reverential expression.

"How does one begin talking about violence?" he said quietly. "You might as well be asking about one's fascination with love. The consideration is that large; no, larger. It is larger than love. Violence is at once mankind's most primitive and sophisticated attribute. We hardly understand it, yet each generation improves on its uses. It is the single red thread that runs through our history, and it looms in our future to the exclusion of life itself as a swelling, red, mushroom-shaped cloud.

"How do we talk about it? There are so many . . . perspectives from which to approach it: historical, anthropological, scientific, philosophical, psychological, political, religious. It is pervasive. Even though it predates nearly every human emotion, man has mostly ignored it as an idea until relatively recently. It has been so much an integral part of his psyche that he could not separate it, hold it out and look at it, examine it as a concept."

Roeg smiled condescendingly.

"Perhaps men dealt with it first through religion. They made the gods responsible for it. Man did not even own up to its presence within him. The gods wrought violence on men. With the evolution of the dualistic Judeo-Christian philosophy, man removed this responsibility from his God and gave it to Satan, or the Devil, still keeping it well removed from himself. Later, when man began to stand back and look at himself within a historical framework, he spoke of violence in terms of societies and governments, armed conflicts between states . . . he spoke of war. War. Aggression involving hundreds, thousands, millions, and the motivation of which was disguised as conflict arising from greed, expansionism, incompatible ideologies, prejudices, religion, defense. Man spoke of violence with averted eyes, never confronting it, never approaching it directly, never isolating it, but always within the context of societal forms.

"Then man stumbled onto the discovery of his unconscious. Freud, after a false start which placed inordinate importance on the libido, finally came to the conclusion that man was dominated by dualistic forces: the life instinct . . . and the death instinct. Man functioned under a driving impulse to destroy, either himself or others. He could do little to escape it. Then Konrad Lorenz gave this frame of thought new dimension by holding that human aggressiveness is an instinctive impulse that is continuously accumulating in the neural centers. When enough of it accumulates, it is likely to explode in the form of destructiveness. Mostly it is activated by outside stimuli, but even when it isn't, the aggressive instinct will spontaneously erupt. And now, with the arrival of today's reigning psychological theory, behaviorism, the emphasis of causation switches from biology to sociology. Violence is seen as arising from man's reaction to disastrous social conditions, to cultural factors, to frustration with his general condition."

Roeg shrugged.

"It doesn't matter. That man is attracted to violence, by whatever motivation, is one of the great truths of life. Whether he is a barbarian or a sophisticate, a pauper or a billionaire, a sniveling weakling who means nothing to anyone or one of the world's power brokers who influences millions of lives, man . . . all men are attracted to violence.''

Roeg came a little closer to the photographs, his eyes ranging over them lovingly. Haydon watched him, noting the strange nature of the black holes of his eyes, taking his time to examine his rare physique. Suddenly Roeg flicked his eyes away from the photographs to Haydon.

"Do you want to hear this? You ask a question, and I am giving you a dissertation. But then, it wasn't a simple question, was it?"

Haydon shook his head. "No, it wasn't. Go ahead."

39

....

Haydon waited silently for Roeg to continue. He did not want to distract him from the murky channels of his thoughts. Whatever passages Roeg's mind was taking, Haydon wanted to follow. He wanted to see all that Roeg would show him of his strangely ordered psyche.

Roeg turned and walked past one of the windows to another section of the wall covered with photographs. He looked at these with as much interest and concentration as if he were seeing them for the first time. He became so absorbed in them that he seemed to have forgotten he was not alone. Haydon waited.

Then, abruptly, Roeg moved away from the wall of photographs. He passed behind one of the sofas, hands still in the pockets of his robe, and walked over to the film projector.

"I've studied violence for a long time, Mr. Haydon. I have . . . become a connoisseur. I have . . . an understanding of the principles; I can discriminate and appreciate the subtleties. Like all connoisseurs I surround myself with my obsessions. You know about these." He took a hand out of a pocket and let it rest on the projector. "It is, admittedly, an esoteric collection. It will eventually go to a major university. The definitive archive of violence on film.

"As my understanding of violence increased so did the refinement of my tastes. While I continued to collect every kind of film depicting violence, I began to pursue more rarefied forms of it. War is a general violence, large-scale. I was curious about a smaller canvas, a more concentrated record. I literally wanted to move in close. How could I do this? Your business, Mr. Haydon, would have been one way. Homicide. But, of course, that was impossible."

He smiled and held up two fingers.

"Two recent newspaper articles. The first I would have paid anything to have had on film. An elderly man, a retired accountant despondent over his health, had killed his wife and then, apparently, had tried to commit suicide by slashing his wrists. He was found before he died and his life was saved. The curious thing . . . the fascinating thing about this was that it took this man four hours to murder his wife. He used a sledgehammer and struck her seventeen times. He told the police, 'I started at eight A.M. and finished around noontime.' He actually said that. Seventeen times in four hours! Remarkable.

"The second article. It was a rather lengthy expression of concern by administrators in the nation's major universities regarding students' acts of 'private brutality,' 'personal violence,' of 'human meanness' that they say manifests itself on campuses 'in mad and infinite varieties.' "

Roeg paused a beat to let the point of the two articles create its own emphasis.

"And you ask me what is my fascination with violence. It is only that I openly acknowledge my attraction to it. Freud made us aware of the power of sexuality in our lives and revolutionized the way we live with it. To speak of sexual freedom now is passé; we take it for granted. It permeates our lives to the point of preoccupation, and this new perspective has literally changed the way we live. But who will do the same for violence? It too permeates our lives, and yet we hypocritically pretend to find it abhorrent, though our entertainment and literature and art and politics and society reek with it. We relish it while pretending to reject it. Regarding our attitudes toward violence, we are whited sepulchers.''

Roeg stopped and pensively reached out and put a single finger on the loose reel of the projector, which was loaded with film ready to be threaded. Very deliberately he turned it one revolution, uncoiling a single ribbon of film, which dangled from the reel like a black thread of something evil threatening to unravel in the room. He slowly reversed the revolution and re-coiled the film. His eyes, with their own peculiar blackness, studied the white screen at the opposite end of the room as if seeing, in an afterimage visible only to them, the scenes of violence that had danced there for so many hours.

"My 'fascination,' Mr. Haydon, is with the Omega of violence. Psychologists readily admit, even if we will not, to the seductive attraction of violence, to its strange and wonderful potency. It is something we crave and to which we will ultimately become addicted. Nothing on earth can equal the sensation and excitement of violence. The energy it generates is like a fabulous heat from another sun, and the human race is attracted to it like the proverbial moth to the flame. We have a deadly fascination with it; we cannot keep away from it. We will go to it again and again, like the moth, until we destroy ourselves in its fire.''

With the flick of his wrist Roeg gave the reel a thrusting reverse spin, and the black polyester film shot off the reel, spewing crazily in glistening coils that jumped and jerked to the floor like disemboweled intestines, the viscera of his obsessions tangling at his feet.

As the reel turned slowly to a halt, Roeg looked at Haydon with a tense expression that was both contemptuous and challenging.

Haydon returned the stare and then said, "By being at the apex of my illustration, Mr. Roeg, you become the central point in everything that has taken place. Everything leads to you. All of the confusion, all of the secrecy, all of the deaths.''

Roeg took his hands out of his pocket and, without

moving a step, began rewinding the film by hand. He did this quite naturally, completely relaxed, unhurried.

"Are you accusing me of being in some way responsible for one or all of these deaths you've enumerated?" he asked.

"I don't accuse. I gather evidence, and when I have sufficient evidence I arrest and indict."

"Then am I being arrested?"

"No. You are being warned."

"Warned?" Roeg looked up from the reel. "Warned in what respect?"

"The way it appears to me is that Ricky Toy had worked for you long enough to discover that you were involved in questionable activities. He filmed those activities and then proceeded to extort a large sum of money from you, in exchange for not going either public or to the police with what he had found. Someone has now murdered one of Toy's girlfriends, and I think that Mr. Toy might believe you are somehow responsible for that death. If this is indeed the case, then I also believe that your life might be in danger. I believe Ricky Toy is fully capable of thinking in terms of revenge. This is a warning in that respect."

Roeg was moving more quickly with his rewinding. He spun the reel with the index finger of his right hand inserted into one of the small holes at the corner of the reel. His left hand guided the film between the disc sides of the reel.

"I have a very good security system, Mr. Haydon, but thank you anyway. I'll have this information passed on to my men."

He continued with the rewinding.

"You might also pass on to your men that Toy has a very elaborate backup system for this operation," Haydon said. "More complex, perhaps, than your men might believe, and certainly too complex to yield to clumsy tactics that will not come close to unraveling it."

Haydon finally left the spot in front of the wall of photographs, where he had been standing ever since Roeg had begun his long discourse on violence, and walked around the projector to confront him. When he spoke, his voice was reasonable, without emotion.

"Tell them too, that if one more homicide occurs in this case, I will follow its 'red thread' all the way to the end of the rope. I am not, Mr. Roeg, in the business of violence as you suggested. I rarely see it because I enter the picture after the fact. My dealings are with the debris of violence. I see the trash in its wake, and it's ugly. But if I'm lucky, Mr. Roeg, I eventually root out its cause, I find the source, and often that proves to be the ugliest thing of all."

Roeg did not turn to face Haydon but continued spinning the reel. The hem of his dark burgundy robe reached to the floor and covered the coils of film, which now appeared to Haydon to be whipping up from beneath Roeg's robe like dancing entrails stripped from his bowels and threaded onto the spool. Like a fourth figure added to the ancient triad of the Fates, his presence formed a modern quaternity. Standing at a spindle of his own devising, he spun from his own viscera a fearful scarlet strand to be added to the string of the Fates, a strand that dealt not with the beginning, length, and end of men's lives, but with the nature of their deaths.

Haydon did not remember turning and walking out of the room, nor did he remember the long hall or the lurking figure of Harvey Gage, who stood back in the entryway and watched him fumble at the heavy wooden door before he tripped the automatic lock and let Haydon outside into the weighted heat of the summer night. He remembered only stopping at the edge of the paving stones and lighting a cigarette that had somehow gotten into his mouth. He inhaled deeply, aware of his trembling hand and the perspiration that seemed to have jumped from every pore of his body as he stood and looked across the courtyard, trying to calm down.

Roeg's security men were nowhere in sight. The Vanden Plas was twenty feet away, where the edge of the woods came right up to the paving stones. A lamp pole stood slightly to one side of the car. Haydon took several more draws on his cigarette and then threw it down and started over. He looked up at the lamp. The globe was almost lost in a flittering swarm of night moths seeking the heat within the glass, clamoring in the blue haze of dust that came from the frantic beating of their wings.

No one appeared to help Haydon get into his car, no one stood where the mouth of the drive entered the woods, no one waved to him as he passed through the already opened gates and drove away into the dark.

Haydon had not kept a hand radio with him as he had promised Mooney, and it was a few minutes before he noticed the red light flashing on his beeper, which he had left lying in the console tray between the seats. He checked his watch. He had been at Roeg's just a little over an hour. It was approaching twelve o'clock.

He pulled up to a service station and used a pay telephone to call the dispatcher.

There were two messages. Ed Mooney was waiting for him at Primo's. Call or come over. Pete Lapierre wanted him to call the number of another pay telephone. Haydon hung up and called Mooney first.

The cashier at Primo's laid the telephone down beside the register and called for Mooney. Haydon listened to her chat with the people who were paying, heard the register bell ring, heard her counting out change. Mooney picked up the telephone.

"Nothing happened with me," he said. "Lam was gone and wasn't expected back until a little after midnight. Kid there about ten years old. I told him I was a friend of Mr. Hoang's and that I hadn't seen him in a long time and wanted to surprise him. Promised him two bucks when I came back if he wouldn't say anything about me coming by."

"The boy didn't say where he had gone?"

"He didn't know. What about your deal?"

"I'll tell you when I get over there."

"Talked to Pete?"

"I'm getting ready to call him now. I'll be there in twenty minutes."

Haydon hung up and called the number Lapierre had left with the dispatcher.

"Pete Lapierre."

"This is Haydon."

"Jackpot here, Stuart. We beat Toy to his cache, but don't get excited. No video tapes. What I found were two false I.D.s. Got a pencil? Two passports and two California driver's licenses. One in the name of Richard M. Kaun, and one in the name of Richard K. Malik. His photograph's on all four documents. And twelve hundred dollars in hundreds, fifties, and twenties. I'd say we've seriously limited his ability to get around."

"Excellent. Where are you?"

"I'm across a parking lot here at an all-night pharmacy. I can see the security company from where I'm standing, and I've got a backup unit hidden around the corner."

"You'd better get those names to somebody back at the office so they can start checking flights, car rentals, everything. And in the morning the banks will have to be checked for all three names. Bob was going to give us some help on that."

"I've already called it in. You want me to stay with this?"

"Yes. There's a chance Toy will try to pick those things up. He's going to be hurt if he doesn't."

"How did it go at your end?"

Haydon explained to him what had happened. "I'm going to meet Ed now and then try to track down Hoang. Let us know if something comes up."

He was only twenty blocks from Primo's, a little Tex-Mex restaurant not far from downtown between Rosalie and Smith that made possibly the best chicken enchiladas and guacamole in the city. Mooney was well into a serving of each of these when Haydon found him at a small corner table. Haydon ordered a guacamole for himself and a cup of coffee. He massaged his eyes, which were beginning to sting, and brought Mooney up to date.

"The interview was long overdue," he said, finishing the rundown and mixing a lot of cream with his coffee. "I wish I had talked to him earlier. It may have triggered something."

"This is a weird story, Stuart," Mooney said. He had finished his food and was nibbling tostadas. Haydon thought his sunburn looked worse. "Something better break on it. Does Roeg think we know more than we do?"

"I think so. I hope so."

"Does that give us an advantage?"

"I'm hoping he will step up his search for Toy. He's going to make a mistake, maybe give us an opening."

"You think so?"

"Somebody will."

"I want a look at that video. You think it's going to blow Roeg out of the water? You think it's big stuff?"

Haydon nodded. He gulped down the coffee and motioned to the waiter for a refill. He took it like medicine, needing the caffeine to pick up his flagging energy.

"Where does Hoang live?" he asked.

"Allen Parkway."

Haydon started on his guacamole, dipping the salad with the chips from the fresh basket of tostadas. When he finished they asked for more coffee and Haydon smoked two more cigarettes. Killing time. When it was almost one o'clock they left.

40
····································

Haydon left the Vanden Plas in the parking lot of Brennan's, which was just around the corner from Primo's, and rode with Mooney, who took the department car along Westheimer and then north on Montrose. Allen Parkway was a broad curving boulevard that lay on the southern bank of Buffalo Bayou on the northwestern edge of downtown. On the other side of the bayou was Memorial Drive, and in between the two was a beautiful greenbelt of parks with hike and bike trails that ran from downtown west, and almost all the way to the vast reaches of Memorial Park. Both streets represented the most appealing routes from the skyscrapers toward the ritzy neighborhoods west.

The Allen Parkway Village was a rather attractive name for an unattractive forty-year-old deteriorating public housing project that sat on thirty-seven acres of prime Houston real estate between downtown and, a little farther in the opposite direction, River Oaks. The project was a festering scab on the northern edge of the Fourth Ward, the city's oldest black community, itself sliding deeper into dereliction. The sprawling complex of orange brick apartments was once largely occupied by blacks, but with the first wave of immigrants fleeing Vietnam in 1975 the Village became predominantly Indo-Chinese. Now nearly three thousand Vietnamese lived in the dilapidated warrens of the project.

It had been a year since the Houston Housing Authority had voted to raze the projects, which had been a controversial eyesore longer than some people wanted to remember, and make the land available for development. Being just across the Gulf Freeway from high-dollar downtown real estate, the rotting slum was in a location that was strategically appealing to developers. But it would be still another year before the residents were moved, and in the meantime there was no great interest by the Housing Authority to maintain even minimal repairs to buildings which had for so long sapped the city's coffers and were already hopelessly deteriorated.

Mooney pulled off Allen Parkway into the project's streets, slowly working his way toward the center, toward Hoang's apartment. After a few turns he pulled to the curb.

"We'd better walk from here," he said.

They got out and locked the car. The projects had an unhealthy reputation for gangs of teenagers, who roamed the neighborhood vandalizing and testing their ability to run petty extortion rackets. This was an imitation of a larger, citywide problem within the Asian community, which was the second largest in the nation. The Chinese tongs were well established in Houston's crime world. They were organized and efficient, and their members commanded a fearful respect within the Chinese community. They were known as "the gentlemen." The Vietnamese gangsters, however, required and received no such respect. They were considered little more than thugs and hoodlums by their own people. Their influence was supported solely by the fear they engendered within the community, which effectively sealed the lips of their fellow Vietnamese victims, making police investigation almost impossible. Though their organization differed from the Chinese, it was a potent force. The four or five gangs that dominated the Vietnamese underworld in Houston had direct links to the Oriental syndicates in New Orleans, Los Angeles, and San Francisco.

The two men moved along a potholed street that served both as a parking area and a sidewalk. A series of short straight cement walks ran under a maze of sagging clotheslines and up to the stoops of the apartments. The doors and windows of the apartments were open, and the aroma of Oriental cooking floated in the gummy night air along with the lilting tonal monosyllables of Vietnamese dialects. In the splashes of light that came out of the apartments, Haydon could see that some of the bare front yards had been turned into little plots of vegetable gardens, their small neat rows presenting a sane orderliness in the sad disorderliness of the declining buildings.

They passed two boys smoking on the hood of a car and cut across a yard and between two buildings. They came out next to an abandoned refrigerator and another block of stoops. Mooney ducked under a couple of clotheslines and approached a ragged screen door. A radio was playing, and Dolly and Kenny were singing "Islands in the Stream."

Mooney knocked on the doorframe. A little boy came from the dim interior.

"Hey, buddy. Remember me?" Mooney asked, bending down. The boy grinned broadly. "Your daddy in yet?" The boy nodded and disappeared. "I don't know if this guy's his daddy or not," Mooney said under his breath.

Silently a man appeared at the door.

"Hoang Lam?" Mooney asked. The man nodded. "Good, good," Mooney said grinning. "I'm a friend of old Ricky's. He was supposed to meet me tonight in a taxicab, but he never showed up. Somebody told me you owned the cab and that you might know where Ricky went to."

The man looked at Mooney soberly. The little boy came up and stood beside him, and the man put his arm around his neck.

"Why you try to fool me?" Hoang asked. "I don't have anything to fear from police."

Even in the frail light Haydon could see Mooney's embarrassment.

Mooney took out his shield and showed it to the man. "Okay, you win. How'd you know I was a cop?"

The man's slight shoulders rose and fell, and he smiled faintly.

"You are looking for Mr. Toy? He has my taxicab. That is all I know."

Haydon moved up on the stoop and held out his shield too. "I'm Detective Haydon, Mr. Hoang. Why does Mr. Toy have your car?"

Hoang pushed open the screen door a little ways and looked up and down the courtyard.

"Come in, please, sirs," he said, and spoke sharply to the little boy, who ran over to the radio and turned it off. The room had only a concrete floor, a sofa, and two wooden chairs. There was a reed mat to one side and several overturned paint buckets used for additional chairs. A handpainted picture of a tropical moonlight scene hung over the sofa, small and lost on the bare wall.

Hoang motioned for Haydon and Mooney to sit on the wooden chairs. He sat on the sofa, on its edge, and his little boy stood beside him, his dark eyes glued to Mooney.

"We are very poor now," Hoang said matter-of-factly. "But we work very hard and everything is very okay. We will not always be poor."

Mooney squirmed on the chair.

"My family want to be good Houston citizen. We want to help the police. But must be careful. Is my friend Mr. Toy in trouble?"

"We think his life might be in danger," Haydon said. "He's missing. We're trying to find him."

Hoang nodded seriously and looked at them.

"Why did he have your taxi?" Haydon repeated.

"The taxi belong to me, my brother Danh and Du. We drive the taxi in turn, eight hour for each one. The taxi never stop. This very good. Ricky Toy ask me to have my taxicab tonight. He pay more I make driving. That is all."

"When did Mr. Toy get your taxi?"

"One of his girlfriend come and drive it away about three o'clock."

"What was her name?"

"Yue."

"You spoke to her?"

"Oh, yes."

"She didn't say what they were going to do with the taxi?" Mooney asked.

"No."

"Where were you earlier tonight?"

Hoang looked at Mooney with curiosity, then answered.

"I borrow car to get my son and friend at Chinatown movie."

"How long have you known Mr. Toy?" Haydon asked.

Hoang's eyes widened as he thought, looking at nothing out the screen door. "One year."

"How did you meet him?"

"I get him at Hobby in taxi. He see I am Vietnamese. He tell me he is there many time. We learn we are in many same place same time. That make us feel like friend. We talk for long time. Now he call me when he want taxi."

"How often is that?"

Hoang smiled. "Mr. Toy don't need taxi. He has two very good car. But sometime he take taxi I think to give me work."

"Where do you take him?" Mooney asked.

"Oh, maybe Chinatown." Hoang was cautious, his eyes floating away.

"Where in Chinatown?"

"Different place. To eat. Other thing."

"Does Ricky Toy go to the illegal gambling clubs there?"

Hoang raised his eyebrows, his eyes diverted. "I think so," he said softly.

"Does he go alone?"

Hoang was very uncomfortable with the questioning now.

"Sometime," he said.

"Do the girls go with him?"

Hoang lifted his shoulders in a half shrug.

"Sometime," he said.

"Both girls?"

This time Hoang just looked at them with no reaction, seeming to be waiting politely for the next question.

"Have you ever seen him with an Anglo, with someone not Asian?"

Hoang shook his head.

"When did you see him last?" Haydon asked.

"One week ago. Yes."

"You took him somewhere?"

"Oh, yes."

"Where?"

"Chinatown."

"Where in Chinatown?"

Hoang shook his head. "No place."

"Was it an old building? A warehouse?"

Hoang nodded. "I think maybe. Yes."

"Was Toy alone?"

"No."

"Who was with him?"

"One of his girlfriend."

"Were they carrying cameras?" Haydon asked.

Hoang's eyebrows went up again. "Oh, yes."

"Do you remember where you took him, Mr. Hoang? Could you find it again?"

"I think so."

"Could you take us there?"

"Tonight?"

"Right now."

Hoang thought about this a moment, then said, "Excuse me." He stood and left the room. Mooney quickly pulled out his wallet and got two dollars, which he handed across to the boy and winked. The boy took the money and looked at him without any change of expression, as if he suspected there was still a catch to it that he didn't understand and that Mooney was just as likely to take the money back again.

"It is very okay," Hoang said, coming back into the room. He had a worried look on his face as if, in fact, it was not very okay at all.

They traveled down Dallas Street and then cut across the southern tip of downtown on Clay until they passed under the Highway 59 expressway and entered Chinatown. Houston's Chinatown did not consist of narrow, densely populated streets and alleyways teeming with people and flashing neon lights like those in San Francisco or New York. Though Houston's Asian population was enormous, like everything else in the city it was spread out. Besides Asian enclaves here and in Allen Parkway Village, there were others along Bissonnet near Bellaire, in the Taum-Milam streets area known as Little Vietnam south of downtown, and still another major grouping in Missouri City far south. But Chinatown was the oldest of these enclaves and occupied a topography typical of warehouse districts everywhere, mostly single-story commercial establishments scattered among littered vacant lots and dreary warehouses that once served thriving rail freight activity.

There were two triple-spurred rail sidings surrounded by warehouses in the immediate area between Clay, Dowling, and the expressway. When Hoang was confronted with the choice of the two locations, he was not sure which of the two had been Toy's destination. They had to cruise through both of them several times before Hoang recognized a landmark and pulled Mooney off the street and onto the crushed-shell driveway of a brick warehouse. It appeared to be abandoned but was directly across from one of the sets of loading docks that flanked each of the three rail spurs. Looking through the windshield from the back seat, Hoang declared that he was sure this was it.

Haydon and Mooney took flashlights from under the seats, and the three men got out of the car and locked it. Haydon and Hoang went to the front door, while Mooney circled the building to see if there was anything immediately suspicious. By the time he got back to the front door, Haydon had gotten a tire tool out of the trunk of the car and wrenched off the padlock that was slipped through the hasp above the doorknob. He pushed the door open, and they went inside.

It was dark except for a cobwebby glow coming through a row of small windows glazed with years of dust and soot near the ceiling on either side of the vast warehouse. The building's flat tar roof had trapped the killing temperatures of the long day's sun, and the heat inside was oppressive. It smelled of wooden skids and shipping crates, of old mortar, yellowed newspapers, and some-thing else.

Haydon turned his flashlight upward, at the bare light bulb hanging from a frazzled wire. A string hung down from the socket. He reached up and pulled it, and a weak yellow light fell on their faces and the stacks and rows of crates. Shadows jittered back and forth from the swinging bulb.

Mooney looked around and took five or six steps away from the light into the warehouse. He turned and looked back.

"Goddamn, Stuart. This is it."

There was an irregular corridor formed by the rows of crates leading farther toward the center of the warehouse. The weak light of the bare bulb penetrated only a short way into it. Haydon flipped on his flashlight again and started into the corridor. There were little narrow aisles branching off in several places, but they were far too small and awkward for half a dozen men to maneuver easily. Haydon stuck to the wide passage as it turned and switched directions. Because the floor of the warehouse was completely covered with packing crates reaching far above his head, Haydon kept his bearings as to his loca-tion in the building by shining the light at the ceiling where the walls converged with the roof. Occasionally they would come upon piles of rubbish, strong with the pun-gent odor of urine, where a transient had bedded down. The deeper they went into the maze of aisles, the more vicious the heat. Sweat pulled at their clothes.

They heard the sound before they actually got to the open space. It was only a faraway whisper at first, almost a remembrance of a sound, but they were aware of it. As they moved on, approaching the end of their search though they were unaware of it, the sound grew distinc-tive, like a great vibration of millions of small wings.

They rounded the corner at the same moment Haydon identified the odor.

"Blood," he said, and their flashlights lit an open area of unspeakable carnage, great swaths of it working with swarms of black flies, grubbing among themselves to get to the source of attraction. Haydon had never seen so much gore, on the floor and splattered on the packing crates that formed the three-sided cul-de-sac nearly twenty feet square in the center of the warehouse. Inside the cul-de-sac the stench was overwhelming.

"Jesus God," Mooney said. "I don't believe this."

Haydon moved farther into the cul-de-sac. Some of the blood was old and black, and the flies mostly avoided it. But in other areas, on the cement floor especially, such huge quantities had been spilled that large smears of it, though undoubtedly drying in the intense heat of the warehouse, were still attractive to the flies and had been ripe enough for breeding grounds. A moil of waxy maggots worked beneath the rind of glossy black flies.

"What in God's name happened here?" Mooney said. He had taken out a handkerchief and was holding it over his mouth and nose.

Haydon moved the beam of his flashlight to the far side of the cul-de-sac and slowly brought it around, following the seam where the stacks of crates met the floor. The beam was more than halfway around to them when a small object caught Haydon's eye, and he stopped the light on it.

"What's that?" Mooney said. He stepped across in front of Haydon and carefully made his way toward the object, negotiating the irregular verge of blood. Without thinking, he bent down and reached to pick it up. Even while he was still in the motion of crouching, an uncharacteristic bleat of horror came from his throat as he tried to get away from it, falling hard against the crates. Before he could stand he was retching, coughing, coming at Haydon, getting out of the cul-de-sac.

"Nose," he choked. "Nose." And he pushed past Haydon and an astonished Hoang. They could hear him vomiting in the darkness of the aisle behind them.

Haydon stared at the black object in the center of the beam and, with a peculiarly clinical detachment, observed the actual sensation of a cold breath start between his shoulder blades and creep up the sides of his neck.

41

....

Half a dozen patrol units were parked at all angles on the crushed shell, along with the lab wagon, a van from maintenance, that had brought the huge fans and floodlights and the necessary electrical cables, a veterinarian's pickup, and several unmarked police cars that had brought Dystal and Captain Mercer. The media vans were there too, their crews kept back by the police. And the crowd. People were standing on the rails of the track, on the loading docks, scattered in the weeds and along the edge of the street.

Someone finally located the circuit switch that turned on six small lights in the ceiling, but because the shipping crates were stacked so high the lights' feeble illumination was useless on the floor. Several teams of uniformed officers had been given the task of scaling the mountains of crates and either opening the windows along the walls at the ceiling or breaking out the panes. The intermittent sounds of shattered glass echoed between the rows of warehouses.

The floodlights were brought in first, lighting the way

back to the bloody cul-de-sac in the center of the warehouse and then, set up on all the pillars of crates surrounding it, shining down into the gore. Each of the men on the maintenance crew stringing the electrical cable and placing the lights took turns coming outside for fresh air. Next, the huge fans were set in place. Already the heat had begun to lighten as it escaped in a natural venting action through the broken and opened windows near the ceiling, but the bricks of the cavernous warehouse had absorbed the summer sun for so long that its contents generated a fever of its own like a living giant.

When everything was in place, everyone cleared out of the warehouse, and the veterinarian entered. He wore a gas mask and carried an exterminator's tank filled with repellent, not insecticide. If the flies died in there, the lab technicians would not be able to work. The veterinarian was accompanied by an assistant, also in a gas mask, a young woman whose blue jeans fit like a second skin.

Outside, everyone waited in silence. The gray-haired Captain Mercer, Dystal, looking sober from having been wakened from a sound sleep and wondering what the hell was happening with the case, Haydon, and Mooney, pale but recovered, standing together and leaning on the hood of Mooney's car. They had all gone in with flashlights before the equipment had been set up. One of the crime lab men had gone with them to take pictures. There was nothing to say until they could actually see what was there. All they knew at this point was that they had found a slaughterhouse.

Suddenly there was an audible deep droning and then they heard the fans kick on.

"Shit, look at that," a policeman said.

The television camera lights came on and pointed at the windows of the warehouse as sooty clouds of flies came boiling out, great regurgitating surges of them, fat and sated from the abattoir inside. They came longer than anyone thought they would, their flight one continuous torrent, slackening, then surging again in a roiling hemorrhage of flying blood.

After a while the flights diminished, but the insects continued to haunt the windows, clinging to the walls around them like clumps of black mold, wanting to get back inside but unable to tolerate the repellent. Finally the veterinarian and his assistant came out of the door, removing their masks. They set their equipment down on the weeds and walked over to Haydon.

"You're not ever going to get them all out," he said. "They're going to be buzzing that place for the next ten years."

He was a little shorter than Haydon, in his late forties, with a grizzled beard that he kept clipped short and which made him look like Ulysses Grant. Both he and the girl, who could have been his daughter, were drenched in sweat.

"I sprayed repellent on the shipping cartons all around the area as well as in the bloody pocket. The flies aren't going to light in it, but they aren't going to leave it alone either. Whoever works in there is going to have to fight them off. I hate it that we couldn't use insecticides. There's billions in there. It's worse than a stockyard."

He turned his head aside and spat, cleared his throat, and spat again. The girl was wiping her face and mouth with her shirttail.

"The maggots are something else," he said. "You couldn't have created better conditions for them in a laboratory. It's rank. You don't want them killed?"

Haydon shook his head. "I think our crime lab people will want to look at them the way they are."

"Okay, it's all yours then. I'll hang around, maybe spray some more repellent later if it's needed. When you're through with your business you'd better notify the health department about it. They'll need to come over and clean the place up. It's an incredible health hazard."

Mooney walked over and told the crime lab technicians they could start and reminded them that Haydon wanted a lot of photographs. Then there was more waiting. A couple of patrolmen drove around to an all-night diner and got doughnuts and coffee. It helped pass the next hour. Mercer went home, saying they could tell him about it in the morning, and Dystal opened one of the car doors and sat in the front seat sipping coffee, his feet outside on the shell drive. Mooney walked over and visited with some of the patrolmen.

After rejecting an impulse to go inside and watch the lab men rake through the gore, Haydon opened the back door of Dystal's car and sat down too. He lit a cigarette. It tasted nasty from the start.

At two-forty, a lab technician came out of the warehouse door and stepped around the corner to vomit. No one said anything or moved to help him. After a while he went back inside.

Shortly after three o'clock, two of the lab technicians came out of the warehouse, one of them carrying an assortment of plastic bags. They were Jake Klein, who led the group, and Dorothy Lea, who held several plastic bags in both hands. They looked around and then started toward Haydon, who was already out of the car.

Klein had been with the police lab for fifteen years and was never, at any time or any place, surprised by what he saw. To him crime scenes were only variations of a theme, and the theme was so old even the variations had begun repeating themselves. Klein did not look too intelligent. His eyes were a little wild and lurked behind eyeglasses with black plastic frames that rose slightly on the outside corners to a small point. His long face always needed a shave, and he favored nylon shirts that were so thin the black glossy hair that covered his back and chest easily showed through. He smelled always of strong, stale tobacco.

"You got a cigarette?" he asked Haydon.

Haydon gave him one, offered one to Lea, and took one himself.

"There seems to be blood in there from several occasions," Klein said. "It's hard to say. Some appears old, a week. Some a few days. There's so much of it it's hard to say. Either a lot of people died, or several people died fighting it. The quantity indicates that. We've taken dozens of samples. The stuff that's mixed isn't going to do us any good. I just hope we can find splashes that haven't been mixed."

He pulled absently at a nostril hair. He turned to the woman and took the plastic bags from her and put them on the hood of the car. Dystal and Mooney had come up, and Mooney shined a flashlight on them.

"The maggots stripped most stuff." He pulled a bag out of the bunch that contained a short length of knotted cartilage. "This is a little finger from a left hand. Just enough flesh to hold it together. It's been cut off, kinda chopped." He pulled out another bag with something black and shriveled. "A nose. Probably male. A whole left nostril, but part of the right one nicked away." Another bag with a concave piece of bone fragment the size of a quarter. "You know, I think this is a piece of kneecap. Here's another piece of a finger, just one joint. A tooth. A little chunk of scalp, Negroid. Got several fabric samples. Some Negroid hair samples. Some sawdust. That's about it."

"What does it look like to you, Jake?" Haydon asked.

Klein shrugged. "Looks like somebody got chopped up. Black folks."

In another half hour everyone was through, and Haydon, Dystal, and Mooney made one more trip inside. They walked the perimeter of the cul-de-sac, trying to make something out of daubs and sprays and smears of blood that climbed the wooden sides of the shipping cartons. Heavy-bellied flies cruised around in the air under the bright lights, constantly slamming into the three men, who steered clear of the mess in the center of the open area where the maggots were also squirming in the heat created by the flood lamps.

When they got around to the right side of the entrance of the cul-de-sac, Haydon stopped. He remembered in Toy's tape that all the men had seemed to bunch up on this side. Then he noticed that for several feet the boxes were shorter, and were arranged in a regular configuration.

"Ed, look at this. What does this look like to you?" The three men looked at the arrangement of boxes.

"Goddamn bleachers," Dystal said. "Those boys were sitting here watching."

"Watching what?"

"Like Klein said, watching somebody get chopped up."

They stood by the edge of the boxes, between the blood and the seats.

"What about light?" Mooney said.

Haydon looked up. "Just that one," he said. Above them, one of the six ceiling lights in the warehouse was installed directly over the cul-de-sac.

"This is hard to believe," Mooney said. He swatted at the flies. "Some silly shit cut people up in here, and those men watched."

"We're going to pull every one of them in tomorrow," Haydon said. "Downtown. None of them will leave until we know what happened here. *All* of them. Roeg. All of them."

Haydon was trembling again. He was aware of Dystal studying him.

Somebody came down the wide aisle and into the glare of the floodlights. It was a uniformed officer.

"Detective Mooney? You've got a call outside, sir."

They all followed the officer, glad for an excuse to get outside, where even the muggy July night seemed light compared to the atmosphere inside the warehouse.

Mooney walked over to a blue-and-white with the patrolman and talked for a minute, then came briskly across the crushed shell.

"You're not going to believe this. Langer and Jennifer Quinn have been found shot over in Memorial Park."

It was four o'clock, still night, yet morning, the time when Haydon's bones felt molded of lead and he longed to see the sun lighten the sky, so he could think of the interminable gruesome night as being over. But it was not over.

Their cars were parked side by side. That's the way the park police had found them. They were both in the Lincoln, the motor was running, and the air conditioner was on high. The park police hadn't touched anything. When they looked in the window they radioed in for the license check.

Quinn was sitting with her back against the door on the passenger side of the car, facing Langer, a hole high on her forehead. The exiting bullet had blown blood and shattered glass outside on the parking lot asphalt and across the left side of her white Porsche. She looked as if she were asleep, her hands in the lap of her emerald silk dress.

Langer was wedged in between the steering wheel and the door. He had also been facing Quinn. His bullet wound was in his right temple, with the exiting bullet splattering the windshield. He was still holding the Charter Arms .38, the force of the charge having flung his arm back so that it rested on his thigh.

The patrol unit flashers lit up the woods as Haydon, Mooney, and Dystal walked around the car in the empty lot. After a minute Haydon raised the tire tool he had brought with him and broke open the door window at Langer's back. He gouged out a hole and reached in and punched the automatic lock button. Then he opened the door, careful not to let Langer's body slide out as Mooney reached across and turned off the motor.

They backed away from the car and looked at it. It reminded Haydon of a nineteenth-century hearse with windows. You could see the dead as they passed you on the street. He looked at Langer asleep and Quinn asleep. Tragic lovers? Romeo and Juliet. Antony and Cleopatra. Tristan and Iseult. David and Bathsheba. Lancelot and Guinevere. Orpheus and Eurydice. Bill and Jennifer? They didn't even come close. It was pitiable and tawdry. A bad ending.

"They've called the crime lab?" Haydon asked.

Mooney nodded. "And the coroner's investigators."

"Has anyone checked with Pete?"

"I called the unit sittin' around the corner from him," Dystal said. "Nothin' happening. I guess Toy got scared off. He don't seem quite as thick-skulled as these other jokers. He's not goin' to come ooching up to bait like that."

"Why don't we send Pete home," Haydon said. He was staring off across the parking lot.

"Good idea," Dystal said. He glanced at Mooney and flicked his head.

"I'll call him," Mooney said, and started across to the car.

After Mooney was out of hearing range, Dystal asked

softly, "How about you, Stu? How you holdin' up? You gonna ride this one out okay?"

"Yes," Haydon said. He was still staring, thinking. "When do you want to start picking them up tomorrow?"

"It's up to you."

"I've got to have some sleep. I want to be there when they come in. They're going to be screaming for their lawyers. It'll be a madhouse. I want to go get Roeg myself. We'd better try to get them simultaneously, or we'll lose some of them."

"What about Toy? I got a man set aside to start checkin' the banks first thing in the mornin'."

"Right. We ought to go ahead with that."

Dystal was feeling a little uncomfortable. Haydon was growing moody. That was dangerous for him, but at the same time it never hurt his work. In fact, it seemed to enhance it. It was as if his emotional agitation and his mental acumen were directly related, and when the former was at its most delicate state, the latter was at its strongest and most resolute. As Dystal saw it, the man was simply hard on himself, but was very good at living with it.

Still, Dystal was concerned about Haydon slipping so quickly into his melancholy ways. It was too soon, and Dystal felt more than a little responsible for his condition. He wanted to get Haydon back to work; he thought it was time and would be good for him. But the stress of the case had come on a little stronger than Dystal had expected. Instead of being the routine puzzler he had hoped would stimulate Haydon's interest in the work at which he was so uncommonly skilled, and which Dystal believed he loved, the unexpectedly brutal nature of the case might have the reverse effect.

Dystal rammed his hands down into the pockets of his bagging double-knit pants, sucked in huge, bulging lungsful of the damp woodsy air, and then let it out slowly. He looked at Haydon. They waited for the morgue van.

42

....

Bob Dystal had thoughtfully called her shortly after twelve
o'clock to tell her that Haydon would most likely be out all
night. He said Haydon had run into one thing after the
other and Dystal thought he probably hadn't stopped
long enough to let her know. He was right. She went to
bed around one after having read for a while and flipped
through all the channels without finding anything interesting. She slept fitfully, waking once when she thought
she heard the Vanden Plas in the drive, another time
when she thought she heard Haydon coming through the
front door, and again when she thought he was in the
darkened bedroom changing clothes.

Then around six o'clock he did come home, but she
didn't awaken until she heard him in the shower. She lay
in bed listening to him shaving, and then he came out and
put on his white *calzones* and walked over and lay down
beside her. He smelled of soap and Kouros. He kissed her
softly at the hairline on her neck and laid his left arm
across her breasts. With his face resting close to her long

hair because, she knew, he liked the smell of it, he went to sleep without ever having said a word.

She lay awake for a while wondering what he had been through, not totally relaxing until he stopped twitching, as he always did when he had had a stressful late-night case. When he finally fell into a deep sleep she dozed too, coming in and out of consciousness, aware of the room lightening with the rising sun, aware of the morning shadows, the warming room. Then the next thing she knew Gabriela's soft hand was touching her arm, and when she opened her eyes the old woman was holding her hand to her ear, her little finger and thumb extended to indicate a telephone. Nina nodded, slipped out from under Haydon's arm, and tied her robe as she went down the steps.

Again it was Dystal. Was Haydon awake? Nina said no and indicated she was reluctant to wake him. Dystal said that was all right, everyone had slept late, but they needed to "have a meet." Would she please have Haydon call him in time for them to have lunch together? She said she would.

Now it was eleven o'clock as Nina climbed the stairs to check on him. She opened the door to the bedroom and stood there looking at him across the sunny room, his chest and shoulders bare on the white sheets, the ceiling fan turning just enough to move the air. He didn't like to sleep in a room without circulation.

Suddenly the buzzer from the speaker at the gates sounded on the intercom in the entranceway. She frowned. No one was expected that she knew. She closed the door and hurried down the stairs. Gabriela was standing at the speaker, a puzzled look on her face. She looked at Nina, shrugged, and backed away. Nina went to the speaker, which was still on.

"Yes?"

"Mr. Haydon, please."

It was a woman's voice, soft. Nina couldn't place the accent.

"I'm sorry," she said. "He's asleep. May I ask who is calling?"

"Wake him, please. Say message from Ricky Toy. He

will know. Most urgent. Okay? Very important. Please hurry."

"Just a moment please. Can you wait?"

"Yes, please."

Nina flipped off the switch and turned and ran back up the stairs, rushing into the bedroom. Even as she did it she didn't want to wake him. She shook him softly. He rolled over and opened his eyes.

"There's a woman out at the gates," she said. "I think she's got an Oriental accent. She says she has a message from a Ricky Toy, and that it's urgent."

Haydon threw back the covers and grabbed his robe from the back of an armchair. He hurried down the stairs with Nina following him.

Haydon flipped on the switch. "This is Stuart Haydon."

"Message from Ricky Toy."

"Who is this?"

"Lai."

Haydon pressed the button that opened the gates.

He waited in the library, self-consciously running his fingers through his tousled hair, smoking a cigarette. When Nina brought the girl in through the hallway door he was not surprised at her beauty. Her long hair was so black it had a cobalt sheen, and she moved with a natural gracefulness. She wore buff canvas pants with military square-cut pockets and a long-sleeved shirt of the same material with the sleeves rolled to the elbows. The pants were tight enough for Haydon to recall the taut long legs of the two girls in the photograph with Toy.

Haydon nodded.

The girl's eyes were sad.

"Ricky Toy want to see you," she said.

"Fine," Haydon said. "When and where?"

"I will take you."

"Now?"

"Yes, please."

"Where?"

"I am sorry." She shook her head.

Haydon glanced quickly at Nina, who left the room.

"I'll have to change."

"Please hurry."

He put out his cigarette and started out of the library. "I must be with you."

He hesitated, then understood. "Come on," he said.

Lai followed Haydon up the stairs and stood in the middle of the room watching him as he washed his face in the bathroom and then took off his clothes and dressed in a suit and tie. He waited for her to stop him when he reached into a drawer and pulled out his Beretta, but she said nothing as he clipped it to his belt in the small of his back.

They went back down the stairs, Lai going first now, where Nina was waiting in the entrance hall. Haydon's eyes met hers, they kissed, and he followed Lai outside to the rental car waiting in the drive.

The day was already hot, and the invisible cicadas keened in the trees like jungle birds.

She took the boulevard to Shepherd and turned north, driving the car with self-assured experience and an attentive urgency. Haydon quickly looked in the back seat. There was a purse back there, rumpled clothes, some maps, plastic bags with toilet articles in them. They had been living out of the car, probably hadn't even risked getting a motel room. Where the hell was Toy waiting for them?

"How does Toy know about me?" Haydon asked. They had stopped at the traffic light on Westheimer.

"He was told."

"Who told him?"

She ignored this and drove through the traffic light as she checked her rearview mirror. Though the air conditioner was cooling the car, Haydon noticed a thin mist of perspiration on Lai's forehead. He wondered if he was doing the right thing. He wondered if, when it was over, he would look back on what he was doing and see that if at some particular point he had done something differently a tragedy could have been avoided. It was as if he were being given a chance in advance to avoid that cruel lucidity of hindsight, but he was still unable to formulate a clear picture of what was happening.

At the same moment he saw the West Gray intersection a block away, Lai put on her turn signal to go left into River Oaks. Good God. He was with Roeg. One of them had the other at gunpoint, he was sure of it, and Haydon was going to have to deal with an unreasonable demand. His mind scattered, trying to see every angle at once, trying to decide if he should stop Lai now, take the car back, and call Dystal, trying to anticipate when it would be too late, and he would not be in a position to decide anything.

They quickly covered the distance along the avenue that led in front of the estates and approached Roeg's gates. He recognized the man he had spoken to the day before. He came up to the car with his clipboard and bent down to Lai's window and looked inside.

"Hello, Mr. Haydon," he said pleasantly. He looked at the list. "Ms. Lai Chung?"

She nodded.

"Very good." He backed away from the car, the gates opened, and they drove through.

Haydon looked at Lai. He rearranged his thoughts. He had expected the place to be under a state of siege, but everything appeared normal. When they came into the parking area he could tell from her hesitation that Lai hadn't been there before. As with him earlier, a security guard in plain clothes stepped out of one of the doors and waved her around to a parking place. He opened the door for her and they got out and were walked to the front door, but no farther.

When the heavy front door opened and Harvey Gage looked at him, Haydon knew his initial impression had been the right one.

Gage's face was a mixture of fear and nausea. He looked at Lai as if she were a snake and backed into the entry hall.

"Goddamn, Haydon, he's insane," he said as soon as they were inside. "He's got a gun taped to Roeg's neck. I don't know how the hell he got in. Can't tell anybody, he'll kill him. Fucking, fucking security. I don't know how—"

"Where are they?" Haydon said.

"In his office down there. I'm supposed to come back with you." He turned and they walked briskly. "I've sent everybody out. Left instructions that Mr. Roeg wasn't supposed to be disturbed today, called instructions up to the gate to let you, both of you, in."

"Why does Toy want me?"

"He said he wanted the man in charge of the case, the Langer stuff. He blames Roeg for . . . the girl."

"You've heard about Langer?" Haydon asked.

"Heard?"

"Nothing."

They were outside the door of Roeg's huge office.

"Wait, I've got instructions," Gage said. He stepped to the door and knocked. "Toy. They're here."

There was a scuffling sound inside, and a thump.

"I'm going to open the door," Toy said. "Send in Lai."

The door opened slowly. Roeg stood straight in front of it, about ten feet into the room. His hands were bound behind his back, his mouth was taped shut, and the barrel of an automatic weapon was secured to his neck with white adhesive tape. Haydon could see about half of the weapon, which he recognized as an HK 94, a nine-millimeter carbine. It was taped to Roeg's neck in such a way that enabled Toy to be either directly behind him or ninety degrees around to his right side. Toy himself was out of the field of vision behind the door.

Lai walked in and immediately said something to Toy in Chinese, as she bent to one side and came up with a weapon identical to Toy's. She turned it on Roeg but kept her eyes glued to Haydon.

"Haydon," Toy said from behind the door, "reach back and get the Beretta, take out the clip, put both the clip and the gun on the floor, and kick them into the room."

Haydon did as he was asked.

"Okay, now you two come in."

They stepped inside, and Toy kicked the door closed behind them.

Toy was dressed in sweat-stained hunting clothes with the kind of canvas boots the military uses for tropical climates. He looked tanned and healthy, as though he belonged in the clothes. Haydon noticed the curtains had been drawn over the tall windows and that every light in the room was turned on. The CRTs behind Roeg's desk jumped with stock quotations from both the New York and American exchanges. The security cameras mounted in the ceiling corners apparently were not operating.

Toy walked Roeg over to his desk and leaned over it and pressed a button. Haydon heard the heavy bolts of the electrical security system chunk closed inside the door.

"Okay," Toy said. "This situation makes me antsy, so to reduce my anxiety I'm going to reduce your mobility. I don't want to have to worry about either of you making unexpected sudden movements, and I don't want to have to be pointing a gun at somebody all the time." He tossed the roll of adhesive to Lai. "Tape their hands behind their backs."

When she had done this Toy said, "Now let's all go over to the sofas."

They moved around the projector to the center of the collection of sofas facing the movie screen. Toy took a knife out of his pocket and reached up and cut the adhesive that held the HK 94 to Roeg's neck. He shoved Roeg down on the sofa and knelt down and taped his legs. Then he shoved Gage on one of the other sofas and taped his feet together, and then his mouth.

He looked at Haydon. "Sit down here."

Haydon sat on the third sofa, facing Gage, Roeg to his left, the movie screen to his right.

"I'm just going to tape your feet. I want you to be able to talk."

Lai stood to one side holding her HK while Toy knelt down and taped Haydon's ankles together. Then he stood, thought a second, and then walked over and stood in front of Roeg.

"There's a psychologist in Amsterdam who specializes in negotiating with terrorists who take hostages. Travels all over the world. He says the first few hours after the terrorists have taken hostages are the most dangerous, because the terrorists' revolutionary juices are still flowing and they might pop a hostage at any moment if they get excited. So these are crucial moments for you and Gage here. Don't piss me off. Of course the only way you wouldn't piss me off is for you to be dead, so it doesn't look too good for you either way."

Toy casually kicked Roeg's slippered feet, the way one might kick a dead animal he was examining.

"This psychologist also says he likes to get the terrorists and the hostages to establish some kind of relationship, to view each other as human beings, not symbols. To do this it's best if they can talk. Now this is bad for you, Roeg, since I've taped your mouth shut because I'm afraid you'll squeal like a monkey for your security men. So that is one point on the negative side of your chances for survival. But the psychologist also says that it's vital for the terrorist and the hostages to maintain eye contact. It's more difficult for the terrorists to kill someone when they're looking into their eyes. That's another point on the positive side, since I'm not going to blindfold you. There're certain things I want you to see."

Toy kicked Roeg's feet again.

"However. There are two main points on the negative side of the scale of your chances of survival that override everything on the positive side. The first point. This psychologist says that *el numero uno* priority in such situations is for the negotiator to establish contact with the terrorists. Initiate a dialogue. Without a dialogue the situation is hopeless. Well. You see, that's bad for you, because there's nothing out there I want. There's nothing to negotiate, no reason for a dialogue. I've already got what I want."

Toy squatted down in front of Roeg, close to his face, and looked directly into jet eyes.

"The second point. I hate you so much, Roeg, that I could pop you every hour on the hour for the next ten years and never get enough of it. Can you understand something like that, you little fucker? The sole object of all the hate I am capable of mustering up is right in front of my eyes, in this stupid . . . little . . . wrinkled tuxedo. That's bad."

Toy let that soak in, his face close to Roeg's, and then he stood again and turned to Haydon.

"Okay. Background. Just to put this operation in perspective for you: I sneaked in here last night because I wanted an uninterrupted and lengthy conversation with Roeg. I didn't think I'd be able to get it any other way. I hid until Gage stumbled past me and offered me a way into Roeg's sanctum without setting off alarms.''

"What about the security?" Haydon asked. "How did you get past it?"

Toy grinned. "One thing I learned in Southeast Asia. One man can get into *any* secured area. He may not get out alive, but he can always get in. I wouldn't have, though, if these fancy high-tech bozos had thought of one more thing: a dog. Just any old dumb Bowser would have caught me. High tech can't smell.''

Toy turned and walked over by the movie screen to a camera sitting on a tripod.

"In honor of Joey Roeg, here, we're going to tape our little meeting today, folks. The violence will be duly recorded."

43

....

Toy did not pick up his HK again, but Lai sat in an arm-chair facing the men with her weapon in her lap. Toy took a straight-backed chair and carried it to the opened end of the U formed by the three sofas. He turned the chair around backwards and straddled it, his back to the screen, and lit a cigarette.

"You want a smoke?" he asked Haydon.

"No."

"I want to unscramble things for you a little," Toy said to Haydon. "I didn't kill poor old dumb Powell. I'm not sure who did, but it was either Langer or Roeg's animals. The night he was killed I had given Powell some video tape I wanted him to process for me. He did it up in Langer's offices. You probably know about all that."

Haydon nodded.

"Okay. That was about twelve-thirty, I guess. Wayne was supposed to enhance the stuff and call me back. It shouldn't have taken him more than an hour. Two at the most. By about two-thirty I hadn't heard a thing. I called his lab, but there wasn't any answer. I got nervous and drove down there. I had a key Wayne had given me. I went in and found him. The video was gone. I left. I figured whoever it was had found the tape, which was the first part of a longer tape I was going to use to blackmail Roeg for big bucks. I figured they recognized the action in the tape, probably knew Powell was doing it for me, put two and two together. I knew this would go straight to Roeg, so I figured I was burned. We moved out of my condo early the next morning and went to that damn place over off Southwest Freeway where Roeg's goons caught up with Yue.''

Toy took his last drag off the cigarette. He dropped it on the Persian rug and ground it out with his foot. It seemed to Haydon to be a calculated gesture, not the sort of thing Toy would do naturally. Perhaps it was for Roeg's benefit.

''I had decided to scam Roeg a long time ago, but it took me a while to figure out the best way. These films I've been humping all over the world to collect for this asshole weren't enough. Most of it was war footage. No crime in having that, right? The closest I came to having leverage was to use some of the death-squad stuff. Roeg here has direct ties with the death squads down there through his investments. Right-wing all the way. He's got a large payroll down there. What's good for the extreme right is good for Roeg's investments. He's tied in with all that. He supports it, directly finances the squads, him and some others, wealthy Salvadorans who live in Miami.

''Anyway, I had all the access I wanted to see these death squads at work. I picked up some serious interrogation footage down there. He's got them in his vault. He loves that shit. There's stuff you wouldn't believe. The little fucker loves it.

''But there was only my word tying it to Roeg. Big deal. So I scouted around, found out as much as I could about this little freak. Spent a couple of months doing it. Then on one of my trips down in San Salvador, I was having a beer with a colonel in the Salvadoran army. At night he moonlights by heading one of the several death squads Roeg finances directly. We were chatting, and this guy starts laughing about something he'd seen when he was up here in Houston. He trains Roeg's security men, which explains a lot about those fucking sadists in the Brooks Brothers suits. He told me about something he'd seen in old warehouses and other places up here. Little entertainments that Roeg arranged once in a while. Real mondo bizarro. Gory. He told me about it. Ha-ha. I said, wow, that's pretty funny. Ha-ha. Neat. I asked him a lot of questions about it, in a chitchatty sort of way. Ha-ha all the time. Maybe I'd get to film some of that, I said. More casual questions, another beer.

"The guy's no fool. I didn't get a lot of information, but I got enough to put me onto a serious search when I got back. That's all I did for about three weeks until I located a black dude who was the key to it. Bam! I set up for the next entertainment. Me and Lai filmed it. It was my ticket."

Toy lit another cigarette. As he blew smoke into the air he looked over at Gage and Roeg, eyed them casually, then turned back to Haydon.

"So I processed the tapes myself and worked out a system for collection that protected me. Made arrangements through Langer and gave the pitch to Roeg. That was yesterday about noon. He agreed to pay, at least he said he would. We made arrangements. Sometime between then and last night they found out where we were living and Roeg's goons 'questioned' Yue. Remember, these were guys trained by that greasy death-squad fucker in San Salvador. I'm glad I didn't find her."

Toy's face grew flushed as he said this. He puffed on the cigarette and looked at Roeg. Smoking, looking. He threw the cigarette on the rug again and put it out as before.

He stood and picked up his HK, which had been lying by Lai's chair. He slid out the retractable butt stock and walked over to Roeg. Kneeling on one knee he held the HK in his left hand and put the barrel in Roeg's right ear. Roeg leaned away reflexively, and Toy grabbed a handful of Roeg's thick black hair with his right hand and jerked his head upright, jamming the HK barrel into Roeg's ear. Roeg's eyes watered immediately from the pain. Toy raised his thumb off the pistol grip of the carbine and flicked the safety down. Everybody in the room heard the click.

"It's only a nine-millimeter," he said to Roeg. "Probably just scramble your brains on the way through, but no big devastation. You'll still look good in a casket."

Haydon didn't think he would do it, not like this anyway. And he didn't. He simply said *bang-bang* and stood up. But Haydon was watching him. Toy had put himself under a lot of pressure. Haydon never doubted that Toy had seen Yue's body in his mind's eye over and over since he had discovered what had happened. The same internal eye that was already sated with atrocities.

Toy laid the HK on the floor beside Lai.

"I'll show you the video we got that night," Toy said to Haydon, ignoring Gage and Roeg again. He walked back to the projector and pushed one button to raise the movie screen and another to dim the lights. Behind the movie screen was a six-foot television screen. Toy came around and turned on the video recorder and popped in the cassette. There were a few moments of static and then the beginning of the tape Haydon had already seen.

"These two black dudes will star later. The dude talking to them is Boney Walker, the guy who finally got me into the warehouse, though not exactly willingly."

With the bigger screen Haydon could see that Walker was wearing a shapeless white suit with cuffs on the sleeves. The cuffs were turned back exposing five or six inches of shiny black shirt. The shirt was open to Walker's stomach, revealing a necklace with some kind of medallion dangling from it.

As Roeg's men came into the warehouse accompanied either by Langer or Grover Ellis, Toy called their names and told Haydon where they fit into the organization. He had indeed done his homework. When the video reached the point where all the men were sitting down, their faces dimly lit, the place where the tape Haydon had already seen ended, Toy stopped the tape, freezing the action.

"I might as well tell you at this point how we did this. Lai and I were using a state-of-the-art thing from Hitachi, an SR-1 VTR. Meant for news gathering. Lightweight,

really handles well. Only thing is the tapes are eight minutes max, which meant we had to keep snapping in new
cassettes. We'd miss, maybe, five seconds of action each
time we snapped in a new cassette. We had seven cassettes
each. Lai and I were shooting from different angles. She
concentrated on the pit, where the action was happening.
I got both the pit and then slow pans over to the men
watching and then back to the pit. I didn't want there to
be any doubt about the fact that these men were sitting
there watching. Unfortunately I couldn't get an angle that
showed both them and the action at the same time. Also
the audio is poor. The acoustics in the warehouse were
hopeless. This one-hour tape is a composite of both Lai's
footage and mine spliced into a continuous narrative. I've
got another one I hadn't told Roeg about.''

Toy punched the play button and the action started
again. He came back over and moved his chair to the side
closer to Haydon. He held a remote control.

After the shot of the men sitting on the packing cases,
there was a bright shot of the cul-de-sac. Walker was standing in the middle fiddling with a rope, while on either side
the two black men were taking off their clothes. They
stripped down to their underwear and tossed their clothes
up on the crates to get them out of the way and then
stepped up to Walker, who tied one end of the rope to the
left wrist of each man. He tested the knots, had each man
step back to the length of the fully extended rope, which
appeared to be about three feet long. Walker moved out
of sight and returned with two short curved knives that
looked like bent machetes.

"Those are Gurkha kukri knives," Toy said to
Haydon. "They're a foot long and weigh about a pound
and a half. These guys have never even seen one before."

Walker gives a knife to each black and talks to them a
little more. They nod and he backs out of the cul-de-sac.
The two men immediately jerk the rope taut between
them and start slowly rotating around an imaginary pivot.
They instinctively hold the knives out to the side and
slightly back. Their bodies glisten with sweat, from the
stifling heat and from fear. One of the men is heavier and
more muscular than the other and starts yanking on the

rope, trying to throw his opponent off balance. The other man resists, not knowing really how to counter this technique. He simply tries to avoid being pulled within the reach of his opponent's weapon. The whole operation seems awkward to him, and his eyes swell with the realization that he is clearly the underdog.

Suddenly the bigger man releases his strain on the rope and lunges at his opponent, who is thrown off balance at this sudden loss of ballast and staggers back. As he falls the bigger man comes down with a wide sweep of the Gurkha blade. He is out of reach with the first chop and only the tip of the blade slices across the smaller man's chest, but the big man's momentum carries him downward before he can bring the blade around for another swing. In the flick of an instant the smaller man raises his blade defensively and the bigger man impales himself by the force of his own weight. The audio catches his scream.

Both men are stunned. The smaller man has been transported from death to victory in a matter of seconds and is dumbfounded. But when the bigger man tries to twist off the blade, more in agony than in an effort to save himself, his opponent comes to his senses, jerks out the blade, and hacks him across the neck with it. With the second swing he decapitates him and releases a squirting flood of blood onto the floor. The big man's body jerks in death, and the winner slashes out at him with a gratuitous blow across his lower back which opens up his kidneys. It is over in less than two minutes.

Then the winner looks up quickly, peering into the dark. He listens as if he is being told something. He nods stupidly and begins dragging his headless opponent by the rope that is still tied to his arm. He drags him out of sight behind some crates, leaving a snail's trail of grume. Walker comes out, trying to keep his spiffy shoes out of the gore, and gingerly picks up the head and runs after the corpse. The camera stays on the corner where they disappear and dimly records the two men wrestling the big man farther into the darker reaches of the warehouse.

Toy stopped the tape.

"Walker tries to recruit real studs for this," he said. "But he can't always match them evenly. He gets these guys from the ratholes of the city. You can hire a killer pretty easy, you know that, but it's something else to get somebody who'll go into a hand-to-hand like this. Putting their *own* life on the line. Losing's a heavy proposition in this game. But there's always someone desperate enough to do it. That's one thing Roeg knows about, desperate people. You can have them cheap, and you don't have to treat them like humans. Some of these poor bastards don't put a hell of a lot of value on their lives.''

Toy punched the button again and the video continued. There was some preliminary cleaning up by Walker, who seemed to be a one-man ringmaster, trainer, referee, and custodian. Some sawdust was sprinkled around. And then two more men, already stripped to their underwear, came into the cul-de-sac. Walker tied them with the rope, which was wet with blood and hard to handle now. One of the men looked down and said something about the floor. Walker went off and returned with more sawdust and scattered it around. He talked to them as he had the previous pair. He went out again and came back with the kukri knives. He gave them to the men, said a few more words, and backed out of sight.

The rope popped tight and they began. But this time it wasn't over so quickly. It became a grisly demonstration of murder through mutual ineptitude. The men went at each other like amateur boxers with no knowledge of technique, just thrashing and slashing at one another in a mad fury to try to kill first. Pieces of flesh literally flew off their bodies as they swung wildly with the razor-sharp blades; blood and sweat mixed and glistened under the feeble light. The pace of the slaughter quickened as panic and a gut drive for survival convulsed their adrenal glands. They spun about in a shower of their own blood like dervishes, like fighting cocks who literally exploded in frenzy. At one moment the fight looked like a mutual effort to get away from each other's deadly blows, and at the next moment it appeared to be an unbelievable effort to kill each other, with total blindness to the dangers of the oncoming flashing blade in the other man's hand. Sometimes they would stupidly step right into the path of the opponent's blade, suffering staggering blows; sometimes they would unwittingly deliver a wicked slash in an effort to ward off a blow that never came. They fell and wallowed and flailed, tried to stand and squealed like pigs, until suddenly a jet of bright arterial blood shot upward with enormous force, once, twice, and both men went down in a heap.

This time the winner could not get up. The hard-working Walker scurried out and cut the rope and dragged away the loser. Then he returned and helped the "winner." Haydon doubted he would live.

The next fight was set up.

"I don't want to see any more," Haydon said.

"Sure you do. These're *homicides*, for Christ's sake. In this next one they use pipes. One guy beats the other guy to jelly."

"I don't want to see it," Haydon repeated.

Toy punched the freeze button and turned around.

"There's two more. They killed four that night. Maybe six. I think two of the winners died. It's another twenty minutes." He was highly agitated.

"I won't watch it," Haydon said.

"You *will* watch it!" Toy screamed. He was furious. He jumped up from the chair and kicked it across the room, where it smashed against the wall. "I-want-you-to-believe-it. I want to burn these deaths into your brain. You *see* the kind of man he is?" He turned and pointed to the wall of photographs. "You *see*? He's an animal. He's a fucking *cannibal*!"

Haydon shook his head.

Toy looked at him. He glared at him. He blinked and stared. Then the tension slipped a little, then a little more, until it bled away. He slumped. He turned to the screen, a freeze shot of Walker cleaning up. He stared at it for a long time, and the only sound in the room was the humming of the video player. Toy punched the rewind button.

"You're right," he said wearily.

He walked around to the projector console and turned up the lights. Then he came back to where he had been sitting and lit a cigarette. He stared at the floor.

Haydon was numb. He looked past Toy's shoulders at Lai, who was sitting straight in her chair with her hands resting on the HK. She seemed as distant as Toy. Neither of them gave any sign of what they wanted to do next. In fact, Haydon was puzzled at what had already happened. If Toy was going to kill Roeg, why didn't he get on with it? Why did he want Haydon there? Toy didn't seem to be vacillating; he didn't seem to be hesitating. He simply appeared to be exhausted and preoccupied. His hunting shirt was dark with sweat, even though the air conditioning was comfortable. Haydon tried to see where it was going.

When the telephone rang nothing moved but their eyes.

44

....

Toy walked over and grabbed Gage by the hair. He shook him. "Listen, suck-ass. You tell them you're still in a meeting. Big-deal stuff. You want to be left alone." He jerked Gage's hair for emphasis. "Remember—as long as I have a chance to get out alive so do you. When my chances are up, so are yours."

He viciously ripped the tape from Gage's mouth and picked up his HK. There was a long wire on the telephone by the projector, and Toy motioned for Lai to hold it to Gage's ear while Toy went over to Roeg's desk. The telephone was ringing for the fifth time when Toy nodded for Lai to pick it up.

"Hel . . . hello," Gage sputtered.

"Mr. Gage, this is Bearden." The man's voice filled the room. Toy had flipped on the speaker phone. "Is everything okay in there?"

"Sure, sure," Gage said. "Why do you ask?"

"Just a routine check, sir. Thank you." Bearden hung up.

"Routine, shit," Toy cursed. "It doesn't matter. I

don't need that much more time. Lai, put the tape back
on him."

Toy walked around the sofas again and squatted down
in front of Roeg.

"Joey," he said, and looked at Roeg. "Joey, do you
think you're going to die now?" He waited for an answer
but Roeg didn't budge. His face had shown no reaction to
anything that had happened since Haydon had entered
the room. His black eyes were no vehicle for understanding his emotions.

"I'll tell you something," Toy said. "There's so many
different ways to die I have a hard time deciding about
you. I've seen so many different ways. Of course you know
almost as much about that as I do. Maybe I should let you
decide."

Suddenly he thought of something. "Wait a minute,"
he said. He stood and walked over to the video recorder
on the tripod and snapped in a new cassette. "I almost
screwed up. Be a shame for Roeg's finale *not* to be on tape
after all he's done to contribute to this field of entertainment."

As Toy walked back, Haydon said, "Toy. I've got more
than enough to convict him. Let it go. Whatever felonies
you might be indicted for as a result of all this can be plea-
bargained off if you will agree to testify against him. It's
over. Don't turn it into a greater tragedy than it already
is."

Toy didn't pay any attention, but squatted down in
front of Roeg again.

"How would you like it? Just nod at your preference.
Bullet in the head?" Pause. "Throat cut?" Pause. "Beating?" Pause. "Strangling, bare hands or garrote? Stab-
bing? Hanging? Or how about torture? I know your love
for that. Maybe a potpourri of methods your boys use in El
Salvador . . . I don't have all the equipment but we can
improvise. Shit, improvisation is what torture's all about.
It's a primitive art form anyway. There's an infinite variety
in this business of dying, isn't there? We could play war,
pretend you've been captured. Stand you up in front of
that white movie screen and empty one of these nine-
millimeter magazines in you, making red patterns a-a-all

over. Jesus, what'll it be, Joey? How do we want to handle your exit, man?''

Toy stood up. He walked over and picked up the white adhesive tape.

"Think about it, for Christ's sake, Toy," Haydon said. "There's no need for this."

Toy ripped off a piece and taped Haydon's mouth.

Without speaking he threw down the tape and went back to Roeg. He took a hunting knife from the thigh scabbard on his camouflage pants and pushed Roeg out flat on the sofa. He inserted the blade in the neck of the wing-collared shirt and brought it down slowly. It was so sharp it hardly pulled at the material. He removed the shirt. Then he inserted the knife into Roeg's tuxedo pants and slit them all the way down one leg. He pulled the pants down to the tape on Roeg's ankles.

Roeg lay on the sofa in his jockey shorts. His limbs were pallid like the tentacles of a squid, soft and muscleless and blue-veined.

"This morning's paper said Yue was naked," Toy said.

He grabbed the waistband of Roeg's shorts and cut it, cut through one leg and pulled them away. Roeg lay naked, totally hairless below the neck. Uncircumcised. Small. He began to make noises behind the tape, the blood veins sticking out on his forehead, his Adam's apple working. He tried to turn away from them to hide his genitals, but Toy grabbed him and turned him back. Roeg's eyes locked onto him, tears forming. He grunted and bucked. Toy put one foot on Roeg's bound legs and with his left hand on Roeg's scrawny chest held him down. Roeg's genitals were bared to the room, absurdly prepubescent and pale.

"They looked at her," Toy said, and everyone in the room was aware that they were looking at Roeg's nakedness, and they were aware of the shame that he felt at having that which he would prefer most to have hidden so crassly regarded.

Toy lowered the point of the hunting knife to Roeg's genitals. Roeg appeared to stop breathing as Toy touched them.

"They did things to her," he said. "Did they report

the details to you, Roeg? Did you ask for them?" Toy used the blade to slowly move Roeg's limp penis from side to side, casually studying it as if there were nothing better to do, as if this amusement might suggest to him some further diversion at Roeg's expense.

"They cut her," he said, and he pressed the cold blade to the base of Roeg's testicles.

Roeg's eyes rolled slowly back into his head, and he began urinating uncontrollably; he could no longer restrain his bowels.

Toy stood back and watched him. He waited until Roeg had finished. He waited until his eyes came back down and focused on him again. He waited until Roeg was alert enough to know what he had done, to know what he was lying in, to know what had not happened to him. Crying, Roeg tried to climb onto the sofa from which he was sliding, but only succeeded in smearing his feces.

"Are you scared, Joey?" Toy asked solemnly, standing before him. "What does it feel like? And nothing's even happened to you. What do you suppose the terror is like when it actually *happens*?"

He waited as if he really expected an answer, but there was only a muffled mewling that choked on and on and would not stop. Roeg had reached the precipice of hysteria and had almost lost his balance. It was a strange and unnerving utterance in the silent room, the sound of humiliation and debasement and shattering defeat. But it was more than that too; it was the sound of spiritual upheaval, of Josef Roeg's revelation. For in the space of a few uncertain moments he had seen his sun from the other side of its orbit.

Toy turned and looked at Haydon. He walked over and took Lai's HK and returned to Roeg.

"I want to show you something," he said. He jerked out the clip and pressed the cartridge spring. It was empty. He picked up his own HK and did the same. It was empty also.

"I was never going to hurt you," he said. There was no rancor in his voice. It was as if he were giving a eulogy. "I just wanted you to know how it felt to wait for it to happen. I wanted you to know what your jollies were cost-

ing. To tell you the truth I would like to have gone ahead
with it, but despite what I've done to you, I can't be as bad
as that.

"For years I've seen too much of it. I thought if I saw
enough, if I got close enough to it, saw the worst of it,
crawled inside it and found the heart of it, then I would
understand. But it never happened. Not until *you* raised
your head from the sewage and put your hands on me.
You're the soul of violence, Roeg, and when all is said and
done you're no different from the rest of us. You're just
our worst impulses indulged to the point of total corruption. So while I would have much preferred to cut your
balls off, I'm not going to do it. I'm not going to do it
because I know it's just the kind of thing you would have
enjoyed seeing done to someone else. I respectfully refuse
the honor, Roeg, and in doing so I take one foot out of
the sewer."

The room was a vacuum. Gage's eyes were closed, and
his head had fallen back on the sofa. Lai was sitting sto-
ically in her chair in front of the curtained windows. Roeg
tried to achieve the impossible. Squirming and twisting on
his soiled sofa, he tried to hide where there was no place
to hide.

Toy walked over and picked up Haydon's Beretta and
inserted the clip. Then he went to Haydon and cut the
tape from his feet and hands, and let him remove the tape
from his mouth. He gave Haydon the Beretta.

"He's all yours. Now, how do we defuse this situation?"

Haydon's heart was rocking his entire body. He
couldn't believe Roeg was not dead. He looked at Toy and
started to say something, but stopped. Instead, he said,
"I'll call out," and started to Roeg's desk.

While he was dialing, he heard the humming sound
of the curtains pulling back, and his blood froze. As he
swung around he saw Toy walking to the light, turning his
back on the dismal room, already retreating into his own
thoughts. Haydon opened his mouth, but it was too late.
The round that hit Toy lifted him off the floor and carried
him back three feet before he dropped and skittered
across the parquet in front of Roeg's desk. His head was

gone. Lai had only enough time to stand before the second round caught her in her right temple, flipping her over the armchair and crashing her into the six-foot television screen.

Roeg's security force sharpshooters had been in place a long time.

Haydon stood still. It was over.

45

"Let's go for a drive. I want to show you something and tell you something."

They were the first words Haydon had spoken in the half hour they had been sitting on the dark terrace drinking iced Tanquerays with lime. He had been in a somber mood, looking out across the black night trees toward the greenhouse. He hadn't gotten away from Roeg's estate until late in the evening and then had spent much of the night downtown setting the paperwork in motion with Mooney and Lapierre. When he finally got home he was tired and preoccupied. Nina had sat with him in silence, knowing he would start talking eventually and that it was fruitless to try to draw him out before he was ready.

They drove for a long time through the flickering lights of the city, going north on Montrose, across Buffalo Bayou, and into the smaller, darker streets of the Heights. After a series of turns among the unfamiliar streets, Nina had no idea where they were. She asked no questions, and Haydon did not explain.

Eventually he pulled the Vanden Plas to the curb

across the street from the small frame house. As always the doors and windows were open to the summer night. He could see, through one of the darkened bedroom windows, a dim saffron illumination coming from one of the rooms farther back in the house. The front door emitted a pale flickering aura that danced on the cement porch and died away on the steps that led to the bare yard. It was late. Probably both the boy and the pup were asleep.

"This is the house," he said. "It was a year, I think, maybe two, before we were married. I hadn't been out of uniform long. I had been pulled to do some decoy work for Vice, and when it was done I stayed with them. I was with them that night. I wasn't even supposed to be there.

"I had worked the Heights in uniform for over a year just before I went to Vice and had been to this place several times. Family disturbance calls and child abuse. The woman who lived here was divorced, living with a man who drank heavily and regularly beat her and the children. He didn't have to be drunk to do it. She worked during the day, and he stayed with the little girl and boy. They were small, six and seven. When I was working the Heights I had gone there on two occasions when it was evident he was burning the kids with hot coat hangers. He said they'd fallen on the kitchen stove grates, got against the oven when he opened it. Things like that. Once the welfare people took the girl out of the home for a while, but the mother got her back. It was a bad situation just waiting to get worse. You can see those things coming, but it's hard to do anything about it."

Haydon looked across the street to the house as he talked. Nina had almost stopped breathing.

"That night was slow for us. My partner and I were riding around, mostly killing time, when we heard the call about a family disturbance on Hyacinth. We were close. I told him about the address and said I'd like to make it. It was fine with him. When we got there the patrol unit hadn't arrived yet so we got out and started up to the front door. I could already hear the children screaming and the woman next door came running out of her house saying he was killing them in there and would we please hurry.

"I ran through the front door and the mother was in

the middle of the living-room floor, trying to sit up. He had beaten her senseless and she was coming around. There were piercing screams coming from the back bedroom by this time. You can't see it from here; it's probably about where that dim light is. I ran back there, and the guy fired a shot that hit the bedroom doorframe. I fell back, pulled my gun, and heard him going out a window.''

Haydon cleared his throat and stopped a moment, his eyes glued to the house.

"There was an old sofa in the bedroom. It was the room where the children slept. All the stuffing was coming out of the sofa, and there was a hole where the springs had broken down. The little boy, he was a year older than the girl, was sitting in this hole screaming, his nose bleeding. He was purple all over. The guy was a true sadist. The little boy died later from internal injuries. But right now he was just screaming and looking down at his sister.

"She . . . she was on the floor. Naked. On her back. Her eyes were glassy. Mentally she was completely gone. The guy had been raping her. I don't know how the roaches got on her so fast. I don't know, maybe he'd been through a while and hadn't touched her. But that's not right. They had just been screaming, I heard them, so it was probably still going on when we got there. Anyway, I remember the roaches. I remember a big one. I remember the girl's wasted little body, and I remember her eyes.''

Haydon reached down on the console and got a cigarette and punched the cigarette lighter. He lit the cigarette and lowered the window and blew the smoke out into the sticky night. The car was still idling, and the air conditioner was on.

"I yelled for my partner to get back there, I think he had stopped a second in the living room to check on the woman, and I yelled for him to call an ambulance. I don't know how I expected him to do both of those things at the same time. I remember going out the window too, and as I hit the ground I saw a muzzle flash, but he was traveling and it went wild again. I don't even know where it went, high or low or what. I started after him.''

Haydon put the Vanden Plas in gear and eased down the street.

"He did an odd thing. This house is not a hundred yards from Holy Cross Cemetery, back that way, and I expected him to go straight for it. But he didn't. Instead he ran this way, toward Marigold. Just the way we're driving now. He crossed it going through back yards and between houses; he crossed Lilac, then Jessamine. Then I thought he was going to cross over into this far end of Hollywood Cemetery and down the bayou or over into Moody Park. I just thought he would go for the woods, but he did another odd thing."

Haydon stopped the car and looked across a narrow neck of Hollywood Cemetery, through the trees toward the bayou.

"I don't know why he didn't continue into the greenbelt. I wouldn't have been able to follow him in there. I would have lost track of him. It was stupid, he should have kept going, but instead he turned back on Goldenrod, firing two more shots at me, and we backtracked, except a block farther over."

The lights of the car panned across the houses, and they followed the same route Haydon had run on foot eleven years earlier, back past Lilac, Marigold, and Hyacinth.

"Before I knew it we were almost back where we started. He crossed Cosmos and staggered into Holy Cross Cemetery, over a low rock wall that runs out from the entrance, this one just a block from Main Street."

Haydon drove through the massive wrought-iron gates of the cemetery, which were always open. The main lanes that wound through the cemetery were paved and shaded over by enormous and beautiful oaks. At night they made a canopy of darkness blotting out the stars, lighted at their far end by patches of sky a little lighter blue than the night, and by small twinklings of city lights. Haydon went a ways into the cemetery and then turned off onto one of the grassy tracks that cut through the ranks and files of gravesites stretching out under the trees as far as you could see. The back of Holy Cross Cemetery joined the southern end of Hollywood Cemetery and went farther north along the black water of Little White Oak Bayou.

Haydon stopped the car and got out. Nina got out too, saying nothing, but entranced by Haydon's narration. He started walking.

"By this time both of us were exhausted, though I was in better shape and, of course, hadn't been drinking. But once he got into the cemetery it became more dangerous for me. There were places he could take cover and still watch me. We came across over there, angling back toward the bayou. Finally he did take advantage of the tombstones and dropped down behind one. I did the same, but as soon as I'd done it I lost sight of the one he had stopped behind. I didn't know what to do." –

Haydon left the path and walked between the graves looking around him as he found the exact spot where it had happened eleven years ago.

"I stopped here. He was perhaps five or six graves away. I could actually hear him breathing. He sounded like he was going to explode. Suddenly I forgot all about the stalking and hiding part of it. I just wanted to get him. I stood up from behind the stone where I had crouched. Here."

Haydon moved from behind the stone and started walking, slowly.

"He must have heard me, because he too stepped from behind his stone. There was enough light, from the city, the stars, I don't know, from somewhere, that I could make out his face. I could probably see yours if you were over there now."

He stopped.

"You see that reclining limestone slab? He was leaning on it. He was heaving for breath so desperately that he couldn't hold his body up. He held the gun in his hand, but he didn't raise it. I don't know whether he was too tired or whether he simply had no fear. I had not yet fired a shot and was holding my own gun at my side. Maybe he didn't see it. I don't know. None of that was registering on me."

Haydon moved one grave closer to the reclining limestone.

"I stopped here, two graves between us. He was looking at me, heaving for breath, reaching down into the bottoms of his lungs for it. In my mind I could still hear the little boy and girl screaming. I could still see the little girl on the floor with the roaches on her. I raised my Beretta, steadied it with my left hand, aimed between his eyes. I fired twice, hitting him in the face with both rounds. I remember the blood jumping, a great black swash of it."

Haydon stepped over to the large stone.

"He fell on this. In the daylight you can still see the stain. For years it had a rusty tinge to it, but now it's just a discoloration in the stone."

He looked across the expanse of the cemetery, the massive oaks casting broad and deep shadows from which the paleness of the stones reflected the amorphous light of the city sky.

"There was, of course, an investigation. The Department's shooting team, the Internal Affairs Division, the Harris County DA. I was no-billed. I never told anyone what really happened, that I murdered the man."

"Your partner doesn't know?" Nina's voice was calm and natural. He was glad to hear it, and he was glad it betrayed no strain.

"I've never told another living soul. Dystal was my partner that night. When he got there I was sitting on one of these stones, my back to the body. I never told him, and he's never said anything. But he knows."

A polished marble bench sat beside a small arbor of grapevines a few feet away. Nina walked over to it and sat down. Both of them were quiet. The night smelled of damp grass and, from somewhere nearby, an occasional waft of gardenia. The rasping cry of a single cicada rose and then subsided.

"The boy died," he said, turned half away from her. "The girl was eventually institutionalized. She's seventeen now. The mother moved away about eight years ago. I don't know where she is."

They both listened to the cicada again. Another joined it for a while, then stopped. It continued alone.

"I'm glad you told me," Nina said.

"I really wanted to tell you early on," Haydon said. "But as it grew more difficult to live with, it also became more difficult to admit. The hypocrisy of it. I didn't have to shoot him, Nina. It wasn't even remotely necessary. I wanted to, and I did. That's all there is to it."

"Why have you decided to tell me now?" Nina asked. "What are you going to do?"

Haydon turned around to face her.

"I'm not going to do anything," he said. "I'm going to keep the secret, and I'm going to live with it. Just like always, only I've got to do a better job of it. But I can't do it without you, and I mustn't go on asking, accepting, your support when you don't know what you're involved in. It's just that I never knew which would be worse, to exclude you from the truth or to make you carry it around with you the way I had."

Neither of them spoke. They were caught up in their own thoughts, each trying to understand the significance of the story for each other and for themselves. Haydon inhaled deeply of the night air, which carried the sounds and smells of a world both ancient and newborn, a world no better and no worse than the best and worst of men could make it.

ABOUT THE AUTHOR

DAVID L. LINDSEY is the author of seven highly acclaimed novels. He lives in Austin, Texas, and is at work on his next novel, REQUIEM FOR A GLASS HEART.

If you enjoyed HEAT FROM ANOTHER SUN, you will want to read David Lindsey's next novel, REQUIEM FOR A GLASS HEART.

Look for David Lindsey's new Doubleday hardcover, REQUIEM FOR A GLASS HEART, at your local bookseller in May '96.

ST. PETERSBURG, RUSSIA

It was nearly ten-thirty in the evening when she emerged from deep within the metro station at the Griboyedova Canal entrance on Nevskiy Prospekt. Normally night would have swallowed the grand Nevskiy boulevard at this hour, but it was late June and the white nights had arrived, a few weeks when the sun never sank more than several degrees below the horizon, precluding darkness, transforming the night hours into an eerie, endless twilight. It also introduced a season of festivities, and throughout the city there were concerts and ballets and parties.

Irina Ismaylov stood momentarily on the sidewalk at the metro entrance and let the hordes of revelers flow around and past her, tourists, hucksters, pickpockets, students, Gypsy urchins sniffing glue and snatching purses, drug dealers, militia, young lovers, and peddlers of every commonplace and oddity. New Russia. In so many ways like the old Russia. Hope in bed with Despair.

She turned toward the Admiralty building, which loomed at the head of the boulevard, its golden dome and spire glowing softly in the rose light of a static dusk, and allowed herself to be dragged along with the throng as they passed over the broad Kazanskiy bridge. On the canal below, water taxis filled with carousers dawdled on the dark stream beneath the dull beads of streetlamps strung along the embankment. At the far end, before the canal met the Moyka river, she could just see the glinting of the harlequin domes of the Church of Spilled Blood.

The crowd moved on, past artists displaying their canvases in twilight porticoes alongside prostitutes—night butterflies—lingering in the tea-rose glow of doorways. They passed cafés open late in this nightless season, where Irina longed to be one of the lucky people in the happy light of those friendly interiors.

Catching a crowded trolleybus near the Narodny bridge, she stood in the opening of the broken door lost in thought, the breeze of the spring twilight tugging at the hem of her cotton dress. As the trolley hobbled across the Palace bridge, she stared down at the leaden water of the Neva in the dusky light and imagined that all the things that had gone wrong with her life were drifting by like flotsam on the swirling eddies of the current.

At the Strelka stop on the northern tip of Vasilievsky Island, Irina stepped off the trolley and, ignoring the milling strollers who lingered along the water's edge in Pushkin Square, headed toward the tree-lined University embankment across the intersection. Keeping to a well-planned course, she hurried past the classical and baroque buildings that faced the Neva, until she drew opposite Rumantsev Square, where she paused to watch a military vessel plow the river toward the Gulf of Finland. She dreaded crossing to the park because it was there she would see the face, or perhaps the faces, that would set in motion the final scenes of a drama in which she had a leading and decisive role. As for the faces, she never knew their names. Krupatin only showed her the photographs of the men who would work behind her and that was all. He was a fanatically cautious man.

Knowing they were already watching her, she turned away from the embankment and crossed the street. She didn't go into the park but entered 2-3 liniya, an adjacent street. This and the other streets that ran into the island from the embankment were among the city's oldest neighborhoods, their sidewalks sheltered by ancient maples and elms, which the season's anemic light had turned into inky silhouettes.

Walking on the park side of the street, she kept her eyes straight ahead as she entered the deepening shadows. The pale green undersides of the dense leaves were dimly lighted by the streetlamps, and Irina could smell the chlorophyll exuding from the moist, fresh foliage of spring.

Someone began walking parallel to her on the murky paths of the park, and just as she got to the corner where there was a streetlamp, he emerged from the hedges and crossed the sidewalk in front of her. With perfect timing his face was caught for an instant in the feeble light, and then he was gone.

To her left now was the Repin Institute of Painting, Sculpture, and Architecture, where she had contrived her first meeting with Vera Vikulov. An art student at the prestigious institute, Vera was a promising painter in the realist style and lived just down the street on Bolshoy Prospekt. Like many women, especially students, who were only marginally self-supporting before the collapse of Communism, Vera had turned to prostitution to help support herself after the disintegration of the economy.

She was a pretty, dark-haired girl of twenty-four who had had the good fortune—or misfortune—to have caught the eye of Piotr Maikov, a midlevel official in the Security Ministry. Mr. Maikov had an irresistible weakness for an ancient pleasure, the ménage à trois. Headquartered in Moscow, he made regular bimonthly trips to St. Petersburg, where he never failed to visit Vera, who was ever on the lookout for a second woman. But Maikov was a man of particular tastes. He didn't want just poor students or night butterflies. Vera had to bring women with an air of respectability about them. On two occasions she even provided the wives of other government officials. (Maikov had secretly photographed these sessions.) Vera had proved to be a procuress of considerable talent, for which Maikov paid her very well.

"Right on time," Vera said, bouncing down the steps at the side entrance of the institute. Approaching Irina, she kissed her on the cheek and grabbed her arm, locking them together affectionately as they began walking. Vera was an irrepressibly optimistic young woman, an attribute that was almost heroic in the face of the recent sorry times.

"Nervous?" Vera asked with a wide grin.

"A little, yes," Irina admitted.

"No need to be. He's not very inventive."

"It's not that. It's just . . . he's a government official, that's a little scary maybe."

Vera laughed. "Look, when he takes off his clothes all of your nervousness will melt away. Luckily, he is a very attractive man. One of the younger bureaucrats."

"I can't complain about the money."

"Nooo . . . neither of us can. And if he likes you—and he can't help but like you—he'll want you several more times. He loves real blondes like you. Too many blondes really aren't when they take off their pants." She laughed.

They continued along the sidewalk for several blocks, until they reached Bolshoy Prospekt at a juncture where art nouveau architecture intermixed with the ornate buildings of the eighteenth and nineteenth centuries.

Turning left on Bolshoy, they walked on the south side of the avenue, passing strollers who lingered here and there under the maples and poplars enjoying the twilight. Still hugging Irina's arm, Vera talked animatedly about a new CD player she was going to buy through Maikov's special connections. She said he was now bringing her Lancôme cosmetics every time he came to St. Petersburg, and that he had promised to get her some Italian shoes next month.

At the corner of 6-7 liniya, they started across the avenue toward a three-story art nouveau building, originally a private home that long since had been broken up into small apartments. It was here that Vera Vikulov lived in a flat that she could afford only by the graces of Maikov's licentious taste.

Sitting at curbside, underneath the brooding trees in front of the building, was a dark-windowed American Lincoln, Maikov's pride and joy.

Irina's stomach tightened, and she furtively scanned the boulevard for Krupatin's faces. There were two. A man carrying a sack of groceries followed a little way behind them, and ahead of them across Bolshoy, another man was approaching on a bicycle, coming along the side of the pink and white St. Andrew's Cathedral.

The two women crossed Bolshoy to the corner and stepped onto the sidewalk. As they approached the front door of the building, Irina counted four men sitting inside the Lincoln. Like many corrupt officials, Piotr Maikov's connections to Russia's Mafia were only too evident in his choice of bodyguards. Most of these thugs were avid fans of American gangster movies and freely copied their posturing and clothes. But their viciousness was something they had learned on their own, and often it beggared anything they saw in the movies.

"What is your name?" someone inside the car demanded.

"Ignore them," Vera said. "The one we have to worry about is upstairs."

As they turned and started up the stone steps to the entry, Irina noticed larkspurs blooming in tidy flower beds on either side of the landing. At the top they pushed open the leaded-glass door and stepped inside the building.

"We're going to be searched by a bodyguard," Vera warned in a hushed voice as they started up the stairs. "A really rude bastard. I've complained to Piotr, but it's no use. They are idiots about security. Just let him do what he wants. What does it matter anyway? It's only touching after all, little enough to put up with for the money."

As they rounded the second-floor landing they were met by a beefy young man with closely cropped hair. Despite the warm weather he was wearing an Italian wool sports coat, and a set of Walkman headphones was clamped to his head like padded calipers. Seeing the two women, he yanked off the headphones and left them hanging around his neck as he planted himself in front of them. Flapping the fingers of his opened hands, he beckoned them to draw closer.

"Let's have a little lookey, sisters." He was somber, frowning.

Taking Irina's purse first, he opened it, felt around inside, his eyes fixed on her. She could hear rock music buzzing from the little pads of the earphones around his thick neck.

"Okay . . . okay . . . okay . . ." he said

slowly under his breath and then dropped the purse on the floor. "Now . . ."

"Be careful," Vera warned him. "You wouldn't want me to tell Piotr you got in ahead of him."

The bodyguard pulled down the corners of his mouth in a shrug of indifference.

"Turn around," he said to Irina.

She did, and he started at her ankles and went up her legs under her dress, his big hands massaging her thighs all the way up. At her crotch his hand paused momentarily and then his thick fingers dug under the tight elastic of the legs of her panties and quickly he was inside her. Irina flinched and froze. But it was not a surprise. This was routine with Mafia body-guards now. Two months earlier a crime boss in Kiev had been decapitated by a woman who had hidden a small roll of piano wire there.

Withdrawing his fingers, he squeezed her but-tocks quickly as he brought his hands from under her dress. Still behind her—he smelled of soured perspi-ration and sweet cologne—he reached around her and unbuttoned the top of her dress. Putting his hands into her bra, one side at a time, he checked the underwiring. After this he plumped his fingers around in her hair, and then pushed her away from him with a thrust of his pelvis.

She stumbled but didn't turn around as she put her breasts in place and buttoned her dress. As she bent down to pick up her purse and the few things that had spilled out on the floor, she could hear him searching Vera behind her. He hissed once, and Vera snapped, "Stupid bastard."

As Irina stood and turned, Vera was squatting to pull up her panties and the guard was flapping his hand loosely at the wrist as if to dry his fingers. Vera's face was flushed with anger.

Vera quickly straightened her dress and the two women walked away, their heels echoing on the wooden floor of the old building, sounding melancholy in the dimly lighted hall.

"Stupid bastards," Vera spat, but even her practiced bravado could not hide the humiliation.

The apartment was in a long, murky corridor with wallpaper blotched with the stains of long, damp winters. At the end of the corridor a window was open to the street below, allowing the bruised glow of the white night to fall upon the wooden floor. The sight of it suddenly brought Irina near tears, an impulse she struggled to suppress. She swallowed hard and, for a moment at least, fought off an unshakable sadness.

Vera stopped in front of her door and took a key out of her purse. She gave a little squeeze of encouragement to Irina's hand, smiled, and then turned and unlocked the door.

In the past two months Irina had come to know Vera's apartment very well, having cultivated the girl's friendship to the point that she was often invited over to listen to music and talk about their common interest in art. They entered into a comfortable living room, to the left of which was a galley kitchen and a small table. In front of them was the bedroom door. To the right was a door to the bathroom, which had a second door that opened into the bedroom.

"Come on," Vera said again, taking Irina by the hand and pulling her after her into the bedroom. Maikov was sitting on the edge of the bed, naked, pouring himself a drink from a half-empty bottle of American whiskey. As he looked around at them Vera said proudly, "This is Irina."

Irina managed a smile as her stomach began to crawl uneasily.

Maikov studied her in silence as Irina tried to read his eyes. But his mind was clouded by drink, and she saw nothing there, only a vacuum.

"How old are you?" Maikov asked unexpectedly, the glass of dark whiskey paused halfway to his mouth. "I don't mean it cruelly. You are very beautiful. I just want to know."

"Thirty-two."

He swallowed the whiskey and eyed her. He was indeed a good-looking man, well built, almost muscular. She guessed he was in his early forties.

"I *told* you I met her in art class," Vera said, already undressing, dropping her clothes on the floor with routine familiarity. She got on the bed and went over to him on her knees, bending over him and trawling a small breast across his back. "I didn't say she was young."

"Thirty-two *is* young," Maikov said, looking over his shoulder at Vera. "You little cow." She giggled. He turned back to Irina. "You want to get your clothes off then?"

"I bought something . . . special," she said, holding up her purse. "Let me slip it on."

"Be my guest," Maikov shrugged, pleasantly surprised that maybe there was to be a little game in this.

Irina stepped into the bathroom and closed the door behind her, then quietly closed the door that opened into the living room. Quickly pulling a wicker clothes hamper away from the wall near the foot of an old cast-iron bathtub, she crouched down on the floor and pried at one end of a loose baseboard. It had taken her many visits to Vera's apartment to find just the right place, and then to make it accommodate her needs. When the baseboard came loose, she was relieved to see the butt of the CZ-75, a Czech-made 9mm automatic handgun. Though she had put it there only two days ago, she had worried about it ever since, fearful that some unforeseen misfortune would cause its discovery. But it was exactly as she had left it, the barrel pointing down in between the wall studs, the silencer screwed into the barrel to keep it from falling out of sight. It was already loaded—and cocked.

Irina retrieved the pistol, not bothering to push back the baseboard or the hamper. She had calculated that she would need at least ten seconds after she opened the bathroom door. During those ten seconds Maikov must suspect nothing. She knew he would look at the door the moment he heard it open, so she laid the CZ on top of the hamper and unbuttoned the top of her dress, slipped her arms out of the sleeves, and removed her bra, letting the top of the dress fall around her waist as though she were about to step out of the skirt.

She picked up the CZ and took two deep, steady

breaths. On the other side of the door Vera laughed a giddy, silly laugh, and Maikov's deep voice mumbled a few indistinguishable words. Gripping the pistol in her right hand, Irina clicked off the safety with her thumb and let her hand hang naturally at her side, the gun hidden in the drape of her dress.

Then she opened the door and stepped into the room.

Maikov and Vera were on the bed facing each other, embracing, and at the sound of the bathroom door Maikov took his face away from Vera's breast and the two of them looked at her. Their heads were close together like two lovers in a photograph, cheek to cheek.

Without speaking, Irina swiftly raised both arms, brought them together to grip the CZ, and fired quickly four times. Each of the four bullets found its mark within the eighteen-inch square that contained the two faces.

She didn't know precisely where the bullets hit— an eye, a mouth, a forehead—only that the imaginary square had exploded in successive scarlet plumes punctuated by the discrete, gassy bursts from the silencer. It was done.

She promptly stepped to the foot of the bed, the gun hanging at the end of her limp arm, and looked at the man and the woman. They continued to die, soft liquidy sounds sighing from their flesh as the two lives continued to slip loose of their tenuous moorings: a tentative drawing of an extended muscle, a shallow movement in the sternum. The volume of blood and the way it continued to surge from the bodies always surprised her. She stood rapt, holding her breath.

On her way out she shot the young bodyguard in the throat, then bent over and put the silencer in his mouth and shot him again. When she got to the front door and started down the steps she saw that Krupatin's faces had disappeared, leaving death behind in the dark Lincoln at the curb.

Outside in the rosy, timeless twilight, she hurried around the corner, past St. Andrew's Cathedral, past the white Church of the Three Holy Men, through the tunnel of locust trees, to the metro station at Sredniy Prospekt.

She rode the metro escalators down, down into the immaculate and brightly lighted subterrain deep below the Russian spring, and within fourteen minutes she had boarded the line to the Finland station. There she caught the last army-green train for Helsinki. It was a six-and-one-half-hour trip, and it would take the remainder of the night.

She leaned her head against the window, and as the lights of St. Petersburg passed away in the everlasting dusk, she wept, wept without ceasing, until she slept.